W9-ANJ-172

"The characters never falter. Each brother deserves a story of his own. These characters you lock within you and cherish."
—*Heartland Critiques*

"Kick up your heels and get set to enjoy a big, boisterous romance. *Rose* is fun, exuberant, and entertaining with a special charm all its own."
—*RT Book Reviews*

### Fern
"Gentle persuasion and passionate loving stirred with the tender, loving pen of Leigh Greenwood present the reader with an unforgettable, high-caliber read!"
—*Heartland Critiques*

### Iris
"Leigh Greenwood continues the standard of excellence that began with *Rose* and continued in *Fern*. *Iris* is a strong, multidimensional novel . . . The character depth and portrayal is nothing short of remarkable."
—*Affair de Coeur*

### Laurel
"Wow! What can I say but magnificent, superb, wonderful, and captivating. The characters are so true to life, I feel they are personal friends of mine!"
—*Rendezvous*

### Daisy
"Fans of the Seven Brides series, as well as new readers, will find *Daisy* a not-to-be-missed keeper!"
—*RT Book Reviews*

### Violet
"Leigh Greenwood writes Americana at its best! Hold these books close to your heart."
—*RT Book Reviews*

### Lily
"If ever there was a happy-ending book, this is it. *Lily* has romance, intrigue, and especially humor with some very lovable characters. Its plot is simply wonderful. This book will capture readers' hearts, making them believe love is possible for everyone."
—*Rawhide & Lace*

## Words of Love

"You want me to say I think you're beautiful," George said, "that I think of you all the time, that I find myself reaching out to touch you?"

"Yes!" the word was a sigh all the way from Rose's soul, the fulfillment of a long-held wish, the period to the open-ended sentence of her love. "That's what any woman wants to hear from the man she . . ."

"She what?"

"Finish what you were going to say," Rose said. She couldn't tell him she loved him. *She wouldn't.*

"I've never done anything as difficult as keeping my distance from you. You can't imagine the number of times I've wanted to touch you, wanted to . . ."

"Tell me," Rose pleaded. "I never thought you had the least trouble staying away."

George came a step closer. "You're a beautiful woman, Rose. I don't think I could live long enough to tell you everything that has passed through my mind since you've been here."

Other books by Leigh Greenwood:

*The Reluctant Bride*
*The Independent Bride*
*Colorado Bride*
*Rebel Enchantress*
*Scarlet Sunset, Silver Nights*
*The Captain's Caress*
*Arizona Embrace*
*Seductive Wager*
*Sweet Temptation*
*Wicked Wyoming Nights*
*Wyoming Wildfire*

The Seven Brides series:
*Rose*
*Fern*
*Iris*
*Laurel*
*Daisy*
*Violet*
*Lily*

The Night Riders series:
*When Love Comes*
*Someone Like You*
*Texas Homecoming*
*Texas Bride*
*Born to Love*

The Cowboys series:
*Jake*
*Ward*
*Buck*
*Drew*
*Sean*
*Chet*
*A Texan's Honor*
*Matt*
*Pete*
*Texas Tender*
*Luke*
*The Mavericks*
*Texas Loving*

# LEIGH GREENWOOD

## Rose

LEISURE BOOKS     NEW YORK CITY

A LEISURE BOOK®

August 2010

Published by

Dorchester Publishing Co., Inc.
200 Madison Avenue
New York, NY 10016

ISBN 10: 0-8439-6436-7
ISBN 13: 978-0-8439-6436-3
E-ISBN: 978-1-4285-0917-7

The name "Leisure Books" and the stylized "L" with design are
trademarks of Dorchester Publishing Co., Inc.

Printed in the United States of America.

10 9 8 7 6 5 4 3 2 1

Visit us online at www.dorchesterpub.com.

# Seven Brides Series

William Henry Randolph (1816–1865)—Aurelia Pinckney Coleman (1823–1863)
m. 1841

George Washington
b. July 14, 1842
m.
Elizabeth Rose Thornton

James Madison
b. Feb. 14, 1845
m.
Fern Sproull

**twins**

James Monroe "Monty"
b. Sept. 16, 1849
m.
Iris Richmon

John Tyler
b. June 17, 1853
m.
Daisy Singleton

Thomas Jefferson
b. Nov. 12, 1843
m.
Violet Goodwin

Juliette Coleman
b. May 21, 1847
died in infancy

William Henry "Hen" Harrison
b. Sept. 16, 1849
m.
Laurel Simpson Blackthorne

Zachary Taylor
b. Aug. 2, 1859
m.
Lily Sterling

# Chapter One

*Austin, Texas, in the spring of 1866*

> **WANTED**
>
> A WOMAN
> TO COOK, CLEAN AND
> WASH FOR SEVEN MEN ON
> A RANCH ABOUT 70 MILES
> SOUTHWEST OF AUSTIN.

### The Women

"I wouldn't do for seven men if they was to offer me every cow between here and the Rio Grande."

"Too many Indians and rustlers in the brush country."

"There's a lot of poor widows in Texas since the war. They gotta find some way to live."

"Seven men! Who's to say they ain't got more in mind than housework?"

### The Men

"He'd be hard-pressed to tell those women from his long-horns."

"They'd take up with any man as long as he had one arm and a leg."

"Ought to get himself a squaw."

Rose Thornton noticed him the minute he walked into the Bon Ton Restaurant. Any woman would notice a man like that. And not just because he stood over six feet or because he looked so handsome you couldn't be a female and not notice him. Something about him said here stood a man who was a man.

"I never knowed anybody to be so slow. You got a man back in the kitchen?" Luke Kearney demanded impatiently.

Rose's gaze never left the stranger. She noticed his pants. Confederate Army gray. She noticed his hat, too, when he hung it on a peg by the door. Cowboys didn't take off their hats indoors. Ex-Confederate Army officers did. He took a table against the wall across the room. He showed no sign of impatience.

"You going to hang on to that plate the rest of the morning or you going to set it down?" Luke asked.

Rose set the plate before Luke. As she turned to see what the stranger wanted, Luke grabbed her wrist.

"You needn't run off so fast." His grip hurt. "How about a little company?"

"I've got another customer," Rose replied. Her quiet, low-pitched voice contrasted sharply with Luke's tenorish twang.

"Let him wait. I ain't through talking to you yet."

Luke's friends, Jeb and Charlie, stopped eating to watch, smiles of anticipation on their unshaven faces.

"I don't have time to talk," Rose said, trying to wrench her wrist from Luke's grasp. It mortified her to be mauled in front of anybody but especially this stranger. "Dottie didn't hire me to keep customers waiting."

"You've kept me waiting too damned long," Luke said, the harsh tone of his voice and the look in his eyes stating clearly what his words hadn't—not yet. "And I ain't giving up my claim for no ex-soldier."

"You have no claim on me, Luke Kearney," Rose stated, her embarrassment replaced by anger.

"You can't hold out forever," Luke said as he attempted to encircle Rose's waist with his free hand. "One of these days you're gonna realize you were made for better things than dishing up grub."

"Slopping hogs would be better than having anything to do with you," Rose replied as she pulled away. "Now let me go."

Jeb and Charlie snickered. That made Luke mad. He jerked Rose's wrist so hard she nearly fell against him.

"I ain't letting go till you promise me more than a plate of hot steak."

"How about some hot grease down your front?"

Jeb and Charlie laughed.

"Watch your tongue. I might take a notion to teach you how a Southern lady ought to behave."

"How would you know?" Rose shot back. "A real lady would cross the street if she saw you coming."

Jeb and Charlie's laughter turned to guffaws.

"I've a good mind to . . ."

"I doubt you have a good mind at all," the stranger said, speaking quietly, unexpectedly. "It certainly isn't occupied with good thoughts."

Spinning around, Rose gaped at the stranger, too astonished at his intervention to remember not to stare. Even leaning against the wall, he made a strong impression. No one could miss the width of his shoulders or the bulge of muscles under his shirt. His large hands and thick, powerful fingers gave the impression of boundless strength.

But his expression affected her even more strongly. His black eyes, utter confidence in their depths, stared at Luke with icy contempt. No muscle quivered in his temple; no muscle emphasized the line of his jaw; no muscle clamped his jaw tight. His face showed no expression at all.

Only his eyes.

"You stay out of this, mister," Luke warned. "This is between me and the lady."

"If you treated her like a lady, there'd be nothing between you," the stranger replied.

The stranger smiled at Rose.

Bemused, she looked away.

"I've been patient with you 'cause you were a Johnny Reb," Luke said, "but I don't put up with nobody butting into my business."

"I have no interest in your business," the stranger assured him. "I'm only concerned with the young lady. She has asked you to let her go."

"This here ain't no lady."

"You just said she was. Are you a liar as well as a bully?"

Rose gulped. Calling Luke a liar was the same as an open challenge.

"Ain't nobody ever called me a liar," Luke growled.

"It seems the good people of Austin have been guilty of neglect," the stranger said, a mocking smile curving his lips.

Luke charged up from his chair.

"Luke, I don't think you ought to . . ."

But Luke paid no attention to Rose. As he moved to confront the stranger, he dragged her along, bumping her into chairs, her wrist still in his grip.

"Now you listen up, mister, and you listen good. You're a stranger in town, so naturally you don't know I don't like being messed with."

"Then you should understand why Miss—I don't know your name," the stranger said, turning to Rose, a smile once again on his lips.

Despite the pain, Rose smiled back. "My name's Rose—"

"It don't matter what her name is," Luke broke in. "She ain't no concern of yours."

The stranger's black-eyed gaze returned to Luke. "I spent four years fighting for the Confederate cause, but I didn't spend so much as one minute fighting for men who mishandle women or interrupt them when they speak."

Luke flushed red with rage. Pushing Rose from him, he reached for the gun at his hip. But before he could bring it up to firing level, the stranger brought his hand down so hard across Luke's wrist he paralyzed every nerve in Luke's fingers.

The gun fell harmlessly to the floor.

"Let the lady alone."

Recovering from his shock, Luke shouted, "I'll be damned if I will." Then he lunged.

The stranger's fist struck a blow that sent Luke crashing into the table behind him. As Rose jumped out of the way of a careening chair, Luke staggered to his feet, stunned, but too furious to see he didn't have a chance against this man.

Head down, Luke charged again.

The stranger merely stepped aside. Luke plowed into the table, and then the wall. He broke the table, a chair, and his collarbone.

A mountain of flesh surmounted by a bulbous face exploded from the kitchen: Dottie, the owner of the Bon Ton. "I won't have anybody breaking up my place," she screamed in a shrill voice as she surged toward the cause of the disturbance. "You'll pay for this."

"Take it out of his pockets," the stranger said, indicating the prostrate Luke with an indifferent glance. "And bring this young lady . . . Rose . . . a cup of strong coffee."

Rose didn't understand why the sound of her name on this man's lips should render her immobile. Or could it be the smile that still hovered on his lips? How about the warmth in his eyes?

"I don't pay her to sit down," Dottie screeched.

"Neither, I imagine, do you pay her to take abuse from your customers," the stranger countered, giving Dottie a look quite as severe as the one he had directed at Luke only moments before. "She needs a few minutes to regain her composure."

"And if I refuse?"

He turned his gaze to the broken chair. "I don't imagine you'd have many customers if all your chairs were reduced to kindling."

Dottie eyed the stranger with malevolent intent, but much to Rose's surprise, she apparently decided it would be wiser to deal with a comatose Luke than this imperturbable man. She rifled Luke's pockets, removing more than enough coins to pay for her broken furniture. "Get rid of him, and I'll bring the coffee," she said, and departed without a backward glance.

"Are you his friends?" the stranger asked Jeb and Charlie.

Both men turned back to their eating without answering. A third man dashed through the door, apparently intent on discovering the cause of the ruckus. One look at the stranger's eyes caused him to slide into a chair on the opposite side of the room.

"You know him?" the stranger asked the new arrival.

"Never saw him in my life."

The stranger picked Luke up by the back of his pants, dragged him through the open doorway, and dropped him in the middle of the boardwalk. Then he stepped back into the restaurant, closed the door behind him, chose a new table, and pulled out a chair.

"I'd appreciate it if you would join me, ma'am," he said to Rose. "You seem to be holding up pretty well, but you'll feel better once you sit down for a little while."

Rose hesitated.

"My name is George Randolph. I just got into town this morning, but I'd appreciate your company."

How could Rose tell him her hesitation had nothing to do with his being a stranger? After her dramatic rescue, she had difficulty thinking of him as an ordinary human being.

"I can't . . . I shouldn't," Rose stumbled, finding her tongue at last. She looked at the litter of broken furniture. "I have to pick this up. People will be coming in soon."

"Don't worry about that," George said. "Luke's friends will get it."

Jeb and Charlie looked up from their food, their expressions impossible to decipher.

"No!" Rose protested. She heard the fear in her voice. "They didn't do anything."

"I know," George said. "And now they want to make amends."

No one could misunderstand his meaning. The gun stuffed in his waist didn't seem necessary to back up his words. But it wasn't unimportant either.

Wordlessly, Jeb and Charlie went back to eating.

George still held the chair. Dottie lunged out of the kitchen and slapped two cups of coffee on the table. "You've got ten minutes," she said to Rose. "You meaning to eat, or you just here to cause trouble?" she asked George.

"I'd like some beef and potatoes. Hot. And some scrambled eggs if you have them."

"Fresh laid this morning. Anything else?"

George turned to Rose. "Have you eaten yet?"

"She don't have time to eat," Dottie snapped.

With one hand, George lifted a chair over his head.

"I'll bring her some eggs," Dottie offered, giving ground, "but that'll have to do. I've got dinners to cook. I don't pay her to dilly-dally with the customers."

"That'll be fine," George said before Rose could answer. He put the chair down. "The sooner it gets here, the sooner she can go back to work."

Dottie turned red in the face, but she rolled from the room like the outgoing tide.

"You'd better sit down," George said, an apologetic smile softening the lines of his face. "I have a feeling your employer will time your ten minutes to the second."

His voice—calm, confident, comforting—convinced her to sit.

"Dottie isn't bad," Rose explained as she stepped up to the table. "She's really good to me, but she's got to feed these men fast if she doesn't want them to go to the place down the street."

As she sat down, George's hand brushed her shoulder. Rose would never have believed anything so slight could cause such an intense reaction. He hadn't actually touched her, just the folds of her dress, but she felt as if he'd given her an intimate caress. Her body responded by becoming ramrod stiff. Her mind reacted by losing the thread of the conversation.

"Is their food better?"

"It's not easy for Dottie to make a go of this place," Rose replied.

"Do the other restaurants have better food than the Bon Ton?" George asked again.

"No," Rose said, her mind suddenly grasping the meaning of George's words. "Dottie's the best cook in town."

"Then what's the attraction?"

"The girls."

"Am I to judge from Luke's behavior that they . . ."

Rose nodded her head.

"And they expect you to . . ."

"Dottie doesn't. She knows I won't."

"Then why doesn't she make sure her customers know it?"

"She doesn't have time, not with all the cooking. Besides, I can take care of myself."

George raised his eyebrows.

"I know it didn't look like it, but Luke's the only one who won't take no for an answer. Jeb and Charlie would help if I needed it."

Rose followed George's gaze as it turned to the two men eating with their heads just inches from their plates, their eyes turning neither right nor left. "I'd hate to have to depend on them," George observed.

Dottie emerged from the kitchen, two plates of scrambled eggs in her hands. "The steak will be ready when you're done with this," she informed George. She slapped the plates down and flowed out again.

"You'd better start," George said. "Four of your ten minutes are gone already."

For a few moments they ate in silence.

"How long have you lived in Austin?" George asked.

"Most of my life."

"Why doesn't someone in your family take care of men like Luke?"

Rose lowered her gaze. "I don't have any family."

"What about your friends? Surely a young woman as attractive as you—"

Rose looked up. "I don't have any friends, either. The family I used to live with moved to Oregon to escape the war." Rose pushed her chair back and got to her feet. "I'd better go. Thanks for breakfast. And for Luke."

George had risen with her. "I don't expect any thanks. No lady should have to endure such treatment."

Rose paused in the act of turning away. "What makes you think I'm a lady? You don't know anything about me."

"I just know," George replied. "My mother was a lady."

Rose's gaze locked with George's. That had to be the nicest thing anyone had ever said to her. That a stranger, a man who knew nothing about her would say it—he knocked Luke down so he must mean it—well, it made her want to fling herself at his feet.

Abruptly she dropped her gaze and hurried away. A moment later she returned with George's steak. Without meeting his gaze, she started to clear away the debris. He stopped her.

"They'll do that," he said, eyeing Jeb and Charlie.

Rose looked nervously in their direction, but neither man spoke.

"I think I'd better . . ."

"You'd better see to that man in the corner. He's waited patiently for quite some time."

With a fatalistic shrug of her shoulders, Rose went to take the order. Two more men came in before she finished.

Jeb and Charlie finished eating just about the time Rose finished taking the last order. Without saying a word to each other, they got up and began gathering up the broken pieces of furniture. They didn't look up until they each had an armload of splintered wood.

"Put it on the woodpile out back," Dottie said, entering with broom in hand. "I'll use it for kindling." She handed the broom to Charlie. "And sweep up the splinters. I won't have the customers saying I keep a messy place."

Rose could have heard a deep breath, had anyone dared take one, as the men swept the floor and set the tables back in order. They left without saying a word or even once looking at George.

"You know you made three enemies this morning, don't you?" Dottie asked.

George finished his steak and got up. His cold gaze appraised Dottie. "I had several million during the war. Three more aren't going to make much difference." He walked over to the wall pegs and settled his battered hat over his eyes. "Good day, ladies," he said and walked out into the street.

"That man's going to get himself killed," Dottie said.

"He survived the war," Rose said. "What's he got to worry about in Austin?"

"Men who'll shoot him in the back and be glad of it," Dottie stated, disgusted that Rose should ignore the obvious. "And Luke'll be at the head of the line."

"I don't think he cares about Luke," Rose said. "He's a gentleman."

Dottie turned on her angrily.

"He may be a gentleman, though I never knew a man who was out for anybody but himself, but that ain't going to help you when you're looking for another job."

"What do you mean?"

"I can't keep you on here. The minute you're done serving, come get your money."

The blunt announcement stunned Rose. "You can't do that. Nobody else will hire me."

"That's not my problem," Dottie said, not meeting Rose's eyes. "I can't afford no more cowboys breaking up the place. There won't always be someone like him to make sure I get paid. Who was that man anyway?" Dottie demanded, turning to her customers.

"Never seen him," one of the men volunteered. "He come into town this morning looking for a woman to do for him and six other men."

"There. Go offer for that job if you think he's so wonderful," Dottie said.

She waddled off to the kitchen.

Through the haze of shock and disbelief, Rose clutched at the only straw she could see. "Do you mean he's advertising for a housekeeper?"

"Guess so. He put up a sign outside the sheriff's office."

"Why doesn't he hire a cook?"

"Go ask him," the man said, a mocking smile on his face. "Seems like he's already got his eye on you."

Rose felt the heat rise in her face, but she refused to let Dawson's gibes get to her. She had to think.

But for the next two hours she had no thoughts to spare for George Randolph or herself. His turn-up with Luke had made the Bon Ton the most popular eating place in town. Everybody wanted to know where he sat and how many tables Luke broke. Long before the rush ended, she began to wish he had gone to another restaurant to eat.

But as she walked back to her room, she caught herself daydreaming of George Randolph somehow making her future bright and secure.

*Don't be stupid,* she told herself as she sank down on the hard, narrow bed in the single room she rented. *He doesn't even know your last name. And you can forget all the fairy tales you read about knights rescuing ladies. If your future is ever going to be secure, you'll have to do it yourself.*

But how?

She opened her drawer and counted her small hoard of coins. Less than twenty-five dollars. How long would that last? What would she do when it was gone?

The men had been getting more bold in their advances, more rude in their suggestions, more persistent in their demands. She didn't know where she could find another job, but she'd starve before she'd let anybody make a whore out of her.

Rose shuddered at the sound of the word. She'd never said it out loud, never even let herself think it. She could leave Austin, but would it be any different in another town? She would still be a woman alone, without family, without money, support, or protection.

She thought of her father's life savings, her only inheritance, lost in a bank failure caused by the Union blockade. She thought of her uncle's family, cold and distant when her father refused to let her live with them on their New Hampshire farm after her mother's death; silent and uncaring after she refused to leave Texas at the outbreak of the war; angry and bitter since her uncle's death at Bull Run.

She felt more alone and vulnerable than ever.

Rose went over to a small table and picked up a hand mirror. What did Luke see in her face that made him so sure she would share her body with him?

It couldn't be beauty. She was always too tired to look her best. Besides, she did everything she could to make herself look ordinary. Her dresses were dark and loose-fitting. She parted her rich, brown hair in the middle, pulled it back from her face until all traces of natural curl were gone, and captured it in a braid at the base of her head.

Did he think desperation would force her to yield? She tried to smile, but nothing could hide the fear in the back of her eyes, the lines at the corners of her eyes, or the tightness of her mouth.

Luke wouldn't be thinking about lust now. He'd be thinking about revenge. And what about Jeb and Charlie? Mr. Randolph would go back to his ranch in the middle of nowhere, and she'd be left here with three men determined to ruin her.

Unless she answered Mr. Randolph's ad.

Rose could hardly credit the thrill that electrified her body.

She had never met a man she liked as much or one as kind, but he was a stranger. How could she be thrilled by the idea of keeping house for him?

She couldn't deny that her whole body trembled at the thought of being near him, but she didn't know anything about him. Any woman who rode off with a man gambled with her fate. A woman who rode off with a stranger gambled with her life.

But it was different with George.

She remembered how she felt while she sat with him at the table. Safe. She hadn't felt that way since the Robinsons left for Oregon. If he would protect a woman he didn't know, wouldn't he be even more ready to defend someone who worked for him?

She remembered the Confederate gray of his trousers and felt her body tense, her hopes dim. He had been an officer, too. No such man would hire her, not once he found out her father had fought for the Union.

But she couldn't stay in Austin, not without a job. She'd soon be forced to beg.

Or . . .

She was desperate enough to grasp at straws.

She would write her uncle's wife again, even though she hadn't answered any letters in five years, not even when Rose had written them of her father's death.

Maybe one of her father's army friends would help. If she went through his letters again, maybe she would find some names. She only needed one.

But even if someone decided to help her, she knew it wouldn't work. It was foolish to expect it—she couldn't wait two or three months for a reply. She needed help right now. Her twenty-five dollars wouldn't last long. She had to do something immediately.

Today.


"Don't know what kind of response you'll get," Sheriff Blocker was saying to George later that afternoon. "Lots of people come by, but they don't cotton to the idea of living in the brush. Too much trouble with rustlers and Mexican bandits."

"We don't have much trouble around our place," George told him. "The boys don't allow it."

"Maybe not, but you ain't likely to convince people around here of that. Not a month goes by they don't hear of a raid by Cortina or the men he protects."

"I'm not asking anyone to go who's afraid."

The sheriff gave him a good looking over. "I imagine you could do a pretty good job of taking care of your own. What about your boys?"

"They're my brothers. We're all pretty much alike."

"That might make it better with the ladies. They attach a lot of importance to family."

Several male spectators had gathered outside the sheriff's office. One of them, an ancient coot with a scraggly growth of beard and a sunken mouth which ejected a stream of tobacco juice every few minutes, climbed up on the boardwalk next to the sheriff. He looked too old and thin to stand by himself, but George could see plenty of life dancing in his eyes and in the wicked expression on his face.

The old man laboriously read the sign, looked at George, cackled merrily, then spat a stream of tobacco juice over the head of the nearest spectator.

"Ain't going to get nobody worth having," he said.

"Go on, Sulphur Tom, clear off," the sheriff said. "We don't need you here putting folks' backs up."

"You listen to me," the old man warned George. "Nothing here you can take to your bed. Not without you're dead drunk first."

"Here," the sheriff interrupted, "I'll have none of that talk. This here is a respectable young man with a ranch and I dunno how many head of cattle."

"Don't matter. Won't get nobody to stay below the Nueces. Sure to get kilt or lose her scalp."

"He doesn't live below the Nueces. Now scram before I put you in jail."

"Won't do no good," the incorrigible said. "I'd slip between the bars."

As the hour drew near, George wondered if Sulphur Tom might not know more about the women of Austin than the sheriff.

Several women had mixed with the crowd, but none had come forward. Much to George's chagrin, he found himself searching for Rose. Even more disturbing, he was disappointed when he couldn't find her. *It's just as well. She's not the kind of housekeeper you need.*

George knew it was true, but the knowledge did nothing to erase his disappointment.

On the dot of five o'clock, the sheriff addressed the crowd. "Anybody here meaning to answer this ad?"

Three women stepped forward.

Only George's military training prevented him from turning tail on the spot.

"This is Mrs. Mary Hanks," the sheriff said of the first, a tiny woman who looked old enough to be George's mother. "She lost her husband during the war."

"I got seven kids of my own," Mrs. Hanks announced. "Don't reckon I'd know the difference if I was to find myself doing for seven more." But Mrs. Hanks's appearance, as well as that of two urchins George guessed were part of her brood, told him her idea of "doing" for a family probably didn't come close to matching his.

Sheriff Blocker turned to the next woman, a strapping blonde of indeterminate age, decidedly unattractive features, and an intimidating ear-to-ear grin. "This is Berthilda Huber. She's German. Her family died on her this winter."

"Ya," Berthilda commented.

"Doesn't she speak English?" George asked, his calm shaken.

"Nothing you could say in mixed company," the sheriff explained.

"Ya," repeated Berthilda.

George turned to the third candidate.

"Peaches McCloud is my name," the imposing woman announced, stepping forward to speak for herself in a manner George associated more nearly with his commanding officer than a housekeeper. "I'm strong and willing. I'll cook and clean for as many men as you like, but you come messing with me in the middle of the night, and I'll put a knife in you."

The crowd laughed. Some men nudged each other. Several of the women nodded their approval.

George knew he had found exactly what he needed in Peaches—a big, strong woman who would work like a horse and expect nothing in return but a roof over her head.

He didn't doubt that meals would be ready on time, the house neat as a pin, and the linens freshly laundered every week. Yet the moment he knew he had found what he had come for, he didn't want her. A woman of Peaches's insensitivity could easily destroy the fragile ties that held his family together.

But where was he to look for someone else? Would things be any better in San Antonio or Victoria or Brownsville?

No. None of those towns had Rose.

George cursed. However much he might be unable to forget her big, brown eyes, he didn't need Rose. Besides, she wasn't here. What he needed and wanted had nothing to do with her.

"Said you wouldn't get nothing but scrubs," Sulphur Tom cackled from the fringe of the crowd. "Peaches is the best of the lot, but she'll wear you down to a nubbin inside six months."

"Shut up, old man, or I'll wring your neck," Peaches threatened.

Sulphur Tom deposited a stream of tobacco juice at Peaches's feet to show what he thought of her threats. When she charged after him, the crowd fell back, most of them laughing. Sulphur Tom danced beyond her reach.

"Take the foreign one," Sulphur Tom advised. "At least she won't talk back to you."

"I don't think any of you ladies would be happy with us," George began. He couldn't go back without someone to keep house for them, but he couldn't hire any of these women.

"I'll be content anywhere I make up my mind to be content," Peaches declared, her expression belligerent.

"Ya," echoed the Fräulein Huber.

George started over. "I'm sorry if I've inconvenienced you . . ."

"We'll have none of your *inconveniencing*," Peaches stated. "You advertised for a housekeeper, and we showed up. Now you've got to choose one of us."

"We may not be what you was looking for," the Widow Hanks added, "but we're the only choices you've got."

"He's got one more."

# Chapter Two

"Clear off," Peaches ordered. "He wants nothing to do with the likes of you."

"You're too late," the Widow Hanks informed her.

"Ya," added Berthilda Huber.

"Now, ladies," Sheriff Blocker said rather nervously, "anybody who wants can talk to Mr. Randolph. This is a free country."

"It ought not be. Not for the likes of her," Peaches stated, dislike, or an even stronger emotion, flaming in her eyes. "If there was any law around here, she'd a been run out of town long ago."

"I'm not afraid of you, Peaches McCloud, or of anything you have to say," Rose said.

She looked so tiny standing between Peaches and Berthilde, her clothes shabby, her appearance tattered. She neither shrank from them nor seemed conscious of her lack of size, but faced George with a China-doll gaze that met his own without wavering.

George felt himself being drawn to Rose, and he instinctively cut his emotions off as clean as a sharp knife slicing through sausage. He had inherited that skill from his father. Though he tried to be like his sire as little as possible, right now he needed all his resources to withstand the almost irresistible lure of this woman.

"I hear you're looking for a housekeeper," Rose said. "I wish to be considered for the position."

After having decided that Peaches would be the perfect choice, George told himself it made no sense to consider Rose. She appeared fragile next to the other woman, even frail. She couldn't have grown more than three or four inches over five feet. Yet a trace of elegance hovered about her, which the other women lacked.

He had to turn her down. To be this captivated by his housekeeper was to invite disaster.

"I don't expect you'd be any happier with the position than these ladies," he began.

"But you can't refuse me without even considering me," she pleaded.

"Of course he can," the Widow Hanks assured her.

"Are you certain you understand what's required?" George asked, trying to give himself time to think. "It's not much of a house, a dog trot I believe you call it, and there are seven of us."

"I understand. It would be a contractual agreement. I would perform certain services in exchange for money."

"Hussy!" the Widow Hanks exclaimed. "You make a perfectly respectable arrangement sound disgusting."

"How's her kind to know what goes on between honorable men and women?" Peaches asked.

"Ya," added Berthilda.

Rose looked about her, frustration, impatience, and desperation taking their turn in molding her expression.

"Could we talk alone for a few minutes?" she asked George. "I have some questions of a private nature about which I need assurance."

"I have no such questions," Peaches announced.

"I won't wait forever," stated the Widow Hanks.

"Ya," added Berthilda.

George told himself he had no reason to see Rose alone, that it would be best to put an end to things right now. But try as he might, he couldn't bring himself to refuse her in front of this hostile crowd.

Besides, he couldn't ignore the appeal in her big, brown eyes.

Yet it was something else that caused him to agree to her request. She had faced them all courageously, but fear hid in her eyes. It peeped out when something caught her off guard; it skittered across her face when one of the women tried to prejudice him against her; it danced wildly when he seemed to be about to refuse her request.

Every instinct George had developed during four years of fighting warned him of danger, and he came instantly alert, ready to do battle.

For Rose.

At the same time, he felt disgusted with his weakness. He'd never make a good army officer if he couldn't make decisions without letting sentiment affect his thinking.

"Would the Bon Ton be suitable?"

Rose nodded.

"Don't have nothing to do with her," Sulphur Tom called out just as George stepped toward the edge of the boardwalk. "She's Yankee spawn."

Yankee! For the briefest instant George froze in his tracks. An impulse made him turn to Sulphur Tom. "Most of us came to Texas from somewhere else. Where were you born?"

For an answer the old man directed a stream of tobacco at George's feet.

George chuckled easily. "Above the Mason-Dixon line, I gather."

The crowd parted to let him pass.

The walk to the Bon Ton seemed endless to Rose. She

turned her words over and over in her mind, trying to decide how best to arrange them. Her future rested on the decision of this now cold and formal man.

Had she made a mistake? He didn't seem anything like the wonderfully strong, cheerfully chivalrous man who knocked Luke Kearney down, or the gentle man who had coaxed her to sit at his table and ordered her to eat while she restored her shattered composure.

Now he seemed more like the intimidating man who had forced Dottie to wait on her and Jeb and Charlie to clean up the mess.

Still, she had seen another side to him. She *knew* another man lived inside that shell. She *knew* the other man came out once in a while. Maybe away from Austin he would come out more often.

"I guess you're wondering why I wanted to talk to you in private," she said as they settled into chairs at one of the tables.

He smiled. "I assumed it was a natural reluctance to discuss your affairs in front of the whole town."

Rose relaxed a little. He didn't seem so forbidding now. "I just needed to ask a few questions about the position."

"There's not much to understand."

"Maybe not for you, but it's a little different for a woman."

George didn't respond.

"You want a housekeeper, someone to cook the meals, keep the house clean, and wash all the clothes."

"Yes, but how do I know you can handle the job? Serving food in a restaurant isn't the same as keeping house."

Rose sighed wearily. "I've been doing those things my whole life. After my mother died, I lived with a family named Robinson. Mrs. Robinson was always having babies, so the housework settled on me. I didn't have to, Daddy paid her to keep me, but she was very kind. Besides, she taught me to cook. She was wonderful at it. There was nobody in Austin any better. I used to cook when I started at the Bon Ton, but Dottie moved me out front hoping I would bring in a few extra customers."

She wouldn't tell him of the humiliation of having to act as a draw for people like Luke. She also wouldn't tell him that Dottie was the only person in Austin who would give her a job.

"That sounds sufficient to me," George said.

"I have a few requirements," Rose said tentatively. "Nothing I expect you'll object to," she qualified when she saw him stiffen up. "Naturally I require a room of my own. I want to be paid each month in gold. I want to be able to come to town at least three times a year. I also expect you to bring me back to Austin when the contract is ended."

"I don't see anything unreasonable in that," George said. He started to rise.

"I'm not through yet."

"What more do you want?"

"I rather imagined you wanted an explanation of Sulphur Tom's remark."

"It's not necessary."

Rose stood. "Then you've already decided against me."

George opened his mouth to deny her accusation, but the words wouldn't come out.

"I know you fought in the war," Rose said, her lower lip trembling, "but I didn't think you would condemn me without at least hearing what I have to say."

"My brother, Jeff, and I both fought in the war, but neither of us would condemn anyone without a hearing." George sat back down. "Tell me."

Rose seated herself again.

"My father was a career army officer," she said proudly, "a graduate of West Point."

Rose noticed the rigidity in George's face, and her heart sank. Okay, she didn't have a chance, but she would tell him her story anyway. At least he would know the truth before he rejected her.

"He was sent to Texas during the war with Mexico. He liked it so much better than New Hampshire he settled here. But when the war broke out, he fought for the Union. He distinguished himself in the battle for Vicksburg. He also died there."

"Then you are alone."

"Yes."

"Why do you want to leave Austin?"

An ironic look filled her eyes.

"Ever since my father died, I have been like a pariah in this town. No respectable woman will speak to me, much less invite me into her home. No man will treat me any differently from the way Luke treated me this morning. No one in this town would lift a finger to keep me from starving."

"But you don't have to worry about that, not as long as you have a job."

Rose hadn't intended to tell George everything—she had wanted to keep this shame to herself—but she could tell he was determined to reject her. She could also tell he was attracted to her. She could feel it.

"Dottie fired me this morning. She said she couldn't afford any more fights because of me."

George swore softly but with considerable vigor. "You mean she fired you because of me?"

Rose nodded hesitantly. Dottie hadn't meant it that way, but it worked out to the same thing. She hated to use George's better instincts against him, but they seemed her only weapon.

"She said she couldn't afford to have people breaking up her place."

After another string of curses, George sat back to think. He found himself on the horns of an unusual dilemma. Duty told him to do exactly what his desire told him to do: hire Rose.

But the common sense that had helped him survive four years of bloody combat screamed at him to take Peaches McCloud, the Widow Hanks, even Berthilda Huber. Choose Rose and he would be tossed into an emotional maelstrom without so much as an oar.

"Is there anything else I ought to know?"

He meant it as a rhetorical question, something to take up time while he tried to force himself to remember all the reasons why he should choose Peaches.

She looked a little embarrassed. "I want you to put what we've said in writing."

Rose seemed to cringe, as though she feared he would get up and walk out. He had a strong impulse to do just that. Why did he continue to waste time on this woman?

"You don't trust me?"

"Yes, I do," Rose said, a little surprised to realize she really did.

"But you would still want a written contract?"

"Yes."

Why did she insist? If he had made up his mind to choose someone else, it wouldn't matter. If he decided to ignore her contract, she probably wouldn't be able to do anything about it. Still, she wanted something on paper, something written out that she could see. When she handed him a pen and some paper she found in Dottie's kitchen, he accepted it without demur.

"Let's see. *I, George Washington Randolph*—yes, I was named after a president—*agree to hire Rose . . .*"

"Thornton. Rose Elizabeth Thornton."

"*. . . Elizabeth Thornton on the fifteenth of June . . .*"

"Make it tomorrow."

"*. . . sixteenth of June, eighteen hundred sixty-six, to keep house for the Randolph men. She will be expected to cook, clean, wash, and generally see that the house runs smoothly.*" George paused, but Rose had no changes to make. "*In exchange she will have a room of her own, be paid each month in gold, be taken to Austin once a quarter, and returned to town if the contract is broken.*" George turned the paper around so Rose could read what he had written.

"Now you need to put down my part," she said.

"Why?"

"I can't expect you to make a promise if I'm not prepared to do the same."

"You'd better write it," George said, pushing the paper toward Rose.

*"I, Rose Elizabeth Thornton, agree to cook, clean, wash, and generally provide for the needs of George Washington Randolph, and his six brothers."* Rose signed her name and date. "There," she said, showing the paper to George.

"I think that covers everything."

"There's something else," Rose said.

"What now?" Impatience and annoyance scraped in his voice. Only the look in her eyes kept him from tearing the paper into tiny pieces.

Rose felt humiliated, but she also felt desperate.

"I owe some money."

"To whom?"

"The undertaker."

There seemed no end to this woman's requests.

"How much?"

"Fifty dollars?"

"How could you run up such a sum?"

"I wanted Daddy buried next to Mother. The army wouldn't pay for it."

Damn those big eyes! Why did every explanation make him feel like a bigger heel than before?

"If I hire you, I'll settle your debts," he said, getting to his feet and handing her the written agreement, this time being careful not to look into her eyes.

He had dismissed her. Rose could feel it. He waited for her to leave the restaurant ahead of him, but she might as well not have been there at all. She wanted to run away, to do anything rather than go back and suffer the humiliation of seeing him choose Berthilde or Peaches over her.

But pride made her walk at his side. Pride enabled her to hold up her head. Pride put steel in her nerves for the announcement she knew would destroy her last hope.

"You sure took a long time," Peaches said when they reached the sheriff's office.

"She didn't tell you any lies about us, did she?" inquired the Widow Hanks.

"Ya," agreed Berthilde Huber.

"Miss Thornton merely had some questions she wished to ask without the whole town as an audience. And I had a few questions to ask her."

"I bet we got a few boys in town who could give you the answers," Sulphur Tom quipped.

George couldn't say what made him react so sharply to the old man's ribbing. But whatever part of his mind Sulphur Tom prodded into action, he got more of a response than either of them anticipated.

"I have a natural respect for anyone who's reached your advanced age," George said, directing a chilling stare at the irreverent Tom, "despite the obvious ill-treatment you've given your body"—howls of appreciative laughter came from the bystanders, including Sulphur Tom himself—"but your longevity will be severely jeopardized if you insult Miss Thornton again. Now if you will hand me your agreement," he said turning to Rose, "I'll sign it before all these witnesses."

Rose handed him the agreement, her surprise lost in the furious response of the people gathered around, most especially Miss Peaches McCloud.

But no one was more shocked than George himself.

Rose couldn't remember when she had been more miserable. Every part of her body ached. After staying overnight in Austin, George had insisted upon leaving at dawn in order to make the return trip in one day. He had given her the choice of traveling on horseback with him or following in a wagon.

Her response had been automatic. She would ride with him. Now she wondered if she hadn't made the wrong decision, on more than one count.

In addition to being certain that she wouldn't be able to sit down for a week, she hadn't been able to carry on much of a conversation. It had been a monotonous trip. George seemed moody, cold, uncommunicative. He had answered all her questions, but he hadn't tried to pretend he wouldn't have preferred to ride in silence. At times his answers had verged on rudeness. Clearly he had another side, one not nearly so pleasant as the face he showed in Austin.

And he had demons, too. She could tell he had been wrestling with something for the last two hours. At first she thought he might tell her about it, but now she knew he wouldn't. George was not the kind of person to confide in others. He rode with his eyes straight ahead, oblivious to his surroundings.

And to her.

Rose had heard about the brush country, but she'd never seen it. Now she wondered how anything, man or beast, could live in such a place. They seemed to be traveling between impenetrable thickets that extended as far as the eye could see. Sometimes miles went by before they came to an opening, a small savannah in this tangle of mesquite, chaparral, prickly pear, wild currant, cat's claw, and a dozen other varieties of low-growing trees, bushes, and vines, all bearing sweet-scented flowers and succulent berries, and nearly all armed with vicious thorns. Rose didn't know how cows and deer, even pigs and turkeys, could hide in such a briar patch. She couldn't conceive of how a man and horse could ride into that tangle and come out alive.

After living in a town all her life, she was unnerved by the isolation of the brush. She hadn't seen a house all day. It was as though they were the only people on the face of the earth. She didn't know if she could survive this far from people. Not with George acting as though he were made of wood.

A widening path drew her attention from the brush. Rose could make out a building in the distance. She felt her pulse quicken.

"It's not much of a house," George warned her. "We had hardly moved here when the war broke out. With Pa and the two oldest boys gone, Ma was lucky to hold things together."

Rose realized, a little surprised, that he had never mentioned his parents before. "I thought . . . you never said . . . you led me to believe . . ."

"Ma died three years ago. The house will be entirely your responsibility." They might as well be discussing some military maneuver for all the feeling she could sense in his voice. He didn't even look at her.

"Your father?"

The hesitation was barely perceptible. "We think he was killed in Georgia, not too long after the battle for Atlanta."

Rose didn't know how to respond. The tone of George's voice exhibited such a mixture of emotions—cold observation and throbbing anger—she thought it better to ask no questions.

The ranch did nothing to support her flagging spirits. It consisted of a house, which at a distance appeared to be made up of two very large rooms with a dog trot in between, and two corrals. A blooded bull occupied one.

George followed her gaze. "A family in Alabama gave us the bull for helping them out. Jeff and I kept him between us all the way to make sure nobody would steal him. At night we slept in shifts. The steers we can breed from him can make us rich."

As they drew closer, the house looked even more pitiful. Bedraggled chickens scratching about for a meager existence didn't improve the landscape. A milk cow grazed a hundred yards from the house. Her sorry condition made her fit right in with the setting. A person could starve and die out here and no one would ever know.

"I'm afraid things have been let go since Ma died. The

twins have been too busy with the herd, and the young ones never mind a mess."

"Young ones? You said seven men."

"We're only six just now. No one's heard from Madison." His voice faltered, but only for a moment. "The twins are seventeen, Tyler's thirteen, and Zac is almost seven."

"He's practically a baby," Rose exclaimed, her sympathy aroused for any child forced to grow up in this barren wilderness.

"Don't tell him that," George cautioned, the first smile Rose had seen in hours fracturing his solemn expression. "He thinks he's as grown as the rest of us."

"There's still one more."

"Jeff."

He said the name as if he deserved an entire chapter to himself, as if all rules no longer applied.

"Jeff lost his arm at Gettysburg. A minié ball shattered his elbow."

Why did each word feel like an accusation hurled at her? He hadn't looked at her, she could hear no condemnation in his voice, but she felt it nonetheless.

"He spent the rest of the war in a prison camp."

Rose couldn't think of anything to say.

"He pretends to have accepted it, but he hasn't. Don't refer to your father's being a hero in the Union Army."

"You mean to keep it a secret?"

"I don't see how mentioning it would cause anything but trouble."

Rose had to agree, but she hated lies, even lies she hadn't told. "Tell me about the others."

"I hardly know them. Zac was a baby when I left, Tyler only eight."

"And the twins?"

"They've grown into young men I hardly understand."

No one came from the house to greet them. The silence of the midafternoon grew oppressive. The enervating heat of summer was still a month away, but Rose felt as if she had stepped into a still life. Nothing moved. Nothing made any sound.

George dismounted, but she couldn't move her lower body. She couldn't even feel her legs.

Like a gentleman, he helped her down. He went through all the motions, said all the words, but there was no warmth in his touch. She leaned on him at first, then decided she preferred her horse. He might kick her, but at least it would be a sign of emotion.

"We sleep on this side," George said, pointing to the left half of the house as she worked some kinks out of her muscles. "This is the kitchen."

She could tell that from the chimney. The yard, if the area around the house could have been dignified by such a name, hadn't been swept in weeks. Rose privately wondered if it had ever been swept. In addition to being the place where they kept their saddles and harnesses, the dog trot seemed to be the place where they threw everything that had lost its use. The windows contained real glass, but Rose doubted she would be able to distinguish much more than daylight and dark until they were cleaned.

Then George opened the door to the kitchen.

Rose's knees nearly buckled under her. The room was in such a state it was scarcely recognizable as a kitchen. A huge iron stove stood piled high with every pot in the house, each covered with remnants of food. Dirty plates and glasses covered the table. On closer inspection Rose discovered that most were chipped and cheap, with a few extremely fine china and crystal pieces. Around the rough board table stood eight ladder-back chairs, slats cracked, rungs worn from use, and cane seats coming loose.

Thrown together, cheek by jowl, were wooden buckets, a crusted Rochester brass hanging lamp, a battered coffeepot, a crude worktable, and a pile of discarded tin cans. The curtains were gray with grease and dust. The woodbox contained little besides splinters.

The strong smell of old grease pervaded the room.

"Tyler has been doing the cooking, but he doesn't know much about food. I'm afraid none of us is very strong on cleaning up."

"Where's my room?" Rose asked. If she didn't lie down soon, she would collapse right here.

"Up there." George pointed to a ladder leading to the loft. Rose's spirits sank to rock bottom. Gone were her visions of a sunny room with chintz curtains and a soft bed with plenty of sunshine and fresh air.

Through the open door Rose could tell the loft was barely tall enough for her to stand up in. She just hoped mice hadn't found their way up there. She was sure doves and owls had already staked out a claim on her bed.

George went out to get her bags while Rose took a closer look at the stove. She shuddered. Dozens of dirty dishes had been piled in a big metal tub. She didn't want to know how long they had been there. She sincerely hoped maggots hadn't hatched. She drew the line at dealing with worms.

George came back with her bags.

"I know it's a mess, but Tyler never washes anything until he has to use it."

"Apparently neither does anyone else," she said as George carried her bags up to the loft.

"Sometimes we're not here for days at a time," George called down to her.

"It's probably cleaner in the brush. At least out there it rains once in a while."

George, descending the ladder, smiled tenuously, but he definitely smiled.

"It does look rather daunting, but I'm sure you'll have things shipshape in a little while."

"Some of these dishes look valuable," Rose said, holding up a bone china plate with an elaborate floral design. "Shouldn't we use something else?"

The appearance of frigid correctness she had seen so frequently on the trip settled over George.

"We don't have anything else. We like to eat about seven. I'll tell the boys you're here." He turned to go.

"You're leaving?" She didn't think she could take being left just at this moment.

"It's okay. Tyler and Zac are around. I'll see if I can scare them up. They'll tell you anything you need to know."

"But the food . . . what do I cook? Where is the pantry?"

"I don't know. Tyler does all that."

"What'll I do until he shows up?" Panic accompanied her developing anger.

"You can start cleaning. It does look a mess in here."

Then he disappeared. Rose stood stock-still for a moment, then rushed to the door, intending to call him back, to ask him to wait just a moment.

Too late. She saw him ride into the all-engulfing brush. A few moments later, even the sound of his horse's hooves had died away. Then there was nothing. Nobody. Not a thing.

She was alone.

Turning back to the kitchen, Rose paused without opening the door. She couldn't face that again, not just yet. She opened the door to the side of the house where they all slept. Even greater chaos reigned there.

The huge room contained a senseless jumble of roughhewn beds, chests, and chairs. Discarded clothes were piled everywhere, even on a shaving stand.

She slammed the door and stumbled into the kitchen. The only good thing she could see in this disaster was that her legs and bottom no longer ached. It was a known fact you couldn't feel anything if you were totally numb.

Suddenly the enormity of what had happened overwhelmed her. She collapsed into a chair, threw her arms down on the table, let her head sink onto her arms, and sobbed her heart out.

She had been a fool. A complete, idealistic, optimistic, head-in-the-sand fool. After years of watching out for herself, of learning to tell the honest and sincere from the deceitful and hypocritical, of hardening herself to snubs and insults, she had let herself be swept off her feet by the first person to treat her decently.

George Washington Randolph might have moments of kindness, moments when he remembered he had been reared a gentleman and a member of the human race, but he clearly intended to waste none of them on his housekeeper. She would be expected to work like a slave from dawn to dusk, and then crawl into her loft to rest before getting up the next morning to start all over again. Was this the only future that waited for her? Would she never have any of the joy and happiness she had dreamed of?

With a noisy and totally unfeminine sniff, Rose sat up, blew her nose, and looked at the room about her. She supposed there might be worse kitchens in hell, but she found it hard to believe. Anyway, this was her own private hell, and George expected her to clean it up. Furthermore, she had insisted he sign a written agreement. That agreement bound her just as securely as it bound George. She might be depressed and ready to burst into tears again, but no one would ever be able to say she didn't stand behind her word.

Rose heard the door hinges protest softly. Images of savage Indians, marauding Mexican bandits, and rampaging rustlers burst into her imagination. She might not have to worry about years of drudgery. She might die in the next instant.

# Chapter Three

Rose whirled about to find herself looking squarely into the utterly charming, thoroughly dirty face of a beautiful little boy. His wide-eyed stare made a mockery of the fright that had caused her heart to pound.

"Are you the lady who's going to cook for us?" he asked.

He didn't step inside the kitchen, just stuck his head in the door.

"Yes, I am," Rose said, quickly drying her eyes.

"You don't have to cry. George won't hurt you. He's pretty mean sometimes, but I don't think he'll hit you. Monty says he's . . ." The child stopped and considered for a moment. "I don't suppose I ought to tell you what Monty says. George says he never heard such language, and he fought in the war."

"I'm not crying because I'm afraid of George."

"Then why are you crying? You're not hurt, are you?" He came a little closer, but kept the door ajar.

Rose figured he intended to keep his escape route open.

"I'm just crying about the house."

"It ain't so bad. It was worse before George came home."

"He doesn't like the kitchen to be dirty?" That, at least, was something in his favor.

"He said if we wasn't going to clean it up ourselves we had to hire somebody. You like cleaning?"

"Not especially."

"Tyler says cleaning is dumb. I don't see how it can be much fun, even for a woman."

"Women like unaccountable things," Rose told him, feeling a little better for having someone to talk to. "But I'm afraid I'm going to need your help."

The boy quickly backed through the door.

"Your name is Zac, isn't it?" she asked as she came around the table toward him.

"Yeah." Only his head showed.

"Well, Zac, I've got to clean up the kitchen if I'm going to fix dinner. I'll need a large tub, a bucket, some firewood, and water. Can you help me?"

"I can show you the well."

"I was hoping for a little more than that."

"That's Tyler's job," Zac told her, his lower lip beginning to protrude. "I only have to do the milking and bring in the eggs, and I don't have to do that until nearly dark."

"Well, I'll make a bargain with you. If you'll show me where to find everything I need, I won't ask you to help. But you've got to find Tyler."

"Okay," Zac agreed. He bounded away and came back almost immediately with a wooden bucket. "Follow me," he said, as he led her around the corner of the house to a well which had been dug within the lengthening shadow of a large oak tree. "You'll have to take the dishes out of the tub. We don't have another one unless you mean to use the wash pot."

Rose had hoped she wouldn't have to touch the dishes until they had sat at least an hour in hot, soapy water, but there seemed no help for it. While she filled her bucket, Zac gathered an armload of firewood. "I have to do the fires, too," he admitted as they walked back to the house. "George shouldn't give me so much work, but when you're little, you can't make anybody listen to you. Especially not Monty. He won't listen to anybody. Not even George."

Zac let Rose hold the door open for him.

Rose set down her bucket of water and started to empty the tub. "Tell me more about your brothers." If she intended to make a place for herself in this family, she had to learn something about them. Besides, she'd welcome anything that would take her mind off these disgusting dishes.

"I don't know nothing about George and Jeff. Madison neither. He left after Ma died, and we ain't heard from him."

"Haven't heard from him," Rose corrected automatically.

"Are you going to be after me like Jeff?" Zac demanded, pausing in building a fire under the tub.

"Sorry, just habit," Rose said.

Zac looked like he didn't quite believe her but was willing to give her the benefit of the doubt.

"Jeff says I talk awful. He says Hen and Monty should have taught me better."

"I'm sure they did the best they could," Rose said, wondering what trap she'd step into next.

"Hen and Monty are gone all the time," Zac continued.

"They shoot people. I want to shoot people, too, but Hen says I can't until I'm older."

"Shoot people?" Rose asked as she poured the bucket of water in the now empty tub and settled it directly over the burner under which Zac was building the fire.

"People who want our cows. If they try to take them, Hen and Monty shoot them. Especially Hen. He likes shooting people."

Rose couldn't think of anything to say to that.

"Jeff doesn't like it a bit. He hollers at Hen and Monty all the time. They won't come to the house anymore because of him."

"Where do they stay?" Rose asked. This family sounded more and more peculiar.

"Out there," Zac said, making a gesture that took in the whole outdoors. "Hen says you can't catch a thief by sleeping in a bed."

"That sounds reasonable," Rose agreed, rummaging around until she found a cake of soap. It had become so hard from disuse she could scarcely cut off a piece.

"Monty likes cows," Zac continued. "Tyler hates them. He hates Texas, too. I don't think Tyler likes much of anything."

"Where is Tyler?"

"Gone. He hates women."

"Oh," Rose said, wondering what kind of nightmare she'd wandered into. "Isn't he going to help me fix dinner?"

"Tyler won't help nobody do nothing."

Rose bit her tongue to keep from correcting Zac.

*That means you have to figure out what to cook. This little boy has no intention of increasing the number of his duties.*

Zac stepped back from the stove. "Fire's going."

"Are you leaving?"

"Yeah. All you got to do is feed it."

"But I don't know where anything is."

"You'll find it if you look."

"Meat," Rose said, nearly desperate.

"In the larder. Potatoes under the house. Some carrots, too." He began backing toward the door. "There's butter and milk in the well. George won't drink it if it ain't sweet. Monty and Hen like buttermilk, but Tyler wants it sour."

"How about you?"

"I hate milk. I drink whiskey." With that he disappeared through the door.

Rose closed her mouth, then burst out laughing. She wondered if Texas had a law against a twenty-year-old woman marrying a little boy. Zac had about ten times as much charm as his older brother.

But as delightful a rascal as Zac might be, Rose had to admit she found George far more intriguing. She didn't know him yet—she had to accept that and start all over again—but she felt something when she was with George that she had never felt with anyone. A kind of peace. Maybe a feeling of belonging. Though how she could feel that way after he had treated her as cold as yesterday's fish supper she didn't understand.

She couldn't forget those ten minutes in the Bon Ton. She had offered to work for the George Randolph she met there. Somewhere, somehow, she had lost him. She must find him again because she had seen in the stranger in the restaurant the kind of man she wanted to marry.

She would never forget her mother's unhappiness during the long months when her father was away. She could still see the tears glistening on her mother's cheeks as she sat and stared at her father's picture. She could still remember her own tears when her mother died and her father wasn't there to comfort her.

His wife and daughter had always been second to his career.

Maybe she had read too many fairy tales, but she had always dreamed of finding a man who would never leave her, who would make her the center of his life, who would always keep her safe.

The kind of man she thought George was.

She hadn't realized it until just now, but she had come perilously close to falling in love with him.

What woman wouldn't?

He had rescued her when danger threatened. He had been concerned for her welfare. He had been considerate of her feelings. He had thrown a cordon of protection around her that no one could breach. She had felt cherished. Well, perhaps that was an overstatement, but she had felt valued, important.

Now all traces of that man had disappeared. She didn't know whether George had been acting the part of the Southern gentleman or whether he had a reason for pretending to be much colder than he really was. Everyone in this family seemed a little peculiar. And from what she'd heard from the two she'd met, nobody seemed to get along with anyone else.

Maybe George *had* been acting a part.

No, her original impression had to be true. Something had caused him to close her out. If she could just discover what it was, maybe she could bring back the man who had made such an indelible impression on her heart.

In the meantime, however, she had dishes to wash, a kitchen to clean, and dinner to fix. And she'd have to hurry if she intended to be ready at seven o'clock. She had every confidence George and his legion of brothers would be knocking at the door at six fifty-nine.

Rose couldn't remember when she had been so tired. Yet a smile played across her lips as she moved about the kitchen. She had managed to wash the dishes, scrub every pot and pan, scour the stove, and put the larder in some kind of order.

She had also managed to cook dinner for seven people.

A beef roast simmered on the stove, its aroma mingled with those of carrots and potatoes in a thick, rich gravy. Two pans of biscuits, one browning in the oven and one waiting to go in, could either be dipped in gravy or slathered with creamy butter.

She had cooked some peas from Tyler's garden. She had picked them herself because he never showed up. She completed the meal with canned peaches and tomatoes from the larder. Milk—sweet, sour, and buttermilk—stood ready for the men to make their choice. And water in case Zac really didn't like milk.

Rose gave the table a final check. She had cleaned it as well as she could, but signs of oil spills and burns remained. She had meant to cover it with a tablecloth, but she couldn't find one anywhere. The Rochester lamp, suspended over the table, its globe sparkling clean, cast its amber light about the room.

Things would look better when she had time to clean the windows, wash and iron the curtains, and scrub down the walls and floor, but she felt pleased about what she had been able to do in one day. It added up to a great deal more than she'd thought possible when she'd stepped into this kitchen about six hours earlier.

The sound of horses' hooves caught her ear. She glanced at the clock, one of the few things in working order. Someone had polished the glass, cleaned the outside surfaces, and oiled the working parts. She hoped it really was three minutes to seven. She quickly cleaned a spot on the window to look out. Four men had ridden up, accompanied by two dogs. Apparently George believed in being punctual. Zac came running up alongside. Obviously he had gone just far enough from the house to escape doing any chores. She didn't see anyone who could be a thirteen-year-old boy. She hoped Tyler wouldn't carry his dislike of women to the point of staying away from dinner.

She hurried to make her final preparations. She would set the roast before George's place just before they entered the kitchen. After the blessing, and while they passed the vegetables, she would serve the biscuits and put in the second pan. Zac could pour the milk. He seemed to know what everyone liked.

She tried to calculate how much time she would have before they were ready to eat. They would have to unsaddle their horses first. She didn't know whether they fed them or turned them out into the corral, but they would need to be rubbed down. Next, they would wash up and change their clothes. That ought to take at least fifteen minutes. Probably closer to half an hour. She still had plenty of time.

Rose sat down to wait.

She had hardly settled into the chair when the door burst open and a stream of men, dogs, and the smell of sweat and horses poured into the room.

"I told you I smelled a roast," said one of an identical pair of blond twins. Before Rose could move from her chair, he grabbed the pot from the stove and set it before him at the table. He immediately began serving his plate with one of the cups Rose had set out for coffee.

"Biscuits!" shrieked a tall, painfully thin boy who had to be the missing Tyler. He whisked the pan out of the oven and dumped the golden brown biscuits along the middle of the table so they would be in easy reach.

In seconds everyone except George had started grabbing for the food. They passed the bowls up and down the table, each person shouting for what he wanted. One of the twins tossed a gravy-soaked biscuit to a bony dog that had followed him into the room. A second dog, not willing to wait his turn, put his feet up on the table and began to eat from the other twin's plate. The man laughed merrily, set the plate on the floor for the dog, and took George's plate for himself.

Not by so much as the flicker of an eyelash did anyone acknowledge Rose's presence.

Anger such as she had never known surged through her body vanquishing her fatigue. She jumped to her feet and charged to the head of the table.

"Stop this instant!" she shouted, her voice shrill with rage. "Don't you dare put another scrap of food in your mouths until you can come to this table like humans."

She might as well have shouted into the wind. She pushed

away a dog intent upon dining in George's place, then pounded on the table.

"Listen to me," she cried. "I won't have you behaving like this."

Still they ignored her. All except the man with blond hair, amazingly blue eyes, and only one arm. His indignant gaze seemed to be asking by what right she complained about their conduct.

Shaking with rage, instinct her only guide, Rose acted. Grabbing hold of the table, she lifted it off the floor and turned it over. The roast and gravy and the hot vegetables crashed to the floor between the twins. As the five males stared at her in stunned surprise, the dogs attacked the overturned meal.

Just then George entered the kitchen. He alone had taken time to wash.

Everyone began shouting at once.

"Stop it," Rose cried.

They paid no attention to her. The dogs continued to eat everything on the floor.

Rose whirled about, grabbed up the full coffeepot, and raised it as though she were about to fling its boiling contents over everyone in the room.

Dead silence.

"Now you listen to me," she said, panting from the force of her rage, "or I swear, by God, I'll never cook another thing for you as long as I live."

"You crazy fool," one twin said. "George, you can't believe . . ."

Rose raised her coffeepot threateningly.

"Monty, you were taught not to interrupt a lady."

George might have decided to strip his relationship with Rose of every vestige of emotion, but she had no difficulty seeing the fury that blazed in his black eyes. She wondered if he had ever hit a woman. She had never seen a man in the grip of such rage. Not this kind. It was pure, cold, and dangerous.

"But you can't let her . . ."

George directed his blazing look at his brother. "Let her speak. Then you may have your say."

Rose didn't know how she would ever learn to tell Monty and Hen apart, but at the moment she didn't care if she never saw either of them again. Only George's anger seemed to have any ability to curb either one of them.

"Okay, tell me what's wrong."

He had given a command, just like he would to a private in the army, and he expected her to jump. Well, she would jump, but she doubted it would be the way George expected. She would get a few things straight right now. She may have made a mistake in assessing George's character, but she didn't mean to make any more.

"My name is Rose Thornton," Rose announced after a pause to control the still-boiling anger which made it impossible to speak with a steady voice. "Yesterday your brother hired me for the express purpose of keeping house for seven"—she groped for a suitable word—"men."

George's glare prevented another outburst, but Rose couldn't be sure whether he intended the look for her or his family.

"I nearly went back to Austin when I saw this place. But I had made an agreement, and I intended to stick to it. However, I refuse to work in a house where people don't even have the courtesy to speak to me before they dive into their food. Your brother led me to believe you'd been brought up as gentlemen." She pointed to the mess on the floor. "I see he was mistaken."

"She can't blame that on us," Tyler said, appealing to his brother. "She turned the table over."

The one who hates women, Rose thought. But he had managed to overcome his dislike long enough to come to the table.

"I couldn't get your attention any other way," Rose pointed out. "Nothing else could stop you from tearing at your food."

"Didn't any of you introduce yourselves?" George asked.

Rose could see the rage remained, but it burned less brightly. Something new lurked in his eyes. She had no idea what it might be.

"I guess we were too excited at the sight and smell of food we could eat."

That was the one with only one arm. Jeff. The one who spent two years in a Yankee prison. He wouldn't speak to her at all if he ever learned her father had fought for the Union.

"They didn't even wait for the blessing," Zac said a little self-righteously, Rose thought. She decided Zac was extraordinarily adept at guessing which way the wind would blow and getting clear of its stiffest blasts.

"It was the food," the other twin said. Hen. He appeared to be quieter than his brothers, but he might be more dangerous. Zac had said Hen liked shooting people.

"But she had no call to turn the table over. Now the dogs got it all."

The other twin. Monty, the one who liked cows. He looked more aggressive than Hen, but what could you say in favor of anybody who actually *liked* longhorns, the most ornery beasts in God's creation?

"I suppose you had a reason for wanting their attention so badly," George said.

His father should have named him Solomon, she thought. He'll probably offer to divide *me* down the middle to keep peace in the family.

"I most certainly did," Rose said, abandoning all her preconceived notions about George or his family. If she had to fight for some degree of consideration, she might as well start right now. They would know she expected to be treated as a human being.

"If I'm going to cook and clean and wash for this family, I expect a few courtesies in return."

"Such as?"

"I don't expect to be ignored. I don't presume to tell anyone what to say, but *Good day* will do when nothing else comes to mind.

"Secondly, I expect each of you to wash and change your shirt before you come to the table. You expect the food to be fresh and good-smelling. I don't see why you can't be, too."

"You've got to be crazy," Monty protested. "I'm worn to the bone when I get in. I don't have time for washing and changing my shirt."

"Nor does he have a clean shirt," Hen added in an undervoice.

Monty gave his brother an evil look but said nothing.

"Any more requests?"

"Yes. I expect everyone to remain standing until I'm seated. And wait for the blessing before they eat. After that, the food will be passed to the right so everyone can have their chance at each dish without reaching across the table or yelling. You will eat with the manners I'm sure you were taught. And the dogs will be left outside."

"I'm not sitting still for that," Monty exploded.

"I told you not to bring a woman here," Tyler said. "I don't mind doing the cooking."

"But we mind doing the eating," Jeff reminded him.

"The woman stays," Monty said, "but she doesn't rule the roost."

"The *woman* has a name," Rose snapped from between clenched teeth. "And if you wish to eat at this table again, you'll learn what it is."

"You voted to hire a housekeeper," George said. "It's up to you to make it work."

Rose spun on her heel to face George. "You *voted?*"

"George kept telling us how he had to take responsibility for the family because he was the oldest," Monty explained. "So Hen and I told him if he was so hot to be responsible, he could find somebody to keep the place clean. I don't like taking orders from him, but an agreement is an agreement."

"I feel the same," George said, turning to Rose. "And you agreed to cook."

"Not unless my conditions are met."

His stare nearly unnerved her. She wanted to hide, say anything to make him look away, but she knew if she didn't win now, she'd never win. Besides, the new look in his eyes had overcome the anger. It had softened it as well.

"Politeness, good manners, and a wash before coming to the table," George said.

"And the dogs left outside," Rose added. She wasn't satisfied with George's condensation of her expectations, but she didn't want to push the point too far. She wanted a good deal more, and at the moment she was mad enough to do just about anything to get it. Still, it might be better if she got an agreement in principle now and worked on the details later.

"What about tonight?" Monty asked. "I'm still hungry."

Rose started to refuse, but one look at George changed her mind. It seemed he intended to consider her demands, but he clearly expected food in the end.

"If you'll sweep up this mess, I'll see if I can't get something ready in about an hour."

"Us!" Tyler exploded. "You threw it on the floor."

"Not much left to sweep up," Hen observed. "At least the dogs have a full stomach."

"If I have to clean up this mess, they'll be the only ones with a full stomach."

Monty. He had the worst temper.

"I don't think we began very well," George said, the look in his eyes more intense. "I suggest we start over again and attempt to forget this."

"I'll not forget it, and I'll not clean up her mess," Monty insisted.

"You'll do both," George said, "or you won't eat."

Their gazes locked, two strong men, two stubborn men. Monty didn't look away, but he made no move to defy George.

"We've been inexcusably rude," George stated, looking from

one to the other. "I, unfortunately, have been the rudest of all. How can I expect you to be polite to Rose when I didn't have the courtesy to introduce her to you?"

"They all started eating before you got here."

Zac again. Rose couldn't tell if he meant to placate George or accuse him of being slow to come to the table.

George ignored him.

"This is Rose Thornton," George said. "From Austin. She has agreed to keep house for us. This is Thomas Jefferson Randolph," he said, indicating the shyest of the Randolph boys. "Jeff and I fought together in Virginia. We don't know what happened to James Madison Randolph, but you'll know him when you see him. He looks like a cross between me and Zac. The twins are James Monroe Randolph and William Henry Harrison Randolph. They took care of the ranch during the war. They're a little wild, but they won't leave you to stand alone. That sour-faced long drink of water is John Tyler Randolph. He doesn't look like anybody. Doesn't like much of anybody either. That little scamp making sure he's on the right side of my temper—"

"I'm not little," Zac protested.

"—is Zachary Taylor Randolph, the youngest and last of the Randolph boys. I don't know what Pa would have done if he'd had any more sons. He had run out of Virginia presidents."

Rose didn't dare laugh. Being saddled with presidential names must have been a serious hardship for growing boys. No wonder Hen and Monty used nicknames.

"I've been looking forward to meeting you," Rose said, making an attempt to smooth over the rift. "Believe it or not, I'm usually rather mild-mannered."

No laughs, not even a smile. Just silent, stoic, forced acceptance. Oh well, they had to begin somewhere.

"Hen, you and Jeff set up the table and chairs," George directed. "Zac, you and Tyler clean up the floor. Monty, the dogs are yours so you get rid of them. I'll clear away the broken dishes. All of you will be washed and wearing a clean shirt when you come back. And you'll eat like you were brought up to eat."

"I'll be damned if I will," Monty stormed, his temper flaring as quickly as it had subsided. He whistled to the dogs as he stomped out of the room. The animals weren't quite through, but Tyler got a broom and soon convinced them they'd be happier outside.

"Sure don't see any need to wash the floor," Zac said as he picked up a bucket to get some water. "It'll just get dirty again."

"No, it won't," Rose said. "You're going to scrape your boots next time you come inside."

"Do you mean to take all the pleasure out of eating?" Hen asked.

"Would you have come to your mother's table reeking of horses and tracking mud all over?"

Hen made no reply, but Rose could tell she had unwittingly touched on a sensitive subject. Nothing about Hen seemed to change, but his expression became set in stone. Rose made a mental note not to mention the late Mrs. Randolph until she had a chance to ask George about his mother.

She looked at him gathering up broken bits of plate and glass. She couldn't tell what thoughts were going through his mind, but she saw a fairness in him, a willingness to support her because he felt she was right. He didn't seem pleased, but then he didn't seem angry anymore. He just didn't seem to feel anything.

Didn't the man have emotions?

Oh well, she didn't have time to worry about that just yet. She had a meal to fix. She'd think about him tomorrow, but George Washington Randolph was a puzzle she intended to solve very soon.

George felt the last of his anger ebb away. He hadn't expected Rose's arrival to be without incident, but he'd never expected her to defy the lot of them the first night.

Her actions had surprised and angered him. They'd also

offended his sense of what was suitable behavior for a proper female. It infuriated him that anyone would treat his family like a pack of mannerless ruffians. They were Randolphs of Virginia, related to governors, college presidents, cabinet ministers, a Chief Justice of the Supreme Court, a United States president.

Even Robert E. Lee.

Who was she but the daughter of some Yankee officer, a girl he had rescued out of the kindness of his heart? It would serve her right if he sent her packing. He wouldn't be dictated to by a woman he had hired to cook and keep house.

But the way she looked at him when he entered the room had melted much of his anger. She was as mad as a cornered bobcat, but she was also scared of what he would do, what he would say, what would happen if he turned her off. But she hadn't backed down. As with Luke Kearney, she knew how she wanted to be treated, and she wouldn't settle for less. He had to admire her courage.

He couldn't hold her defiance against her. His determination to keep a safe distance had caused him to be thoughtlessly rude. He had meant to be late. He thought he would be less affected by her presence if the boys were already at the table.

He had gotten that one wrong.

When he saw them ranged against Rose, he had wanted to protect her, to shield her with his body. He had to consciously stop himself from taking her into a protective embrace.

The strength of his feelings had so surprised him, he had wanted to withdraw, to let them fight it out while he got himself under control. But doing that had caused the present trouble. He had no recourse but to find a way to be fair to Rose, to be objective about his brothers, and to keep his feelings under control. He had done it in the army. It was hard with his brothers. Harder with Rose.

The men under his command hadn't looked at him out of soulful eyes, engaged his chivalry by their helpless condition, or aroused his physical need with the alluring curves of their bodies.

Playing peacemaker between Rose and his brothers was different. He'd have to explain to the boys how she must feel. They were basically good. He was certain they would try to change their attitude if they just understood.

In the meantime he would talk to her.

She didn't know how hard they tried. She couldn't. Not without understanding what they had gone through, being torn from the familiarity of their Virginia home and abandoned in the alien world of south Texas. Not without understanding the shock and terror of being left to run a ranch in bandit-infested country where they had to kill just to stay alive. Not without understanding the pain and rage of seeing their gentle, aristocratic mother die, deserted and nearly destitute, in a wild and savage land she could never like or understand.

Rose didn't understand that being a son of William Henry Randolph was an excuse for almost anything.

George closed the door behind him.

"The boys are ready when you are," he said to Rose.

She took her eyes off the pots on the stove long enough to check the bread in the oven.

"It'll be just a few more minutes. The biscuits aren't done yet."

"They're not happy about it."

Rose looked up. "I doubt they're any more unhappy than I was."

"I shouldn't have let them come in alone."

"They're big enough to know how to behave without you being here to tell them."

"I know, but they've been left to themselves too long."

"That's no excuse."

George knew it wasn't, but he was irritated at Rose for saying it.

He wondered what had gone through her mind as she prepared dinner for the second time that evening. She had said very little while the boys were in the room. She said nothing after they left.

"Anything I can do?" he asked. He hated doing nothing. Not even four years in the army had taught him to wait patiently.

"Sit down. You're paying me to fix your dinner."

So she was still angry.

"This is different. I hired you to prepare only one dinner a day."

She ladled the gravy over a second roast before setting it on the table in front of George's place. "You can pour the milk. Zac says everybody likes something different."

He began filling the glasses from different pitchers and setting them beside the appropriate places. "The boys really aren't so bad," he said. "Boys their ages never take well to discipline under the best of circumstances."

"I wouldn't know," Rose replied, taking the biscuits from the oven. She placed them in a bowl and covered them with a towel. "The Robinson boys were a lot younger."

"Then I imagine our family will take some getting used to."

"I'm willing to try if they are."

She wasn't backing down. She was braced for trouble, and he couldn't blame her.

Rose set the butter on the table, shooed away a fly showing an interest in the roast, stood up, straightened her dress, and pulled an errant lock of hair behind her ears.

"Everything's ready. You can let them in."

# Chapter Four

They walked in like condemned men.

They had washed and changed, but Rose noticed their shirts were neither clean nor new. They moved to their places and stood waiting for her to be seated, but they either looked at her with anger in their eyes or didn't look at her at all. George held her chair. Rose sat down, but a second look at their faces changed her mind. She stood up, her chair scraping angrily on the still damp floor.

"I think it would be better if I ate later."

"No, you don't," Monty exploded, all rigidity vanished. "You made this fuss about us washing and dressing up. If we have to be miserable, you do, too."

"It wasn't my intention to make anyone miserable," Rose tried to explain. "A certain standard of behavior is expected of gentlemen when they come to the table. If you continue eating as you did before, no one will ever believe you've been properly reared."

"Have you ever spent the night out in the brush?" Monty demanded. "Have you seen Cortina's men when they come? Have you watched your friends fall dead from the saddle, their bodies trampled beyond recognition?" His shouted words didn't lessen the earnestness of his questions.

"No."

"Gentlemen don't live like that. Only animals. It's not easy to change just because you walk through a door."

Yet George had changed. He must have seen even more terrifying, brutalizing sights during the war. Still, he managed to put it aside when he came to the table. But Rose couldn't say that to a boy who had been fighting brutal, vicious men since he was twelve.

"I'm sure Miss Thornton doesn't need a graphic description of what it means to live in south Texas," George said,
"but it is possible for men to put aside their battle manners
when they come home. They've been doing it for centu-
ries."

"If you weren't so anxious to murder those poor farmers,
you—" Jeff began.

"You self-righteous ass!" Monty exploded. "If you'd had to
crawl on your belly through the brush, or swim through a
cottonmouth-infested stream to keep one of those *poor farmers*
from killing you, you'd sing a different tune."

"That's enough," George said.

"You can't mean to listen to his bleating."

"No, but I don't imagine Miss Thornton wants to listen to
you either."

"She'd better. Our guns is the only thing that'll keep her
safe in her bed."

"Are," Jeff said.

Monty threw his milk across the table. He aimed for Jeff's
head, but his brother dodged, and the glass shattered against
the far wall. Fragments fell into the woodbox and scattered
under the stove.

"If you don't keep that bastard's mouth shut, I'll shut it for
him."

"Jeff, I've told you not to correct the boys."

"I can't stand to hear them sound like untutored fools."

"Then don't listen. If Pa didn't think their education was
important enough for him to see to, then you leave it alone.
How do you think they feel knowing we got special tutors
while they got nothing?" George cast a meaningful glance in
Rose's direction. She knew he was telling Jeff not to air the
family's dirty linen in front of her.

"Monty, apologize to Miss Thornton."

Rose's startled, protesting gaze flew to George's face. She
didn't want to be made part of this confrontation.

"I'll be damned if I will," Monty swore. "Let Jeff do it."

"Apologize, or leave the table. We've already ruined her first dinner. It's inexcusable to ruin a second."

"Go to hell!" Monty shouted and left the room.

Hen half rose in his chair, his coldly furious gaze fixed on Jeff.

George motioned him back in his seat. "Jeff, if you can't leave Monty alone during dinner, you'll have to eat some other time. You don't have to like the way the twins looked after Ma or this place, but you have no right to complain. You weren't here."

"Of course I wasn't doing anything important, only defending my country and losing my arm," Jeff stated, furious.

Rose didn't know who to sympathize with more. It must be awful for the twins to suffer from a perpetual feeling of inferiority, but that was nothing compared to Jeff's loss of his arm.

"Clean up the milk," George said to Jeff. "It's your fault it's spilt."

*It's also your fault Monty has to go without dinner,* Rose thought.

They finished the meal in silence.

Tyler was the first to get to his feet.

"If you're finished, ask Miss Thornton if you may be excused," George said.

"Why should I ask her?" Tyler demanded, looking at George like he'd lost his mind. "She's nothing but the cook."

"She's as much somebody as you are," George replied. "If you enjoyed dinner, say so. Then ask her permission to be excused."

"You may go if you're finished," Rose said, not waiting for the mutinous boy to ask. She wasn't sure he would, and she didn't think she could stand another confrontation tonight.

"Everything tasted mighty good," Hen said as Tyler made a hasty exit. "Mind if I go?"

"Not at all," Rose said.

"Me, too," Zac said, jumping up. "Don't mind Tyler," he whispered in Rose's ear. "He's just mad you took away his job. Now he has to chase after cows, and he hates cows more than anything."

"Don't forget to fill the woodbox," Rose reminded Zac before he could make good his escape. "I'll need more wood if I'm to cook breakfast in the morning."

Zac looked like he wanted to argue, but one glance at George's stern expression, his thick eyebrows virtually drawn together, caused him to change his mind.

"I'd better be going, too," Jeff said. "The food was excellent. George did well when he hired you."

*Just like I'd been a cow or a horse.* Jeff was more of a snob than all his brothers put together. She'd never be more than the hired help to him.

"I hope you don't mind if I don't go right away," George said.

"Stay as long as you like." Rose hoped she didn't sound as breathless as she felt. That she could feel anything beyond relief that such a horrendous evening was over was a mystery to her.

What was it about this man that appealed to her so much that she could virtually forget the most miserable meal of her life? He hadn't done anything romantic since they left the Bon Ton. Neither had he gotten excited nor allowed his emotions to run away with him. He had supported her, but she was sure he had done it for practical reasons rather than any liking for her.

Yet she still felt drawn to him.

He made her feel safe. He was fair even when he didn't want to be. And after her years in Austin, she knew just how important these qualities were.

*Fine. Campaign for him if he ever runs for governor, but you're thinking about feelings, not qualifications.*

"Would you like some coffee?" she asked.

"No, thank you. But I'd like a little more milk." He smiled at her surprise. "I'm afraid I'll never make a true Texan. I don't like coffee. I couldn't drink it strong and black to save my life."

"I don't suppose it's required."

"I apologize for the way the boys behaved. I'm afraid it's been an unpleasant evening."

"Tempers are bound to fly at the end of a hard day. Then I came along and upset everything."

"It's not that."

"Then what is it?"

"I doubt I could explain it to you. You'd have to be part of the family to understand."

"Try." She wasn't going to be shut out that easily. She didn't know if her knowing what bothered them would change anything, but she wanted to understand why they kept snapping at each other, if only to keep from unwittingly starting a fight.

"We moved to Texas six months before the war broke out," George began. "Pa sent Jeff and me off to fight. We never knew he meant to leave right behind us. That left seventeen-year-old Madison to take care of four younger brothers and a ranch he hated. Mother's health was too poor to allow her to help him."

"What happened to your mother?"

"She died within the year. Madison left as soon as they buried her. That meant Hen and Monty had to take over. They never forgave Pa for leaving Ma. I don't think they forgave Madison, either."

"Where did he go?"

"Nobody's ever heard from him."

Rose could imagine how that must hurt George, especially when coupled with the fear that Madison might have died in the war.

"The rustling got pretty bad at times," George continued. "I'll never know most of what the twins had to do. Certainly things no fourteen-year-old boys should have to go through. They fought for their lives as much as for this place. Naturally they resented it when I came back and started telling them what to do.

"I know Jeff shouldn't antagonize them, but he's bitter over the loss of his arm. He thinks that no matter what the twins went through, it doesn't compare to his years in a prison camp."

Rose thought of her own miserable years in Austin. They would probably seem like nothing compared to the dangers of a war or rustlers, yet they were very real to her. Would Jeff feel she had nothing to complain of? Probably, but she knew that in some ways she would rather have lived in fear of her life than have to face the hatred and anger of the citizens of Austin.

"None of us is capable of judging the suffering of another human being," she said. "What's easy for one person might be impossible for another."

"I don't think Jeff will understand that until he starts to accept the loss of his arm."

"I hope it won't be too late. It won't do him a lot of good to come to terms with his loss if there's nobody left to care."

"Maybe I should let you talk with him."

"I'll do the dishes," Rose said, rising. "I have a feeling it'll be the easier task."

"I'm not my brother's keeper."

"Yes, you are. Whether you know it or not, you're the only one with any real desire to bind the six of you into a family once more."

"Seven."

Rose reminded herself to be careful to talk of Madison like he was still one of them. Regardless of her own private certainty that he was dead or would never come back, George obviously expected him to return.

She wished there were something she could do to lift the burden of worry from his shoulders. There was so much she didn't know, so much she didn't dare ask about.

One thing she did know. There was something inside George that he was afraid of. He was too busy with his family to deal with it just yet, but it lurked there just the same. She didn't know what it was, but it was the something that made him keep his distance from her.

The responsibility for his brothers hung over George like a pall. There were times when he was tempted to throw it all over and head for the nearest fort and a commission he knew would be his for the asking. It was there just for the taking, the rank, the command, the career he had always wanted, doubly bad after his father's last scandal had cost him his appointment to West Point.

The war had given him a second chance. If he joined now, he'd have his choice of commands. If he waited until the boys were settled and Zac old enough to get about on his own, he would probably be too old to work his way up through the ranks.

But he couldn't leave. The only people he really cared about were here.

Did that include Rose?

He hadn't meant to say so much to her. More than that, he hadn't expected so much understanding. He had been able to control his attraction to her only by cutting himself off from her.

But one evening had changed that.

He wished he'd been in the room when she turned the table over. He could just see his brothers' faces. Jeff was used to weak women who never stood up to a man. Why shouldn't he be? Their mother never stood up to their father. Monty expected people to listen to him, but he respected anyone who fought back. George didn't know what Hen thought. He never had.

It would take them a while to get used to Rose's willingness to stand up for herself.

He remembered her profile as she moved to put away the dishes. He felt a familiar warmth begin to stir in his groin. Odd she should set him off so easily. He had met hundreds of women before and during the war, some of them very beautiful, some of them ready to do just about anything for the son of tall, handsome, infamous William Henry Randolph, and he'd been able to ignore them all.

But he couldn't ignore Rose.

He remembered the endless trip from Austin, the hours he spent trying to concentrate on the ranch, the numberless times his eyes had sought her out, the struggle to keep the heat flaring inside him out of his voice, his actions, his every thought.

It was like that now. Everything faded until he could see nothing but Rose, think of nothing but Rose, want nothing but Rose. It was like she had bewitched him, made him do things he didn't want to do.

It would be so easy to reach out and touch her.

And so stupid!

"Does George know you're out here?"

"I told him."

"What did he say?"

"I didn't ask."

Monty chuckled. "You don't mind getting into the middle of any kind of fight, do you?"

"I don't like fights," Rose answered, surprised he would say such a thing.

Monty laughed again. "You throw a whole dinner on the floor because you don't like our manners. Then you bring me dinner after George and Jeff have exiled me, and you say you don't like fights."

"George didn't exile you."

"Yes he did—he and that sanctimonious prig."

"You must try to be patient with Jeff."

Monty made a rude noise.

"Losing an arm must be a terribly difficult thing to accept. As for George, he was only trying to see that you treated me properly. He didn't enjoy sending you from the table."

"I can't believe that."

"You should. He's the one who told me where to find you."

"Why would he? He doesn't care whether I go to bed hungry or not."

"You're wrong. He also told me I'd better bring your dinner in a bucket or the dogs would get it before I got halfway here."

Rose was exhausted, but she couldn't sleep. She had twisted and turned in her bed until the sheets were in a knot and the thin blanket had fallen to the floor. She listened for any sound, but silence had settled over the house more than an hour ago. She doubted she would have heard the men even if they'd been talking loud. The house didn't look like much, but it had been very well built.

She had locked the kitchen door below. She wasn't sure whether she was keeping the men out or herself in, but she needed the security of knowing she was safe from rustlers.

Monty was sleeping out. It seemed one of the boys always spent the night somewhere in the brush. It was a little like standing watch. That made her feel better, but it also worried her. She had never feared attack, not even during the war. Now nothing but Monty stood between them and the dreaded Cortina. And Hen, who shot people when they tried to take their cows.

And George. Rose didn't imagine that George liked shooting people, but she couldn't see him allowing anybody to harm his family or take his property. And for the time being she was part of his family. Knowing that made her feel safer than she had felt since her father left for the war.

George felt strongly about his family—as far as Rose could discover, it was the only thing he did feel strongly about—but she didn't see them showing a similar interest in him. They didn't realize they had a corridor straight to his heart, that everything they did, everything they wanted, everything that hurt them affected George, sometimes more than it affected them. Jeff and Monty would soon forget their fight. They would have other fights. They wouldn't remember any of them for very long.

But George would. He would agonize over ways to bind the family together while they mindlessly went on tearing it apart. It made her so mad she wanted to tell them that if they didn't want to try for their own sakes, at least they could try for George's.

But she didn't have the right. She was an outsider. She would only make things worse.

She had already said too much. She shuddered when she thought of the things she had said to George about his own brothers. She was lucky he hadn't fired her on the spot.

Rose got out of bed and walked over to the tiny window. She looked out over the countryside. There wasn't much to see. An impenetrable wall of brush reaching miles in all directions ringed the house. Anything could be out there and she wouldn't know.

A chill ran down her spine.

The moon flooded the land with an amazing amount of light. Odd. In town it always seemed so dark at night. She could see other buildings only by the light that shone from their windows. Now she could even see the leaves on the trees as they hung listlessly in the warm night air.

Everything seemed absolutely still, so peaceful and quiet, so far removed from all the things that used to threaten her.

The people in Austin didn't seem frightening now. She wondered why she had been worried about the looks the women gave her when she walked down the street, the things they whispered behind her back, the things Luke and his friends might do.

None of it frightened her anymore. Unpleasant, irritating, but not frightening. Not as long as she was here. Not as long as she had George to protect her.

Even this past evening didn't seem so bad anymore. These were strong, stubborn men doing a difficult job, trying to get used to other strong men, trying to curb their tempers and bend their wills for the good of all. That was bound to make things difficult from time to time, but it also was exciting to watch. These were no weaklings bullying people weaker than themselves. These were no cheating, deceitful men turning against the loyalties and beliefs of a lifetime just to get on the right side of the Reconstruction officials.

Just good, strong men trying to sort out what was right for all of them.

She couldn't imagine anything more rewarding than being part of a huge family that worked together for the good of all. She could do without the fighting, but she wouldn't shy away from it. She was a fighter herself.

The three years following her father's death had hammered every bit of softness out of her. The successive shocks of the Robinsons leaving for Oregon, her father's death turning her into an outcast, and the bank failure making her a pauper would have crushed almost anyone else.

But even when things were most bleak, she had never given up hope that she would someday have a home and a family of her own.

And this was the kind of place she wanted.

*You're just the housekeeper,* she reminded herself.

Rose felt her excitement wane. How was it possible she could have become so involved with this family so quickly? It wasn't like they had welcomed her. She didn't feel the anger they felt any more than they seemed to have experienced the fear that stalked her.

They were fearless. Nothing and nobody daunted them. Maybe that's why she liked them. Even Zac rushed to spend his day in that menacing brush without a moment of hesitation. It must be nice to feel that confident, that secure. She couldn't remember what it was like to be completely without fear, to know with perfect certainty that tomorrow would come, and that it would be another beautiful day. These men didn't realize what a blessing that was.

But she did, and she knew that if she had her way, she would never leave this place.

* * *

George decided he wouldn't get up just yet. He needed some time to think. His dreams disturbed him.

George considered himself a very sensible person. He took pride in being able to look at life with a critical eye, and to make decisions without emotional foot-dragging. From time to time he had to make some unexpected adjustments to his plans for his life, but he had never let himself get derailed, never let himself lose sight of his objectives.

Until Rose.

Not that she had actually done anything. Except look as captivating as any woman he could ever remember, fight like a bantam when she felt slighted, and cook the best meal he'd ever tasted.

And start juices flowing which hadn't stirred in his veins for five years.

Maybe that's what caused the dream. He'd had plenty of dreams about women. Sometimes they were set off by the things men said around a campfire. Sometimes because his body was trying to remind him that Nature hadn't intended him for a life of celibacy.

But he'd never had a dream quite like this one.

He'd been married. To Rose. He couldn't tell where they lived—the house was a mixture of Ashburn, the Randolphs' Virginia home, and several of the houses he'd been quartered in during the war—but he thought they lived in Virginia. Oddly, his brothers were their children. They squabbled, but the mood of the dream had been happy. He was content to be married to Rose, to look after his vast estate, and to raise a large family of boys.

That dream represented everything George feared most in the world.

That was what caused him to wake up before dawn, his heart beating double-time. It was what caused him to lie in bed searching his mind for an explanation.

Only Rose could account for it. He would have to be very careful that her seductive presence didn't lure him into thinking he wanted the very things he knew would end up making him miserable. He would never have thought he could be so weak-minded, even about a woman as attractive as Rose. He wouldn't make much of a head of the family if he didn't learn to be less impressionable.

The creaking door ended his self-examination.

"Time to get up," Hen said, entering the room with a basin of hot water and a bucket of cold.

Tyler turned over. Zac didn't move. Jeff sat up and swung his feet to the floor. Monty charged to his feet and headed for the door, apparently intending to go straight to the kitchen. Hen handed him the basin.

"What's this for?" Monty demanded irritably.

"Miss Thornton sends it with her compliments. I take it to mean we're to shave before we show up at the table."

"I'll be damned—"

"You probably will," George interrupted, "if you don't make some attempt to get your temper under control. Why don't you try accommodating Miss Thornton rather than blowing up at everything she does?"

"Dammit, George, I thought you hired a housekeeper. That woman's worse than a nanny."

"Maybe you could use a nanny," George said. "Have you taken a good look at yourself lately?"

Hen obliged by taking the mirror from its hook on the wall and holding it before Monty.

"Good God," Monty exclaimed. "I'd scare a Spanish whore."

"I been telling you that for years," Hen said. "That's why you can't get any—"

Monty jumped his brother, and they went down in a tangle on the floor. George rescued the mirror.

"Tyler, since you and Zac don't have to shave, you can get dressed and go help Miss Thornton."

"I got a beard," Tyler said. "I need to shave as much as you."

George put out a hand to stop Jeff from uttering the words

on his lips. "Okay, it looks like Zac gets to help Rose. Tyler can share my basin."

"I ain't going in there by myself," Zac declared.

"You make Monty and Hen stop fighting, and you can share my basin," Jeff said.

Zac looked at the boys still wrestling on the floor. They were several times his size. Many more times his strength. Before George could stop him, Zac took the bucket of cold water and poured it over them.

Shouts of profanity reverberated throughout the room.

"Fetch some more water before you get torn apart," George said, barely able to hold back his laughter. "And see if you can find another mirror. We can't all be looking in one at the same time."

"You put him up to that," Monty accused Jeff.

"It's not Jeff's fault," George said. "Zac will do anything to stay with us. More than anything, he wants to be treated like a man."

"It's an overrated state," Monty said. "I'd be just as happy to be the one to help with the breakfast."

"Do you think she'd have you?" George asked. "You gave her a right rough time last night."

"I don't think she minded it much."

"Of course she did," Jeff argued. "Females are delicate. They can't stand things a man would hardly notice."

"Not every female is quite so fragile," George said, cutting off what he feared would be an ill-chosen reply from Monty. "I get the impression Miss Thornton is capable of taking care of herself."

"There's only one more mirror," Zac announced as he came into the room and slammed the door on the dogs trying to follow. "It's hers, and she said she ain't giving it up."

"Isn't giving it up," Jeff corrected.

"Rose don't correct me, and she knows more than you," Zac shot at his brother.

"What do you mean, she doesn't correct you?" George asked.

Zac looked like he'd said too much. "She did it yesterday, after you left. I told her I didn't like it, that Jeff did it all the time, and she promised she'd never do it again. And she hasn't," he said to Jeff. "I said some awful terrible things just to see if she'd break her word. But she never did."

"I doubt Rose ever breaks her word," George said, more to himself than his brothers. "She seems to be a woman of clear ideals and strong character."

"All we wanted was someone to cook and clean," Jeff said.

"I have a feeling one day you'll be glad we got more," George said.

"Why would you say that?"

"I don't know. Just a feeling."

"Stop jawing and get shaved," Monty said. "I'm starved, and I'll bet you ham to potatoes she won't let a one of us inside the door unless we're shaved close as a baby's bottom."

"And wearing a clean shirt," Zac reminded them.

"We don't have any clean shirts," Hen pointed out.

"Wear the same one you wore last night," George said. "It'll have to do."

"How about tonight and tomorrow night?" Hen asked.

"We'll worry about that later."

"You didn't have to worry about shaving and clean shirts when I was doing the cooking," Tyler said.

"We only had to worry about dying," Monty said.

"We appreciate what you did," George said, hoping Tyler believed he valued his effort, "but you have to admit Rose is a much better cook."

"She looks better, too," Monty added, relishing needling his younger brother.

"Outside, all of you," George said. "I'm not putting off my breakfast so you can start a free-for-all."

"Comb your hair, Zac," Jeff said. "She won't want you sitting down at the table looking like you were scared out of your wits by a bobcat."

"I ain't afraid of no bobcat."

"No more fights," George intervened. "I'm hungry."

The six men spilled through the door to be brought up short by the sight of Rose building a fire under the wash pot.

"Before you sit down to the table, I want this pot filled with water. And I want everything except the clothes on your backs in it."

"Dammit to hell!" Monty cursed.

# Chapter Five

"Can't it wait until after breakfast?" George asked. He had been anticipating his breakfast almost as much as Monty, and to be ordered to fill the wash pot and search out every piece of clothing they owned before they could eat made him irritable.

"I thought about that," Rose said, "but what's to keep everybody here after they've eaten?"

"You could ask them."

"I could," Rose admitted, "but it's easier to do it now."

"Are you going to let her get away with this?" Monty demanded.

"Get away with what?" George asked, his temper short. "You voted to hire a housekeeper. The washing is part of her duties. If you want the job done, you've got to let her do it."

"Then let her do it herself. I don't mean to stop her."

"You don't mind her going through your things?"

It was obvious that thought hadn't occurred to Monty.

"I don't want anybody going through mine," Hen stated.

"She can do anything she wants with my clothes," Zac said. "I don't even like to wear them."

"Ain't no woman touching anything that belongs to me," Tyler declared.

"I'm sure she doesn't want to," Jeff said. "She probably intended to use a stick."

"You boys collect the clothes," George said. "Jeff and I will get the water.

"You mind digging out my stuff while I bring the water?" George asked Hen.

"Naw. I'll give you a hand as soon as I'm done."

"Aw, hell, I'll help with the water," Monty said.

"Jeff will do that," George said, giving Monty a particularly penetrating look. "You just make sure Zac and Tyler don't leave half their clothes buried under a floorboard somewhere."

"You shouldn't let her get away with this," Jeff said as they walked toward the well.

"Get away with what?" George asked.

"Ordering us around like she was a general and we were the recruits."

"I don't suppose she will when she feels she can ask and get our cooperation," George answered.

"You shouldn't encourage her to give orders. You should do that."

"Dammit, that's what I hired her for," George snapped, dropping his bucket in the well. When he heard it splash bottom, he started hauling it up. "I don't want to have to worry about the cooking and cleaning and what needs doing next."

"Okay, but she's getting above herself."

"If she does, we can fire her and hire someone else." George handed the first bucket to Jeff and dropped the second in the well. The bucket splashed and he hauled it up. "This is our place, Jeff, and we decide what happens. But when you hire someone to do a job, you can't crowd them too hard and expect them to be happy."

"I'm not interested in whether she's happy."

"Then you're making a big mistake." George hefted his bucket out of the well. "Come on. The sooner we fill up the wash pot, the sooner we eat."

"It's going to take another couple of trips to fill up the pot,"

Monty said after they had emptied their buckets into the pot. He still stood where they'd left him, glaring at Rose.

"Then you'd better get a bucket and help."

"You think she's got breakfast ready, just keeping it warm, while she gets all this work out of us?" Monty asked as they walked back to the well together.

"Yes."

"Damn. That's what Hen said."

"Don't imagine you'd want to wait twenty more minutes, would you?" George asked.

"Hell, no, but having it just sitting there, waiting, while she keeps us hopping about like a bunch of Chinese coolies galls my butt."

Rose watched as George and his brothers emptied the last buckets of water into the wash pot. Hen was helping Zac lay the fire so the heat would be distributed all the way around the pot. Tyler had taken to finding dirty clothes with a vengeance. He probably thought by finding more work for her, he could force her to go back to Austin.

Rose didn't care. They were going about it with pretty good humor, much more than she expected. She knew she owed that to George.

She wondered what he thought of her. She had noticed the sharp, angry look he cast her way when she issued her command. He had supported her, but it was clear his devotion to his family was unchanged.

Rose loved to watch him with his brothers. It reminded her so much of the Robinsons.

She had lived with them until she was seventeen, long enough for their family to grow from three to eight children. They never had much money, but all they needed to be happy was to be gathered around Mr. Robinson, all talking, laughing, and competing for his attention.

"They crawl over him like puppies over a brood bitch," Mrs. Robinson would say.

Rose used to think wistfully of the family she wanted when she grew up. Three boys and three girls. The boys first so they could help their father and the girls last so she could spoil them. She didn't want them too far apart. They ought to have companions as they grew up. The loneliness of her childhood still hurt.

And of course they would all be strong-minded, each struggling with the others for his place in the sun, each depending on their father to be there to sort things out when they got too complicated.

And he would. Always. Because his family was more important to him than anything else in the world.

George would do that. Only when he was sorting out his brothers' problems did he seem to forget his own demons. He didn't know it, but his family might be his salvation.

Rose didn't know how to tell him that. Even if she did, she doubted he would believe it.

She wondered if the boys had any idea how much they meant to him. Probably not. They all seemed to be too busy with their own anger. Only George could put his own interests aside to concentrate on those of someone else.

*I wish he would concentrate on me.*

She had tried to avoid letting that thought cross her mind. It was a waste of time. She was bound to this family by their mutual need. She mustn't make the mistake of thinking she could remain here on any other basis.

But it hurt to know he was interested in her only as long as she worked for him.

*If you can't stand it, ask him to take you back to Austin. But before you do, remember that no matter how badly they behave, it's not half as bad as Austin.*

But she wanted more. She wondered if anyone would ever look at her with the love and concern she saw in George's eyes when he looked at his brothers. She wondered if anyone would ever give up something they wanted, or even a little of it, for her.

Not in Texas. Not where she would always be that damned Yankee woman.

"You're making a real nuisance of yourself, but you sure can cook," Monty said, digging into his breakfast with such enthusiasm that George had to remind him of his manners.

"Then she shouldn't cook so good," Monty answered, his mouth full. "I never knew eating could be this much fun."

"You eat like that every day, and your horse will soon refuse to carry you," Jeff said.

"Hell, I'd walk all the way to the Rio Grande for food like this."

"How about you, Hen?"

"It's good, but I wouldn't walk that far. I'd have blisters the size of possum eggs."

"You know there ain't no such thing as possum eggs," Zac said.

"Of course I do, but maybe Rose doesn't. I was planning to ask her for a possum egg omelet tomorrow, and now you ruined it."

Zac laughed happily. "Even a town girl knows possums don't lay eggs. Don't you, Rose?"

"It's Miss Thornton to you, young man," George corrected.

"It will be easier if everyone calls me Rose," Rose said. "And yes, I do know possums don't lay eggs. Did you know a bear's favorite food is pork?"

"You're pulling my leg?"

"Am not," Rose assured him. "You eat up your breakfast. If I have to throw it out, there'll be bears here before suppertime."

"I ain't seen no bears."

"You don't want to see one that loves pork. They like to snack on little boys."

"You *are* pulling my leg," Zac complained.

"Just a little. But I'll make a deal with you. You tell me when Hen's about to pull my leg, and I won't tell you any more tales."

"Hen wouldn't do that, but Monty would."

"Then we'll band together against Monty."

"You keep on cooking like this, and you can do anything you like," Monty said, popping the last bit of biscuit in his mouth and gulping down the last swallow of milk. He started to rise. "I'll be back at seven hungry as a bear."

"You forgot to ask to be excused," Zac piped up.

"Cow dung," Monty mumbled under his breath at his little brother as he sat back down. "May I be excused, ma'am?"

"Yes, and 'Rose' will do."

"Guess I'd better go, too," Hen said, getting to his feet. "I can't let Monty have all those rustlers to himself."

"I imagine the McClendons are too busy trying to feed their families to try stealing our cows," Jeff said.

"Do you have any special requests for dinner?" Rose asked hurriedly when she saw both twins turn toward Jeff, murder in their eyes.

"Turkey," said Monty. "I know where a whole flock of them roosts in some live oak trees down by the river."

"You bring them home tonight and I promise you roast turkey tomorrow."

"Hot damn, you might not be so bad after all."

"See, we're not so hard to get along with," Hen said.

"Just as long as I keep you full of food."

"You might want to start making a list of the supplies you'll need," George said to Rose. "Monty can't be bringing home turkeys every night. I'll send somebody into town next week. Jeff, I need to talk to you." George turned back to Rose. "Zac and Tyler can stay and help with the washing."

"I'm not toting water like a baby," Tyler exploded. "I can do as much work as you can."

"Don't be ridiculous," Jeff said. "You've been doing the housework for years. What do you know about range riding?"

"More than you ever learned locked up in some Yankee prison," Tyler shot back.

Jeff went dead white.

Monty and Hen quietly slipped out.

"I only need one person to help me," Rose said. "Zac will be just fine."

"Why is it always me?" Zac whined.

"Because we have to plan what trick we're going to play on Hen for the possum eggs," Rose said, "and we can't do it with you gone all day. Besides, I don't know anything about living in the country. There's all kinds of things I've got to learn. I might even try to milk the bull."

Zac treated that remark with the scorn it deserved.

"I won't have to stay home every day, will I?" he asked George.

"Not every day."

"All right. But I still don't like it."

"Tyler, you and Jeff get saddled up. I'll be along as soon as I have a few words with Miss Thornton."

"Can I saddle your horse?" Zac asked.

"You can't—" Jeff began.

"Of course," George said. "Just don't saddle that bad-tempered paint. After yesterday, he's probably just waiting to take a bite out of my leg."

"Beat you to the corral," Zac said and lit out the door running. Tyler followed close on his heels.

"You'd better keep an eye on them, Jeff."

"Why? They won't listen to a thing I say."

"You watch real well. It's just when you talk that you cause trouble," George said.

"I know he doesn't mean to," Rose said after Jeff had gone, "but it's almost as though he looks for the one thing that will hurt them the most."

George's frown caused her to bite her tongue. She would have to remember not to be so outspoken. It was bad enough she was always ordering them about, telling them what to do. Nobody liked to have his brother criticized by a near stranger, even if it was justified.

"You're not comfortable around him, are you?"

"No, but not because of his arm. You like your brothers, even when you disapprove of them or are angry at them. Jeff doesn't."

She had done it again. Would she ever learn not to blurt out everything she thought?

"You're wrong there. Jeff's the one with the sense of family, not me. In fact, I wouldn't have come home at all if it hadn't been for him.

"What would you have done?"

"Joined the army to fight Indians."

His words shocked Rose so much she could hardly respond.

"But that would mean joining the Union Army." She could hardly believe he would have done that after four years in the Confederate Army.

"The *United States* Army," George corrected. "I've always wanted an army career. I mean to rejoin as soon as I can leave here."

"Won't it be difficult to support a wife, especially raise a family, under those conditions?"

"I don't mean to get married or have a family."

He might as well have knocked the breath out of her with his fist. His every thought was bound up with his family. It seemed only natural he would want one of his own.

"It's just that I thought . . . with so many brothers . . . you have taken on so many responsibilities . . ."

"That's exactly the reason I don't want a family," George said. "I know the kind of burden we were to Ma and Pa. And what for? Seven sons who can't get along with each other? It's not something that appeals to me."

"But why the army?" Rose asked, unable to absorb either his words or the shock of their meaning.

"It's a job I'm good at. And it allows me the freedom to do what I want."

"But won't you miss the love and companionship a family gives you?"

"You haven't been in the army, or you'd know that combat forges extraordinary friendships between men. You trust your life to a comrade because you know he would give his life for you. Those feelings are just as strong as any between a man and woman, yet they carry no suffocating ties. Wives and children hold onto you forever, drain you of your strength. They feed upon you like beasts upon prey. Other men don't."

Zac came running up with George's horse.

"Did I do it right?" he asked, his eyes shining with excitement.

"Looks shipshape to me," George said, ignoring a loose cinch and the near-certainty there was a crease in the saddlecloth.

"Hen bridled him, but I did the rest."

"It's obvious I'm going to have to give you your own horse."

"Really?" Zac was so excited he released his hold on the bridle and threw himself into George's arms. Hen took the opportunity to tighten the cinch. Rose imagined George would stop just past the first thicket and readjust the saddlecloth.

"As soon as we get a chance, we'll go after some mustangs. Monty said he saw a big herd just across the river."

"Can I go with you? I want to pick out my own horse."

"Of course you ca—" Jeff began.

"We'll see about that," George interrupted. "But someone has to stay here to protect Rose in case any bandits show up while we're gone."

"I want a black one," Zac said, apparently unmoved by any possible danger to Rose. "Then no one can see me when I sneak up on them at night."

"We'll talk about that later," George said.

"When you say that, you don't mean to take me," Zac complained.

"I certainly won't take you if you throw a tantrum," George said, his tone severe. "Now I have to go. You be sure to do everything Rose asks. We'll talk about your horse tonight."

Feeling a lot like a drowning man about to go under for the third time, Rose watched them ride away. George had told her he wanted an army career. He was also set against anything that smacked of home and family responsibility. He wanted no ties whatsoever.

Rose had sworn she would never marry a soldier.

Her father had rarely been home. He never took his family with him because he said it was dangerous and it distracted him. Her whole life had been spent waiting for him to come home on his short visits and counting the days until he had to go back.

And now she discovered George wanted an army career and didn't want a family.

She was surprised at how much this disheartened her. She knew she liked George, depended on him, had built daydreams in her mind and heart with him at the center. Only now did she realize these were more than dreams. They were hopes. She had placed her future in George Randolph's hands without even knowing it.

And now he had quite positively handed it back to her.

She felt lost. Like a ship whose rudder had been wrenched off in a collision with a hidden shoal. Her future yawned before her, empty and somehow dangerous.

"We sure got us a heap of dirty clothes," Zac stated, intruding on her thoughts. "You mean to wash them all today?"

"Every piece," Rose said.

"You don't have to. Nobody will mind."

"What you mean is you don't want to do all that work," Rose replied. She felt a little better. She always did when she talked to Zac.

"Yeah, that too," Zac admitted with a brash grin. "Seems like an awful lot."

"Once we get everything clean, we won't have to do this much again."

"Why are women always carrying on about being clean? My ma was forever pestering me about it. Ever since she died I don't wash no more than once a month, and I've growed just fine."

"But you don't smell so fine," Rose said, wrinkling up her nose. "Now rustle about and get me some more wood. It'll take boiling water to get this dirt out."

"I don't see nothing wrong with dirt," Zac grumbled as he headed off. "God must have liked it, too. He sure made lots of it."

Rose looked around the kitchen. Something about the room bothered her, but she couldn't decide what it was. That annoyed her. This was her first full day at the ranch, and she had too much work to do to get distracted by vague feelings. It would take every minute she had to be ready by the time the men came home. If her plan was to succeed, she had to stay ahead of them.

Still, when she stepped into the pantry to look for some canned fruit, the feeling settled over her again. The moment she stepped back into the kitchen, she knew what it was. The room was too small to account for all the space in this half of the house. It was so obvious she wondered why she hadn't noticed it before.

*Because you've been too busy and worried and upset and frightened to notice anything that wasn't shoved under your nose.* She stared at the inner wall and almost immediately saw the door. It was nearly covered by heavy coats and rain slicks hanging on a series of wooden pegs. She would have to change that. The kitchen was no place to keep such clothes.

She moved one coat and tried the handle of the door. It turned, but she had to take down two more coats before she could get the door open.

She stepped into Mrs. Randolph's bedroom.

The room was fully as large as the kitchen itself and filled with furniture such as Rose had never seen. The few pieces of china and crystal had told her the Randolphs had once been rich. This room showed her what the inside of their Virginia mansion must have looked like.

Apparently Mrs. Randolph had brought everything from

her bedroom, from an enormous canopy bed covered in satin and mounded with pillows to the several rugs that covered the rough board floor. Someone had even tried to wallpaper the room. The attempt had been given up after the smooth inner walls had been covered. The log-and-mortar outer wall was covered by furniture and curtains. Brocade curtains and swags hung at windows made small and high for defense rather than beauty. Chairs, chests of drawers, wardrobes, and a daybed competed for the limited space in the room. A door at the end of the room, roughly adjacent to the pantry, must lead to a storage closet.

Rose stepped into the middle of the room even though she felt she was violating some unspoken taboo. Dust and the fine grit of Texas dirt covered everything. They probably hadn't disturbed the room since their mother's death. Rose wondered whether this was some sort of shrine or just a corner of their lives they had shut away. She knew she wouldn't ask George. If he wanted her to know, he would tell her.

It crossed Rose's mind that this should have been her room, but she knew she would never sleep here. It would remain closed, a monument to all that had gone wrong in the Randolph past.

A thin trail of smoke curled across the horizon.

"I thought she would have been finished with the wash long before now," Hen commented.

"She probably didn't have time, what with keeping an eye on Zac," Jeff said.

"We did have a lot of dirty clothes," George pointed out.

"If she's waiting for us to hang them up for her, I'm leaving," Monty declared.

"Good God," George exclaimed. "We don't have a clothesline. She can't have dried anything."

"Christ! That means everything I own is wringing wet," Monty groaned. "What am I going to wear?"

"What's wrong with what you've got on?" Jeff asked. "You've only worn it a week."

"Shut up," Monty growled. "You don't smell so sweet your-self."

"If you two are going to start arguing again, you can stay out here until you're done," George said. "I've had enough for one day."

"Me, too," said Tyler. "You're worse than a pair of girls."

Monty jumped his horse at Tyler, but the boy was already off and running toward the corral.

"Wouldn't be any arguing if Jeff would lay off Monty," Hen said.

"I wouldn't bother him if he would just think before he opened his mouth," said Jeff.

"You should have stayed in Virginia," Hen said, his eyes bright with anger. "I don't think you're going to like Texas too well. It sure as hell ain't going to like you." He jabbed his ankles into his horse's side and cantered after Monty and Tyler.

George and Jeff rode in silence for about a minute.

"You agree with him, don't you?" Jeff demanded angrily.

"Dammit, Jeff, when are you going to stop letting your bitter-ness poison everything you say? The boys are convinced you hate them."

"I wouldn't say anything if I wasn't concerned about them. They ought to know that."

"They don't. Even Rose commented on it."

Jeff stiffened so alarmingly George knew he'd made a mis-take by bringing Rose into the discussion.

"You can swell up like a toad if you want, but if an outsider can see it in just one day, it's worse than you think," George went on.

"I don't intend to take her as a judge."

"You apparently don't intend to take me or the boys, either."

"I didn't mean—"

"You got a raw deal, Jeff, nobody's denying that, but you're alive. You can walk. There are hundreds of thousands of men who'd count themselves lucky to be able to do that."

But Jeff's angry silence didn't occupy George's thoughts for long. As he rode into the yard, he saw Monty and Tyler angrily shouting at Rose. Hen and Zac also seemed to be lined up against her. With an exasperated sigh, he spurred his horse forward.

# Chapter Six

"You've got to get rid of her," Monty shouted.

Tyler agreed. "She's crazy."

"I did what you said. I asked them," Rose told George, "but it didn't do any good."

"I should think the hell not," Monty exploded.

"What did you ask?" George said.

"She wants them to take a bath and put on clean clothes before supper," Zac announced. "And you gotta make them do it. She already made me."

Exasperated as he was, George couldn't help but smile at Zac's indignation. The little boy would never forgive him if he ended up being the only one to take a bath.

"The bathtub is already filled with hot water," Rose said, "and I have plenty more in the wash pot. Your clothes are folded on your beds."

"What did you use for a clothesline?" George asked.

"Zac found some wire. We strung it between two trees, but the clothes would dry faster in the sun."

"I didn't even think about it until I was nearly home," George apologized.

Clearly the woman was ingenious. She might be bossy—she *was* bossy—but she could be depended upon to do her work without a lot of fuss and bother.

Not like Ma. With her, nearly everything was a crisis. She needed help deciding what to wear.

Just thinking of his mother made him feel guilty about not having been home to take care of her or to relieve the twins of a responsibility which must have been too much for their young shoulders.

"Do we have to take a bath?" Tyler demanded, bringing George's thoughts back to the point of contention.

"I intend to," George said. "I can't count the times during the war when I would have given almost anything for a decent stream to bathe in. I can't resist the temptation of a hot bath, especially when it's already waiting in my room."

"Hell!" Tyler exclaimed, apparently taking George's desire for a bath to mean he had to take one, too.

"Wait a minute," Monty said and headed for the kitchen. He came back a moment later, surprise and indignation on his face. "You don't have dinner ready. You really mean to starve us if we don't wash."

"If it were ready this early, it would be cold before everyone finished their baths," Rose told him.

"No, it wouldn't. I'd eat now."

George could see *I told you so* written all over her face.

"I'll go first," Hen announced, stunning his twin by heading for the house without further comment.

"I'm next," Tyler called, apparently resigned to the inevitable. "Before the water gets too dirty."

George nearly laughed at a boy as filthy as Tyler being concerned about dirty water.

"How about you?" Monty demanded.

"What about me?" Rose asked.

"You ought to take a bath, too."

"I'll have my bath in the kitchen after I've cleaned up."

"How do we know you'll really take one? Nobody will see you."

"You'll know because she says so," George said, impatient with Monty's teasing. At least he thought Monty was teasing.

He looked truly angry, even vengeful, but then Monty hated to be forced to do anything he didn't want to do.

"I think one of us ought to make sure," Monty said.

"Don't be stupid," George said.

"We can supervise her. I'll take the first watch. It shouldn't be a bad duty. Sure beats watching for rustlers." Monty took Rose by the arm. "Come along. Might as well get it over with."

Rose resisted, but Monty was stronger. He pulled her toward the house.

"I don't think Rose finds this amusing," George said. He found it surprisingly difficult to hold his temper.

"I do," Monty replied.

"Let her go. Nothing in her contract says she has to bathe."

"It ought to." Monty kept his hold on Rose.

"Maybe you should take your bath after Hen," George suggested, his calm voice belied by the look of sternness in his ebony eyes.

"You going to make me?" Monty said.

"I don't care if you never take a bath," George said, "but I'm afraid you will have to let go of Rose."

"And if I don't?"

"Don't be a fool. You can be as mad as you like at me, but you can't go about mishandling women. There's been enough of that in this family already."

Monty let go of Rose with a curse, shot George a look of cold fury, then stalked off toward the house.

"I'm next," Tyler protested, as anxious to defend his place in line as he had been moments ago to avoid the bath altogether. Monty shoved him aside.

"We'll throw the water away after Monty," George said. "Why don't you see if Zac needs help with the milking or picking up the eggs? You might ask Rose if she needs anything from the garden."

"That's not my job."

"Do it or stay home tomorrow," George snapped.

The younger boys went off, Tyler complaining loudly, Zac crowing in triumph. Jeff drifted off toward the corrals.

"You do seem to have a knack for turning things upside down," George remarked, his irritation at Monty causing him to speak sharply to Rose.

"I did ask them," Rose said.

"I know," George said, upset he was taking his irritation out on Rose. But he was even more upset by the suspicion that he was angry at Monty not because he had been rude, but because he had threatened Rose. He had been ready to fight his own brother. He didn't want to feel that strongly about anybody, especially not Rose.

"You've worked awfully hard since you got here. You must be exhausted."

"I am a little tired."

"Why don't you take tomorrow off."

"Do you mean to ask Tyler to do the cooking?"

He could have sworn he saw imps of amusement in her eyes. "I didn't mean the cooking."

"You don't think that's work?"

Now he knew she was teasing him.

"I guess I didn't say that very well. Why don't you take a book and sit under a tree tomorrow. I'll leave the boys here to do the chores."

"We'll see."

Her smile made him wonder how it was possible to mix coquettishness and innocence in the same expression. He also wondered how such a tiny movement of muscles could have such a strong effect on him.

"In the meantime, I've got to see about getting supper finished. If Monty's not fed soon after he's finished with his bath, he's liable to throw me in the tub yet."

Her effort at humor barely eased the tensions inside George. "Thanks for remaining cheerful despite so much opposition. Now I'd better get inside and hurry the twins along, or you'll be midnight getting out of the kitchen."

Rose felt a pang of disappointment as she watched George walk to the house. She was certain he was more concerned about not being left alone with her than about the hour he sat down to his dinner. He was prepared to thank her, appreciate her work, support her decisions, but that was as far as he would go.

*Forget the notion you're ever going to be more than a housekeeper to him. He's told you what he wants.*

But hope didn't die that easily. George's brothers weren't anything like the Robinsons, but she felt a kinship with them. They were all lonely souls looking for a place to keep warm. She would love to help if they would only let her.

"This has got to end now," Monty shouted.

Jeff agreed. "You've gone too far this time."

"I don't mind stripping the beds and hanging the blankets on the line to air," Rose informed them, "but I can't lift the mattresses."

"Who says they have to be lifted?" Monty demanded.

"They need to be aired out."

"Then open the windows."

The clamor of angry voices outside woke George. Realizing that Monty and Jeff had set aside their mutual antagonism long enough to become embroiled in a new argument with Rose, he felt tempted to sneak out the back door, saddle his horse, and head for any army fort west of the Mississippi and north of the Arkansas River. Just once, why couldn't Monty do what he was asked without kicking up a fuss? And why on earth did Jeff have to join in? What was it about Rose that made him so antagonistic? George couldn't find a single thing to object to about Rose.

Except that he thought about her too often.

He hadn't known her four days yet, and it seemed she was on his mind all the time. And he didn't mean her cooking or her running battle with Monty.

He meant Rose herself. He had dreamed about her. And the things they did in those dreams would probably turn Rose's cheeks crimson. George had tried to look at her as just a housekeeper, but a few more dreams like last night and he wouldn't be able to think about her without his body stiffening immediately.

It had happened three times yesterday, twice while he was in the saddle and once at dinner. During the enforced abstinence of the war years, his body had seldom reminded him of its unsatisfied need. Now he was feeling almost as randy as he had in his teens.

If either Jeff or Monty noticed, he'd never hear the end of it. Hen probably wouldn't say anything; he didn't know if Tyler would understand. Zac wouldn't care even if he did understand.

And of course he didn't want Rose to know. What could she think except that he had lured her out here into the wilds of southern Texas to take advantage of her?

George didn't intend to take advantage of her, but he didn't know what he did want to do. At one moment he wanted nothing more than to be alone with her so he could satisfy his hunger for her. At another time he wanted to be far beyond the reach of any woman, especially a woman as domestic as Rose. He could see babies in her eyes. And the last thing on this earth George wanted was to become a father.

"I'm going to ask George." That was Tyler. The little worm.

"Get up, Hen," George said to his brother.

"Time to quell another domestic rebellion?" A rare smile lifted Hen's lips.

"Sounds like it. Unless you want to handle this one."

"No. I hear Jeff."

"He is your brother, too. You don't have to treat him like a leper."

"You tell him that."

"I have."

"Doesn't seem to do much good."

"Nothing I've done around here seems to have done much good. I might as well have gone straight into the army."

"I'm glad you didn't."

George had his back to Hen, but he turned back to face his younger brother.

"Zac needs somebody to look up to," Hen explained. Then, much to George's surprise, Hen drew on his pants, picked up his mattress, and carried it outside.

"Shut up, Monty, and get your mattress," Hen said to his twin. "You're getting to be a regular jaw-me-dead. Where do you want this, ma'am?"

Rose had to close her mouth before she could reply. "On the corral fence."

"You can't mean to knuckle under just like that," Monty protested.

"If we'd helped Ma more, she might not have died," Hen said as he walked away.

"Well, I'll be damned and double-damned," Monty muttered.

Just then George came out with his mattress over his shoulder.

Monty took one look and broke into an ear-splitting grin. "By damn, Rose, if you haven't outmaneuvered me again. Slipped around my left flank and routed the whole damned column without me even knowing. Maybe I should have brought you half a dozen turkeys instead of just three." He walked over to his horse and untied from his saddle three large birds that he had shot that morning after his watch.

"Three are quite enough," Rose said, as bewildered by her success as Monty. "You can bring me more some other time."

"I sure will," he said as he hung the turkeys on a nail in the porch roof, out of reach of the dogs.

"Okay, you scamps," George said to Tyler and Zac. "If you want a hand with those mattresses, you'd better get off your hindquarters."

"But, George—" Tyler began.

"Give it up," Monty said. "We're in full retreat. We've been beaten by a better man."

"She don't look like no man to me," Zac pointed out.

"That's why we've been beaten," Monty said, looking first at George and then at Hen with an inquisitive gleam in his eyes. "I made the mistake of ignoring her most obvious weapon."

"What are you talking about?" Tyler asked.

Monty threw his arm over his brother's shoulder. "It seems we've seriously neglected your education, my boy. You'd better ride with me today."

"It might be better if he rode with me," George said. "I doubt his understanding will be much improved by anything you would tell him."

"Zac, put the sheets in the wash pot," Rose said. "Tyler, you can hang the blankets on the line. I'll have breakfast on the table by the time you're finished."

"I can't bring you my mattress or my sheets," Jeff said, waving his stump at Rose.

Rose knew he was registering his objection to her victory rather than complaining about his arm.

"I'm sure you could if you made up your mind to try." She spoke as normally as she could into the uncomfortable silence. "But you can get me some water from the well, if you like. I'm going to need more to wash the floors."

George hadn't expected Rose to confront Jeff's opposition as she had, or to understand the real meaning of what he said. Her deft handling of his remark increased his growing respect for her.

"Come on," George said to Jeff. "The sooner we get the water, the sooner we eat."

As soon as they got beyond hearing distance of the others, George turned angrily on his brother. "I think it's about time you decided what you want."

"All I said was—"

"You're the one who demanded a housekeeper. The others

would have been happy with a range cook. Well, I hired her. And not even you can deny that Rose has done more work in two days than we ever thought possible. Yet all you've done is object to everything."

"I can't help it. I don't like her."

"Well, I do, so start giving her a little cooperation."

"Are you telling me you'd choose that woman ahead of me, your own brother?"

"I'm telling you to start pulling with the family and not against it. And as long as Rose is working for the family, I mean her as well."

"I suppose you'll want me to leave if I refuse."

George swore in exasperation. "I want no such thing. This is your home as well as mine."

"It'll *never* be my home. We should go back to Virginia. We could get Ashburn back if we tried."

"What for? The house is a near ruin. The land has been fought over until I doubt there's a barn, fence, or tree left standing. This is our home now. You have to learn to accept that."

"I can't."

"You give yourself too many battles to fight, Jeff. Come on. Rose is waiting for the water."

"I'm going to need someone to help me with the heavy work around here," Rose announced. The men were almost through with breakfast. They were full of ham and gravy and grits and milk. Too contented to get upset. Yet.

"What work?" Zac asked, his black eyes apprehensive.

"Someone needs to build a coop for the chickens. I'm surprised the coyotes haven't gotten them all."

"Would have if the dogs didn't keep them off," Monty said.

"I need a garden dug," Rose continued. "There's plenty of time to plant corn, potatoes, beans, peas, squash, strawberries—"

"I hate squash," Zac informed her.

"—tomatoes, and pumpkins. I'd also like some fruit, nuts,

and berries if there are any trees around here. I can make jam."

"We have berries along the creeks," Monty said. "Pecan trees, too."

"Zac and Tyler can help with that," George said.

"I don't see why I have to go berry hunting," Tyler objected.

"What about meat?" Rose asked. "Do you buy it, grow it, or kill it yourselves?"

"Why don't you stay home today?" Monty suggested to George. "That'll give you plenty of time to discuss all the things she wants done."

"You're just trying to get out of doing it yourself," George said.

"Sure he is," Hen said, "but it's a good suggestion anyway. We can't get much done over the breakfast table. And we're too tired at night."

"Okay, but I mean to give you two all the worst chores."

"Can't," Monty said with his most irresistible smile. "I can't use an ax without cutting myself, and I can't use a hammer without hitting my thumb."

"You can milk the cow," Zac suggested. "She don't care how clumsy you are."

Zac dived behind George when Monty made a grab for him.

"I'll be expecting roast turkey tonight," Monty reminded Rose as he and Hen got ready to leave. "I like it with stuffing and lots of gravy."

"You'll get what I can fix," Rose informed him.

"See if you can find me some eggs," she told Zac when he tried to leave with the twins.

"I don't collect the eggs until near 'bout dinner," he informed her.

"I used all the eggs I had for breakfast, and I need more for the stuffing. I have to start the turkeys early."

"Those stupid old hens ain't laid anything yet," he protested.

*"Haven't,"* George corrected him, "and you'll never know until you look. Now get going."

"When I get big, I ain't never going to look for eggs," he swore.

"I don't blame you," George commiserated. "Now I'm going to heat water to scald the turkeys. I want you back with those eggs before we finish plucking them."

Pretending to look for the egg basket, Zac hung back after George left. "I'm going to New Orleans when I grow up," he announced in a whisper, as though he were telling Rose an important secret.

"My father used to tell me it was the most beautiful city he'd ever visited," she said. "If you want to help George pluck the turkeys, I'll look for the eggs."

"I'm the only one who knows where they hide their nests," he said, not without an element of pride.

"I can learn."

"A girl can't go all those places. You'd get dirty."

"I wouldn't mind."

"Yes, you would. Girls hate dirt worse than anything."

"I hope you won't leave for New Orleans before I learn where all the nests are."

"You done told George you wanted a chicken coop. All you'll have to do is look inside."

"I guess I forgot. You'd better get the eggs quick before I forget what I wanted them for."

"You didn't forget nothing," Zac said. "You're just trying to make me feel better about being little and having everybody tell me what to do. George does it, too."

"I think that's nice, don't you?"

"I suppose so, but I don't need no special looking after. I'm going to tell him to stop."

"I wouldn't if I were you."

"Why?"

"Well, big brothers like to have somebody to take care of. You'd take away all his fun if you didn't let him look after you."

"Monty and Hen don't do it. Neither does Jeff."

"Of course not. Middle brothers are supposed to plague you. Your biggest brother protects you. It's written in the big-brother book they give little boys when they're born."

"I didn't get no book."

"Little brothers don't get one."

"I think that's rotten."

"Girls don't get one either."

"I think that's rotten, too."

"So do I, but that's how things are. Now I have to help George with the turkeys, so you'd better look for those eggs. I bet I'll have the dressing ready before you get back."

"No, you won't," Zac said, and raced from the room.

"He's a scamp," Rose remarked to George as she came out of the house.

"He's the only one Pa and the war didn't ruin," George said. "At least I don't think he's ruined."

"I don't understand," Rose said.

"Never mind. The water's hot. Want to hand me one of those turkeys?"

"Do the boys bring home wild game often?" Rose asked. She took the turkeys down from the hook, weighing each carefully with her eye and the pull on her hand.

"I don't really know. It probably depended on what Tyler could do with the meat. We could try to get more if you like."

"It would help. A diet of bacon and dried beef can get monotonous."

George dipped the turkey in the pot long enough for the scalding water to loosen the feathers. Then he handed the dripping bird to Rose. He dipped a second bird, then tackled it himself.

"I want to save everything but the wing and tail feathers," Rose said, pointing to a woven basket she had brought with her from the kitchen. "I plan to make some more pillows."

"Are you always thinking about something practical?" George asked.

"That's what you pay me for."

"I thought women liked to dream."

"Some might, but I hate dreaming about things I can't have. It makes me irritable."

"But don't you think about them in spite of knowing better?"

"Of course," Rose said. She tossed a handful of wet feathers into the bucket with a little more energy than necessary. "But as soon as that happens, I make myself concentrate on something else until I forget."

"How old are you?"

"You didn't ask that before you hired me. Why do you want to know now?"

"Curiosity, I guess. I'd say you were twenty, still young enough to indulge in all sorts of dreams. And pretty enough to have a hope they might come true."

Rose tugged at a handful of stubborn wing feathers. They held tight. She was forced to pull them out one at a time. Even then she had to pull hard.

"I used to daydream," Rose admitted, "before the war. The men looked so handsome in their uniforms it was hard not to make up stories about them. But all that ended when my father decided to fight for the Union."

Rose remembered with painful vividness how she felt when her father told her of his decision. It had destroyed her world. She respected his allegiance to the army which had given him his career, as well as his belief that the Union should never be divided, but he couldn't seem to appreciate that it would alienate her from the people she had grown up with.

He never understood her feeling for Texas. She guessed he was too much a son of New England for that.

He had been so certain he would be able to set everything aright after the war. Well, he wasn't around to see what happened or to fix it.

But then he'd never been around.

"The good people of Austin soon made it clear that neither they nor their sons would be part of my dreams."

She finished plucking her turkey. Holding it by its neck and feet, she held it over the low flames to singe the hairs. Then dipping it into a bucket of clean water, she began to scrape the skin clean.

"As things got worse, I found myself having nightmares about the terrible things that could happen to me."

"Didn't you ever dream of some young soldier coming to save you?"

"Of course I did. My mother once read me a story about an English knight who slew a terrible dragon to save a princess. Of course I knew it was all make-believe, but when things were at their worst, I would imagine him coming to save me." She paused in her work and looked at George. "The knight was named St. George. You can't imagine what a shock it gave me, after you'd beaten up Luke, to learn your name was George."

George laughed. "St. George rescuing Princess Rose."

Rose smiled a little sheepishly. "Something like that."

George handed her his plucked turkey to singe and clean. He dipped the last turkey into the still scalding water and started to remove the feathers.

"Is that why you accepted this job, to get away from Austin?"

"Yes." Rose didn't tell him that was only part of the reason.

"Weren't you worried about what might happen after you got here? I did say seven men."

"I knew you'd protect me."

"How could you know that?" George asked, surprised.

"I could tell the minute you stepped into the Bon Ton."

"How?" asked George, stunned that anyone could feel they knew him so well after just one look.

"I don't know, but a woman can always tell."

George wasn't sure he liked being so transparent. It was hard to defend yourself when other people could read you so easily, and he had too many secrets he wanted to keep.

"What else can a woman tell?"

"When it's time to stop talking," Rose said with a smile that rocked George off balance. "I just told Zac that girls don't get a book when they're born, but they do. They get one about boys. And the first thing it tells you, right on the first page, is not to tell everything you know. Hand me that last turkey. If I don't get them cleaned, I'll never have the stuffing started before Zac gets back. And he won't let me forget it."

"You don't have to spend so much time with him," George said. "He can be an awful nuisance."

"I don't mind. Besides, he makes me laugh. It's a nice break from all the fussing around here."

Rose hadn't meant to say that. She had made a promise to herself to stop criticizing so much.

"I'm sorry. I guess we don't see it. You'd have to have known our father to understand. Monty's not half so bad."

Rose felt chastised.

It turned out to be one of the busiest days of George's life. While Rose dressed the turkeys, prepared the giblets for gravy, and mixed the stuffing, he and Zac beat the blankets, turned the mattresses, took up the rugs, and washed the bedroom floor. Then he chose and cleared a site for the chicken coop. After that he cut four posts and set them in the ground to form the corners of the coop. Next he cut some saplings from the creek bank, dressed the trunks, and built the roosts. Then taking a pencil and making a rough sketch, he figured out how much lumber he would need for the roof and sides.

Later he and Rose walked over every foot of ground within a half mile of the house trying to decide on the best place to locate the garden. Tyler had placed his garden on top of the ridge. It was safe from floods, but the ground was hard and dry and the crops exposed to the wind. Rose meant to plant her garden in the rich soil of the creek's floodplain.

They came upon Mrs. Randolph's grave in a small grove of live oaks just beyond the well. Only her name and the date of her death were carved into the weathered board that marked her final resting place.

"I mean to carry her back to Virginia someday," George said. "I think she lost her will to live when she had to come out here."

Rose could only wonder how the mother of seven such vital, vigorous sons could give up on life. Rose would give almost anything to have such sons. And she would fight to her last breath to see them grow to manhood.

But it wasn't fair to judge Mrs. Randolph. There was so much Rose didn't know about the family. Besides, any woman who could inspire her children to wallpaper a log cabin deserved her respect.

By the time she and George had spent more than an hour deciding what they wanted to plant, how many rows they needed, and how many seeds they required, it was late afternoon. The sheets were dry, so George carried the mattresses inside so Rose could make up the beds. Then while Zac looked for the eggs a second time that day, George tried to milk the cow. The cow might not have minded clumsy, but she minded George. Zac finished the milking while George split wood for the stove.

"I think it would have been easier to go with the boys," George said as he sank into his chair at the head of the table. Rose was fixing dinner. He wasn't especially hungry, but the smell of roast turkey was enough to tempt even the most lethargic appetite.

"There are still a lot of things around here I can't do by myself," Rose said.

"Make a list, and we'll start working our way through," George told her, but without much enthusiasm.

He wasn't thinking about chores. He was thinking about Rose. It had been years since he had been around a woman for more than a few minutes. He couldn't remember their effect on him in any great detail, but he knew it was nothing like his reaction to Rose.

He felt no chivalrous desire to protect her from bandits or rustlers. He wanted to take her to his bed and make love to her until he didn't feel this burning inside his loins. He wanted to lose himself in her sweetness until he stopped having the queasy feeling all over when she brushed against him. He wanted to bury himself in her body until he was certain he would never want a woman this badly again.

He also felt desperate to break the hold she had on him.

He wanted to be free of any ties that would keep him from going where he wanted, doing what he liked, being what he wanted to be. He didn't want to endure the same difficulties and frustrations his father had. True, his father had been weak and selfish, but George had watched unending demands wear at him until he lost his control, his dignity, his self-respect.

And George was his father's son.

Even before the war, he had known he had the same weaknesses. He swore he wouldn't make the same mistakes. He knew this meant giving up much he might have enjoyed, but he also knew a man had to be true to himself.

The boys didn't stand in his way. At least they wouldn't for long.

It was Rose. That was where the danger lay. That was where he had to keep a watch.

He tried to figure out what it was about her that made her so appealing. How could a woman look absolutely delicious with her hair up, her brow moist with perspiration, and her body shrouded in a loose brown dress that covered everything from her chin to the tips of her toes and her fingers? It didn't even have the advantage of being pretty or of fitting her body suggestively.

She had her back to him, her attention centered on the meal she was preparing. Yet he wanted to stay with her so much he offered to set the table. He didn't know how to set a table. He'd never done anything more than pour a glass of milk.

# Chapter Seven

"Zac deserved a chance to play a little while. I've worked him hard all day."

That was just an excuse to be alone with her.

"Turn the plates over," Rose told him. "I don't want flies getting on them."

George discovered a woman's back could be a very sensual part of her body, even when shrouded in an old brown dress.

The lace-trimmed collar reached almost to the hair on the nape of her neck. The tiny area of white skin dusted by a fine mist of hairs that would not remain in her bun made him want to see more.

He didn't know why he had failed to notice it that morning in Austin, but she had a very tidy figure. Not even the dress could hide that. And she was pretty. Well, more than pretty. He couldn't find the exact word he wanted, but then he wasn't used to expressing himself about women.

"Turn the glasses and the cups over, too."

"What do I do with all these forks and knives?"

"You need the napkins first."

She reached into the drawer of one of the cabinets and pulled out napkins, washed, ironed, and folded.

"The boys won't know what to do with these. I doubt Zac's ever seen one."

"Then it's time he did."

Piquant. That was the word he wanted. Pretty, too, but piquant. There was a liveliness about her, a kind of charm which had a greater impact than mere beauty. Not that George was about to spurn beauty. But he had found that beauty needed spice to make it come alive. He had met too many debutantes before the war who had been taught that being beautiful was primarily the art of *being*. Tables, chairs, and hearth rugs could *be* just as well as women, but you never found men tripping over themselves to get a second look at them. But piquant, that caused people to take a second look, ask questions, remember.

"Maybe you don't think a housekeeper should concern herself with manners and napkins," Rose said.

"I guess it's a good idea. The boys need to learn how to behave. Their wives will thank you someday."

"I don't expect to be here long enough to meet their wives."

Much to George's astonishment, her words jolted him. Five days ago he'd never heard of her. Now he was surprised to find he hadn't thought of her job coming to an end.

"If you mean to turn Zac and Tyler into perfect gentlemen, you'll be here forever."

"Zac will do just fine," Rose said. She opened the oven to check the turkeys. "That boy is clever enough to do anything. And charming enough to get away with it, too. I don't know about Tyler. He stays as far away from me as he can, but I don't think he much cares about people, or what they think about him."

"You've reached a pretty fair estimation of the boys' characters. What about Jeff or the twins?"

She had just broken her own promise.

"I've said enough for the time being," Rose replied. She tried to remove the turkeys from the oven, but it wasn't as easy to handle a hot pan as a cold one.

"Here, let me help you," George said. But when he tried to take the pan from Rose, there wasn't enough room on the handles for both their hands. His hands covered hers.

George doubted he would have felt the pain if the handles had burned him. The jolt he received from touching Rose was more powerful than a mere burn.

"I can't let go," Rose said.

*Neither can I*, George thought. His muscles refused to respond to any message he sent them. But common sense warned him he had to do something before they dropped the turkey and spilled the boiling juices over themselves and the floor.

George forced himself to concentrate on the pan rather than Rose. He loosened his grip. "I've got it. Slip your hands out."

"You can't put it on the table in that pan," Rose cried when he turned toward the table. "Set it on the stove. I've got to put it on a serving platter."

George helped her lift the turkey and set it on the platter. They stood shoulder to shoulder, elbow to elbow, hip to hip. It was all he could do to keep from dropping the bird and taking Rose into his arms. Never in his life had he experienced anything so powerful, so overwhelming, so completely beyond his control. It was like a physical force, one much stronger than he, forcing him to do what it willed. He was only just able to control himself long enough to take the second turkey out and transfer it to a platter.

His eyes scanned Rose's face and he knew immediately she had felt the force of their nearness just as strongly as he. She looked stunned, maybe even slightly scared. She stood still, seemingly unable to move.

Like a man hypnotized, George reached out and touched her cheek. It felt soft and warm, just as he knew it would. He wanted to touch more of her, to absorb her through his fingertips, but his hand wouldn't move. It just stayed there, cupping her cheek like something precious.

"I think I hear the boys riding up," Rose said, her voice more breath than tone. But she didn't move. Her gaze remained locked with George's.

The sound of hooves brought George out of his trance as quickly as if a hypnotist had snapped his fingers.

"You'd better get ready. Monty can unsaddle a horse quicker than you can shuck an ear of corn."

"He still has to wash and change his clothes," Rose said, struggling to pull herself out of her dazed state.

But George had hardly set the second turkey on the table before Monty burst into the kitchen. He had neither washed nor changed. Considering his haste, George was surprised he hadn't ridden his horse right into the kitchen.

"I swear I could smell those turkeys a mile down the trail," he said, going straight to the closest platter.

"Wash up, and you can have all you can eat." It seemed odd to Rose to be saying words that had nothing to do with the feelings that engulfed her body or with the thoughts that whirled about in her mind with the speed of a hurricane.

"You expect me to walk back out that door with the smell of turkey pulling at me harder than a rope on a calf?"

"I expect you to wash and change before you put a leg under this table." How could George have recovered so rapidly? She still felt numb.

"And I imagine your horse would like you to unsaddle him and put him in the corral," George added.

"Just this once?"

"No."

Maybe she was the only one genuinely affected. Maybe he did this every time he found himself alone with a woman. She couldn't imagine too many of them objecting.

"But I can't move."

"I told your brother a lie when I said Zac had the charm of a dozen cats," Rose said. "You're twice as bad."

*I told you not to place any reliance in that foolish dream of yours. It meant nothing to him. The moment was just that to him, a moment.*

She tried not to let her disappointment show as she took a large, sharp knife and cut a slice from the golden brown breast. The juices dripped down her fingers.

"Here," she said, handing the steaming meat to Monty. "But you don't get another bite until you wash and change."

Monty had barely strode away with his prize when Zac burst in the kitchen.

"You gave Monty a piece of turkey. That's not fair."

She couldn't remain mired in her own cheerless thoughts, not with this dynamic, vividly alive family about to wash her away on the tide of its exuberant energy.

"Probably not," Rose confessed, a smile announcing the return of her self-control and her good humor, "but it's Monty's turkey. He shot it."

"But I found the eggs for the dressing," Zac insisted.

"So you did. And you shall have the first serving. Here, I'll set the bowl in front of your place."

Zac plopped down in his chair.

"Are you washed?"

"Yep. Hen said he hardly recognized me this clean."

"How about pouring the milk?"

Zac groaned and got up. "A little kid has to do everything. I sure ain't doing it when I get to New Orleans."

*"Am not,"* George said, "and you won't be going to New Orleans for some time yet."

"George can pour the milk," Zac said. "He knows what everybody wants."

"George has to carve the turkey before Monty tears it apart," Rose replied sternly. "The milk."

Zac made a face, but he poured the milk double speed so he could be back in his chair before anybody else entered the room.

The Randolph men poured through the door like miners from a tunnel at the sound of the closing whistle, but Rose's calm "Good evening" slowed their rush to the table. The sight of napkins at their plates slowed them even more. Jeff stared at Rose, looked at George, and back at Rose.

"You're supposed to put them in your laps," Zac said, unable to resist imparting his newly-acquired knowledge. "It keeps the food from messing up your clothes when you drop it."

*"If* you drop it," Rose corrected.

"They will," said the irrepressible Zac.

"Hurry up and pass the turkey," Monty said. "I can taste it already."

"The turkey's too big to pass," Rose said. "Tell George what you want, and he'll carve it for you."

"I shot three of them. That's enough so that every two of us can have one."

"George will carve," Rose repeated. "We'll pass everything else."

Monty looked like he was going to protest, but since George cut off a huge slice of breast and passed it to him first, he didn't complain.

"I want a drumstick," Zac reminded his brother.

"Why did you cook all three turkeys?" Jeff asked.

"They won't keep," Rose said, faintly irritated that Jeff would question her.

"What will we do with them?"

"Eat them. We'll have sliced turkey, turkey and gravy over rice, or turkey hash until it's gone."

"Then I'll kill three more, and we'll start over again," Monty said.

"I don't like turkey that much," Jeff said.

"Then I'll feed it to the dogs," Rose answered so sharply George looked up from his carving.

The younger boys may have missed the look George gave Jeff, but Rose didn't. Neither did Jeff. He turned his attention to his food.

"We have to send to town for supplies," George announced. "Anybody in particular want to go?"

"Rose ought to go," Hen said. "She's the only one who knows what she needs."

"I have too much to do to spend several days going into town," Rose said. "I'll make a list." She didn't mean to tell them she had no intention of going back to Austin until she had to. She was even considering asking George to take her to San Antonio when her quarterly trip came due.

"We need lumber and nails for the chicken coop as well as a month's supplies," George said.

"We'll need a smokehouse if you mean to cure your own meat," Rose reminded him.

"And seeds," Zac said, his mouth full. "Rose wants a garden full of everything."

"You ought to send Tyler if it's building you want done," Hen said. "He's a terrible cook, but he's the best builder we got."

"Okay, but he can't go alone."

"Don't look at me," Monty said. "I haven't lost anything in Austin."

"Same here," said Hen.

"That leaves you, Jeff."

"Is driving a wagon all you think I'm good for?" he demanded.

Rose didn't know what got into her. Maybe the encounter with George rattled her nerves so much she forgot her promise to herself. Maybe Jeff's question about the turkey had irritated her more than she thought.

"Are you going to force George to send the wrong person just because of your sensitivity about your arm?"

There was an audible gasp, and everyone in the room seemed to freeze in place. George looked at her, shocked.

"Even I can tell you're the obvious choice," she went on. The look in George's eyes scared her, but it was too late to stop now. "Monty doesn't know how to talk to anything but cows, and Hen is bound to find somebody to shoot. That leaves George, and you know he's the only person who can get this cantankerous, pigheaded, stubborn bunch to work together."

Monty's face split with a roguish grin. "You like us a lot, don't you?"

"It has nothing to do with liking you. It's just the way things are. Just as your arm is the way things are," she said turning back to Jeff. "If you keep seeing what everybody says as having to do with your arm, your whole life is going to be upside down. And if you can't give George credit for thinking of you rather than your arm, how are you going to believe anyone else can?"

Okay, so Jeff would never like her, but she wasn't worried about Jeff. George was looking at her like he wanted to strangle her. She knew it wasn't her business to tell Jeff to stop striking out at everyone, but even Hen and Monty, who if looks could kill would have slain their brother days ago, walked around him like they were walking on eggshells.

"I wasn't telling you to do anything," George said to Jeff. His quiet tone as much as his manner eased the tension in the room. "I just asked you if you wanted to go."

Jeff ignored Rose. "You ought to go," he said to George.

"I thought you might like a chance to get away, see some people, maybe even buy a few things for yourself."

"Do we have enough money?"

"For the time being. While you're there," George continued, deciding it would be easier just to assume Jeff was going, "ask about bloodstock. The bull will make a big difference in our herd in a few years, but we could improve our stock a lot faster if we had twenty or thirty good heifers."

"Are you looking for breeding stock?" Rose asked.

Jeff looked at her as though she were intruding in family business, but George answered readily. "We've been talking about it."

"I've heard Richard King is doing exactly what you want to do. I don't know if he'll sell you any breeding stock, but if he won't, maybe he'll know somebody who will."

"Where does he live?"

"Somewhere south of Corpus Christi."

"How do you know so much?" Jeff asked. His tone implied he doubted that her information could be trusted.

"People in restaurants never pay any attention to who's serving them. They'll say anything."

"See if you can find out anything about King when you're in town," George told Jeff. "We can sell some of our steers to get the money."

"When should I leave?"

"Tomorrow."

"We don't have a mule or a wagon to bring back the lumber."

"Then buy one."

"Or a barn to put the mule in."

"I expect we'll have to build one sooner or later, for the bull if nothing else. He's too valuable to leave out."

"All of a sudden we're doing a lot of buying and building," Jeff said. He looked at Rose. It was clear he held her responsible for a situation he didn't approve of.

"That's normal, considering nothing's been done for five years," George pointed out, his temper getting rather short. "It's my turn to sleep out. Anybody want game?"

"Venison," Tyler suggested. "Hen says there's plenty of deer eating our grass."

"Don't shoot anything until dawn," Hen warned. "There's panthers in some of those creek bottoms. You kill a deer at nightfall and you'll have three or four panthers nosing about your camp before midnight."

Rose shivered. "You didn't say anything about panthers," she said to George accusingly.

"They won't come near the house. They don't like the dogs."

"Shouldn't George take one of the dogs with him?" she asked. The idea of George sleeping out with panthers all around him upset her.

"They're my dogs," Monty said. "They won't go with anybody except maybe Hen once in a while."

"Maybe you should buy a dog, too," Rose said to Jeff.

"I don't need a dog to let me know if a panther is around," George said, touched that Rose would worry about his safety. "My horse will do just as well."

But Rose had never met a horse that inspired her with that kind of confidence. Something would have to be done about these bandits and rustlers, as well as the panthers. Preferably all three. She didn't see why they should be allowed to terrorize people, especially at night when people couldn't see to defend themselves.

"You've got to anticipate which way the calf will turn," George told Zac. "He won't stand still while you throw a rope on him."

"It don't make no difference," Zac complained, disgusted with himself. "Nobody's going to let me rope no old calf no way."

Rose had been watching George try to teach Zac to ride and rope. Without too much success. Zac was much longer on wanting to ride than on desire to learn how to do it correctly.

"If you don't start paying more attention to your grammar, you'll stay home and practice your sentences with Rose."

"I done . . . I already practiced them all week," Zac argued. "I can't do no more."

George cast his little brother a stern glance.

"Any more," Zac corrected himself.

"You can't rope properly until you ride so well you don't have to pay attention to anything except the calf you're after. And you can't ride through the rough parts of the range until I feel sure you can stay on your horse."

"I can," Zac assured him. "I can stick like glue."

"Maybe we'll go for a ride this afternoon and see."

"Promise?" Zac said. He had the skeptical look of a little boy who had seen too many promises come to nothing.

"I promise, as long as you get all your chores done and don't give Rose any reason to complain about you."

"I like Rose," Zac said. "It's Tyler and Jeff that cause all the trouble."

George looked embarrassed to have led Zac into making a statement he didn't want Rose to hear.

"They'll come around," George assured him.

"Jeff's mean. I don't like him," Zac said.

"You don't mean that," George said.

"Yes, I do. He's mean to Monty and he's mean to me. He's mean to you, too."

"Jeff isn't mean. He's just unhappy. It's hard to get used to having only one arm."

"It's hard to get used to being the littlest and getting told what to do all the time," Zac argued. "But I don't say mean things to nobody because of it."

"Yes, you do, you little scamp," George countered, scooping his brother up and tossing him up on his shoulders. "You complain about every chore I give you."

"But I don't mean it."

"Neither does Jeff."

The days when Tyler and Jeff were away were wonderful for Rose. Their absence didn't remove all dissension—Rose decided no two members of this family could be together without arguing—but the spirit of anger left with them.

She understood Jeff's resentment, but she had no idea what caused Tyler to be so antagonistic. He hated helping her. He particularly hated having to pick berries or gather nuts with Zac. Rose decided he must be going through a difficult time, no longer a boy but not quite a man. It couldn't be easy to feel grown but not be treated that way. He was almost as tall as George, but he was so skinny he looked more like a prisoner of war than Jeff. His clothes hung off him, and he shuffled along like a boy grown so fast he had left his coordination a year behind.

The others had begun to accept her. Zac was young enough to still enjoy a woman's softness. In fact, he was constantly underfoot. She suspected he was the one brother who was truly born to live indoors.

Monty and Hen had warmed considerably. Well, at least Monty had. Nearly every day he brought her some game he had shot. With so many mouths to feed, she was glad for the fresh meat, but she wasn't glad of the work of cleaning, dressing, and preparing it.

Hen never said much, but he had the best natural manners of anybody except George. He remembered to thank her, say good morning, and hold the door. Little things, to be sure, things he usually did without speaking, his face showing no expression, but touches of thoughtfulness which she appreciated.

But the greatest change was in George.

At first she had feared his interest might be the same as Luke Kearney's. Despite the way he looked at her, despite the quality of his character, he said nothing to make her think he liked her. Her work maybe, but not her personally. How could she *know* he was interested in anything more than her body? It had been a physical touching, an accidental brushing, which turned the heat up to a blaze.

Had she left Austin and Luke Kearney only to discover that George was just like him?

If so, she would have to leave. It wouldn't be as easy to refuse George as Luke.

It mortified her to think she was so weak that she would hesitate for as much as a moment. She wouldn't mean to. She would struggle against it, but she had had a taste of the havoc George's touch wrought in her body. She didn't know if her willpower could withstand a prolonged attack.

But as the days passed, Rose's fears began to recede. George was avoiding her once again, but his control was no longer absolute. Under his stiff manner she could see signs that his feelings were no longer cold.

He hardly took his eyes off her when he was at the ranch. He talked to each brother during each meal, but most often his eyes would be on her at the opposite end of the table. Whether he knew it or not, he included her more and more often in their conversations.

But it was the way he looked at her that made the difference, as if he couldn't get enough, as if he wanted to learn everything about her there was to know, as if he had never seen such an entrancing woman before and he wanted to look his fill.

Rose tried not to attach too much importance to it. After

all, she was the only woman in sight and she wasn't exactly ugly. Yet it did make her feel better to know he couldn't ignore her, even if he meant to.

But the thing that caused her heart to beat a little fast, her limbs to tingle with excitement, was the warmth she noticed in George's eyes.

And it wasn't merely lust.

It amused her that stoic George—in her daydreams she had dubbed him St. George of the Texas plains—should have to struggle with his physical appetites like ordinary men. She didn't want him to lose the struggle, but it would have hurt her vanity if he hadn't been a little unsettled by her continual nearness.

And he liked her.

Despite the fact that she was a stranger, that he got angry with her at least once a day, he liked her. She could see it in the friendliness he showed when he didn't remember to act cold. She could see it in his gaze when he looked at her when his mind was on something else. She could see it in the many little things he thought to do to make her work easier, her day more pleasant, her relationships with his brothers more smooth.

He might remember he didn't mean to act so friendly—it was amusing to see him catch himself in the middle of some little act of kindness and struggle over whether to continue or bow out gracefully—but he couldn't keep the warmth from his voice. Rose doubted he even knew it was there.

Rose was aware that her determination not to marry an army man was growing weaker. It wasn't something she had done consciously, and it shocked her to find she was actively considering ways to make her dreams compatible with the life of an army officer's wife. After all, hundreds of other women managed it. Why couldn't she?

She had already thought of a dozen reasons why George wouldn't act like her father.

Rose repeatedly cautioned herself to keep a tight rein on her feelings—George had told her he didn't want to be married—but it was a losing battle. She realized now she had lost it that morning George came into the Bon Ton Restaurant.

"Why would you want to leave a town like Austin to come out here?" Monty asked Rose. They had fallen into the habit of relaxing around the table after dinner.

"Not everybody likes living in a town," Rose replied.

"I know that. Tyler wants to live in the mountains. But you're different."

"What makes you say that?"

"You're a woman."

Rose chuckled. "Don't men who live in mountains need women who want to live in mountains?"

"Sure they do, but you're too pretty for that."

"Can't a pretty woman like to live in the country?"

"Yes, but not until after she's married."

George could see that Rose was uncomfortable with the drift of the conversation, but he was reluctant to interrupt. It was inevitable the boys should become curious about her. He was curious, too.

"You aren't running away from some man, are you?"

"Not the way you mean. If you spent more time in town, you'd know men don't look at an unmarried woman the same way they do a married one."

"I should think not," Monty said, a devilish gleam in his eyes.

"Don't be stupid," Hen said. "She's not talking about men wanting to marry her."

"You mean they . . ." He couldn't find any words he wanted to use.

George almost laughed at Monty's indignant response. He wasn't as sophisticated as he liked to believe.

"Yes," Rose said, coming to Monty's rescue.

"Why didn't your brothers shoot them?" Zac wanted to know.

"I don't have any brothers," Rose said. "I don't have any family at all."

"Then you can be part of our family," Zac offered.

"Thanks," Rose said, her lips quivering slightly, "but one of your brothers would have to marry me for that to happen."

"George can marry you."

Zac's words caused chills of excitement and dread to shoot through George. The notion that Rose would continue to be near him gave birth to a feeling of pleasant anticipation from deep within. But the realization that he would be bound to one person *for the rest of his life* caused an even greater feeling of apprehension.

"You can't expect George to marry me just to protect me," Rose said to Zac. "Men get married for quite different reasons."

"What reasons?" he asked.

Rose didn't want to answer that question, especially not in front of George.

"Why don't you ask your brother?"

"You made the statement," George said, the suggestion of a smile on his lips. "You ought to answer it. Besides, I'd be curious to know why a woman thinks a man marries."

"You're just trying to embarrass me," Rose objected. "All three of you will probably pounce on anything I say."

"I promise we won't crack a smile."

"Speak for yourself," said Monty. "I can't wait to pounce on her."

Monty was obviously trying to be provocative, but Rose couldn't take him seriously. How could any woman be interested in a seventeen-year-old boy, no matter how well-grown and handsome, when he had a twenty-four-year-old brother like George sitting in the same room? George's shoulders would make two of Monty. And all Monty's youthful enthusiasm paled before George's masterful calm. Monty was as transparent as still water. George was a tangle of dark secrets, suppressed passions, and barely restrained tensions, an irresistible challenge to any woman.

Rose ignored the others and looked straight at Zac. "A man has to like a woman so much he doesn't want her to leave."

"I don't want you to leave. Can I marry you?"

Rose had to turn away to hide her watery eyes. "Thank you, Zac, but there are rules against little boys getting married."

"There's rules against everything I want to do," he said, disgusted. "You'll have to marry Hen. He'll shoot those fellas."

Rose got up from the table. "I'm sure he would, but he's too young, too."

"Is George old enough?"

"Yes."

"Then why—"

"I think you've asked enough questions for tonight," Rose said. "It's time to get ready for bed."

# *Chapter Eight*

"Wonder why she isn't married," Monty said later when they were settling into bed.

"I guess nobody asked her," George said.

"With that face and body! If they had any notion how she can cook, there'd be a line from here to Austin. I'm tempted to ask her myself."

"You!" George could hardly credit how much the idea of Monty's marrying Rose upset him.

"You needn't say it that way. I'm not bad looking, and she likes me."

"What makes you say that?"

"She's nice to me."

"She's paid to be nice to you."

"I know, but there's a difference."

George didn't want to own up to the rising tide of irritation within himself.

"I'm not going to dignify that remark by asking what you mean. Besides, she's older than you."

"No law against a man marrying an older woman. Seems like a good idea in Rose's case."

George wished he could enlist Hen's aid in making his twin talk sense, but it was Hen's night to sleep out.

"I agree it's unusual for such a nice-looking girl to be unmarried, but I can't see why that should make you want to marry her."

"Nice-looking!" Monty exclaimed. "Girl! That *woman* is beautiful, and you know it. I don't know what tale you told her to get her out here, but if you weren't such a cold-hearted bastard, I'd be sure you were after her yourself."

"I'm not planning to get married. I didn't know you were either."

"I was just joking," Monty confessed, "but it's not a bad idea. Then she could go on cooking for us forever."

"Go to sleep, Monty. And for God's sake don't let her guess you thought of marrying her just so she could cook for you."

"What's wrong with that?"

"You'll know one of these days, and then you'll squirm every time you remember what you said."

"I can't go to sleep with you talking," Zac complained.

"We're done," George said.

But George couldn't sleep either. The feelings hurtling around inside him were too numerous, strong, and unexpected to allow him to rest. The thought of anybody marrying Rose had thoroughly upset him.

But why? What business was it of his who she married? Besides, marrying Monty would solve just about all his problems.

But it was a solution he would hate.

He was jealous. Monty had said Rose liked him. That implied a very special kind of liking, and George realized he wanted Rose to like him more than anyone else.

No. He wanted her to like him *and no one else.*

George was suspicious when Monty held Rose's chair at breakfast. He became irritated when he kept telling her how good everything tasted. He grew furious when he told her how pretty she was.

"For God's sake, Monty, shut up. How can you expect Rose to swallow your overblown compliments with her breakfast?"

"It's not hard for a woman to accept compliments any time of the day," Rose informed him. "I haven't gotten all that many."

"I can't imagine why," Monty said. "You're certainly the prettiest woman I've ever seen."

*He came out with that awfully quick,* George thought. *Probably just said it so I couldn't.*

"You didn't seem all that bowled over that first evening," Rose pointed out.

"I like having my way," Monty confessed, flashing his ingratiating grin. "But it didn't take me long to see that you were just what this family needed."

*You saw it so quickly you threw a temper tantrum at nearly everything she said,* George thought.

"If I remember your exact words—"

"Never mind my exact words," Monty said. "I've seen the light."

"Bullshit," Hen muttered.

George couldn't stand it any longer. "For God's sake, Monty, shut up."

"George doesn't think you're beautiful," Monty said. "I'm not even sure he likes your cooking."

It was obvious to everybody that Monty was out to provoke him, but George could take only so much. His fork landed on his plate with a noisy clatter. "I'll thank you not to put words into my mouth, especially words which can get me poisoned."

"You think I'd do that?" Rose exclaimed.

"You'd have every right if I said such things."

"Now George is being gallant," Monty said. "I think I do it better. You ought to have me, not him."

"Miss Thornton is not *having* anybody," George stated, barely keeping his temper. "I'm certainly not going to enter into a contest with you for some woman's attention."

"George can't like you as much as I do," Monty said. "Not if he's going to call you *some woman*. He doesn't like me much either." The devil gleamed in his eyes.

"You are right about the latter point," George said between clenched teeth. "To set the record straight once and for all, I think Miss Thornton is very pretty, I like her quite a bit, and I very much enjoy her cooking."

"So you are going to compete with me for her affections," Monty said, a gleam of devilish pleasure in his eyes.

George threw down his napkin and pushed back from the table. "What I'm not going to do is stay here and listen to any more of your twaddle. If I do, I'm liable to break your neck."

George stalked out of the kitchen. It was the first time Rose had seen him lose his temper.

"George didn't deserve that," Hen said, disapproval in his voice. "You did that intentionally."

"Considering how George and I met, you ought to be blushing with shame," Rose said.

The brothers looked at her expectantly.

"George saved me from a man who was trying to force me to become his mistress," she explained.

"He was just showing off," Monty said, guilt making him angry at himself.

"Luke drew a gun on him. He would have shot George if he hadn't been faster and stronger."

"What happened?" Zac asked, enthralled to see his adored brother in this new light.

"George knocked Luke down and tossed him into the street. Now you go out there and apologize," Rose said, turning back to

Monty. "If you don't, you'll be a lot older before you taste any more roast turkey."

"George beat him up?" Zac asked, his eyes wide with excitement.

"He chopped him up into little pieces," Rose said, pandering shamelessly to the boy's thirst for gory details. "It wasn't a pretty sight."

"Yippee!" Zac shouted. "I wish I had seen it."

"And George complains about me exaggerating," Monty muttered.

"Do what Rose told you," Hen said.

"I'm going," Monty said, getting up, sulky, "but I wasn't just kidding. I do think you're the prettiest woman I've ever seen. And the nicest. I don't understand why there weren't dozens of men wanting to marry you. If I were the marrying kind, I'd be proud to have you for my wife."

"Thank you, Monty."

"He didn't mean any harm," Hen said after his twin had left. "He just likes to aggravate George."

"He shouldn't. George never thinks of anything except this family."

"Monty knows that. He's just not very good at showing gratitude. He's better at fighting. I am too."

"But you understand."

"So does Monty," Hen said. He paused. "Do you mind if Zac and I sit here for a while? Monty will get along better if there's nobody watching him."

"Stay as long as you like," Rose said.

Zac held out his biscuit. "If I got to stay here, I want some more jam."

George could have kicked himself. He had known all along that Monty was only trying to annoy him, and he had let himself get angry just the same. He was acting as jealous as a spurned lover. Ever since Monty mentioned the possibility of

Rose being in love with anybody else, he had been as sore as a bear with a bee sting on the end of his nose. He didn't know why he had felt so angry and jealous, but he had. He had been ready to fight Monty.

Maybe it was time he figured out just what his interest was in Rose. Surely it wasn't normal for a man to get this upset just because his brother said the housekeeper was pretty.

Not unless he was in love with her.

He wasn't in love with Rose, but he obviously hadn't been able to keep from developing feelings about her. Ever since he touched her cheek, he hadn't been able to get her out of his mind. He liked her. He liked her so much he wanted her to like him back. Clearly he'd passed the point of merely desiring her body.

But how could an honorable man say he had become this attached to a woman in little more than a week? He thought of his father's numerous affairs. Did he want Rose only because somebody else wanted her? Would he lose interest as soon as he met a new, more attractive, and more exciting woman?

He had known many exciting and attractive women, but he'd never become emotionally attached to one before. Did it mean his interest in Rose was deep and true?

His father had fought a duel over a woman who bored him just six months later. Would he do the same?

George had never kidded himself. Every time he looked in the mirror he saw William Henry Randolph all over again. He saw the same appetites that had ruined his father's life, the same aversion to responsibility that nearly destroyed his family as well. Whatever his feelings for Rose might seem to be now, no matter how hot the passion might flame, in the end it would fade just as it had with his father.

Knowing that, George couldn't take a chance on falling in love. Even worse, he couldn't allow Rose to fall in love with him. He must never do to any woman what his father had done to his mother.

\* \* \*

"Rose said you beat up some man because of her."

George was checking his guns in preparation for saddling up.

"He was hurting her."

"I guess I looked pretty foolish in there, talking about men lining up wanting her."

"Yes, you did."

"I didn't mean to hurt her feelings."

"You never do, Monty," George said, looking up. "But you never stop to think, either, before you blow up or say something just to get a rise out of people."

"But she is pretty, and I do like her. She'd make someone a wonderful wife."

"That's all the more reason not to say anything. She's got to feel it, being twenty years old and unmarried."

"Why? What's wrong with her?"

"You'll have to ask her that."

"I may be unfeeling and stupid, but I'm not that dumb."

"I never thought you were," George said, all the anger draining out of him. "I don't think Pa meant to be, either, but you know what he was like."

"Son-of-a-bitch!" Monty swore. "If you ever say I'm like that damned bastard, I'll kill you."

"We're all like him," George said. "And we can't ever forget that."

"You just say that because you know you aren't."

George laughed, a mocking, hollow laugh. "I'm exactly like him, and it scares me to death."

Four days later Rose was surprised to see Tyler return alone with the wood and supplies. Jeff had decided to stay in town a few extra days to learn more about Richard King. Over the next two days all the boys took their turn plowing the garden. Since none of them knew how to manage a plow, and the mule didn't seem to know any more than they did, the job took the better part of a day and the combined efforts of George, Monty, and Hen. Rose was certain this part of Texas hadn't heard so much cussing since the Spaniards came through more than three hundred years earlier looking for gold.

The boys finally resorted to leading the mule with two of them struggling to hold the plow straight. It tossed them about like rag dolls.

Zac spent most of his time pitching clods at his older brothers and then trying to stay out of their reach. Tyler worked on the chicken coop.

Rose laughed until her sides hurt.

There were no straight rows when they finished. There were patches of untilled sod throughout the garden, but enough of the deep, rich soil had been turned for Rose to plant her vegetables.

"I want to plant the garden today," Rose told George next morning. "Do you mind?"

"Not at all. What do you want me to do?"

"Dig the rows so I can drop the seeds in. Zac can cover them."

"You always give me the hard job," Zac complained.

"The hard job is making the rows," Rose told him.

"I'll dig the rows," George agreed, "and put up the poles when the vines begin to grow, but don't ask me to pick anything."

"That's Zac's job," Rose said.

Zac made a face.

"Or shell or snap or peel," George added.

"That's my job," Rose said.

Zac looked relieved.

George couldn't remember feeling so contented, not even when he had lived in a household staffed by servants and supplied with the best that money could buy. He knew he'd be hoodwinked into digging potatoes, picking beans and squash, and he didn't know what else, but he didn't mind. Already he had uprooted berry bushes and grapevines and planted them along the corral fence. There were enough pecan trees along the creeks to supply a household much bigger than theirs, but Rose had already talked to him about ordering fruit trees.

"There's no substitute for fresh fruit," she had said.

"Don't you think this is an awfully big garden?" George asked, surveying the full acre of ground. They had put the garden in the old corral to protect it from the ravenous longhorns, deer, antelope, wild horses, or anything else that might want to dine off its succulent plants. The mule and cow would be staked out until they could build a corral for them. Maybe a shed would come sometime after that.

"You have no idea how much you men eat," Rose said. "I have to put up enough to last through the winter."

"We can buy what we need from town."

"You can't carry squash and tomatoes and beans from town," Rose said. "Besides, I thought you might like some fresh corn instead of corn mush for a change."

So they proceeded to plant the garden, George digging the rows, Rose carefully spacing the seeds as she dropped them, and Zac happily pushing the soft dirt over the seeds with his bare feet.

And George continued to wonder at the feeling of contentment which seemed to seep out of the soil into his body. He felt more relaxed, more optimistic, more at peace with the world than he could ever remember. Wouldn't it be wonderful if things could stay like this forever?

Of course nothing stayed the same forever. It rarely lasted a day, even a few hours. This serenity would be destroyed when his brothers came home. Monty's energy, Hen's intensity, and Tyler's moodiness would be enough to dispel it completely.

Would he feel this way again tomorrow, next week, or was it just a passing mood?

Now that he thought about it, he realized his brothers' moods had become less extreme during the past weeks. Was that because of Rose, too?

\* \* \*

"Now that Tyler's got the chicken coop finished, I'll stay and help Rose," Monty offered next day.

George regarded his younger brother steadily, skepticism in his gaze.

"When did you find you could do any work except from the back of a horse?"

"You said we were all going to have to help out," Monty reminded George. "You and Tyler have done more than your share. Hen stayed yesterday. It's my turn to lend a hand."

"When did you develop such a democratic attitude?" Jeff asked. He had returned from Austin the night before, and the tension had returned with him.

"When I realized I liked looking at Rose better than looking at cows," Monty replied. "Besides, the work's got to be easier."

"I think it's good for us all to take turns," Hen said. "Then everybody knows how hard everybody else works."

"A good point," George said, getting up.

"Can I go with you?" Zac asked.

"No, you have too many chores to do."

"Monty can do them."

"I'm not doing your work and mine too," Monty said.

"Tyler can stay," Zac said.

"I've been here all week," Tyler protested.

"I've been here all my life," Zac said.

"You'll get to ride with us soon," George assured Zac, "and when you do, you'll probably wish you were back here."

"I wish I was in New Orleans," Zac said. "I wouldn't have to milk cows and fetch eggs then."

George cursed himself for the weakness which made him give in to his need to know what was happening between Rose and Monty, but he kept the cows moving. He did need to bring them back to be bred to the bull, but they usually did that at the end of the day.

The fact that they had located more cows than usual that

had just calved or were about to calve wasn't really an excuse. He just wanted to see Rose. And that was that.

He wondered if it had anything to do with her ability to make the ranch seem like a home. Recently he had noticed a subtle difference in how his brothers talked about the ranch. Their discussions were more relaxed; they seemed more anxious to be together for meals. Sometimes they even spoke as though the ranch would be part of their future.

She had helped bring them closer together as a family.

She constantly went out of her way to do things for each of them. She fixed the game Monty brought home and carefully avoided touching anything in Hen's part of the room. She never called Tyler a boy or drew attention to his gangly, uncoordinated body. She had become even fonder of Zac. She saw to it he did his chores properly, but she spent hours talking to him as she did her work, answering the hundreds of questions all six-year-olds ask and giving him individual attention when he felt rather overwhelmed by five brothers who towered over him.

She also understood that Jeff felt less of a man because of his missing arm. It was beyond her power to do anything about that, but neither did she coddle him.

And she spoiled George. He knew he only had to state a wish, even a preference, and it was his. She looked to him for approval. It seemed the more he praised her, the harder she worked. It made him feel guilty to have her value his opinion so much.

And it made him feel wonderful.

He was finally able to admit he hungered for this kind of attention. His father had never given him any affection, and his mother hadn't made up the difference. She never had any thought for anyone except her husband. If George dared to criticize his father, she would reproach him with tearful reminders of his own broken promises.

Rose was so different. She was strong and vital, ready to stand up for herself and perfectly willing to scold his brothers when they got out of line. Equally willing to tell him when she thought he was wrong.

He found it hard to think of the two women as being at all similar. He had found Rose's attitude uncomfortable in the beginning, but it wasn't nearly as hard to get used to as he first imagined. Probably because she was an extremely sensible woman. He wondered what his life would have been like if his mother had been more like Rose.

George cast all thought of his parents out of his mind. They had lived their lives, made their choices, paid their penalties.

Nothing could be changed now.

"Thank God you're back," Monty said, erupting from the house the moment the first cow reached the lane. "Do you know what that woman has had me doing? Laundry! I've fetched and carried and stirred until I can't see straight. If I have to stay another hour, I might join Cortina's bandits."

Monty stayed long enough to help George herd the cows into the corral, then he rode out as fast as his horse would carry him.

Rose came out of the house as George walked up. She wore a wide-brimmed sunbonnet tied under her ear with a large bow. Totally impractical for the south Texas plains, but definitely eye-catching.

She also wore a dress of yellow calico which hugged her shoulders, breasts, and waist as no dress she had worn since she arrived at the ranch. The sight of her breasts, full and high, mesmerized George. He forgot about piquant, innocent, or charming. Lust had him wriggling frantically in its toils.

"What did you do to Monty?" George asked, trying to keep his mind off Rose's body.

"I told him he had to work as much as he talked. The effort wore him out." She laughed. "I'll never let him forget he wasn't strong enough to do woman's work. Have you seen Zac? He's supposed to help me pick berries." She carried two woven reed baskets.

"He probably took my arrival as an excuse to disappear. Want me to go with you?"

"Aren't the boys expecting you back?"

"Monty took my place."

"Then I'd be happy to have you go with me." George thought she looked a little flustered.

"Where are the berries?"

"I was just going down to the creek. But now that you're here, we can go to the place Monty told me about, the one a mile below the ford."

"That's a long walk."

He looked forward to that. He'd make sure he had to help her across as many creeks and fallen logs as possible.

"We'll have to ride, or I won't be back in time to start dinner."

George was able to keep his mind off Rose's breasts for the time it took to saddle two horses, but the moment he put his hands around her waist and lifted her into the saddle, it came crashing down on him again. He felt his body tense and his groin begin to swell. Climbing into the saddle was uncomfortable. Remaining there was a minor misery.

"It's nice to get away for a few hours," Rose commented as they rode. "I feel as if I've been tied to the house ever since I got here."

George wondered how he had been able to keep his hands off her for two weeks. He wondered even more why the need to touch her should suddenly overwhelm him. Maybe it had been this way with his father. If so, he understood why his father had failed so often.

"I'll take you into town if you would like."

"Maybe soon. I'm content to stay here for the time being."

George didn't realize he had been anxious about her answer until he felt himself relax. Apparently his jealousy extended to every man who might look at her. He waited for the wonderful feeling of contentment, but it didn't come today. His whole body felt as taut as his groin.

"What do you plan to do with the berries?"

"I want to make a pie. Zac wants jam."

Talking about jams and jellies, canning vegetables, digging

potatoes, drying peas and beans, planting collards and spin-
ach so they would have something green to eat during the
winter, should have bored him.

But it excited him. It meant Rose was planning to stay.

George forgot he was like his father. He thought of nothing
but Rose's beauty and how much he longed to hold her in his
arms and kiss her until they melted into one another.

They reached the berries too soon. George was out of the
saddle and next to Rose in a flash.

"I can get down by myself," she said.

But he already had his hands around her waist. They stayed
there, and Rose stayed in the saddle.

"Are you going to let me down?" she asked.

She tried to turn it off lightly, but George could see she felt
the tension between them just as much as he did. He lifted
her down. Rose turned within the circle of his hands to untie
her baskets from the saddle.

"Do you mean to keep me pinned against this horse all afternoon?"

George let his hands drop slowly. "I'll let you go, but I'd
rather not. I never realized how lovely you are."

"It's hard to look attractive slaving over a stove or a boiling
wash pot," Rose said, moving away from George toward the
berries that hung heavy on the vines. She smiled at him, a little
coquettishly, George thought. "It's surprising what a new hat
and a pretty dress can do."

"It's not the clothes—"

"Not that this hat or dress is new," Rose continued, her gaze
on the berries she had begun to pick rapidly. "I haven't been
able to buy anything this nice since Daddy died. Get a basket
and start picking," she directed when she looked around and
saw George still standing by the horses. "We'll be here all afternoon if I have to do it all myself."

George staked the horses, picked up a basket, and started
picking. But he spent so much time looking over at Rose that his
fingers soon bore the marks of dozens of thorn pricks.

"They're supposed to be blackberries, not red," Rose said, noticing the drops of blood welling up on his hands.

"I don't seem to have your skill at avoiding thorns."

"You would if you'd watch what you're doing."

"I'd much rather watch you."

George's directness flustered Rose, but not enough to slow her work.

"Maybe I should have waited for Zac. He picks faster than you do."

"He probably eats more, too."

"Probably," Rose agreed.

But the tension remained between them. The sky was cloudy and the breeze cool, but George's blood grew hotter.

"He can't appreciate you the way I do."

"I don't know. You ought to see the way he devours blackberry jam. I wonder what happened to him."

George threw his basket down and marched over to Rose. He spun her around to face him. "You can't prefer the attentions of a six-year-old to mine."

"He's safer."

"I thought I was St. George, slayer of dragons and protector extraordinaire?"

"I always wondered what he did with the princess after he killed the dragon. My book didn't say."

"If she looked as lovely as you, he must have carried her off to his castle."

George never intended to kiss Rose. He wanted her so badly his joints ached from the tension, his screaming nerves made his skin protest against the roughness of his clothes, but he never intended to touch her. Now it seemed impossible not to. She seemed to fit naturally into the circle of his arms. Her head seemed to automatically lean back to meet his lips as they descended on hers.

Everything seemed so natural, so right. Her lips felt soft and warm under his. Just as he had dreamed so many times. Her lips quivered in hesitation, then met his lips firm and eager.

They tasted sweet. He wondered why he hadn't thought to kiss her before. He wondered if his father had felt this way.

"Do you think the princess minded?" Rose asked breathlessly.

# Chapter Nine

"Minded what?" George asked, his mind empty of everything except Rose.

She stood on tiptoe, her whole body leaning against him. George felt his groin swell in response to the pressure of her breasts against his chest, the rubbing of her thighs against his own. How could he have thought he was immune to women when just one kiss could demolish his resistance? His arms tightened around Rose as his lips took hers in a feverish kiss.

"Being carried off to his castle," Rose said, when she finally managed to disengage herself. "Maybe she loved someone else."

"Princesses are only allowed to love the knight who rescues them."

"Mmmm." Rose seemed to find nothing to object to in George's reasoning. Nor with the kisses he planted on the corner of her mouth or the end of her nose. In fact, she seemed to be in total agreement with his program of action. George felt her arms go around his neck.

George felt as though something inside him burst loose from its bindings. He could never remember feeling so absolutely wonderful in his entire life.

As much as it stirred his physical need of her to the breaking point, holding Rose tight against his chest fulfilled another need deep inside him. It was almost as though she were holding him, as though her arms were enfolding him in a protective embrace.

Rose sighed with contentment and leaned her head against George's chest. "I thought you didn't like me."

"How could anybody not like a woman as pretty as you?"

"You never said anything."

"I was trying to stay away from you."

"I was afraid you were angry at me for getting the boys upset."

"I couldn't be angry at you, at least not for long."

George kissed the top of her head and pulled her back into his embrace.

"I've got to finish the berries," Rose said, attempting to break away.

"They can wait a little longer."

"No, they can't. I'll have to start dinner soon."

"That can wait, too," George said, his arms still firmly around her. "I won't be able to think about food for hours."

"What about Monty?"

But George kissed her again, and they both lost interest in Monty.

"George, why are you biting Rose?"

Neither of them had heard Zac come up. They jumped apart.

"Where did you come from?" George demanded, his mind rapidly reorienting itself.

"I followed you. Rose promised I could help her pick blackberries. She's going to make jam."

"I thought you meant to stay gone until I'd finished picking," Rose mumbled, unable to regain her composure as quickly as George.

"I wouldn't do that. Not anymore," Zac added. "Why was George holding you up? Did you fall down?"

"You might say I lost my balance," Rose said.

Zac looked at the creek bank which fell sharply away to the sluggish, brackish water below. "You ought to stay away from there. George and I will pick those berries. You pick the ones over there."

"Do you know if there was a St. Zac?" Rose asked George, hardly able to keep her amusement bottled up.

The heat still raged in George's veins. So did irritation at Zac's interruption. "I doubt it. Dragons gobble up little boys who sneak up behind their big brothers."

"How can it if you've just slain it?" Rose asked, her eyes dancing with laughter.

"There are other dragons that specialize in devouring little brothers," George replied.

"Have you been making wine out of these berries?" Zac asked, his cherubic face screwed up in confusion.

"What are you talking about?"

"Monty wants Rose to make wine out of the blackberries, but she won't because she says it makes people act funny. You sure are acting awful peculiar."

George and Rose struggled to hold back laughter.

"I must have chewed on some loco weed."

Zac had no intention of being treated like a little boy. "I know you didn't chew on loco weed. You probably ate too many berries and didn't want anybody to know. Rose said it makes your stomach queasy."

"That must be it."

"You can't eat any more or there won't be enough to make jam."

"If we don't get back to picking, there won't be enough for anything," Rose said.

Zac looked into George's basket. "You don't have very many."

George didn't look at Rose. He didn't want to see her laughing at him, not when his body was still hot and tense. "Rose has already made that complaint. Maybe you'd better show me how."

As Zac chattered away, proudly telling his brother which berries were ripe and showing him how to twist through the vines to reach the choicest fruit, George allowed his eyes to wander to where Rose picked, safely back from the creek bank. He continued to receive thorn pricks for his inattention until Zac sharply adjured him to stop looking at Rose and watch what he was doing.

"There's nothing going to happen to her as long as she stays back from the creek," he told his brother.

But he couldn't. Those kisses, so few in number, had blasted a hole in the fortifications he had built around his heart, a breach he knew he could never repair. He was vulnerable now. He would never be able to forget the feel of her in his arms as they kissed.

But he would have to make himself *act* like he could. And he would have to begin by not looking at her every five minutes. He forced himself to keep his eyes on his work, to listen to Zac, to concentrate on avoiding the thorns. Slowly his body relaxed, the tension left his groin.

He didn't like it, but he did it anyway. As Rose had said, there was no point in dreaming about what you couldn't have. It only made you feel sorry for yourself. And George refused to do that.

"I want to apologize for my behavior back there," George said to Rose. They had reached the house, their baskets full.

"There's no need," Rose said.

"Yes, there is. I employed you to work here. I had no right to take advantage of you that way."

"You didn't—"

"You're a lovely woman, and I admire you tremendously. You're kind to Zac, you placate Tyler and Jeff, you put up with Hen and Monty. I certainly have no right to ask you to put up with my attentions."

"Is that all you feel about me?" Rose asked. She seemed hurt. "I'm kind, tolerant, and a good housekeeper?"

Why did she have to ask him that question? Did she have any idea how hard he tried *not* to think of the way he felt about her? How hard he was struggling this very minute to pretend he felt nothing, or not much?

"I feel a lot more."

"Such as?"

He should have sent her into the house and busied himself unsaddling the horses. He should have kept his mind on his work and off his feelings for Rose.

"I like it when you're around. I feel more at ease. We're a happier family. You've brought a kind of magic, something we lacked."

"So now I'm a chemical reaction."

But George didn't hear her. He seemed to be talking to himself more than her.

"I keep thinking how nice it is to have you here when we come home. I wonder what it would be like to hold you close on a winter's evening when it's snowing outside and the fire's dying down. I wonder what it would feel like to witness the birth of your first child. What you'll look like when you're a grandmother. What it would be like to love someone, knowing you will love them even more forty years from now. I wonder all sorts of improper things."

Rose swallowed. "There's nothing improper about those thoughts. Any woman would be fortunate to have a husband who felt that way about her."

Rose lay in her bed, unable to sleep. With all the work she had to do, she couldn't afford to lie awake. Yet restless nights were getting to be a habit.

Why had she let George kiss her? More importantly, why had she enjoyed it so much she had kissed him back? Why had she let him think it was all right?

For days she had been telling herself not to read anything into his actions except kindness. He had no interest in her except as a housekeeper. *He had said that.* There was no chance of a future together.

She couldn't get the memories of her father out of her mind. George would be just as bad. Maybe worse.

She couldn't stand that.

Yet she hadn't stopped him.

It wouldn't have taken much, just a word or a gesture. But

she had done nothing. Worse, she had encouraged him to think she welcomed his attention.

If he now thought she would sacrifice her virtue for him, she had no one to blame but herself. If he thought her a strumpet, it was her own fault. Worse still, knowing all this, she longed to feel his arms around her again.

She must have fallen in love with George.

There could be no other reason for her behavior. She would have fought, kicked, and screamed if Luke had dared kiss her. Yet she had melted into George's arms as if she belonged there, and she hadn't wanted to leave.

There could be only one end to this.

To give in to him, only to be abandoned later, would break her heart. She would have to be the one to exercise control. Though she could think of nothing more wonderful than to spend the night in his arms, one night, no matter how blissful, was not worth the rest of her life.

Still her hope remained suspended by a slender thread.

In George's last words, she finally got another glimpse of the man who had come to her rescue in the Bon Ton. No man still in his prime could think of being in love with the same woman for forty years unless he was the kind of man that dreams were made of. Nor wonder about the magic of giving birth.

This was the George she had first seen, the George who had caused her to take this job, the George she had fallen in love with. Could she rescue him from himself? She didn't know, but as long as she knew he still existed, she would try.

"Make sure you do everything your brothers tell you."

Zac looked mulish. "I won't listen to Tyler."

"Nobody but Hen and Monty will give you orders," George said, "but if you get into trouble, you latch on to the person closest to you." This was the first time Zac would be going out without him, and George was a little nervous. Anything could happen with longhorns.

Zac's expression didn't change.

"If you don't promise, you'll have to stay home."

That threat broke Zac's resistance. George was certain he would have agreed to obey a girl in order to go with his brothers.

"Don't let him out of your sight," Rose said to Hen. "You know Monty is too impatient to keep an eye on him."

George found himself feeling jealous of the bond of understanding he saw developing between Hen and Rose. She allowed Monty to flirt with her, even tease and flatter her, but she depended on Hen.

*She depends on you more than anyone else.*

But knowing that didn't eliminate the feeling of jealousy. George groaned inwardly. He was tired of being jealous and feeling bad about it. Would it always be this way with women, or was it just Rose?

"Bye," Zac called back as he rode away, his sunny mood restored by getting to ride between Monty and Hen.

"You realize you won't be able to keep him home after this," Rose said.

"He should never have been kept here this long," George said, his thoughts taking a leap back through the years. "My father gave me my first horse on my second birthday. On my third he taught me how to jump. I fell off. He cursed me and my mother when I cried."

"I'm surprised you ever got back on a horse again," Rose said.

"He put me back on before I'd stopped crying, and made me take the jump again. I'm told I fell off a total of eleven times that afternoon, but I learned to jump. Before I was four, I was following my father over some of the roughest country in northern Virginia."

He was certain Rose could hear the rancor in his voice. After all this time, it was as strong as ever.

"My child won't be put on a horse until he's old enough to know how to stay there," Rose stated emphatically. "And he won't be put over any jumps until he wants to."

"Then don't marry a Virginian or an Englishman," George warned. "They believe a man should come into the world knowing how to jump."

George found it difficult to concentrate on the tasks Rose gave him. All he could think about was her nearness. Her appearance had changed as she had become more relaxed around them. She now wore her hair loose. Though it deprived him of the opportunity to glimpse the tempting spot at the back of her neck, it made her look even prettier. Younger and more innocent. More piquant.

Exercise had put color in her cheeks. Working under the hot Texas sun had given her a fine dusting of freckles across the bridge of her nose and her cheekbones. Her ears disappeared under the cascading ringlets of her hair, but she wore tighter-fitting dresses of thinner material with lower necklines. Apparently she had quite a store of clothes purchased before her father's death.

George noticed that fine droplets of perspiration had caused the dress to mold itself to her body and become nearly transparent. At such times, no matter how hard he tried to concentrate on his work, his attention kept coming back to Rose.

And her body.

Every night since they had gone berry picking, he had lain in his bed dreaming of her lips, her kisses, the feel of her in his arms. It was driving him mad to keep his distance, not to touch her.

"Why don't we go for a walk?" George suggested. "It's too hot to work."

Rose didn't look at him. "I can't. I've got a stew on the stove. And I still have to put the dishes up, straighten your room, and change the beds."

"I'll help."

"No." She didn't look at him, but she sounded definite.

George put his hand under her chin and lifted it until their gazes met.

"Why not?"

"It can't lead anywhere."

"Does everything have to lead somewhere?"

"Doesn't it?"

"I like you, Rose. I like you very much."

"I like you, too, but that's no reason to go walking together."

"Why not?"

"People sometimes say things they don't mean. They might even do things they don't want to."

"Like this?" George tried to kiss Rose, but she backed away.

"I don't think we ought to do that again."

"Why?"

"Be reasonable, George. I'm your housekeeper. Suppose I let you start kissing me, catching me in corners, and . . ." Rose couldn't finished that sentence. "Zac caught us. One of the other boys soon would. Then what would happen?"

"It was only a kiss."

"I couldn't stay here." Rose meant to stop there. She didn't know what made her say the next words. "It would be different if you wanted to marry me."

"I don't intend to marry anybody."

"I know."

"But I didn't mean any harm."

"I know that, too, but I can't let you kiss me."

She made him feel guilty, and that made him angry. "Why didn't you stop me at the creek?"

"You caught me by surprise."

"Is that all?"

"I guess I liked it."

George started forward, but Rose stepped back again.

"I won't do it again."

"Why not?"

"Once something like this gets started, there's no way to stop it except . . ."

"Except marriage," George finished for her, an edge on his voice. "Is that all women think about? Can't they imagine two people just enjoying each other?"

"Maybe I could, but other people can't."

"Are other people so important to you?"

"I'll have to leave this ranch someday. What kind of work am I going to find if people think I've been carrying on with you? That would be worse than being a Yankee."

"You don't have to leave."

"Yes, I do. You'll leave, and the boys will find wives."

"There'll always be a place for you." Why was he always saying that? They'd never intended her employment to be permanent.

"To do what? Be a nurse for other women's children? To cook and clean so they can spend more time with their husbands? I want a husband and children of my own. I don't want to be on the outside looking in."

George couldn't imagine Rose being anywhere without being the center of attention. It wasn't just her looks or the fact she had a knack for organizing their lives and making them like it. She would be a very special person anywhere she went.

"Where are you going to find a husband?"

"Don't be cruel," she snapped.

"I didn't mean it like that. You've already said nobody in Texas would have you. Where will you go?"

"I don't know, but it's not your concern."

"Maybe not, but I am concerned."

"Don't be," Rose said, fighting to hold back her tears. "Don't pretend you care."

"I do."

"No, you don't. You like me, and you want me. That's not the same thing."

Wasn't it? Liking and wanting. Because he felt both very strongly.

One of the horses in the corral neighed.

"Somebody's coming," Rose said, dashing a tear from her cheek. "No matter what you or I feel, there can be nothing between us. Not unless you mean marriage."

She fled to the kitchen.

George felt like a skunk. He had warned himself against this from the start, yet he'd gone right ahead, knowing he couldn't offer marriage, knowing he planned to leave within a year. Rose should have slapped him. She should be packing to leave right now.

A feeling of self-loathing swept over him. If his selfishness caused her to return to Austin and the likes of Luke Kearney, he was truly his father's son.

George wanted to go after her, but the rider, a stranger, had reached the house. George walked forward to meet him.

He was nearly as tall as George, but he had none of his size. He had narrow shoulders, was whipcord thin, and rode bent over from the waist. He looked dirty and unshaven, but his worn and patched Confederate uniform guaranteed him a welcome.

"Howdy," the man said. "I'm looking for a job. I heard your ranch had come through the war better than most."

"Look around you," George said. "Is this your idea of better than most?"

For the first time since his return, George looked at his home with a stranger's eyes. The results staggered him. The rough logs of the house, the mud that filled in the cracks, made it look like the home of a poor dirt farmer, something George's grandfather would have been ashamed to let his slaves live in. The scattered corrals, thriving garden, and brand-new chicken coop couldn't negate the effect of clothes hanging on a line in the front yard, chickens scratching for grubs, and a wash pot nestled on a bed of ashes only a dozen feet from the front steps. Steps led to an open breezeway between the two halves of the house, not the elegant wallpapered passage of Ashburn with its polished heart-of-pine floor and winding double staircase.

Suddenly George felt poor. He had always faced the world against the backdrop of an elegant mansion; he'd extended hospitality that depended on the work of a dozen servants. He'd always been a Randolph of the Randolphs of Virginia, privileged, courted, his name a household word from Massachusetts to Georgia.

But this stranger saw only a poor Texas rancher, hardly better off than himself, with no reputation, no standing in society. He was plain George Randolph.

He was nobody.

But quick on the heels of that devastating realization came another. For the first time in his life, he was free of the Virginia Randolphs; he had no reputation to live up to, or pull him down. And if he made something of himself, he would have earned it himself.

If he failed, he would disappear without a trace. In Virginia, a Randolph could never entirely disappear from society's view. In Texas, plain George Randolph already had.

He was so taken by his thoughts he was almost unaware that the stranger was answering his question.

"You've got a roof over your head. That's more than a lot I've seen."

Rose had stepped out on the porch beside George to take up the burden of conversation.

"Won't you get down and come inside?" she asked. "I've got a pot of stew on the stove. You're welcome to have some."

"Thank you, ma'am. It's sometimes hard for a man to get a full belly. Ain't no way he can keep it that way."

"Why don't you unsaddle your horse," George suggested, ashamed of his lack of hospitality. "The least we can offer you is a few hours' respite from the trail."

"Mighty obliged," the stranger said. He swung down and George helped him unsaddle his horse and turn him into the corral. When they entered the kitchen, Rose had a bowl of stew, some cold cornbread, and a big glass of milk waiting on the table.

"Have you come very far?" she asked.

"All the way from Georgia," he replied. "There wasn't much

left of the home place, so I started to drift. Things were better in Alabama, but they don't have any money. It was even worse in Mississippi. Things seem a little better in Texas."

Rose refilled his glass with fresh milk.

"I don't mean to pry," she said with an ingenuous smile, "but who do I have the honor of serving?"

"Things must have got real bad when I forget my manners," he said, returning her smile. "The name's Benton Wheeler, but I'd rather you call me Salty."

"How did you get such a name?" Rose asked.

"The men in the company gave it to me for liking too much salt on my food. My old ma always said it would kill me someday."

"My brother and I got home just a few months ago," George said, sitting down to the table himself.

While Salty ate a plate of the venison stew Rose had simmering for dinner, three chunks of cornbread left over from breakfast, and drank two more glasses of milk, he and George talked.

"I must have passed a thousand ex-Confederates along the road, all looking for work. Lots of them have their families with them."

"We're not much better off here," George said.

"Then I guess I'll keep moving," Salty said.

"I wish I knew where to tell you to go. You might try Austin or San Antonio."

"Already been to Austin. That's where I heard about your place. I thought I'd drift farther west. Maybe go as far as California or Oregon."

They discussed the merits of looking for gold against farming, ranching against fighting Indians, homesteading against starting up a business in a new town.

"I guess I'd best get going," Salty said, coming to his feet. "I'd like to be a good fifty miles west of here before sunset. Thanks for the food, ma'am. I never tasted anything better in my whole life."

They walked outside. For several moments Salty stood looking into the distance, apparently reluctant to get back on the trail.

"Old Bony sure is going to be mighty disappointed to feel the weight of that saddle again today."

Rose and George walked to the corral with Salty. "I thought you said you wanted to round up some cows to sell this fall," Rose whispered to George when Salty slipped through the rails to catch his horse.

"I do."

"You ever been on a roundup?"

"No."

"Has Hen or Monty?"

"No."

"Then you're going to need help, first with the roundup and then with the drive."

"I planned to hire men when we got ready to hit the trail."

"You'll need more help with the roundup and the branding than you will on the trail. They wouldn't expect to be paid until you sell the herd. All you need to do now is feed them. They'd probably do most of their own cooking."

"I don't know if I can afford it. We won't get more than a few dollars each selling them for hides."

"Then trail them north to Missouri. A man came through Austin a few months ago saying he got thirty dollars a head for steers in St. Louis."

"Thirty dollars!" George almost choked. "At that price I can afford to buy a hundred heifers from Mr. King. Are you sure they won't expect to be paid now?"

"Ask him."

"Just a minute," George called out to Salty. The man had led his horse up to the corral fence. "We've got some rounding up to do. I'm thinking about sending a herd north to Missouri. Would you be interested in something like that?"

"Sure."

"There might be shooting."

"No more than in the war."

"I won't be able to pay you until I sell the herd."

"Eating regular is more than I'm doing now."

"I can't even offer you a bed. The house is hardly big enough for us."

"It ain't rained but once since I crossed the Trinity," Salty answered with an easy smile. "And I dry out real fast."

"Okay. Leave your horse in the corral. You can go out with us tomorrow and get the lay of the land."

They headed back to the house.

"I almost forgot," Salty said. "I got a letter here. I'm told it's almighty important, but I can't seem to find the young woman it's addressed to. I was told she stayed over this way, but I must have been given the wrong information."

"I haven't heard of any women living out here, young or old," George said. "The Indians or bandits drove nearly everybody out during the war."

"What's her name?" Rose asked.

"Miss Elizabeth Thornton."

# Chapter Ten

"But my name's Elizabeth Thornton."

"Now what a coincidence," Salty said. "No wonder people got confused thinking you and this Elizabeth Thornton were the same one."

"But we must be. I mean, we are."

"This can't be you, ma'am. This young lady is unwed."

"I'm not married," Rose told him.

"I thought . . ."

"I keep house for Mr. Randolph and his brothers." Rose hated the silence that fell. "My father always called me Elizabeth, but I prefer to be called Rose," she explained.

"Then I guess this is yours," Salty said, handing the letter to her.

Rose looked at the postmark and lost a little of her color.

"Anything wrong?" George asked.

"No," she answered. "It's just from somebody I thought had forgotten me." She tucked the letter in her pocket. "I expect you men have a lot to talk about. I need to get back to the kitchen. There'll be seven mouths to feed tonight."

"You got five brothers?" Salty asked, startled.

"Six. One hasn't come home from the war yet."

"She a relative?" Salty asked, after Rose had gone.

"No."

"She hiding out from somebody?"

"Exactly what are you getting at?" George asked, his temper and curiosity beginning to rise.

"Nothing much. Just that it's unusual for a young woman to be staying with so many men. You know, women being such gossips and all."

"There aren't any women around to gossip."

"Good thing."

George didn't pursue the conversation, but he didn't have to in order to know what Salty meant. By coming to work for them, Rose had ruined her reputation.

But she must have understood the risks when she offered for the job. Whatever happened, it was none of his concern. Certainly not his fault.

But that didn't soothe George's irritation. People had no right to judge Rose. They hadn't thought any worse of Peaches or Mrs. Hanks. But Rose was a Yankee's daughter. She was young and single and prettier than their own daughters.

"There's not much to show you," George said to Salty. "Outside of the house and a chicken coop, all we have is corrals. And a bull we hope to use to upgrade our herd."

"I know something about bulls," Salty said. "Let's have a look."

\* \* \*

"Did George say we could go this far from the house?" Zac asked.

"I didn't ask him," Rose replied.

"He said he'd chain me to the porch if he ever found me past the creek."

"Do you think he'll chain me?"

Zac giggled. "George wouldn't chain a lady."

"Who says I'm a lady?"

"George."

He would, Rose thought, and ruin all her arguments for putting him out of her mind. She had gotten herself pretty much in hand after telling George she wouldn't kiss him again. He wanted nothing permanent, and she wanted nothing to do with an army man. He was keeping his distance and she was keeping hers, but she had felt the need to get away from the house. Sometimes she felt as though the house was suffocating her.

"Keep an eye out for flowers," Rose told Zac. "I want a bunch for the kitchen."

"Do you like flowers?" Zac asked.

"Sure. Doesn't everybody?"

"Men don't," Zac said, putting a bit of a stiff-legged strut into his walk. "That's girl stuff."

"Now who told you a thing like that?"

"Nobody had to tell me," Zac stated. "I just knowed it."

"Well, girls like flowers, so look sharp."

"I'll bet we'll find thousands by the creek," Zac said, running ahead. "Monty says they's daisies everywhere."

Rose refrained from correcting his grammar. They were on an outing. Both of them deserved to feel completely free to enjoy themselves. She particularly didn't want to be thinking about George. That's what had driven her from the house. If it ruined the countryside for her as well, she'd have no place to go.

She hurried ahead to catch up with Zac, pausing only to make a mental note of the berries or nuts she saw along the way.

Rose could never accustom herself to the brush—it seemed a cross between a desert and a jungle, all of it covered in thorns—but today it seemed friendly and welcoming. She started to wish they had brought a picnic lunch. The day was warm without being too hot. About a mile from the house, a thicket of live oaks beckoned invitingly. After the long walk, she was content to wander into its shade. She sat down on a fallen trunk and let her body absorb the cool. Zac followed moments later and immediately waded into the stream. She wondered why it was that little boys never could resist water, especially if it had mud in it. The two oldest Robinson boys seemed able to locate every mud puddle in Austin within ten minutes.

Next minute Rose found herself thinking about George, wondering if he'd enjoyed getting dirty when he was a little boy. Wondering if he had been as charming as Zac. Wondering if his sons would be like him.

Heaving a sigh, Rose got to her feet. She refused to think of George today. It only gave her a headache and solved nothing.

"Come on, Zac," she called to the boy. He had climbed a tree and was crawling along a limb that extended out over the stream. "It's time to head back." They had come a long way, and she had plenty of work waiting for her when she got back.

Looking back to make sure Zac was climbing down from the tree, Rose started up the bank. She raised her hand to pull back a branch blocking her path and froze in her tracks.

Indians!

It was only one Indian, a Comanche she guessed. He sat his horse about a hundred feet up the trail, scanning the horizon. What was he doing here? What was he looking for? Was anybody else with him?

She foolishly hadn't brought a rifle, and she had no idea where George and his brothers might be. If the Indian meant to raid the house, she was glad she wasn't there. But he didn't seem interested in going upstream. He looked around a moment longer, then waved to someone she couldn't see.

There were more Indians.

"Wait for me," Zac called, running up behind her.

Rose turned and slammed her hand over Zac's mouth. The boy immediately struggled to free himself, but the single word "Indians!" hissed into his ear stilled his struggles.

Rose looked through the foliage, petrified that the Indian was even now galloping to where they hid in the trees. He hadn't moved, but he was facing them. Before she could wonder what to do next, she heard the sound of hundreds of hooves on the hard earth. Moments later, several Indians emerged from the brush followed by a large herd of horses. Hundreds of them, Rose decided as she watched them go by.

"They're stealing horses," Zac whispered.

"Maybe they're mustangs."

"Look, they're branded."

Rose didn't want to look. Just like anyone else, Indians were free to capture the thousands of mustangs that roamed the plain. But stealing horses was a hanging offense, and these Indians would be prepared to shoot anybody who interfered with them.

Rose became so fascinated with the horses streaming past she forgot the Indian sentry until Zac pulled on her sleeve.

"He's coming."

Rose didn't have time to panic. "Climb back up the tree," she hissed to Zac as she turned and ran back into the trees. She searched frantically for a place she could hide. The Indian was close to them now. If he pulled the branch aside, he couldn't help but see them. Zac was already halfway up the tree when Rose decided the fallen tree was her best chance. She climbed over the log and hurried along the trunk hoping to hide among the tangled roots at its base. The tree had torn a big hole in the earth when it fell over, raising a ball of roots more than a dozen feet in diameter. Rose jumped into the hole. Chancing discovery, she looked back long enough to make sure Zac had disappeared among the upper branches of the tree.

Rose drew back as the Indian pulled aside the branch. Did he know they were here? Did he only guess?

Rose nearly stopped breathing when he rode his pony into the shadowy depths of the oaks, his rifle leveled. He must know they were here. She looked up into the treetops, but couldn't see Zac. She hoped the Indian couldn't either. She looked around for an escape route in case he discovered her hiding place. She could beat him across the creek, but she couldn't get away, not when he was on horseback and she on foot.

Suddenly she noticed that the silence was so deep she could almost hear herself breathe. The horses and the other Indians were gone. Just the sentry remained. He looked at the ground. They must have disturbed the leaves. Maybe he could follow her trail to her hiding place.

She heard a strange animal sound, and the Indian looked back. His friends were calling him. The Indian looked over his shoulder, but didn't turn his horse. He continued to study the ground.

The call came again, more impatient this time. Muttering something angrily under his breath, the Indian turned his pony. At the edge of the grove, he turned back once more.

Rose held her breath.

Digging his heels into his pony's side, the Indian rode out into the sunlight and cantered off to join his fellow warriors.

Rose almost fainted with relief. She had known there were Indians and outlaws roaming over most of Texas, everybody knew that, but her days at the ranch had been so peaceful she had come to feel that no danger threatened her. George had made her feel safe. Now she realized that not even George could shield her from every danger.

She waited a few minutes to make sure the Indian didn't mean to come back. It seemed as if she waited for hours, but she knew that only a few minutes had passed. Finally, she emerged from behind the roots of the fallen tree. She searched the trees overhead, but try as she might, she couldn't see Zac.

"Zac," she called softly. She was afraid to call too loudly

for fear the Indian was close enough to hear. "Zac," she called again when nothing happened.

A bit of bark fell at her feet, and she looked up to see Zac descend to the joint where the oak's huge trunk divided in two.

"Is he gone?" Zac asked.

"I think so," Rose answered, glancing nervously about to make certain the Indian wasn't trying to sneak up on them from a different angle.

"Wait till I tell George," Zac said, dropping to the ground. "He told me I wouldn't see no more Indians."

Rose didn't want to tell George. She was going to have to think of a good reason for being so far from the house. George had never told her not to leave the house, but she had known it was a dangerous thing to do. Thinking about George had caused her to forget caution. It was a stupid thing to do, and she couldn't expect George to think much of her intelligence after this.

"They must have had a million horses," Zac told his brothers that evening.

"Closer to a hundred," Rose corrected.

"I wonder where they got that many?" Hen asked.

"Must have been Hewson's place," Monty said.

"But that's more than fifty miles from here."

"Hewson probably thought he was safe. That's why the Indians were able to steal so many."

"Are you sure the Indian wasn't doing anything more than serving as a lookout?" George asked Rose. "Was he wearing war paint?"

"His face wasn't colored, if that's what you mean," Rose answered. "And he didn't come up to the house. Do you think he knew you lived here?"

"Yes," Monty answered her. "They know every rancher in the area."

"Someone is going to have to stay at the house from now on," George said. "It was stupid of me to think we could leave it unprotected."

"We'll take turns," Hen said.

"And I don't want you or Zac to go any farther than the creek or the corrals unless one of us is with you," George said to Rose.

"Those old Indians won't find me," Zac stated proudly. "I bet I can go all the way to Austin without nobody seeing me."

"We're all going to have to be more careful," George told his youngest brother, "even you."

"But—"

"If you want to go with us again, you'll do exactly as I say."

"But—"

"How would you feel if some Indian shot Rose while you were playing in the brush, all because you weren't here to warn her?"

Rose hated for George to make Zac feel guilty before he had done anything, but she realized it was probably the only way to make the boy stay close to the house. After years of doing pretty much as he wanted, he was having difficulty accepting discipline.

"Okay, but if any old Indian comes sneaking around the house, I'll blow his head off."

"You do that," George said. "As for you," he said turning to Rose, "I don't want you to leave the house unless it's necessary."

"You don't have to worry about me," Rose assured him. "Today was enough to keep me quaking in my boots for months to come."

"I don't believe a word of it," Monty said. "If any Indian was stupid enough to come after you, you'd have his clothes in the wash pot and him in the bathtub in five minutes. Wouldn't any Indian ever come around here again."

Rose laughed along with everyone else, but as far as she was concerned, the Indians could stay dirty.

* * *

Rose had a bad feeling about the six men the moment she spotted them through the kitchen window. There wasn't supposed to be anybody out this way except rustlers, bandits, and ex-soldiers down on their luck. These men rode strong, well-fed horses and wore good clothes. Their eyes seemed to dart from one spot to another as though they were making a mental inventory of everything they saw.

She couldn't believe they were thieves come to check out the ranch before they tried to rob it. There was nothing to steal. But they wanted something and probably weren't too concerned about how they got it. They looked the type.

Whatever they wanted, George was here, in front of the house. He had seen them, too.

But the tension along the back of her neck twisted a few notches tighter when she saw George move toward a rifle he had leaned against the house. They were alone today. All the boys, including Salty, were working a little-used part of the range. Much too far away to hear gunshots.

Almost without thinking, Rose reached for the shotgun that George had made her keep in the kitchen since the Indians appeared.

"This your place?" the man who appeared to be the leader asked as they drew their horses to a stop in front of the house.

"It belongs to me and my brothers," George told them. "Why do you ask?"

"We're from the land office."

"You got any proof?"

The man seemed shocked at George's question. And annoyed.

"We don't need no proof. We're here to—"

"Either you show me proof or get off my land," George said. He reached out to rest his hand on the barrel of his rifle.

The men stirred restlessly in their saddles, their hands not far from their guns. Rose knew that George wouldn't have a chance if they started shooting. She eased the end of the shotgun through the open window.

"Show him the paper, Gabe," the man next to the leader said. "Ain't no use making a fuss unless we have to."

The man's cooperation didn't allay Rose's fears. She didn't like his eyes. They looked tiny and mean. Worse still, he spoke with a more pronounced Yankee accent than the other.

Carpetbaggers.

"Dammit, Cato, ain't nobody else asked for papers," Gabe complained.

"They ought to," George said. "Anybody could ride in here and pretend to be anybody they wanted to."

"They look okay," George said after he'd looked over the paper thrust at him, "but I'll check when I go into Austin. Now what's your business?"

Gabe looked disposed to argue, but Cato said, "Get on with it."

"It's our job to check on everybody who owns land in the county. And you seem to own a whole lot."

"I told you, it belongs to me and my brothers. There are seven of us."

"We don't have no record of no brothers. All I see is one William Henry Randolph."

"He's dead."

"Then I suppose we need to talk to Mrs. Randolph," said Cato. "Could she be the young woman looking out the window there?"

Rose wanted to leap back into the shadows, but it was too late. She shouldn't have been listening—George had every right to be angry with her—but it was too late to pretend she hadn't been.

"No," George answered. "My mother died three years ago."

"Do you have any proof of your parents' deaths?"

"I can show you my mother's grave if you like. As for my father's death, all I have is the word of witnesses. Written confirmation might be hard to get. He fought for the Confederacy."

"You don't have that long," Gabe said. None of the men

seemed anxious to get down from his horse. There was a strained feeling about them that made Rose uncomfortable.

"I don't see none of these brothers of yours about."

"They don't happen to be here at the moment, but they'll be back tonight if you want to meet them."

Gabe looked at Cato. Rose had no idea what they might be thinking, but she was certain they didn't mean to be around when the boys got back.

"You haven't paid your taxes," Gabe said.

"I just got home, but I'm sure my brothers have paid all the taxes required of them."

"We'll check on that when I get back."

"If you don't know whether we've paid our taxes, how much, and when, you're not from the land office," George stated flatly, "and you can ride out now."

"We didn't mean your back taxes," Cato said. "We mean you ain't paid for this year. We're here to figure out what you owe and collect it."

Rose knew the taxes weren't due until the end of the year, but she doubted George did.

"Why don't you get down and come into the kitchen," George invited.

"We'd rather stay where we are," Cato said.

Rose saw George's expression harden. He knew these men were going to try to cheat him.

"Our records show you own about sixty thousand acres."

"We own the ranch jointly."

"You can't do that. It has to be in one person's name."

"Yes, we can, and no it doesn't."

"We know the law—"

"So do I. What else do you want to know?"

The men looked a little disconcerted by George's confidence. Rose guessed that none of them had bothered to read the laws they were talking about.

"The tax is two dollars for every hundred dollars of value. Now let me see. For sixty thousand acres that comes to . . ."

Rose gasped. They had quoted a hugely inflated rate. They must have heard about Jeff paying for their supplies with gold and come to see how much they could get out of George. She doubted any money would ever reach Austin.

". . . I can't figure that high without paper," Cato said with what Rose thought was a greedy grin, "but it's thousands, all payable in gold."

"I don't have that kind of money," George said, "and certainly not in gold."

He had lost color. From the enormity of the sum, Rose was sure.

"That's not what we heard," Cato said.

"It doesn't matter what you heard," George snapped, "I don't have that much gold."

"How much do you have?" Gabe asked.

"Not even a tithe of that."

Rose could see they were disappointed.

"The tax has still got to be paid. And today."

Rose noticed that the other men had gradually shifted their positions until they formed a wide circle around George. Too wide for him to keep them all covered. One of the men had his hand awfully close to his gun handle.

Rose gradually shifted the direction of her shotgun and tightened her finger on the trigger.

"If that's the tax, we'll pay it," George said, his eyes never leaving Cato, his hand never leaving the rifle, "but you'll have to wait until we can gather our cattle and make a sale."

"We got orders to collect the money today," Gabe said, reaching into his pocket and handing George a folded paper. "Look for yourself."

Rose could tell from George's expression that the directions were painfully clear.

George had only recently returned home. How could he know Texas law? She couldn't allow him to be cheated. But would they believe her if she spoke up?

"If you ain't got money, we got to have something of equal value."

"I don't have anything worth that much."

"Maybe we'll look around, just to make sure," Cato said, "but that bull will make a start."

Rose stiffened. Losing the bull would take the spine out of George's plans for the ranch. She couldn't let that happen.

"If you'll just wait until we can sell some cattle, even some land . . ."

"That paper says we can't wait," Cato said, starting to dismount. "Now if you'll just step aside . . ."

George's rifle was pointing at Cato's heart before his foot reached the ground.

"Nobody searches my house," George said, "not today or any other. You'll get your money, but you'll have to wait."

Cato paused in the uncomfortable position of one foot in the stirrup and one on the ground.

"Now look here, Mr. Randolph," he said, "there's no use getting riled. We got our orders. We can't do nothing about that. You let us take what we have to. You can buy it back once you get your money."

"Get back in that saddle."

"Now why would I do that? There's only one of you and six of us."

"I'll get you and Gabe first," George said. His gaze never wavered.

"I'll get the others," Rose said.

Shock registered throughout the group. Rose had come out of the house to take up a position in the breezeway. Several hands paused in midair.

"Your figures are wrong, Mr. Cato."

She wanted to call them liars, yellow-bellied carpet-baggers, but it was crucial that there be no shooting. No matter what the outcome, George was certain to be killed.

"Now look, Mrs. Randolph—" Gabe started.

Rose flushed involuntarily, but she decided it would be better if they continued to think she was George's wife.

"The tax is twenty cents for every hundred dollars of value."

"The taxes have been raised—"

"I know. They were raised this past winter. They doubled it from ten cents."

"Lady, you can't know, living out here—"

"I lived in Austin until just a few weeks ago. I know exactly what the taxes are."

"Our orders say—"

"Then your orders are wrong. Go back and get correct ones."

George stared at Rose, fully as surprised as Gabe and Cato.

"I can't change no orders just like that," Gabe said, snapping his fingers. "You got to pay up now. You can talk to the land office about your refund."

"No." It was George, and he was adamant.

"It's got to be paid today," Cato repeated.

"No, it doesn't," Rose contradicted. "We have until the first of the year."

"Ma'am, I'm telling you, our orders say the taxes have to be paid now. The laws have been changed."

"They couldn't have been," Rose stated. "The legislature isn't in session, and they're the only ones who can change tax laws."

"Okay, let's say it's only twenty cents," Cato conceded. "At five dollars an acre you'll have—"

"It's not worth one dollar per acre," Rose contradicted.

"Look here, woman—"

"The term *lady* is still appropriate," George said.

The men looked uneasy now. Having been thrown for a loss, they struggled to regain their confidence.

"Look, ma'am—"

"River bottom land along the coast is selling for less than three dollars. Land west of here has been going for sixty-five to seventy cents. I saw it in the paper. I heard people talking about it."

"Tax value ain't made up from land sale prices," Gabe said, attempting to intimidate Rose.

"I know that," Rose said. "They're placed at about half of the real value. If your *paper* says differently, it's wrong."

Silence. A deadlock.

What should she do now? She knew they weren't going to calmly turn around and go back to Austin. She had heard about groups like this showing up at outlying homesteads and taking everything they could carry off, including food. George wasn't going to let them raid his home. She could see that.

But could George stop them?

She could. But if she did, if she divulged her secret, she would have to leave the ranch right away. Maybe even tonight. Just the thought of leaving caused her pain, but she knew there was no future for her here. It would be better to help George and leave before it became any more difficult to tear him out of her heart.

Before anyone could do anything, they heard the clatter of hooves, and the boys came into view. Between Salty and Hen, tied to a pole whose ends rested on their saddles, hung the carcass of a wild boar. Monty carried a wounded dog across his lap.

"Look what we got," Zac said as he galloped up to the small gathering. "Salty says he knows how to make real Georgia barbecue."

"I know I brought everybody home too early, ma'am," Salty apologized when they reached the steps, his eyes surveying the men gathered in front of George, "but we got to cure this pig tonight or it'll spoil. Pork just won't keep when it's this hot." Rose noticed that he had maneuvered the pole so his shooting arm was free.

"I have no idea how to cure a pig," Rose said, staring at the huge, black, mud- and blood-flecked carcass.

"I'll see to it, ma'am," Salty offered. "All I need is a little help now and then." He and Hen maneuvered the boar between George and Gabe and Cato.

"I need to keep Homer home for a few days," Monty said, sliding out of the saddle. He lifted the panting dog off the saddle and carried him to his favorite resting place on the breezeway. "He strained something in his leg." He took up a position just behind Rose, his hand inches away from his gun.

"You shoulda seen us chasing it," Zac said, excited to tell Rose all the details, impervious to the tension all about him.

"You can tell Rose later," George said. "I'm talking to these men on business."

Gabe and Cato didn't look very happy to find themselves suddenly facing six men, all of them armed and fearless.

"What are they doing here?" Jeff demanded, coming to stand next to George. "I saw them hanging around Austin."

"They're from the land office," George said. "They're here about our taxes."

"They've been paid," Monty said.

"We settled that. Rose is trying to help them figure out the new tax figures."

"Rose?" Jeff said, surprised. "What can she know?"

"Apparently quite a bit," George said.

"We still haven't settled on the tax value," Gabe stated.

"What is it?" George asked, turning to Rose.

She had been prepared to step back inside and leave the rest of the negotiations to the men. But she couldn't refuse George's invitation.

"If the land's worth a dollar an acre—and that's about twice as high as it ought to be, check when you go into Austin—you've got six hundred one-hundred-dollar values. At twenty cents per hundred, that comes out to something over a hundred dollars."

"One hundred and twenty," Jeff said.

"Cut that in half," Rose finished.

"Sixty dollars," George said.

The men looked angry at the small sum mentioned, but they didn't leave.

"There's another problem," Gabe said to George.

He looked belligerent now, his telltale New England accent stronger than ever. Having had his game spoiled, Rose figured he was going to cause as much trouble as possible.

"Did you fight in the Confederate Army?"

"Yes."

"Did any of your brothers?"

"I did," Jeff volunteered.

"Then you can't vote or hold any public office. You're also subject to a special tax."

"You're lying," Rose said. She had thrown down a challenge. There would be no easy way out now.

"You're obviously here for no other reason than to see how much trouble you can cause," George said. "Get off my land."

"I don't think we ought to let them go," Hen said.

"If you so much as lay a finger on us," Gabe warned, "I'll send the army in here."

"You can't let the army come here," Rose whispered to George. "They burned down Brenham, and not a single person was arrested. They even attacked Brownsville."

"Couldn't nobody do anything about it," Gabe bragged. "In fact, I think I'll notify General Charles Griffin as soon as I get back. He ain't been at all friendly with ex-Confederates."

The Randolph men stood in a line with George flanked by Rose and Salty. Zac had been pushed to the rear.

"General Griffin won't be coming if there's nobody to send him a message," Monty said.

"There's a lot of open prairie between here and Austin," Hen added.

"They know where we are," Gabe said. Rose could tell that the line of seven stern faces had shaken his courage.

"I say we shoot them right here," Monty said.

"You'd hang," Gabe replied, a little desperately, Rose thought.

"If anybody ever found your bodies, they'd believe it was Cortina's bandits," Hen said.

That was no idle statement, and the men knew it.

"There are too many of us. You'd never kill us all."

"There's something I think you ought to see," Hen said. He drew his gun so fast it seemed to materialize in his hand. The men just stared at him.

"See that wasp's nest hanging from that eave?" Hen asked, pointing to a two-inch nest about fifty feet away.

The men nodded. In the next instant Hen shot. The nest vanished. And the wasps with it.

"I would advise you to go back to Austin and forget you were ever here," Rose said.

"We can't let them go," Monty objected as he drew his gun. "We got to kill all of them."

"General Griffin will be here before the week's out," Gabe threatened. "There won't be a stick left standing on this place when his men get through."

Rose knew she couldn't hold back any longer. She had seen what the army could do. Everything the boys had worked for, everything George had sacrificed for, could be destroyed forever. She took a deep breath.

"Then General Grant will have every one of them court-martialed and hanged."

"You're crazy," Gabe exclaimed.

"General Grant has sent word to General Sheridan in Louisiana that he's to see that the army takes particularly good care of me," Rose announced. "He also said he'll send full presidential pardons for George and Jeff as soon as he can arrange it."

"Your wife's insane," Gabe said to George. "General Grant would never help no Southerner."

But no one was listening to Gabe. Everyone was staring at Rose.

"I have the letter from General Grant in my pocket," Rose said to George. "It's the one Salty brought."

# *Chapter Eleven*

"You're lying," Gabe said. "You've got to be."

"You call her a liar again and you won't—"

Hen's elbow stopped Monty in midsentence.

"My father and General Grant were in the same class at West Point. They later fought in the Mexican War together," Rose told him. She didn't dare look at any of the boys. "General Grant is my godfather."

"You're a Yankee!" Jeff said. The hate and rage that Rose had so often seen near the surface suffused his face.

"I was born right here in Texas," Rose told him proudly. "But that's not important," she said, determined not to get sidetracked until she had convinced Gabe and Cato that any attack on the Randolphs would mean grave personal danger to them. "I want your names, and a full copy of your authorization," she said to Gabe. "I intend to forward it to General Grant along with your assurance that you won't take any action against this family until the pardons arrive."

They handed over the papers without protest.

"Make a copy," George said to Jeff.

"I still think we ought to shoot them," Monty said.

"They're going to go back to Austin to tell the land office there's no need for further investigation," Rose said. "They're also going to report that they have been given incorrect information. Then they're going to see that the correct figures are written into all the proper documents. Is there anything I've left out?"

"I think that about covers it," George said, unable to take his eyes off Rose.

"Would you like to see my letter?" Rose asked as she took

an envelope from her pocket and handed it to Gabe. "I don't want you to have any doubts about the truth of what I've said."

Gabe took one look at the first line, then the signature, and turned dead white.

"Your father was that Thornton?"

"Yes," Rose replied.

"Holy shit! Griffin will skin us alive if he finds out we bothered this woman," Gabe hissed to Cato, who took one glance at the letter and agreed.

"I would like the letter back."

"Sure, Mrs. Randolph. And you can be sure we'll get the tax records straight. Might not be no more than thirty dollars tax on this place. Nobody can believe anybody would own so much land. Most people just run their cows on it for free."

"Remember, I plan to write that letter tonight."

"You won't be bothered, ma'am. Ain't nobody anxious to annoy General Grant or General Sheridan. Everybody knows his temper is something awful."

"And the taxes?"

"You don't have to pay them till next year."

"That man must have a mighty comfortable job to protect," George said when the land officers had ridden off.

"One that lets other people's money find its way into his pockets," Salty added.

"I still think we should have buried them both under the nearest creek bank," Monty said.

"Rose dealt with them much more effectively," George said.

All eyes turned toward Rose.

Why did she feel as though she should slink away in shame? She fixed her gaze on George. There was none of Jeff's rage or hate in his face. Only stunned surprise and speechless silence.

And questions.

"I wrote him after you hired me and posted the letter that night," she said to George, sure of what he wanted to know. "I never thought he would answer. He left Texas after the war.

Daddy thought he'd never hear from him again after he was asked to resign his commission. He probably wouldn't have if he hadn't needed Daddy to write a letter to get his commission restored."

She took a deep breath and let some of the tension flow from her body. Now they knew. They could do as they would.

"I was bluffing about writing a second letter. He wouldn't answer."

"But the pardons?" George asked.

"I knew about the *ironclad* oath. I figured you'd need the pardons someday. I didn't see any harm in asking."

"But why would he go to so much trouble for two ex-Confederate soldiers?"

There was no reason not to tell him the truth. Not now.

"I told him I was going to marry you. I didn't think he'd send them otherwise."

Rose nearly choked on the words. He would certainly be furious at her now. It was bad enough that she had made them beholden to Grant, but to do it with a lie!

"Now that's what I call clever thinking," Salty said.

Rose knew he was trying to help her, trying to dispel some of the tension, but it wouldn't work. Jeff would never forgive her. She didn't know about the twins, but George was the only one who mattered to her. She expected to have to leave, but it would break her heart if she had to go with him furious at her.

George still looked somewhat stunned, but he pulled himself together. The knot in her stomach loosened a little when she saw a trace of warmth flicker in his eyes. "There's no way we can thank you for what you've done," he said, his voice noncommittal, his smile only slightly mechanical. "You have our eternal gratitude."

Just like he was making a speech, Rose thought. Maybe he would use this as an excuse to get rid of her. Well, they wouldn't do it just yet. She'd make them think about it. They had that boar to dress and dinner to eat. The Randolphs weren't men to do anything on an empty stomach.

"I don't have time to get dinner ready before you start on that hog," Rose said, "but I'll heat up some stew to tide you over. It'll be ready by the time you've washed up." She disappeared inside the house.

"Did you know her father was a Yankee officer?" Jeff demanded of George. He had barely waited for Rose to leave before he questioned his brother.

"Yes," George answered, his mind more on Rose than his answer.

"And you still hired her?"

"Yes."

George realized there was a threat to Rose, and he felt a calm settle over him as his mind prepared to lay a protective cordon around her.

"Then you can be the one to get rid of her, right now," Jeff stormed.

"We should talk about this," Hen said.

"There's nothing to talk about," Jeff said.

"I think there is," Monty added.

"Let's wait until after dinner," George suggested. "We'll think better on a full stomach."

"How can you eat when a Yankee's cooking our dinner?"

"Jeff, you lost your arm, not your brain. If you think she's going to poison you, don't eat. But I don't see how her father being Grant's friend is going to affect her cooking."

"I'll still wait outside."

"If any of you feel like Jeff, just say so."

"I don't care about no Yankee. Rose is nice," Zac stated. "You're not going to send her away, are you?"

"It looks like we're going to have to talk about it."

"It's all your fault," Zac said, turning on Jeff. "I hate you." He pummeled his brother with his fists, then ran inside when sobs threatened to overpower him.

"I don't care what you do about her," Tyler stated before following his little brother inside.

"Why did you hire her?" Hen asked. "You know how Jeff feels."

"She was the only person for the job."

"But—"

"And I never planned for any of you to find out about her father."

"But—"

"It doesn't matter. She was born in Texas. She's more Southern than we are."

"You don't have to yell at me," Hen said. "I'm not trying to throw her out."

George realized he had raised his voice, but he couldn't help it. Just thinking about the injustice of the situation made his temperature boil.

"You've already judged her. Her father fought for the Union so she's a Yankee. What about other families with divided loyalties? They haven't been judged guilty by association."

"What are you getting so mad about?" Monty asked. "You sure you aren't starting to like her?"

"Monty, there's a lot to be said for you, but there are times when you're as insensitive as that boar. She knew who those men were when they rode up today. She also knew all of you hated Yankees, because I told her. Yet she chose to use her connection with Grant to protect this family even though she knew we might force her to go back to Austin.

"Now I consider that an act of courage, the action of a person of character and deep convictions. I admire that in anyone, and their being a Yankee doesn't change it. You can stay out here if you like, but I think in light of what Rose has done for us, you owe her your courtesy and respect. If you can't give it, then by all means, stay outside."

George turned on his heel and marched inside without waiting to see what his brothers would decide.

"He's got us across a barrel there," Monty said.

"Yeah," Hen agreed.

"You can give in to George if you want, but I won't," Jeff said.

"I never expected you would," Monty said, his habitual antagonism toward Jeff back in his voice. "You always were too stubborn to do what's best for you, even when you weren't too blind to see it. You coming, Salty?"

"In a minute. I've been so enthralled by the eloquence of the Randolph boys I haven't remembered to wash up."

Monty laughed heartily. "You must mean George. Hen doesn't talk enough to be eloquent, and Jeff will tell you I don't talk much better than an ignorant dirt farmer."

"You don't have to stay out here to keep me company," Jeff said to Salty as Hen and Monty turned to go inside.

"I'm not," Salty said. "I'm staying to make sure you go in to dinner."

"I won't. Not as long as she's in there."

"Suit yourself. Just know it's not Rose you're standing against now. It's your brothers."

"No, it's not. It's that damned Yankee woman."

"Your brothers understand your feelings and respect them. They've all agreed to talk about it tonight. But they've told you they feel you're wrong to treat Rose this way. They all agree on that point. If you stay out here, you'll be slapping them in the face as much as Rose."

"No, I'm not."

"If you ignore their opinion in this matter, how do you expect them to respect yours in the other? You can't have it all your own way."

"What do you think about Rose?" Jeff asked.

"My opinion doesn't matter."

"I want it anyway."

"Okay, I think she's one magnificent woman. If I thought she'd have me, I'd propose right now."

"But her father fought for the Union!" Jeff said, unable to believe that no one agreed with him.

"I wouldn't care if her father was Grant himself. She's a damned fine woman, and Texas ought to be proud of her."

"You sound like George."

"Your brother is a smart man. Now make up your mind. If you wait any longer, it won't matter what you decide later."

•

George was surprised at himself. He was so angry he was shaking. He knew his appreciation for Rose had increased with each passing day, but he had no idea his feelings for her had grown to such proportions. What he felt for her had gone past simple appreciation.

He liked her very much.

Maybe even more than that. If not, how could he account for his reaction to Jeff's attack?

It had taken a lot of courage to ask Grant for pardons for two Confederate officers. When he thought of the agonizing hours ahead before she would know their decision—of the long hours it would take to process the boar, of having to put on a brave face all during dinner—he got angry all over again.

She didn't deserve this. After what she'd done, she deserved their thanks, their unstinted approbation, their sincere gratitude.

He entered the bedroom. Zac and Tyler were inside.

"You're not going to send Rose away, are you?" Zac asked. He had changed his clothes, but he was obviously waiting for George.

"We're going to discuss it later."

"Tyler wants her to go back."

"I never wanted her here," Tyler said. But after one glance at George's expression, he decided to leave without saying any more.

"Well, I do," Zac called after Tyler. "I like her a lot better than you. You like her, don't you?" he asked George.

"Yes, I like her."

"Don't let Jeff make her go away."

"We will all vote. You too. Now scoot. You know Rose depends on you to pour the milk."

"She'd rather have you do it."

"Well, I'm late. She'll have to depend on you."

Zac almost ran into Hen.

"Slow down, you little cyclone."

He didn't. "I got to help Rose," he tossed over his shoulder.

"What's gotten into him? I never saw him so anxious to do any work in his life."

"He's afraid we're going to send Rose away."

"I didn't know he liked her that much."

"We tend to forget he's still a little boy. No matter how much he likes to think he's grown up, he needs the kind of attention and tenderness Rose gives him."

"I never thought about that."

"Neither did I, I'm ashamed to say."

"Why should you? He's always busting his britches to show us how big he is."

"Which probably makes what Rose gives him all that much more important."

The door crashed open. "I know Jeff doesn't look a thing like Pa, but he gets more like him every day," Monty exploded.

"He's not very easy to live with," George agreed, "but I try to remember we're more fortunate than he is."

"So he keeps reminding us," Monty grumbled.

"Hurry up," George said. "I don't imagine the next several hours are going to be very easy on Rose. They won't be any easier if she has to spend the first hour wondering if we're going to come to the table."

"She knows I'll be there," Monty said. "With me, food comes before anything else. And that includes Jeff."

Rose was glad to have Zac in the kitchen. Anything was better than her own thoughts.

"George said he was going to be late so I was to pour the milk."

"Am I supposed to wait?"

"Naw. They'll be here any minute. George was just getting mad at Jeff."

Rose would never have believed how much her heart would leap at that news. She realized her fate depended on more than George's opinion, but she also realized his was the only opinion that counted with her.

"We're going to have a meeting, and I get to vote," Zac announced.

"You're not supposed to talk about that," Tyler said. He was already seated at the table.

"I expected it," Rose told both boys.

"See, she already knows, so I can talk about it."

"I imagine George would prefer you didn't," Rose said.

"I'm going to vote to keep you," Zac stated boldly. "I don't care what Jeff says."

"You little sneak," Tyler shouted. He made a dive for Zac. The boy took refuge behind Rose's skirts. "You wait until I get my hands on you."

"Both of you sit down," Rose commanded. "If you're going to fight, you'll have to go outside."

"I've got to finish the milk," Zac said, smiling in a superior manner at Tyler.

"Hurry up. I think I hear your brothers."

George, Hen, and Monty entered together.

"Salty is washing up," Monty announced. "I don't know what Jeff is doing. I don't mean to wait for him."

"It'll be a couple more minutes before I'm ready," Rose said. "Maybe they'll be here by then."

The silence in the room was deafening. Rose thought she could hear the seams in her dress stretch each time she breathed. She tried not to be too tense, but she couldn't help it. She only had to look at George's countenance to realize how upset he was. Hen rarely talked, but she couldn't recall a single meal when Monty had been quiet. Tyler never said much either, but she could tell Zac was bursting to talk.

But he didn't.

Zac used George as a barometer for his behavior, and right now the prospects were for heavy weather. Zac wisely decided to keep his sails trimmed.

Rose guessed she had always known this day would come, but she hadn't expected it so quickly. She had barely been here a month, hardly time enough for them to get to know her. It would be like deciding the fate of a stranger.

She was also anxious for George. She knew how important it was to him to strengthen the bonds that held his family together. Jeff's not coming to dinner would be a difficult hurdle to overcome. She knew from her years with the Robinsons that as long as a family pulled together, as long as they all felt they were working for the best interests of the family, they could overcome almost any disagreement.

But Rose wasn't sure the affection the Randolph boys felt for each other was strong enough to hold them together through even a minor confrontation. In fact, there were times when she wondered if the Randolphs were capable of love. Even family loyalty seemed beyond their grasps.

The door opened to admit Salty. Rose breathed a sigh of relief when she saw Jeff behind him.

It was nearly midnight when Rose got up from the table. "You'll be more comfortable if you have your meeting here. It's a nice night. I think I'll sit in the yard. Maybe the stars are out."

They hadn't finished the boar until after eleven o'clock, and she would have to clean up the kitchen after they made their decision. Still, it was nice to think of the hams and rings of sausage in the larder. They really needed to build a smokehouse. She didn't think pork was at its best when cured in salt alone. She'd speak to George about that tomorrow.

If she stayed.

"I'll keep you company, ma'am, if you don't mind," Salty said, getting to his feet at the same time. "I know a bit about the constellations."

George felt a pang of jealousy. He'd never sat in the moonlight with Rose, or talked of the stars. It seemed hardly a day passed that he didn't find something new he wanted to share with her. He might not have an opportunity after tonight. He pulled his mind back to what promised to be an unpleasant confrontation.

"Each of us will have a chance to say what's on his mind," he said. "Make sure you say it all now. No matter what we decide, I don't want to hear it again. Nobody can interrupt or ask questions until the speaker has finished. Okay?"

"Okay with me," Monty said.

Jeff nodded his agreement.

"I want to go first," Zac said, bouncing in his seat with excitement.

"You're too young," Jeff objected.

"Rose's presence affects him as much as anyone else," George stated. "He gets to have his say and cast his vote."

Zac stood up on his chair and surveyed the room like one getting ready to make a far-reaching announcement. "I think she ought to stay because I like her," he said and sat back down.

"You birdbrain," Tyler said. "Is that all you have to say?"

"Let's get one thing straight right now," George said, giving Tyler such a severe look the boy subsided. "No one is to make slighting remarks about anyone else's opinion. Regardless of what you think of their reasoning, it's their opinion and they have a right to it, just as you do to yours."

"But—" objected Tyler.

"If you can't follow the rule, you lose your right to speak. Agreed?"

Everyone nodded except Tyler and Jeff.

"Who's next?"

"I'll go," Tyler said. He stood up, looking all the taller because he was so thin. "I didn't want any female here in the first place. I can do anything she does."

George had to frown severely at Monty to prevent an outburst.

"I certainly don't want any Yankee woman cooking my food. I also don't like being bossed around. She's been telling us what to do ever since she got here, and that ain't right."

Tyler paused.

"Do you dislike her?" George asked.

"Whether he likes her isn't the point," Jeff objected.

"It will make a difference in how I vote," George said.

"I don't dislike her," Tyler admitted grudgingly. "She hasn't been so bad lately."

"That's not the point," Jeff interrupted.

"You through, Tyler?" George asked.

"I guess so."

"Okay, Jeff, you can speak."

The words started tumbling from his mouth before he got to his feet.

"It's not a matter of whether we like her or whether she bosses us around. It's a matter of principle. It's a matter of what the Yankees did to us during the war. What they're still trying to do to us through Reconstruction. I can't see that woman, or think of her father, without seeing thousands of brave Confederate boys lying in the torn-up earth, their bodies ripped to bits by cannon fire, their life's blood poured out in the dirt of one battlefield after another.

"How can you think of that woman in the kitchen and not think about the families whose husbands and sons won't come home? What about Madison? Will he come home?"

George objected. "You can't hold Rose responsible for Madison."

"Then what about Pa? We know Yankees killed him. Shot him to ribbons."

Jeff paused to look at his brothers, but none of them spoke.

"I don't see how you can even consider for one moment keeping that woman here. I would never have believed it of you, George, not in a hundred years."

George realized Jeff's objections had nothing to do with Rose or her father. It was the war and what it had done to him and others like him. He would never accept Rose until he learned to accept his loss.

George wondered if Jeff would ever be able to do that.

"Have you got anything else to say?" George asked.

"Yes. I don't see how I can stay in this house if Rose stays." Jeff sat down.

"I think it would be better if we refrained from making threats," George said. "It's unfair to the rest of us. Also, who knows when any one of us might want to change our mind? Casting down the gauntlet in that manner will just make it harder to do an about-face."

"I won't change my mind."

"Which of you wants to go next?" George asked the twins.

"I guess I will," Monty said. He didn't stand up. "I wasn't the least bit pleased when Rose got here. As you may remember, I said we had to get rid of her. I said it rather loudly."

"You say everything loud," Zac said.

"Well, I changed my mind. Laying aside that she's pretty as a picture and just about the greatest cook in the world, she's a real nice lady. I appreciate what she did for us out there this afternoon. I'd have shot the damned scoundrels out of the saddle, and we'd have had the whole army down on us. She knew they were trying to cheat us, and she knew what to say to put a stop to it.

"Only thing is, I can't forget she's a Yankee. I know she didn't fight, but her pa did. I don't have nightmares about dead soldiers like Jeff, but I do think of the bandits and rustlers they let come in here just to keep us too poor to fight back. I don't want us fighting over her. We've finally started to feel like a family. I'd hate to see that go." Looking a little embarrassed at his show of emotion, he sat down.

George could hardly believe his ears. He would have said Monty valued the family less than anybody except Tyler.

All eyes turned to Hen.

Hen remained seated. "I didn't like her at first either. It stuck in my craw that she turned the table over that first night. I always took Ma to be how a woman ought to act, and Rose didn't measure up. Then I remembered going to Ma's room one day. She was crying about something Pa had done."

"She was always doing that," Monty said, anger at remembered slights making his voice tight.

"She was saying to her mirror, *If I could only stand up to him.* Ma never could stand up to Pa. But if she could, I bet she'd have acted just like Rose."

"We're not—" Jeff started.

"I'm not finished," Hen said. The cold look in his eye encouraged Jeff to keep quiet.

"I yield to nobody in disliking Yankees. If it hadn't been for Ma, I'd have been out there with the rest of you. But I don't hold any child liable for the sins of his parents. I thought Pa was the meanest, lowest, most cussed son-of-a-bitch who ever walked the earth, but I don't hold it against any of you that he's your Pa. By his own lights, Rose's pa was an honorable man. That's a whole hell of a lot more than you can say about our old man. I can't hold his serving in the Union Army against her. And I agree with Monty about it feeling good to be a family again. I just wonder if we would have done it without Rose. We weren't doing too good before she got here."

A surge of affection for his stoic brother warmed George's heart. He knew how much Hen adored their Ma. Comparing Rose to her was the greatest compliment he could give any woman.

Everyone turned to George.

"I answered this question when I hired Rose," George began. "She told me about her father and I knew how you would feel. But I hired her because I thought she was the best for the job."

"Anybody can cook and clean," Jeff objected.

"I chose her for two other reasons. I thought she was the only woman of the four who wouldn't break the slender bonds that hold this family together."

"You were wrong there," said Jeff.

"No, I wasn't. What Hen and Monty just said proved it. Also,"

George continued when Jeff tried to interrupt, "I chose her because I thought she was honest and courageous. But we're not talking about Rose now. We're talking about her father. I don't care about her father. I didn't hire him."

"You don't care about her father?" Jeff repeated, aghast. "You don't care about all the honest and courageous Southern men he killed?"

"I killed honest and courageous Yankees, Jeff. You did, too, but now the fighting is over. I'd like to think if our sister had lived and if she had found herself alone in Pennsylvania or New Hampshire, she wouldn't have been turned out to starve, or to stay alive at the expense of her self-respect."

"It's not the same thing."

"I think it is."

"I've had enough of this," Monty said. "Let's vote."

# Chapter Twelve

"It's nice out here," Salty said.

Rose sat on the chopping block. Salty stood, looking at the starry canopy overhead. They had sat in silence until the volume level of the argument inside unexpectedly plummeted to an indistinct murmur.

"Yes, it is," she agreed, trying to concentrate on talking to Salty rather than straining to make sense of the fragments of sentences escaping through the kitchen window. "I'd never lived outside a town when I agreed to come out here. I was afraid I would miss the people and shops, things going on."

"And you haven't?"

"I wasn't happy in Austin. Things would have to be much worse than they are for me to want to go back."

"Are they bad? I thought everybody pretty much bowed to your commands."

Rose laughed, a sputtering sound which indicated her amusement as well as her surprise. "Look again. They're really very nice, especially when I forget my place and start handing out orders, but I'm an outsider. I always will be."

"At least George thinks you can do no wrong."

Rose wasn't about to explain how things stood—or didn't stand—between her and George. But before she could think of an answer to disarm Salty's curiosity, the kitchen door banged open; they both spun toward the house as Jeff stomped out and strode off into the darkness.

"I take that to mean you'll be cooking breakfast for some time to come," Salty said, turning back to Rose. "I expect George will be here to deliver the verdict any minute."

George didn't get a chance. Zac exploded through the doorway almost on Jeff's heels.

"You're going to stay!" he shouted, racing toward Rose and throwing himself into her arms. "Jeff is as mad as a castrated bull. Aren't you glad?"

Rose gave Zac a big hug. "I'm glad you want me to stay, but I'm not glad Jeff is upset."

"Jeff don't matter," Zac stated. "Not as long as George wants you to stay."

Unable to think of a judicious answer, Rose decided to ignore Zac's remark and his bad grammar. Neither did she want to read too much into George's approval. That had gotten her into enough trouble already.

"I'd better start on the dishes," she said, getting to her feet. She took Zac's hand in hers and headed toward the house. "Much longer and they'll be as bad as the day I got here."

"I got to go to bed," Zac said when they reached the house. He very primly disengaged his hand from Rose's clasp and turned toward the men's bedroom. "Hen said he'd tell me a story if I promised not to nag him to death tomorrow."

Rose couldn't tell whether Zac was running *toward* the story or *away* from the dishes. But the question didn't engage her mind for long. George was clearing the table when she entered the kitchen.

"You don't have to do that," she said, hurrying to take the plates from him.

"You'd have been through long ago if we hadn't run you out."

"It won't take long."

"I'll help."

"Okay," Rose said, a flutter of excitement making her stomach feel almost queasy. George hadn't helped since that first night when she threw dinner onto the floor.

"I suppose Zac told you the news."

"Was Jeff very upset? He went past me like the north wind."

"He'll get over it."

"Maybe I shouldn't stay." She didn't know why she said that. The last thing she wanted was to leave, no matter how Jeff felt.

"He's not really mad at you," George said as he settled the dirty plates into the tub of water Rose had left to heat on the stove. "He just can't forget what the Union soldiers did to him."

Rose felt despair close in on her. "It'll be like it was in Austin. Everybody started out hating something else, but they ended up hating me."

"No one will hate you. I won't let them."

Rose felt some of her alarm melt away. Silly man. Didn't he know he couldn't control people's feelings? But he would protect her.

"You needn't worry about Tyler either. He doesn't even dislike you."

"I'm still uncomfortable."

"Don't be. The rest of us want you here. Monty can't say enough about your cooking. And Hen admires you."

"I didn't think he approved of any female except your mother," Rose said, surprised.

George's smile left his face.

"I'm sorry if I shouldn't have said anything, but I never know when it's safe to mention your mother. Sometimes you don't seem to notice. Other times you turn as stiff as dried leather. You didn't even tell me that was her bedroom," Rose said, nodding toward the door still hidden behind the coats. "I had to find out by accident."

"I guess it's about time I told you about my mother."

But George didn't appear anxious to begin. He just stood there as though the memories were drawing him back in time. Rose had to take the dishes out of his hands.

"Ma was a beautiful, gentle creature. She came from an old family long on respectability and short on money. Pa mesmerized her with his good looks and charm and dazzled her with his boundless energy and wealth. But she married him because she loved him. It was the biggest mistake of her life."

Now that he had started he seemed to relax a little.

"Ma thought Pa hung the moon. No matter how scandalous his behavior, the disgrace he brought on us, or the misery his gambling caused, she never stopped loving him or trying to make us love him just as much."

He paused.

"After a particularly nasty scandal, a group of family, neighbors, and past friends bought this ranch and forced Pa to come out here. But he never meant to stay. He figured he'd soon find a way to get back. And he did. The war started just months after we arrived. He must have loved it. It was the only thing whose violence matched his own."

Another pause as the lines in his face hardened.

"Ma was in poor health and Zac still a baby. The boys were too small to look after a ranch, but he never considered that. Hen says they never heard from him. You can imagine what that did to Ma. She died a year later."

Rose knew George would never understand. To him responsibility was everything.

"Monty merely curses at the mention of Pa's name, but I

think Hen would have killed him if he had come home. He worshiped Ma."

George might not hate his father, but he could never forgive him. The tragedy, Rose knew, was that he wanted to.

"Your mother must have been a remarkable woman."

"She never wanted to come to Texas—she considered it a foreign country—but it never occurred to her to oppose Pa." George paused again, remembering something he didn't share with Rose. "I don't think any of us will ever forgive him for what he did to her."

"You know that's exactly what you have to do, don't you?"

"Could you?"

Rose wanted to think she could, but she knew better. She hadn't forgiven the people of Austin for much less.

"I don't think so."

"Maybe I could if I didn't see the consequences staring me in the face every day. Have you noticed that faint scar around Monty's neck? It's a rope burn. Two bandits had just strung him up when Hen found them. Monty was fourteen. *Fourteen,* for God's sake, and he thought he was going to die. Hen killed two men that day. He was fourteen, too. If you want to know what that did to them, just look into their eyes. They're only seventeen, but they're older than I am."

Rose didn't say anything. She couldn't.

"Jeff didn't want to join the army. He was afraid he wouldn't measure up, but Pa shamed him into it. He lost his arm, and now he feels even less a man."

Rose had never felt so useless. She had looked deep into George's heart and seen the heat of his passion. She had also seen the iron bands that held it in check. She finally understood, and she felt more helpless than ever.

With a hiss of exasperation, Rose threw back the covers and sat up on the edge of her bed. She was exhausted, but she hadn't gotten a wink of sleep. She couldn't stop thinking about last night. Not about George's father or the vote. About George.

She had made the mistake of asking him how he felt about her staying.

"I've told you all along how much I appreciated the job you're doing," he said. "That hasn't changed."

She didn't know why she asked. She had told him to keep his distance. What did she want from the man?

She knew exactly what she wanted.

She wanted him to say he wanted her to stay more than anything else in the world. She wanted him to say he would be devastated if she left, that he would come after her and bring her back, drag her back if necessary. She wanted him to say he couldn't imagine life without her, that she was as necessary as the sun or the earth beneath his feet. She wanted him to say she filled his dreams at night and his hopes during the day. She wanted him to say she would be an inseparable part of his life for as long as she lived.

She wanted him to say he loved her.

She wanted him to talk about her eyes, her hair, her lips, her skin, her nose, her ears, even her breasts. Anything except her cooking, how well she kept house, or her wonderful knowledge of Texas law. She wanted him to think of her as a woman. A desirable woman. A woman who caused him to lie awake at night. A woman whose beauty and charm had become an obsession, whose nearness tortured him, body, mind, and soul. A woman who had so thoroughly worked her way into his life he could never feel complete until he possessed her.

Utterly and completely.

She wanted him to be so filled with raging desire when he was around her that she would have to lock her bedroom door to protect her virtue. She wanted his passion for her to utterly vanquish his maddening control, his need for her to be so great he would do anything to win her love.

She longed for him to ache for her as much as she ached for him, to know the agony of spurned love, of unacknowledged love, of love forced into the ignominy of hoping for compliments on cooking and cleaning just so she would know he thought of her. She wanted him to look into her eyes, search desperately for a sign of warmth, a sign of genuine feeling, and find only cold appreciation.

She wanted him to be as miserably unhappy as she was.

During the following week it became clear that Jeff's anger was affecting the mood of the whole family. Monty turned almost savage; Hen grew morose; Tyler might as well have taken himself out of the family.

Rose's heart went out to Zac. The child knew that something was wrong, but he didn't know what. He looked to his two anchors, George and Rose, for reassurance. It was an assurance Rose couldn't give. It was an assurance George didn't give.

That was why Rose decided to go back to Austin.

It really was a simple decision. There was no future for her at the ranch. George had made that plain from the first. His attitude during the past week reinforced it. She was young and pretty enough to cause desire to occasionally overcome his restraint, but she wanted more than naked passion. She wanted love and a family; she would get neither from George.

Besides, her presence was tearing the family apart. All the ease and comfort had disappeared. Only tension, anger, and bitterness remained. It didn't matter that it was unfair, that no one wanted it.

It just happened.

She couldn't stand to see what it was doing to George. It didn't matter that Jeff was responsible. Jeff was part of the family. She wasn't.

She never would be.

So she decided to leave. She wouldn't tell George. She didn't think she could.

"If you're going to Austin anytime soon, I'd like to go with you," she said to George next morning at breakfast.

She had trouble actually saying the words. They seemed too final. They meant giving up any hope that George would come to love her. She didn't kid herself into thinking her absence would achieve what her presence hadn't.

She knew she loved him. Despite her vows to not marry a soldier, she loved him.

She didn't want to. It was a waste of good, honest emotion, but her heart hadn't consulted her brain, nor taken advice when it had been offered. It had settled on George and wouldn't have anybody else. She didn't expect it ever would.

"Are we running out of anything?" George asked.

"No."

"It hasn't been three months yet."

"There are some things I need, things I can't very well ask anyone else to purchase for me."

"Very well. We'll go tomorrow."

He knew. She could tell. After one penetrating look, he knew.

"I'll ask Salty to come along. He offered to find us some hands. I think it's time."

"Hands for what?" Jeff asked.

"We can't round up and brand a couple hundred crazy wild steers without help. It would wear us down before we even started for Missouri."

"Are you sure we should take them to St. Louis?" Jeff asked. "We only have *her* word there's any market."

"It's already been decided," George said. "We can get nearly ten times the price."

"But how do you know she—"

"We're taking them to St. Louis," Monty snapped. "If you don't like it, you don't have to come. As a matter of fact, I wish you wouldn't. It'd be a damned relief not to have to look at your sour face."

"I need a volunteer to do the cooking while we're away," George said, trying to divert Monty's anger. "Tyler?"

"I ain't cooking nothing for this lot, not after what they all said."

"Let Jeff do it," Hen said. "He's the reason she's leaving."

"You know I can't handle the cooking," Jeff said angrily. "And what do you mean I'm the reason Rose is leaving?"

"You don't think she means to come back, do you?" Hen demanded, anger making his eyes agate hard. "Not after you've been a bastard to everybody, acting like we're responsible for that damn stump of yours."

"Hen, that's enough," George said.

"The hell it is," Monty exploded. His twin's outburst blew the lid off his own smoldering resentment. "It's about time somebody told him what a pain it is to live with him, lashing out at everybody all the time, thinking he's better than the rest of us because he's got a little education, thinking the rest of us ought to crawl on our bellies to him for the rest of our lives because he lost a goddamned arm. It's a damned shame that bullet didn't take off his head. Then he could have been a real martyr, not just a penny-ante imitation."

Rose thrust back her chair, jumped to her feet, and fled from the room. She couldn't stand to hear another word, see another face twisted by anger, feel another hot wave of rage. Especially not when it was her fault.

The dogs, disturbed in their slumber, jumped up barking. But Rose was too familiar to be worth more than two or three listless howls. They sank back to the floor, their heads dropped on their paws, before she had disappeared into the dusk.

She couldn't stop the tears running down her face any more than she could stop her feet running aimlessly into the night. She had to get as far away from the anger and the bitterness as possible. It seemed her whole life had been filled with it. No matter where she went, it followed her.

She caused it. She carried the seeds with her.

No, she wouldn't accept that. She had been happy until the war brought an end to everything kind and gentle. The anger, hate, and bitterness had come with the defeat and the Reconstruction that followed. And regardless of how unfair it might be, she was inexorably bound up with these powerful feelings, feelings so strongly imbued with their own energy that no one, individual or government, could control them. They ripped through towns and families, destroying lives as wantonly as the guns had destroyed people and property.

It was time she stopped trying to fight it. It was time she stopped being foolish enough to think she could win.

The pain in her chest forced her to stop running, to sag against the corral fence. Her chest heaved as her breath came in short gasps. The bull, chewing its cud in the moonlight, turned his head to stare at her out of vacant eyes.

Over the sound of her ragged breath, she heard footsteps. George. She should have known he would follow. She desperately wanted him to. He was the only one who could heal the wounds in her soul. And her heart. Only his arms would make her feel safe and secure.

God, when would she ever learn? She was such a fool!

George's family came first. That was the reason he had remained silent all week. That was the reason he hadn't told Jeff to curb his behavior or leave.

That's the reason he hadn't given in to his desire to hold her in his arms or kiss her. That was also the reason he agreed to take her to Austin even though he knew she wasn't planning to come back.

Why had he followed her now? There was nothing he could say that wouldn't cause her more pain.

"Are you all right?"

She didn't turn around. She didn't need to. Even as a disembodied sound coming out of the night, his voice was comforting. How could anything that deep and solid not be an unfailing support?

"I'm fine. I just didn't want to sit through any more fights."

"Monty always—"

She whirled to face him. "It's not Monty or Hen, and you know it."

"I don't know what to do about Jeff."

"There's nothing you can do. He has to do it himself. And don't you even think of mentioning his arm."

She was too angry to choose her words, think about his feelings, or remember not to criticize. She had held her silence too long.

"Jeff has used that arm like a whip ever since he got back. I know you don't want me to say this, but I can't help it. He's used it to keep you defending him, to keep you from being as close to the twins as you want. You said your father was selfish. So is Jeff. Don't interrupt," she said when he started to speak. "I've listened until I can't listen any more. Coddling isn't going to make him feel differently. You've got to cut him loose. Let him sink or swim by himself. If you don't, he'll pull you down with him. And your family as well."

"I know that."

"Then why haven't you told him?"

"Because he's my brother. I can't turn my back on him."

"So you'll turn your back on yourself, your other brothers, your career, and me. You'll let him make everybody miserable."

"You're not coming back from Austin, are you?"

"Do you want me to?"

"Yes."

"Why? And don't you say a word about cooking and cleaning. Peaches McCloud would do it better than I can."

"Peaches can't do anything half as well as you."

Why couldn't he talk like that all the time? Why did he have to wait until she was leaving to say something nice?

"It would be pointless to come back. Nothing will have changed. I'll still be a Yankee. Jeff will still have lost his arm. You'll still be waiting for your chance to go off and join the army."

"We need you, and not just for your cooking. You've helped us start to feel like a family."

"Until Jeff found out I was a Yankee."

"Zac needs you. I never realized how important it was to a little boy to have a woman around, someone who wouldn't expect him to be anything but a little boy."

There were times when she wanted to hit him, to shake

him until his back teeth rattled. Didn't he ever think of her? Or of himself? She wasn't sure he *could* think of himself without thinking of his brothers as well.

"I'm very fond of Zac," Rose said, her voice unsteady. "I think he's adorable, but I can't come back just to be his mother. One of you will have to get married if you want that."

"There's no chance of that."

"I know. The twins are too young, Jeff is too bitter, and you hate women. I'm sorry, George, but I can't prop up your family. I tried, but I can't anymore."

"I don't hate women."

"You're dead set against marriage, so it comes to the same thing."

"I'm very fond of you. If it wasn't that . . . If things were different . . ."

"Well, they aren't. You're saddled with your family and some terrible fear which gives you cold chills whenever you think of marriage."

"What do you mean?"

"I'm not stupid, George. You're a perfectly normal man. You've got perfectly normal urges and desires. And don't tell me you don't want a wife and family. You'll never be happy without one. You've talked yourself into thinking you aren't fit for marriage, that you hate responsibility, but it's all a lie. And don't tell me again you wouldn't have come home if it hadn't been for Jeff. You haven't listened to Jeff since I've been here."

She had done it again, spoken out when she should have kept quiet. Only she had nothing to lose this time. It wouldn't make any difference if George got mad enough to throw her out. She was leaving.

"You came to take care of your family because you wanted to. You stayed here because you liked it. You even took me under your wing. Now you've got Salty and you're about to add more ex-Confederates. You're a man who can't live without dependents. They make you stronger."

"You're mistaken. I don't know what gave you the idea that—"

"Tell yourself all those lies if you must, but I don't want to hear them."

"Well, this isn't a lie. I don't want you to leave. I came out here to ask you to reconsider."

Rose felt as if the ground had given way under her feet. She had gotten her wrath stoked, her anger going full throttle, and then he tripped her up.

"Why do *you* want me to stay? Not because of Zac. Not anybody else. Just you."

Rose almost wished she hadn't asked. Maybe his only reason for coming had been his brothers. She didn't think she could stand that.

"I like you," George admitted reluctantly. "I think I always have. I admire your courage and energy—"

"I've had enough of admiration. Can't you feel just one purely spontaneous emotion?"

"My admiration has deepened my liking for you," George said, insisting upon his own words. "I've had too many lessons in the importance of courage to overlook it again."

"Okay, you like my courage and my energy. Isn't there anything you like about *me?*"

"But they are you. You wouldn't be you without them."

"Maybe I was wrong," Rose said, frustrated. "Maybe you are completely unsuited to be a husband."

"You want me to say I think you're beautiful, that I think of you all the time, that I find myself reaching out just to touch you?"

"Yes!" The word was a sigh all the way from her soul, the fulfillment of a long-held wish, the period to the open-ended sentence of her love. "That's what any woman wants to hear from the man she . . ."

"She what?" George asked.

"Finish what you were going to say," Rose said. She couldn't tell him she loved him. *She wouldn't.*

"I've never done anything as difficult as keeping my distance from you. You can't imagine the number of times I've wanted to touch you, wanted to . . ."

"Tell me," Rose pleaded. "I never thought you had the least trouble staying away."

George came a step closer. "You're a beautiful woman, Rose. I don't think I could live long enough to tell you everything that has passed through my mind since you've been here."

"You haven't told me *anything*."

"I started to, but you told me it could never come to anything."

"Forget what I said."

George came closer still.

"I hardly know how to put my feelings into words. I've never met a woman like you. You don't want me to speak of my admiration, but how can I begin to make you understand if I don't? You don't want me to speak of your courage or your energy, but they are just as much a part of you as your eyes or your lips."

He reached out and touched her, barely brushed her cheek, but Rose could hardly concentrate well enough to answer.

"I know, but somehow your talking about my lips doesn't make me feel like a beast of burden."

"I've seen many beautiful women. It seemed the world was full of them only a short time ago. But for them, beauty was an end in itself. They were the eyebrows and lips and skin and hair and nose you so want to hear praised. But that's all they were. A collection of beautiful parts."

His hand trailed down the side of her arm. The feeling was so intense it was almost painful.

"You don't think I'm nice to look at?"

"Yes. Even Monty thinks you're pretty. And if you can stop him from thinking about cows for as much as five minutes, you must be stunning."

Rose laughed in spite of her hypersensitive arm. "I never

thought I'd be pleased to have a compliment phrased exactly that way, but a lot of things have happened I never expected."

"I'm not doing this very well, am I?"

"No. As a matter of fact, you're making a pretty wonderful mess of it."

George let his hand slide all the way down her arm until he took her hand in his.

"What I'm trying to say is you're beautiful. But your beauty means so much more because of the person you are inside, what you're willing to give of yourself, what you're willing to share without demanding something in return."

She could feel the pressure of his thumb as it traced circles on her skin. Even in the face of such a small attention as this, it was hard to think of leaving.

"You're doing a little better now."

"The more I got to know you, the more I found myself drawn to you. I thought of your lips. They seemed to haunt me almost as much as your eyes. But they haunted me because they were *your* lips, not just because they were so beautiful I couldn't stop thinking about them."

"You're doing much better," Rose murmured, her eyes closed, her starved soul rejoicing in the nourishment of his words.

"I wanted to hold you in my arms and kiss you, and not just because it felt so wonderful. I wanted to hold *you* because of the little things you did to please me, the times you stopped what you were doing to pay attention to Zac, because of the times you were too tired to go on but you did because you were doing something for us."

"Go on."

Pulling gently, he drew her close to him.

"I found after a while I didn't feel quite as content, quite as comfortable, if you weren't around. Out on the range I would find myself wondering what you might be doing now. When I'm at the house, I find myself looking up to see where you are. When I have a decision to make, I wonder what you might think about it. You have invaded my mind and thoughts so thoroughly I can't imagine your not always being here."

He pulled her closer. They didn't touch, but Rose could feel his body heat.

"I got angry, then jealous, when Monty started flirting with you. It was a shock to think somebody else liked you. It was even worse to think you might like him. I knew then I wanted you to like only me.

"I told myself it wasn't fair to say anything when I had nothing to offer. But that day at the creek, I guess I forgot about being fair. I wanted only to kiss you, to know you liked me a little."

Through the material of her dress, Rose could feel their bodies brush. Her breasts became more excruciatingly tender than her arm.

"You've always known that," she said.

"It wasn't enough when neither of us could speak of it."

"You told me from the first you never wanted a wife or a family. Why should I talk about something I could never have?"

George put both his hands on her shoulders. Instinctively Rose leaned toward him.

"For the same reason I wanted to hold you in my arms and kiss you. Because I couldn't help myself. What did you mean just a minute ago when you said *That's what any woman wants to hear from the man she . . . ?*"

Rose tried to pull away, but he wouldn't release her.

"It's not fair . . ."

"Nothing's fair. You wanted the truth from me. Now I want the truth from you."

Rose was tempted to tell him a lie. Why should she bare her soul to a man who seemed to have none? Sure, he admitted to liking her, being attracted to her, drawn by the quality of her character, but that wasn't a warm emotion, one capable of igniting a passion which would last a lifetime. It wasn't strong enough to build her life on. It wasn't tough enough to shield her from Jeff's abuse.

But there was something there. Something which had sustained her feeling for him all these weeks. Something which had caused the feeling to deepen into love. Did she know what it was? Could she tell him if she did?

She leaned against him once more. It would be easier to tell him if she didn't have to look him in the eye.

"I don't suppose I'll ever forget the morning you walked into the restaurant. You made me feel like a real person, not just someone who took orders and served food."

A slight increase in the pressure of his arms encouraged her to go on.

"I know I came here with unfounded expectations. I knew that from the first. I told myself to do my job and keep my feelings to myself. But I couldn't. It's impossible for anybody to be around your brothers and feel nothing. It's like living in the center of a whirlwind. But it was a whirlwind that never went out of control, because you stood at the center.

"You kept a loose rein on Monty. You kept watch over Zac. You never forgot Jeff suffered more than you. You even understood Hen and Tyler. And you never forgot that even though he was absent, Madison was still part of the family. You put aside your own career for your family. Not by even the slightest word or action did you lead anyone to think you might resent it. You are kindness and thoughtfulness personified, and you don't even know it."

She looked up at him, expecting a frown. The look of tenderness, of wanting, nearly caused her tongue to lie still in her mouth.

In that look, she found the courage to tell him the one thing she'd sworn he'd never know.

"You always protected me. Even when I made you mad, you were fair. You leavened your orders with humor and caring. You were quite simply the most wonderful man I'd ever met. And I fell in love with you."

George reacted as if he'd been jabbed with a cattle prod.

"You fell in love with me?"

Rose would have broken away if she could, but George held her in an iron embrace. How could he be so sensitive to his brothers and be so unaware of her feelings toward him? If she needed any proof he didn't love her, she had it now.

"Is that so hard to imagine? You're handsome, kind, and wonderfully reassuring to be around."

George put his hand under her chin and raised her head until their eyes met. "Why didn't you tell me?"

She felt herself relax. She never could stay angry at him, not even when he deserved it.

"Why should I? I have lain in that miserable loft for weeks dreaming of being held in your arms, of being kissed, of being told you loved me. And all you could say was you didn't see how it would cause any harm since you liked me a lot."

George wasn't listening. He was kissing her face, planting dozens of kisses on her eyelids, nose, and mouth.

"You said you thought we could *enjoy each other* without making any sort of commitment. You couldn't have been more cruel if you'd tried."

Somehow Rose's arms found their way around George's neck.

"You are too much like my father. Even though you seemed to be everything I was looking for, I tried not to fall in love with you."

George's kisses became more insistent, and her sentences started coming in fragments.

"Only I made one . . . mistake. This wonderful man had no room in his . . . heart to love anyone but his . . . family. He had closed the door . . . sealed himself off from the rest of the world. This . . . wonderful man was afraid of a . . . little thing like . . . falling in love."

George paused. "What if this man could fall in love without wanting to get married or have a family? What if he wanted more than anything else to make a woman know how much he loved her?"

Rose felt some of the fire go out of her limbs. Her fingers

unclasped and her arms slowly slid from around George's neck. She put her hands on his chest and pushed until she could look straight into his eyes.

"That man would be confusing love with desire. Desire has all the heat of love with none of its warmth. It has a need to consume without any need to build. It considers the moment everything and the future an unpleasant afterthought. Desire flames high and burns out quickly. Love strives to build a nourishing warmth which will last through the years."

"You don't believe that that man could love you?"

"He could, but he won't let himself."

"Then you won't stay?"

"I can't."

# Chapter Thirteen

"I thought southern Georgia was a Godless country, but this place sure has it beat."

They had traveled for hours—along narrow paths deep in the brush, across several clearings, through dozens of shallow creeks—without seeing a house or any other sign of human habitation. George drove the wagon. Rose sat next to him. Salty rode alongside. All morning he had entertained them with a steady stream of genial chatter.

"We had a jim-dandy briar patch back home, but it was nothing compared to this stuff," Salty said, indicating a towering thicket that stretched for miles. "Can't understand how your cows get in and out with those horns. Ma had an old milk cow once with horns no longer than a pig's tail. Got tangled up in a wisteria vine and broke her neck. Shame, too. We never did get another cow that gave as much cream."

George wasn't interested in Salty's wisteria vine or his cow. He was aware of only two things: Rose's nearness and a dawning awareness that his resolve to remain a bachelor wasn't nearly as firm as he had thought.

Rose had never looked lovelier, or more desirable. He didn't know whether it was because he knew she was leaving or because her dress clung to her body with revealing intimacy. A row of buttons running up to Rose's neckline preserved her modesty, but her bosom was outlined as never before. Her stiff posture only accentuated its thrust.

The temptation to reach out and cover her breasts with his palms was almost too strong to be withstood. George hated to be such a slave to his lust, but there was nothing he could do about it when Rose sat just a few tantalizing inches away.

She might as well have been a thousand miles away. He could feel the tension between them. He knew she was reluctant to talk about what was on her mind. And he didn't encourage her to break her silence. She had said too much last night.

But he hadn't said enough.

He had told her of his admiration, of his liking, but he hadn't told her of the pain her leaving would cause.

He couldn't because he hadn't known until this morning. Until the moment she had come out of the house carrying her bags he hadn't truly suspected its magnitude. He hadn't expected to like her leaving, but neither had he expected to feel like getting down on his knees and begging her to stay.

She was probably right in feeling he would never be happy or contented if he didn't marry, but he had no choice, so it wouldn't help either of them to know they wanted the same thing and couldn't have it. Far better to separate quickly. The pain would be easier that way.

And there was pain. Anger, too. A surprising amount. He should have become used to it by now. It seemed his entire life had been a series of promises made but never kept.

But it hurt most of all to know she would leave believing he felt nothing for her beyond lust. That would make him no better than Luke Kearney in her eyes. He couldn't stand it if she despised him, too.

Maybe it would have been better if he had told her why he couldn't marry, why he didn't want a family. Last night didn't seem to be the right time. Neither did now. Since she had decided she must go back to Austin, it seemed unfair to undermine her resolve.

And he knew she had to go.

He had lain awake all night looking for another solution, but there wasn't one. They would hire another housekeeper, one with no connection to the Union Army.

The army. Odd. Coming home from Virginia he'd spent weeks going over the territorial forts in his mind, trying to decide which ones offered him the best chances for advancement. When he'd asked about Texas, he never asked about cattle or ranches. He asked about the Indian wars, the forts, and the men who commanded them. Even after he'd reached home and realized it would be some time before he would be free to leave, he worried that the longer he waited, the harder it would be to build a career.

Now he realized he hadn't thought of the army in weeks. He had spent all his time thinking about the roundup and setting up a breeding program for the herd. He was even planning to build new corrals, a shed, a barn for the bull, maybe enlarge the house.

He had thought of Rose.

And he had been happy.

Happier than he could ever remember. Could it be that Rose was right, that he was merely running away from something he was afraid to face?

No. The evidence was beyond question.

He could never marry.

Located on the north bank of the Colorado River, Austin had been chosen as the capital of Texas in 1839. Edwin Waller laid out the town in a square with all the streets running at right angles. The streets running east and west were named after Texas trees such as Live Oak, Cypress, Pecan, Mulberry,

Mesquite, and Bois d'Arc. Those running north and south were named after rivers. Congress Avenue, the street running through the middle of town, was the only exception. A Capital Square had been laid out, but the public buildings went up along the southern part of Congress Avenue. The armory, barracks, warehouses, barns, and corrals were across Waller Creek near the southeast corner of town.

The heat of summer had turned the streets into dust bowls. It had also driven the inhabitants indoors.

George pulled the wagon to a halt in front of Bullock's Hotel. Situated on the corner of Pecan and Congress Avenue, it was the biggest and finest hotel in town.

"What are you going to do?" George asked Rose. He couldn't just let her down and forget about her. He had to know she would be safe.

"I thought I'd see if Dottie would give me my old job back. Maybe things will be different now."

"Where are you going to stay?"

"There's my old room."

That's what he'd thought. She didn't have a job or a place to stay.

"You'll stay at the hotel until you have a job and somewhere to live."

"That might take days."

"I'll be in town for a while hiring hands." It wouldn't take more than half a morning, but he'd stay a week if necessary.

Rose hesitated.

"I'll pay for the room. It's our fault you had to come back so soon."

"I can't let you do that."

"Let him," Salty advised. "I always say there's no point in using your own money when you can spend someone else's."

"I'd rather pay my own way," Rose said.

"I'd rather have a farm of my own than work for George," Salty responded, "but there's nothing I can do about that either."

George took some gold coins from his pocket and handed them to Rose. "Three months. That's the minimum we agreed on."

Rose looked at the gold coins winking in her hand. Then she looked at George.

"Is this all your gold?"

"No. I've got plenty more."

He could tell she didn't believe him.

"As soon as I get a job, I'm going to pay you for the hotel."

"I won't let you do that."

"Then I won't stay in the hotel."

She had made up her mind, and George could tell she wouldn't change it.

"I wish my mother had had some of your stubbornness. She'd have been a much happier woman."

"I doubt your father would have been pleased."

"Pa could go to hell. I'm sure he's there already."

George reined in his anger. This wasn't about his father. It was about him and Jeff and circumstances; it was about Rose's leaving.

"Will you be sure to tell me if you need anything?"

"Yes."

"Promise?"

She nodded.

He took her hand. He shook it. Only iron restraint kept him from taking her in his arms and kissing her right there.

Then, without a word, he turned and walked away.

But it was impossible to just turn his back and forget Rose. It wasn't fair to ask him to try. Every fiber of his being screamed in protest. It seemed wickedly cruel that, after being forced to make a vow to remain unwed, he should have been fated to meet the one woman who could make him want to break his promise.

He turned back toward the hotel. But no sooner did he prepare to take the first step to follow her, start to open his mouth to call her back, than nightmarish visions of his own life filled his mind. If he followed her, if he called her back, was he fated to play those same scenes over again with himself in the lead?

He couldn't take that step.

She deserved to find a man who could love her and give her the family she so desperately wanted. She deserved a husband who could come to her with an unfettered spirit, not a man handicapped and shortchanged by his heritage.

George had thought he would never again feel as heartsick as he had the day Lee surrendered to Grant.

Today he felt worse.

George was at the livery stable when Salty found him. "Have you seen Rose?" Salty asked.

"No. Is anything wrong?"

"You're not going to like this."

"Spit it out. Bad news never improves with keeping."

"Dottie won't give her back her job."

"I was afraid she wouldn't."

"And nobody will rent her a place to stay."

"Why?"

"This is the part you're not going to like. It seems some woman named Peaches is spreading it around that Rose wouldn't be back here so fast if she hadn't done something she shouldn't. She's insinuating it couldn't have been anything nice or she wouldn't have been paid off in gold."

Rage so overwhelmed George he hardly knew what he did. He headed straight to the hotel. He had no idea what he intended to do, but he had no intention of allowing anyone to mistreat Rose. Especially anyone in this town.

It infuriated him even more that Jeff's blind hatred and his own selfishness should have made her situation worse than it had been two months ago. He thought of Rose's kindness, her sweetness, her outpouring of affection when anyone treated her kindly. There must have been dozens of times when she had tried to bridge the gap of hatred and misunderstanding in this town and had been repulsed. Just thinking about it made him furious. By the time he neared the hotel, he was in a lethal mood.

He spied Peaches McCloud across the street in front of Taylor's Drygoods. Without looking right or left, without acknowledging the shouts from drivers and riders who had to jerk up their horses to keep from running over him, he plunged into the street and marched straight up to her.

"Ma'am," he said, interrupting Peaches's conversation with a matron of similarly imposing stature, "I've never laid a hand on a woman in my life, but if you say one more word against Miss Thornton, I'll take a strap to you right here in the street."

Peaches and her companion gaped at him as if he had taken leave of his senses.

"It's absolutely none of your business what she does, but if it will help set this town's mind at rest, you can present yourself at the hotel lobby at nine o'clock tonight. You'll be able to see her become my wife."

George turned on his heel, leaving his auditors, Salty included, speechless.

*You've done it again. You've let this damned town's attitude toward Rose stampede you into doing something you had absolutely no intention of doing.*

George marched down the boardwalk to the Bon Ton. He had just wrecked every plan he'd ever made for his future. Dozens of unanswered questions buzzed in his mind. He had no idea what he was going to say to his brothers. Yet even as he cursed his foolish impulse, while he stared into the future with horror, even as the folly of what he had done made his knees feel weak, he felt exhilarated.

He felt as though a weight had been lifted from his shoulders. There was a buoyancy of spirit he had never experienced before, a sense of reckless abandon, of freedom from restrictions. Even though he had done something on the spur of the moment, without a single instant of thought, he was happier than he'd been in a long time.

But he had to find Rose quickly. "If she hears this from anyone else, she'll never believe I mean it," he said to Salty, who was practically running to keep up.

"That Peaches woman sure looked convinced."

George delivered himself of a description he hoped would find its way back to Peaches. "Of course if Dottie had given her a job . . ." He charged into the Bon Ton, leaving the sentence unfinished.

Several men sat over their dinners, but Dottie was nowhere in sight.

George went through to the kitchen. The sight appalled him. He couldn't imagine how Rose had managed to work here so long. Grease blackened the walls and every surface in the room. Including Dottie.

"I'm not giving her a job, so don't come trying to make me," Dottie said as she ebbed and flowed around the stacks of dirty plates.

"I wouldn't let her work in this foul pit for as much as one hour," George said. "Where is she?"

"Gone looking for a room."

"Where?"

"The Widow Jenkins. To the left when you go out the front door. Down Walnut to the edge of town. It's a log house sitting out on the prairie."

George was spared asking strangers the whereabouts of one log house among dozens. He almost bumped into Rose coming around the corner.

"Come with me," he said without explanation or warning.

"What's wrong?" Rose asked. "Has something happened to one of the boys?"

All George would say was, "I'll explain when we get to the hotel."

Though she was suffering under the shock of being refused

a job and a place to stay, Rose wasn't too upset to notice the looks of passersby. George's thunderous expression caused some to smirk, others to stare in naked curiosity. Refusing to give them the satisfaction of thinking she was in disgrace, Rose walked with all the assurance and the appearance of contentment she could muster.

She *was* glad to see George. Ironically, she felt he could solve everything.

No one spoke to George. His expression was so fierce even the hotel clerk swallowed his habitual cheery greeting.

Rose was confused when George followed her into her room. She was even more perplexed when Salty followed on his heels.

"I know this is going to sound a little strange, coming as it does at this particular time," George began the moment the door was closed, "but I want you to marry me this evening at nine o'clock."

Rose lost color. She reached for a chair and sank onto it.

"Do you know what you're saying?" Her voice sounded calm, but she felt as if she were about to explode.

"Of course I do. I'm asking you to marry me."

What was wrong with her! George had just said the most precious words in the world to her, and she could only collapse into a chair with her mouth open. But this didn't feel right. Now that some of his anger had subsided, George looked stiff. He sounded as if he were reciting words he had memorized. Even Salty looked stuffed, as though he were being held up by a bamboo pole down his pants.

She had to think. She took a deep breath, hoping to slow the furious beating of her heart.

"Sit down, George. You, too, Salty. Now tell me what this is all about. You can't have changed your mind so fast."

"But I have. I spent nearly the whole trip thinking about it."

Rose's mutinous heart thumped crazily in her chest. Her breath felt shallow, her eyesight dim, but she struggled to hold back her elation.

George *never* changed his mind.

"George, I'd love to believe that my entrancing smile or my delightful sense of humor, even my cooking or the way I wash your shirts, had caused you to come begging to marry me, but I know you. You don't do anything without a reason."

"I've told you. I realized I wanted to marry you."

Rose felt the hope building inside. She didn't know how long she could hold it down.

"Why is Salty here?"

"I don't understand."

"If you just wanted to tell me you realized you wanted to marry me, you wouldn't have marched me in from the street like I was about to be put in handcuffs. And you wouldn't have brought Salty with you."

"It hit me all of a sudden. I guess not seeing you, knowing I might never see you again, made me see some things I'd never seen before." George pulled up a chair, sat down directly in front of Rose, and took her hands into his. "I missed you already. I don't know why I didn't see it before today, but I didn't. I want you to marry me. I've got it all arranged."

That was another false note. George would never have arranged a wedding. Men never did. Rose felt her hope begin to fade. Whatever the explanation, she was certain it had nothing to do with love. She disengaged her hand from George's grasp.

"Something happened. I know it did. You might as well tell me, because I'm not agreeing to anything until you do."

"You might as well tell her," Salty said.

George looked up at Salty, disgust written all over his face. "Remind me to be on hand when you propose."

Salty looked abashed.

"I didn't want to tell you because it really has nothing to do with this except that it made me so mad I decided to marry you. That's when I realized I *wanted* to marry you. That I'd been wanting to all along without realizing it."

"Tell me." Rose felt her control start to go again. He had to get to the truth soon.

"Salty heard that Dottie wouldn't give you your job and that no one would rent you a room."

"That's true," Rose said.

"Well, it made me furious that anyone should say shameful things about you."

"What things?"

"I don't know," George lied, "but they must have thought something or they'd have been happy to have you back. That's when I got mad and decided to show them all by marrying you. Only I realized I wasn't interested in showing anybody. I wanted to marry you."

"Is that the truth?" Rose demanded, turning to Salty.

"As God is my witness," Salty swore. He looked ready to swear to anything Rose wanted.

"Are you sure?" Rose asked, turning back to George. "Are you absolutely, positively sure?"

"If I didn't know better, I'd swear you didn't want to marry me."

"I do," Rose said, feeling the warmth of happiness rising in her heart, "but I never thought you'd ask me. For weeks I've been conditioning myself against the day you would leave and I'd never see you again."

"Then let's be glad I woke up in time."

George kissed her. The kiss felt wrong. She knew it would.

"Now I imagine you have some shopping you'd like to do. I don't know much about these things, but I always understood women had to have bride clothes."

"Yes," Rose said, thinking of the fabricated enthusiasm in George's voice rather than the hours she could spend shopping.

"Here's some money . . ."

"I have all I need."

"Are you sure?"

"You paid me more than enough."

"Okay. I have some things I need to do, like get the license. Don't be gone too long."

"I won't," Rose assured him.

After the door closed, Rose sank back into the chair. She didn't kid herself. She wanted to believe that her dream had come true, that her knight had finally come to her rescue, that she would live happily ever after, but she knew better. George didn't love her. He never used the word at all.

She couldn't understand why she didn't feel sick at heart. Her world had just come crashing down around her.

No, she had never had a world to crash down. George had never loved her. He had never pretended to. She had always known his interest was a mixture of gratitude, liking, lust, and protectiveness. Each fine in its way, but all falling far short of love.

She had lost nothing by agreeing to marry him.

Yes, she had. She had lost the fairy tale. She had lost the dream that he would sweep down and carry her off to a magical kingdom where everything was wonderful. She had always known that such a world didn't exist, but she had hoped it might.

Now she knew it didn't exist for her.

So she had a choice. She could marry a man who didn't love her, or she could take her chances and stay in Austin. She thought of the money in her pocket. She could go to San Antonio or Brownsville. She was a good-looking woman. Surely she could attract the notice of some honest man, a man of principles she could learn to like and respect.

Like and respect! Had she drifted that far from her dreams? Was there no chance she would find someone she would *love*?

Even if she found such a man, how would he feel when he learned her father had fought for the Union? And he would learn of it. Somebody would tell him.

She felt her heart grow heavy. She knew she'd never escape the Yankee epithet. If she went north, she was a Rebel. If she stayed in Texas, she was a Yankee. If she did find a man to marry her, he and his family would always look down on her. Maybe even her own children. She couldn't stand that.

Wouldn't it be better to marry George? He respected her. She loved him. Wasn't that better than marrying someone she didn't love?

It might be better not to marry at all.

But she wanted to marry George. She could feel her pulse beat a little faster at the thought.

She could accept George's offer, or she could continue to struggle to escape the Yankee epithet and the townspeople's persecution.

For a moment Rose felt like screaming with rage. Why should she be forced to choose between two kinds of hell? Why couldn't she be given the chance to live her dream?

Rose made herself calm down. Screaming wouldn't solve anything. Neither would complaining about her lot in life. She had a choice to make.

George had offered to marry her. She might never know what prompted him, but he had undoubtedly done it to protect her. If she were going to refuse him, she owed him the courtesy of doing it quickly, before it made him look ridiculous in the eyes of the town.

Just thinking about it made her feel like crying. He was always getting himself into trouble because of her. He had hired her to protect her. And now he had offered to marry her for the same reason. What could she do for him in return?

She could protect him.

Not just from the Reconstruction officials. She could protect him from his brothers. They would use him all his life if someone didn't stop them. Especially Jeff.

And she could also protect him from himself.

That was a fair trade, wasn't it? Pragmatic. Logical. Unemotional. Rational.

She stifled a sob of pain. She wanted to fling herself down, wail aloud that she wanted to be loved and cherished, to be the center of his universe, but it would be a waste of time.

He liked her. He admired her. He wanted her. That ought to be enough.

It had to be. It was all she had.

But even as she prepared to go out, even as she checked her face in the mirror to make sure her eyes showed no sign of crying, she realized she hadn't given up hope that George would come to love her.

Her hope would never die. Regardless of the obstacles, regardless of how impossible it seemed, as long as she was alive, she would hope.

As long as she could be near George, there was a chance her dreams would come true.

The moment the door closed behind George, his expression of happiness changed to one of disgust.

He was sickened by what he'd just done.

He had known for years why he had to remain a bachelor. It wasn't a decision taken lightly. Nothing had changed, yet he had asked Rose to marry him, even though he knew he was a disaster waiting to happen. And now it was waiting to happen to Rose, the one woman above all others he didn't want to hurt.

How could he ask her to marry him, even to protect her? If he really cared for her, he would move heaven and earth to keep her from wasting her life on somebody like him.

As much as he needed her, as much as he enjoyed being with her, as much as he liked and admired her, as arresting as he found her beauty, as much as he desired her body, he didn't love her. There was no excuse for what he'd just done, even to protect her. If he'd been as smart as he thought he was, he would have found another way.

Knowing how she felt about him, what he had just done went beyond thoughtlessness. It transcended all his doubts about himself, his family, and his career. He had asked her to share a life he had no intention of making. It didn't matter that he'd done it without thinking, just like his father used to do. It didn't matter that he'd done it for all the right reasons.

He had still done the wrong thing.

He should go back in there right now and confess everything, but he knew he wouldn't. Even worse, he didn't want to. The evil inside him wouldn't let him. It would take advantage of his weakness and of her love to despoil her for its own pleasure.

He wanted her for himself. He couldn't do without her. Call it weakness, call it deviltry, it didn't matter. He had to have her.

He hated himself.

They still hurt. The hate-filled glances. The angry turnings away. Noses raised in the air. It seemed to have gotten worse since the news had flown around town that she was getting married.

Rose tried hard not to remember past slights and hurts. But it was impossible when the women made a point of letting her know that even though she was about to become a married woman she would not be welcomed into their midst.

The men didn't seem so unbending. A couple winked at her, but most respected George enough to not want to anger him by insulting the woman he was about to marry. Especially not on his wedding day.

She had the unrewarding pleasure of knowing that even though she had finally risen in the men's estimation, it was due to George's credit rather than her own.

The injustice of it all angered her so much that she resolved to give the people of Austin a wedding they wouldn't forget. Or at least a bride they wouldn't forget. She would spend every penny in her pocket if necessary, the money she had saved to leave Austin and the money George paid her, but she would be the most spectacular bride possible.

Rose turned purposeful steps toward Dobie's Emporium, the largest and most expensive purveyor of ladies' clothing in Austin. Up until now she had never dared do more than stand at the window, looking at the articles of feminine apparel on display. Today she would have the pleasure of looking over their entire stock. And she meant to inspect each piece before she decided how to spend her money. This might be the most important investment of her life. She wanted no mistakes.

Once inside, Rose found it hard to concentrate. Rows of merchandise seemed to stretch for miles. Everything from shoes, coats, dresses, and fine undergarments to items of decoration. Frivolous things like shiny stones, billowing feathers, and imitation flowers. Fantastic things like an artificial branch with a mother bluebird on the nest. Apparently this concoction was meant to be worn on a hat. Rose decided it would take a more imposing stature than hers to support such an arrangement.

For the better part of an hour she wandered up and down the aisles studying each garment, fingering the material to test its weight and the tightness of the weave, turning the garment inside out to inspect the craftsmanship of its construction, weighing the merits of the various articles which caught her eye, going over and over in her mind the number and cost of the items she needed for her purpose.

Rose enjoyed the delicious feeling of knowing she had fifty-four dollars to spend for anything she wanted. She was only barely aware of the stares or whispers of the other women in the store. To be able to shop for exactly what she wanted was a pleasure too intense to be spoiled by censorious or curious glances.

She was in a world of her own.

She would have loved to discuss her purchases with another woman, someone like Mrs. Dobie, the proprietress of the establishment, but she could tell from that lady's pursed lips and crevassed forehead that Mrs. Dobie wasn't happy with Rose's success. She probably felt, as did most of the women in town, that women like Rose should be prevented from mixing with their betters.

After all, there was only one way for a woman like her to catch a respectable man like George Randolph. And what more could you expect? Any fool could have told you Rose was going to do everything she could to get her claws into him while she had him to herself. Why not? The man had his own ranch, and gold he was willing to waste on this hussy.

At least, Rose thought, that's what Mrs. Dobie's expression seemed to say. Her compressed lips didn't utter a single word.

Rose picked up a soft cotton chemise decorated with a bit of pink ribbon, two more just like it trimmed in blue and green, a pair of shiny black button-up shoes with two-inch heels, a new Sunday dress, a hat with a wide upstanding brim lined with gauze, and two nightgowns, the prettiest in the whole store. She also chose a pair of dainty white slippers, an ell of yellow ribbon, and two bunches of artificial flowers.

She took her purchases to the front of the store.

Mrs. Dobie's frown grew even more pronounced when Rose laid her choices on the counter. Her lips became so pursed she looked as if she'd just sucked on a lemon.

"Spending the man's money before he's even married you, I see," she remarked. "Suppose he backs out?"

"This is my money," Rose said with quiet dignity. "If he backs out, I've only bought things I need."

"You won't be needing all these nightclothes," Mrs. Dobie said, malice shining in her eyes. "Nice girls don't go parading about dressed like this, not even after they're married."

"I don't intend to *parade about*."

"Think you'll keep him faithful that way?"

Rose had tried to keep a civil tongue in her head. She had tried to remember she had been raised a lady. She'd tried to remember her father's warning not to let other people pull her down to their level. But now she wanted to get down on their level. She *wanted* to give them a taste of what they had done to her all those years.

"The ladies of Austin have proved to me it isn't necessary to keep a husband faithful to keep him," Rose answered.

Mrs. Dobie swelled up so much Rose could hardly keep from laughing. She knew she shouldn't feel such pleasure at being able to return a dig, but she did, and she wasn't sorry.

"If women like you didn't go about enticing decent men—"

"I never enticed a man in my whole life, married or not," Rose declared, too angry to care whether people in the store heard her. "I only wanted to be left alone. But all of you made it plain you wanted me to leave. Well, I left. You said I ought to get married. Well, I'm getting married. You ought to be happy."

"Every decent woman will sleep better for knowing you're married and gone," Hetty LeBlanc announced, coming up behind Rose.

"You'll sleep alone regardless of how well you sleep," Rose snapped. "Horace will simply find a new skirt to chase."

Oblivious of Hetty's crimson face or Mrs. Dobie's furious displeasure, Rose continued with her purchases. "I want some of your rose water . . . no, the large bottle . . . and three cakes of your violet-scented soap. And I want that dress off your model up front."

The women had been incensed by Rose's profligate purchases of what they considered luxury items, but her mention of the dress stunned them.

"Do you mean the white dress?" Mrs. Dobie asked.

"It costs fifteen dollars," Hetty LeBlanc exclaimed.

"I know."

"What could you possibly want with such a dress on a cow ranch?" Hetty demanded. "You'd ruin it the first time you put it on."

Rose slapped her money down on the table as if she spent fifty-four dollars every day. "It won't matter if I do. George has promised to buy me new clothes every year *and* give me money to spend as I like."

Neither Mrs. Dobie nor Hetty had a response for that. Texas men weren't in the habit of giving their wives money to spend on themselves. As for buying clothes, well, they were more likely to tell them to make their own.

Rose didn't bother to tell them this was part of her contract. George had made no promises to her as his wife.

"Wrap everything up very securely," Rose instructed Mrs. Dobie. "It will have to stand a long trip."

"What about the white dress?" It still remained on the model.

"I'll take it with me. Put it in some wrapping paper."

While Mrs. Dobie busied herself wrapping up her purchases, Rose continued to look around, acting as though she might buy something more. Out of the corner of her eye, she watched Mrs. Dobie take the white dress off the model.

"Fold it very carefully. I don't want it wrinkled."

Mrs. Dobie scowled more than ever, but she exercised care with the dress.

"Have someone send the package around to Bullock's Hotel," Rose said when she accepted her change. "I'm in room seven."

"Hussy!" Hetty exclaimed even before the door closed behind Rose.

Rose could hardly suppress a smile of happiness as she walked back to the hotel. And it had nothing to do with her momentary pleasure at being able to return a fraction of the unkindness that had been heaped on her for so long. She had just decided the white dress would be the first shot in her campaign to get her husband to unbend toward her. George Washington Randolph might not realize it, but Rose intended to invade every corner of his heart and mind. And that included the dark secrets he still held hidden somewhere within himself.

George hadn't given any thought to who might attend the wedding, but if he had, he never would have expected so many people to attempt to pack themselves into the hotel lobby. Not even Bullock's could hold everybody who came. It seemed the whole town was trying to crowd inside. And the women weren't shy about jostling with the men for position. Several forced their way to the front even though they arrived after all the spaces were filled. Dottie sat in the front row.

Dottie *was* the front row.

"I'm going to see she's married right and proper," Dottie announced to everyone. "He asked for her, and I'm going to see he gets her."

The other women exhibited the same grim determination, but George couldn't decide to what end. It didn't seem to be anything that pleased them very much. Like an avenging angel, Peaches McCloud stood in the middle of the entire group. George couldn't figure out why she had decided to come—the Widow Hanks and Berthilda Huber were also there—unless she intended to be present in the unlikely event George changed his mind at the last minute.

The emotional temperature of the room was so highly charged that George started to wonder if the seventy miles that lay between Austin and his ranch would be enough.

"Here she comes," someone called out. The spectators began shoving to make room for Rose to pass. George hadn't seen Rose since she returned from her shopping.

The transformation took his breath away.

Nothing remained of the crushed, tired, worn-down woman of yesterday. The white dress had become her wedding dress, the dainty slippers her wedding shoes. The yellow ribbon had been braided into a net which supported her long hair, pulling it back from her face and causing it to cascade down her back. She wore the bunches of artificial flowers in her hair. But the smile that transformed her face made the greatest difference of all. That and her enormous brown eyes.

She looked like a bride.

Like a bride he was seeing for the first time.

He had expected to marry the woman who made his home comfortable, who was kind and thoughtful to his family, who did her share of work without complaint, who was strong and dependable, the kind of woman a man needed but so rarely found.

The Rose descending the stairs was the kind of woman every man dreams of marrying.

Her radiance was beyond his meager words to describe. It had that timeless quality he had previously associated only with the Southern beauties before the war. The elegance he had noticed from the first was given full play by the simplicity of her clothes, the starkness of the white. Her smile was the smile of a woman who knows more than she's willing to tell.

Seeing Rose descend the stairs with angelic grace made George feel like a true bridegroom, fearful he wasn't worthy of this extraordinary creature, nervous he would do something to mess up the ceremony, and anxious for the whole thing to be over.

Rose's effect on the spectators was nearly as great. The rumble of whispered remarks, too-loud asides, and hissed observations continued even after the preacher began the words of the service. But George didn't hear them any longer. He only heard the words of the preacher.

Why had he never read the marriage vows? Why had he thought he could get married and nothing would change? He had just promised to love and cherish and protect this woman. To honor her with his body as well as his mind and spirit.

George wrenched his mind away from his inner thoughts. The preacher was speaking to him.

"Do you have a ring?" the preacher repeated.

It had never occurred to George he would need a ring, not for himself or for Rose. He hadn't thought of wedding clothes either. He had on the same clothes he'd worn all day. He felt thoroughly ashamed.

George wrenched a family ring off his finger. "Use this," he said as he handed it to the preacher.

Somehow the act of giving the preacher his ring brought home the finality of the wedding more than the words.

He had married Rose.

He had just taken a vow he had no intention of honoring.

# Chapter Fourteen

"To your bride," a stranger said, holding out a drink to George. "May she live long and give you many children."

"To my bride," George repeated, accepting the drink with only a slight hesitation. There was no point in trying to decline. He must have drunk a toast with every man in Austin in the last two hours. He had retreated to a corner hoping he'd be unnoticed, but each man seemed to find his way over to his table within ten minutes of entering the saloon, a smile of congratulations on his lips and a drink in his hand.

George had come to the saloon to try to figure out how he was going to handle his desire for Rose without taking advantage of her love, her vulnerability, or her generosity. But by now his alcohol-fogged brain was having trouble remembering anything except that his body was on fire with desire.

"You can't stay here all night," Salty said. "This is your wedding night."

"Goddammit, I know what night it is," George replied, his words slurred.

They were in the Golden Nugget, one of the dingy saloons along Waller Creek near the army corrals. It was a long room with a low ceiling and dark walls. The mirror behind the bar reflected the meager light of two coal oil lanterns suspended overhead. Customers playing cards in the far corners needed to squint in the poor light.

George didn't drink. Period. And the alcohol had gone straight to his head. It was too late to tell himself he'd allowed the people of Austin to cause him to make still another mistake. It was too late to try to explain to Rose that he had never intended to get drunk, that he'd only been trying to find a way to be fair to her and to himself at the same time.

Any ordinary bride would be hurt to learn her groom had gotten drunk within an hour of getting married. After the way he had proposed, Rose would be devastated.

"Can you imagine how Rose must feel, waiting in that room, not knowing what's happened to you, not knowing when you mean to come back?"

Go back to what? He couldn't go to her and not make love to her. He wasn't that strong.

Several times this evening he'd been on the verge of forgetting all his scruples and running straight into her arms. If he could lose himself in her love, maybe he could forget the conscience which nagged him so unmercifully. If he could satisfy this physical need which tore at him until his control had been picked raw, maybe he could look for answers with a clear mind.

But he couldn't do that. He owed it to Rose to stay away until he could make a full and honest commitment to her and to their marriage. It would be cruel of him to take her body and reject the rest of her. After all she'd done for him and his family, he damned well owed her that much.

"I told her I might not be back until late. I told her she might want to go to bed."

What was he to tell her? To wait up for a husband who didn't know if he could come back, and didn't know what he would do if he did? For a husband who knew he must not touch her, but who knew he couldn't resist?

He thought of the many nights he had spent dreaming of Rose, the countless hours spent thinking of her, imagining her in his arms, imagining himself making love to every part of her body.

A few kisses had just as much power to overset his calm now as they had that afternoon. But now there was no barrier, no fear of ruining her reputation. In the eyes of God and man, she was his.

"You did what?"

"You heard me. I'm not repeating it."

"Why?"

"None of your goddamned business."

"You're right, it is none of my business, but it sure as hell is Rose's business, and I think she deserves to know what you're doing and why."

George tried to force his brain to think. He had to decide what to do before his mind ceased to work altogether.

"Rose is none of your damned business either. She's my wife."

"Nobody could tell it."

George started up from his chair, but he stumbled. Salty had to help him back to his seat.

"I don't know what's eating you," Salty said, "but no matter what it is, I wouldn't let it cause me to shame my wife."

"I'm not shaming Rose."

"What do you think all these men are thinking with you drunk as an Indian on white lightning? They think there's either something wrong with you or something wrong with Rose. Can't be any other reason for a man spending his wedding night getting drunk, not when he's got a bride like Rose waiting in his room."

"I don't care what they think about me."

"Didn't think you would, but I thought you might care what they thought about Rose."

George sat up and turned to look at the other men in the saloon. They were gathered in assorted groups about the room, some drinking, some gambling, others just talking. Many of them watched George out of the corners of their eyes.

"Every woman in town will know of it first thing in the morning. If they're all like that McCloud wench, it'll mean a dog's life for Rose."

George pulled himself up straight in his chair.

"Rose won't have to run from any more dragons," George said, almost as if he were making a declaration. "I'll see to that."

Rose had put on the prettiest of her new nightgowns, but she hadn't been near the bed. How could any bride sleep on her wedding night when the bridegroom wasn't by her side? When she had no idea where he might be. And she had no idea when, or if, he would return.

As a surprise, George had instructed the hotel management to move their things during the wedding ceremony from their separate rooms to the nicest corner room in the hotel. They had a view of Pecan Street from two windows and Congress Avenue from a third, tables with whale oil lamps, upholstered chairs, two washstands, and a large brass bed. The staff had even put their clothes away in the enormous mahogany wardrobes.

But Rose hardly noticed the luxurious room. Her thoughts were completely absorbed by George. It wasn't likely anything could have happened to him, not with Salty along. No, he was staying away intentionally. But why?

*You have no idea, and you aren't likely to figure it out by sitting up all night. The sensible thing to do is go to bed, get a good night's sleep, and be ready to deal with it in the morning.*

Suppose he didn't come back?

She didn't have to worry about that. George would be back. He took his responsibilities seriously.

But suppose he didn't want to tell her what was wrong. How could she convince him to confide in her? He had to. No marriage could prosper when such secrets existed between husband and wife.

Her husband! She still couldn't get used to it. She was married. To George. She was his wife. Their marriage had happened so suddenly and unexpectedly, it was hard to believe. Maybe George felt the same.

Maybe he had mistaken his feelings and was now drowning his sorrows in strong drink. Maybe he had married her for convenience and didn't care about his wedding night. It was possible he was fond of her but that his feelings were very tepid.

Hers were powerful. More powerful than she had realized. Rose had had no idea how much she loved George until he had escorted her upstairs after all the congratulations were over and told her he would be back after a while.

Only then did she realize how much she had looked forward to being alone with him. Only then did she fully realize how keenly it could hurt to know he didn't return her love, that living with George might be far more painful than living without him.

Had she made a mistake in marrying a man who didn't love her? Had she fixed her gaze too firmly on her dream and failed to see the man? Had she been too absorbed with her hopes for the future, the sounds of happy children filling every corner of the house, George's love and devotion filling every corner of her heart?

*Wake up, princess!* Rose said harshly to herself. *The dragon is dead and the knight has gone home. It's time to get on with the rest of your life.*

But without George's love, there was no reason to bother.

Rose was startled awake by a knock at the door. She had been dozing. The lamp burned low. It must be long after midnight. She turned up the wick and reached for her wrap. "Who is it?" she said, her lips close to the door.

"It's George." It was Salty's voice.

The fear she had pushed aside all night gripped her. Something had happened to George. In her haste to get the door open, she fumbled the key in the lock, then dropped it. She was almost frantic by the time she flung the door open.

Salty and George stood before her, Salty holding George up.

George had been drinking. She didn't know how much, but it didn't look as if he could stand by himself. Her fear changed to despair. It was useless to be angry.

"Bring him in," she said, stepping back. "Where did you find him?"

She didn't really want to know. She didn't want to hear that George had gone through every saloon in town trying to forget he'd gotten married, that not even the lure of his wedding night could make him face his bride before he was practically insensible.

"You shouldn't have waited up," George said. His words came out slowly, with great effort.

"I was worried about you," Rose said.

"Everybody in town had to drink his health," Salty explained. "He's got to have a head of steel just to be conscious after all that."

Rose added another item to her list of barbaric customs men seemed to enjoy.

Salty started to help George enter the room, but George waved him away. "Would you see if you could find me some coffee?" he asked Salty.

"You hate coffee," Rose said.

"I hate feeling drunk even more," George said, sounding a little more like himself. "Besides, I only kept drinking to avoid having to face the truth. Any man foolish enough to do that deserves a worse punishment than coffee."

"I'll get some if I have to get the cook out of bed," Salty promised. Then he disappeared.

George carefully closed the door behind Salty. He wasn't entirely steady on his feet, but he could walk. He crossed the room and carefully lowered himself into a chair. Rose didn't dare offer to help him. She sat down on the edge of the bed and waited, her hands in her lap.

Waited for the ax to fall. For George to tell her he didn't love her, that their marriage had been a mistake, that he was going back to the ranch and leaving her in Austin.

Waited for him to say her life was over.

Yet despite her own heartache, she couldn't help but feel some sympathy for him. He looked as miserable and unhappy as she felt. She had never seen him drunk. She hadn't even seen him take a drink. He must feel truly desperate to go to such an extreme.

"My head isn't working too well, so this may not make any

sense," George said. "It was stupid of me to drink all those toasts, especially when I don't drink. I knew I'd have to explain everything to you in the end." George fell silent. He seemed to be looking at something only he could see. "My father never got drunk. He just got mean. And reckless."

George looked at Rose. "I didn't come here to talk about Pa. Wanted to say something else."

He looked so miserably unhappy, she wanted to go to him, cradle his head against her breast, promise him it couldn't be as bad as he thought.

"I don't know how to say this. I can't find the words I want. They keep slipping away. They're like Zac. Never where you want him."

She didn't know whether to laugh or cry. Here he was, about to tell her everything was over, and he was making her laugh.

"I always knew I shouldn't marry," George began. He spoke slowly and deliberately, almost as though each word had to be hunted down and captured before he could use it. "You ought to have good stock for marrying. I'm not good stock. Got rot at the heart. Just like a big black oak we used to have at home. People used to say how pretty and green it was. Ma had parties under it in the summertime. One day a wind came up and blew it down. The inside was all rotten. That's me. Inside all rotten."

Rose didn't have any idea what George was talking about. True, he was pretty on the outside. But she had no idea what kind of rot he could possibly be referring to. It obviously wasn't a liking for drink. He wasn't enjoying this evening any more than she was.

"That's why I tried to stay away from you," George continued. "Do you know how hard it is to keep yourself from doing the one thing you want to do more than anything else?" He transfixed her with his gaze, its intensity heightened because of the struggle to fight his way through the cloud of alcohol. "It's the worst kind of hell."

Rose felt an upsurge of hope. He was telling her he *wanted* her. He was saying he had to *force* himself to stay away from her. Still, she warned herself not to build up false hopes. The whiskey had muddled him. He could still utter those fateful words.

"Pa was prettier than any oak tree," George said, going off on a tangent Rose couldn't immediately follow. "But he was rotten. Mean and rotten. Ma tried to hide it, but I could see it. All of us could."

Rose felt she was living with two people she couldn't see, people she couldn't talk to, argue with, drive away. Two people who stood between her and George. Between all the Randolph boys and happiness. They were like ghosts haunting the living out of anger at their own ruined lives.

"It's in all of us. It's what makes Jeff so bitter, Monty ready to defy the world, Hen enjoy killing, Tyler dislike people. It's what caused Madison to turn his back and walk away."

"What's in you?" Rose asked. If she didn't understand something soon, she was going to lose the thread of his conversation altogether.

"The rot," George told her. "It's there, eating away, just waiting for a storm. Then it'll break through and destroy us."

"There's nothing wrong with you or your brothers," Rose hastened to assure him. "Even Jeff."

"I'm the worst of all," he said, ignoring her. "I'm just like Pa."

"That's ridiculous," Rose said. She would have been furious if anyone else had made that statement.

"I won't be a good husband. Pa tried, but he made us all hate him. The worst thing I can think of is having you hate me."

A glimmer of understanding pierced the fog. George saw some of the same faults in himself he had seen in his father. He was afraid he would make the same mistakes.

"You're not the least bit like your father," Rose assured him. "You may not always want to take responsibility—no one likes it all the time—but you accept it because you love your brothers."

"But—"

"You know no one else can do what you're doing. If you join the army, you won't leave until they can take care of themselves."

"Pa left us," George muttered.

"You could have stayed away after the war, but you didn't. You could have gotten fed up with Monty or Jeff and left, but you didn't."

George didn't look convinced.

Rose decided it was time to get to the core of the problem. If George wasn't willing to mention it, then she would.

"If you're trying to tell me you made a mistake in marrying me—"

The transformation was instantaneous. There was nothing confused or apologetic about the George who sat before her now.

"I never said anything about not wanting to marry you. I didn't, did I?"

"No, but I thought you meant—"

"I wanted to marry you more than I ever thought possible. But everything ought to be perfect for you. You ought to have a husband who loves you more than life, who's worthy of the love you have to give, who wants the same things you want, who won't destroy everything he touches."

"There's nothing destructive in you."

"Yes, there is. The most deadly of all."

"What?"

"My blood."

"I don't understand."

"There's bad blood in my family. It's in all of us."

If she hadn't known he was deadly serious, she would have thought the alcohol had completely clouded his brain. A knock sounded at the door. Salty came with a pot of steaming coffee and two mugs.

"I thought you might want some."

Rose shook her head. She waited impatiently for Salty to pour the coffee. She was anxious for George to sober up so she could understand what he was talking about.

Even though he hated coffee, George swallowed it down. It was probably too hot to taste. It must have burned his mouth and throat. Maybe he was too drunk to feel it.

"I'll be next door if you need me," Salty said, and he let himself out.

"What do you mean about bad blood?" Rose asked the minute the door was closed.

"I can't give you children."

"I don't understand."

"Just that. I can't give you children."

Did he mean he was physically incapable of being a father? Was he afraid she would stop loving him if he was?

"Explain it to me."

For a moment she thought he would refuse. It was obviously something he didn't want to share with anyone, even his wife.

"There's bad blood in our family, and it's getting worse with each generation. Pa was a rotten father, and he had seven rotten sons. I can't give you children knowing the kind of father I'd make or the kind of sons I'd sire."

"You mean—"

"Do you think I could knowingly put you through what my mother endured?"

Ghosts again. The past had a more powerful influence on George than the present.

George went on talking, but Rose didn't listen any longer. She didn't have to. She wasn't afraid of ghosts. Nor George's fears. She knew they were groundless. She could have laughed aloud with relief.

Only she didn't. No matter how ridiculous she might think they were, they were very real to him. She couldn't see the damage their parents had inflicted on him and his brothers or judge the severity of the scars. Neither could she measure his fear that he would do the same to his children, especially if they were to be as difficult as his brothers.

Though he might see every ugly attribute of his father in himself, she knew he'd make a perfectly wonderful father. Hadn't she seen him be just that with his brothers?

It was up to her to help him feel the same way.

But she couldn't change everything at once. She had to take it one step at a time.

"So you understand why I couldn't come to your bed to-night," George concluded.

Rose throttled her excitement. She had to be very calm. There was no room for error. There was always a chance that if he didn't come to her bed tonight, he might never come. She must remove this barrier first. She would have to leave the ghosts for another night.

"I realize you don't love me—there's no need to feel guilty. You never said you did—but are you still certain you want to be married to me?"

George came out of his chair with a rush. He paused to grip the arm until he got his balance, but he reached her side rather quickly. He sank down on the bed next to Rose, took her hands in his, and looked into her eyes.

"More than anything I've wanted in my whole life. I tried not to marry you. I tried to keep from thinking about it, but I couldn't. That's why I kept drinking those toasts. I kept putting off coming back, telling you I'd done the one thing I couldn't do."

"Could you be happy with me if I agreed to have no chil-dren?"

"But you've always wanted a family."

"Answer my question."

Rose had made up her mind. She knew there would be times when she would bitterly regret this decision, but experience had taught her she couldn't have everything. She had George's affection, loyalty, and support. She felt certain that one day she would have his love as well. For that she would endure any sacrifice.

George was shocked to realize that not once during the whole evening had he considered leaving Rose. He couldn't imagine being without her.

He wondered if his father might not have felt the same way when he met and married the young and beautiful Aurelia Juliette Gascoigne. He could remember when they seemed happy together.

He shivered. Could it happen to him?

"Yes."

He meant it now.

Rose said, "There's something else I want you to promise me."

George felt the chill of iron fetters winding about him, binding him, restraining him, tying him down.

He resolutely forced down the apprehension trying to seep into his veins. Rose loved him. She wouldn't expect him to do anything he couldn't. And he would want to do anything that would make her happy.

"Promise you'll tell me if you ever start to feel our marriage is suffocating you."

"What will you do?"

"I'll let you go. I want you to stay with me because you enjoy being with me, because even though you have the freedom to go anywhere on earth, there's no place you'd rather be. For the happiness that would bring both of us, I will be willing to give up having a family."

"I couldn't let you do that."

"We all have to make choices, George. You asked me to marry you even though you were afraid that rot would topple you in the end. I'm willing to take the chance I can be happy without a family. Isn't that fair?"

George nodded. He didn't trust his voice.

"And for the record, there's no rot in you. I'm not trying to change a word of what I just said. I just want you to know I believe you're the strongest man I've ever met. I believe you can do anything you want."

Even after too much whiskey, George marveled at how wonderful Rose's confidence in him felt. He might be his father's son, but with Rose's help, he wouldn't have to turn out to be like his father.

Rose dropped her eyes and looked at her hand, held tightly in George's grasp.

"In case you want to come to bed, you can't father a child tonight."

"You mean . . ."

Rose looked up. "I'll always tell you."

Rose withdrew her hand. Deliberately, she removed her robe.

It took George a moment to understand what she meant. She'd offered to be his wife on his terms, without the fear of children, without the fear of failure. The magnitude of her gift, the selflessness of her sacrifice, nearly overcame him.

Nearly.

His conscience reminded him that he still didn't love her, that he shouldn't take her innocence when he had nothing to give in return, but he clubbed the noisy little bastard into silence. Rose had invited him into her bed. As long as it was all right with her, he meant to accept the invitation.

George's body responded immediately. He felt a little guilty that his needs should intrude on such a nearly holy moment, but he had become aware that Rose sat before him in nothing but her nightgown. The pull that had always existed between them leapt into full strength.

George staggered to his feet and threw open the door. Salty's door pushed open in almost immediate response.

"More coffee," George shouted. "And hot water for a bath. This is my wedding night, and my bride is waiting." He had to lean against the doorway to steady himself.

"Ssshh!" Salty hissed. "It's past one o'clock. You'll wake up the hotel."

"Wake 'em up," George shouted.

"Can't you do something with him, ma'am?" Salty asked Rose.

Rose couldn't suppress a smile. "I already have."

Salty grinned back. "He'll be back here in half an hour even if he has to take a bath in the creek."

"Don't know why he can't get his bath in the morning like everybody else," the attendant grumbled as she hauled two buckets of hot water up to the tub in Salty's room.

"You only get married once," Salty explained. He carried two buckets as well.

"Don't know what he wants a bath for anyway," the woman grumbled. "He won't do it regular, so she needn't expect it. He'll just come to her in all his dirt and sweat, take his pleasure rough like, and be snoring inside five minutes."

"Gentlemen behave differently," Salty said.

"Humph! He's a man, ain't he? He's drunk, ain't he? What's so all-fired different about him?"

George didn't feel very steady on his feet when he opened the door to their room. His bath had been warm and the coffee hot, but his head still felt like the inside of a bell tower during the ringing of the tocsin.

Worst of all, he felt terribly sleepy, almost as if he had been drugged. He wasn't used to whiskey. Unable to forget his father's violent behavior when he drank, George had stayed away from alcohol. It was a relief to know it didn't affect him the same way, but this feeling was bad enough.

Rose was waiting for him. In bed.

God, she looked lovely in the lamplight. He'd never thought much about hair. He'd always pictured beautiful women pretty much like his mother. Her blonde hair had been the color of new corn silk. Long and straight and thin, it had added to her fragile appearance.

Rose's masses of curly brown hair flowed over her shoulders

and the pillow like the spilling of a cornucopia. It was like an invitation to bury his face in its bounty. He'd always thought she was beautiful, but now, in the dim light, against an all-white background, he realized her greatest beauty lay in her simplicity. Her lashes weren't overly thick, her lips weren't overly full, her eyes weren't deep and hypnotizing. But everything fitted together as a part of the most enchanting, human, kind, warm, and inviting face he'd ever seen.

He noticed the dusting of tiny freckles over her nose and cheekbones. He ought to keep after her to wear her sunbonnet every time she left the house, but he would hate to see her face and hair covered up for the sake of a few freckles. He didn't mind them. In fact, along with her riot of curly hair, the freckles made her seem girlish. When the imps of mischief danced in her eyes and she started to play with Zac or tease Monty, she was just like a tomboy.

But there was nothing tomboyish about her tonight.

Like some earth mother, she invited him to lean his head against her breast, to rest for a moment in her arms, to replenish his strength from her deep well of constancy. Even as she surrendered herself to him, admitted her weakness, she became his strength.

George didn't understand how that could be. Maybe he would understand better when his head didn't feel like a block of wood. He did understand that Rose had issued an invitation he wanted to accept, but his senses had started to feel dull, his body heavy. He tried to revive the surge of desire that had coursed through him when she issued the invitation, but his body only felt more leaden. Even his mind seemed to want to give up the struggle, to save it for another day.

Rose smiled to herself. She had always seen George as a commanding personality, sure of himself, impressive because of his size and his self-confidence. She had felt relatively small, weak, and ineffectual.

Now the roles were reversed.

"I never thought about my wedding night," George said after

he'd closed the door behind him. "But if I had, this certainly wouldn't have been the way I'd have come to my bride." He didn't approach the bed but remained standing a few feet away.

Rose felt as if he were asking permission to come to their bed.

"It's more important that you came." She folded back the covers and patted the sheet.

He hesitated.

"I'm ashamed to come to you this way."

Rose patted the bed again. "You haven't, yet."

George crossed to the bed. "The husband you deserve would have come to you full of pride and confidence."

"The husband I want *has* come to me. But like the rest of us, he carries a load of guilt, mostly heaped on him by someone else. I want to help make that burden lighter."

George dropped down on the bed.

"I don't deserve such understanding."

Rose reached out and grasped his hand, pulling him gently toward her. "Let's not talk of deserving. Let's talk instead of what I want to give you, what you want to give me."

George leaned toward her until his cheek rested on her shoulder.

"I hardly know what I can give you," he said. "As far back as I can remember, I made up my mind never to marry. The change came so quickly it caught me unprepared."

Rose pulled him down until he rested against her. The feeling was absolutely delicious. She had waited so long to cradle him in her arms, to have him close, to know he belonged to her. She wanted to savor the moment, to wrench every bit of sweetness from it. She wanted him to make love to her. She wouldn't feel their union was complete without it, but she realized that this feeling of closeness, of sharing of himself, this opening the door to the past which still tormented him, was even more important than sharing his body.

"I wouldn't even let myself daydream about being married to you," George said.

He spoke softly, slowly, one arm under him, the other across her belly, their hands clasped together. She wiggled a little until his head rested more comfortably in the hollow between her breast and her shoulder.

"But I used to dream about it." He chuckled softly. "My brothers were always our children."

"I don't think Monty would like that." Rose felt reassured. If he wanted children in his dreams, it wouldn't be too long before he wanted them in real life.

Her feeling of contentment continued to grow.

"We lived in a big house, a lot like Ashburn. You had servants and all the dresses you wanted."

"I never wanted those things."

He didn't respond right away. Rose thought he sounded a little sleepy.

"You were so beautiful. We would sit at the table and talk long after dinner had ended. I ordered the servants to always place two branches of candles near you so I could watch the light play on the gold in your hair, the sparkle in your eyes."

Rose twisted around until she could see his face. His eyelids were drooping. Between the liquor, the hot bath, and the excitement of his wedding, George had been drained of all energy. He was going to sleep right here in her arms.

Surprisingly, she didn't mind.

"But there was something I wanted to say to you. I wanted to say it every night, but I never did. I can't figure out why."

"What was it?" Rose asked. Her voice was as soft as his.

There was a pause.

Rose looked down at George. He was asleep, his head resting on her breast, his hair rough against her tender skin, the weight of him making it difficult for her to breathe. She wouldn't have moved for all the riches in the world. She was content to be where she was even though nothing about her marriage had gone the way she had dreamed.

She smiled to herself. She'd have been horrified a year ago if anyone had described her wedding day. She might even have sworn she wouldn't get married. She could never have imagined she could still be content.

But she was.

She had married the man of her dreams. George wanted and needed her. She had his trust, his admiration, and she was on the way to acquiring his confidence. What more could a woman want from a man?

She would have his body. Tomorrow, or the next day, or the day after that. George was too hot-blooded to hold off for long. Tonight had been lost somewhere between liquor and his fear of fathering a child. Tomorrow would be another day.

His love? That was a more difficult question, one that depended on his past almost as much as his future. But he would say those words one day. Of that she was certain.

As for children, that would come, too. She just felt it. George would want them. Lots of them.

But as much as she wanted a family, she had told the truth when she said she would give it up. She wanted to free him from his fears for his sake, not for hers, or for the sake of the children they might have.

He thought he was made of the same timber as his father. Rose knew her task would be to show him he had all of his father's and mother's strengths without their weaknesses.

Except perhaps an inability to look at himself and see just how wonderful he was.

She had every intention of doing her best to make the Randolphs feel like a family once again. It was important to George, therefore it was important to her. But she had no intention of standing by while they took advantage of him. If Jeff didn't put a cork in it, she would see that his ship soon sailed to another port.

But for the moment she had no battles to fight, no one to defend. She only had to lie here, holding George, and wait for him to wake up.

# Chapter Fifteen

The feeble light of morning pierced the gray of the room. George stirred and opened his eyes. Nothing came into focus. Where was he? He felt disoriented. At least he knew he wasn't in his own bed. He had to sit up. He had to find out where he was.

Movement brought a vicious stabbing pain through the center of his head. George collapsed on his pillow, his hands gripping his throbbing head. He tried once more. The pain was just as terrible. A groan escaped him. Was he hurt? Did he have a wound he didn't remember?

"How do you feel?"

He wasn't alone. It was hard to tell with his head pounding so, but it sounded like Rose. He must be at home. He must be sick.

He opened his eyes again. Her face slowly materialized out of the sea of mist which seemed to surround him. Gradually the room came into focus. It wasn't his room. He wasn't at home.

"You must have drunk more than I thought," Rose said. "I've been trying to wake you for nearly an hour."

What was she talking about? He never drank. He remembered what it did to his father. It made him angry and mean. He got into fights, said cruel, vicious things. George had sworn he would never drink.

"I'm sorry you feel so rotten, but you're going to have to get up. Everybody expects to see the new bridegroom."

Maybe Rose had been drinking. Nothing she said made any sense.

"There's already a line outside wanting to know how you survived the whiskey *and* your wedding night."

With the impact of a mule's kick, the events of the previous day came rushing back. He was married!

And he'd passed out cold on his wedding night.

He didn't know whether to laugh or slink away in shame.

He decided to laugh. Maybe he wouldn't feel so humiliated. But the pain was excruciating. Even the movement of the muscles in his face hurt.

"What time is it?" he managed to ask. His voice sounded thick, the words slurred.

"It's past ten. It's hot, but it's going to be a beautiful day."

"Then why is the room so dark?"

"I thought it might be easier on your eyes." She walked over to the window and raised the shade. A blinding light caused a splitting pain to drive to the center of George's brain. He grabbed his head again, the palms of his hands pressed hard against his eyes.

"Yes, a lovely day to be sure." He meant to sound good-humored, even if a bit reluctant. He just sounded angry.

Rose laughed softly. "I don't imagine you feel that way at all, but you can't lie in bed all day. Do you think you can sit up?"

No, he didn't. He thought the effort would kill him, but he knew he had to try.

"They just sent up a pot of coffee."

If sitting up didn't kill him, that would. He hated coffee. If he remembered correctly, he had drunk a hell of a lot of it last night. Somewhere he'd heard the wages of sin were death. Well, he had sinned, but apparently the angels thought death wasn't punishment enough. They were going to keep him alive until every possible bit of agony had been squeezed out of him.

There was no use putting it off any longer. He had to sit up. If he died in the process, it might not be a bad thing.

George sat up.

He thought his eyes would fall out of his head and yank out the center of his brain. Rose faded into the mists. It was a full minute before he could bring her into focus again.

"I must have really tied one on," he said. That was obvious to any fool, but his powers of conversation were extremely limited at the moment. He was surprised he remembered enough words to put together a sentence.

"According to Salty, you drank a toast with every man in town."

"Did anybody think to remind me I don't drink?"

"Nobody knew."

"Why would they, when I was busy piling up proof to the contrary?"

George sat on the edge of the bed, his head resting on his hands, his elbows on his knees. He didn't even want to think of the impression Rose was getting of her new husband. It couldn't possibly make her chirping merry. He raised his head and was rewarded by new circles of pain boring into the base of his skull.

"Are you ready for some coffee?"

"No, but give it to me anyway. I might as well start paying for my sins."

George had forgotten how much he hated the taste of coffee. Especially Texas coffee. It tasted as if it had been boiled for hours in a pot with acorns, pecan hulls, and some weed which made it taste like alkali and acid at the same time.

He drank it anyway. He kept hoping someone would soon collect his debts, but it seemed the angel of death had slept late as well. He took another swallow. At least the taste helped him forget some of the pain. Now if he just didn't get sick.

"Would you like some breakfast?"

"No." It was a groan rather than a spoken response.

"Good. I've got enough here for three people. Mrs. Spreckel said you're to eat it all. She's convinced that after last night you need to build up your strength."

"Mrs. Spreckel?" The name made him think of a hen. A black and white one, all fussy and broody.

"You woke her up at one o'clock wanting hot water. Remember? You were determined to come to your marriage bed fresh as a daisy."

If the coffee did kill him, it would be no less than he deserved. Surely his ignominy had already been broadcast far and wide. George breathed a deep sigh, swallowed the rest of the coffee, and handed the cup to Rose.

"Apparently I've made an impression that can only be countered by bold action. Bring on the breakfast and gallons of coffee. If I survive, and at the moment I sincerely hope I don't, we shall parade through the town proud as peacocks, brazen as carpetbaggers, our heads held high, our gazes crossing swords with anyone who dares frown at us. And I shall do my best to pretend I know exactly where the ground is."

Rose giggled.

George smiled in spite of himself. "Are you ever going to let me live this down?"

"Maybe."

"You can't tell the boys. Monty would never let me forget it."

"You don't think I would tell anyone, do you?"

"No, but I'll have to remember not to make Salty angry. Or half the male population of Austin."

"Salty says the men are rather in awe of you. I'd never think of celebrating my marriage that way, but men are strange, unaccountable creatures."

"Yes, we are," George agreed.

Once his eyes adjusted to the glare of the sun, George thoroughly enjoyed himself. He made it a point to stop every female he saw with a frown on her face or a crease on her forehead. He smiled and chatted and flattered until each of them went away with their wits knocked acock by his floodtide of nonsensical prattle. He stopped people he'd never seen before and told them he was on his honeymoon. He stopped people Rose had never seen before and introduced his new wife. He was determined to look stupidly, blissfully, irritatingly happy. He wanted everyone in Austin to know he had married "that Yankee woman" and was proud of it.

He took Rose to Dobie's Emporium and tried to buy her clothes she didn't want. He took her to Hanson's Wholesale and tried to buy furniture he didn't need. He took her to the Bon Ton and made Dottie wait on her former waitress. He didn't have to make sure everyone in Bullock's Hotel knew he had come in close to midnight demanding a hot bath before he could go to his bride.

Mrs. Spreckel had made sure of that.

They walked arm-in-arm, shopped side by side, whispered in each other's ear, laughed at jokes only they would understand, and pretended to be completely unaware that anyone else was in the street.

"Sure I'm looking for hands," George said when Silas Pickett introduced himself and told him he was looking for a job. "But I can't pay wages until I sell the herd. I'm just providing mounts and food. You have to provide all your own equipment."

"Fine with me."

"Ever do any work with cattle?"

"A bit."

"Then you're ahead of the rest of us," George said. "Go talk to Salty. He's been doing my hiring. I've been busy with other things."

George's gaze strayed to where Rose had stopped about twenty feet up the boardwalk. She was looking in one of the windows, her attention apparently caught by something. Whatever it was, George made up his mind to buy it for her.

"I heard. I guess congratulations are in order."

"Thanks," George said, shaking the hand offered him.

"I guess it won't be too long before you're building a place in town."

"Why do you say that?" George asked, surprised.

"I just assumed," the ex-soldier said, clearly aware he'd said the wrong thing. "You selling your herd, just getting married. A beautiful wife doesn't seem to belong on a dirt farm in the brush country."

"I'm selling steers to buy breeding stock. In five years my six brothers and I plan to have a lot more than a dirt farm. Salty's back at the hotel. I've got to join my wife."

George put the man out of his mind. It was much more pleasing to think about Rose.

She turned away when she saw him coming. She even tried to position herself between him and the window, but he saw it nonetheless. It rested on a piece of black velvet cloth and winked wickedly in the sunlight.

A gold ring set with a large, yellow topaz. It was beautiful. It would be perfect with her coloring. He knew she wanted it. The effort she made to distract his attention only underlined how much.

But he couldn't afford it. They had barely enough money to last until they sold the herd. And it was the family's money. He had none of his own.

George tucked her arm in his and guided her over to the jeweler's window. "Do you like that ring?" he asked. He had to mention it. She never would.

"Which one?" Rose asked. But her eyes found the topaz ring immediately.

"The one with the yellow stone. I think it would look pretty with your eyes."

"Maybe," Rose said, turning away, "but I can't wear it in my eyes. Besides, it's much too expensive. I never knew topaz could cost so much."

"Would you like it?"

"I don't know. I'm not sure I like that shade of amber. It's so dark."

George thought it looked perfect.

"Besides, I'm waiting for you to sell the herd. Then you can buy me something really expensive. How do you think I would look in rubies and sapphires?"

He thought she'd look just lovely, but she was still trying to draw his attention away from the ring. He cast one last glance at it as they walked away. He'd love to give it to her, but he'd have to wait until he had some money of his own. He didn't know how many years it would be before he could spend that kind of money on a ring.

He knew Rose wouldn't mind waiting, but he would.

It was the shaking earth that woke her.

Rose sat up with a start. She couldn't see anything in the inky darkness that surrounded her. They were on their way home, and George had insisted they make camp in a nearly impenetrable patch of brush. She turned to where he had bedded down next to her.

He was gone!

"George!" It was a strangled cry.

"Shhh!" Silas Pickett hissed from nearby. He and the other men were standing with the horses to keep them quiet. "George and Salty went to see what's going on," Silas said. "He said we were to stay here no matter what."

Rose waited, huddled in her blanket, fear causing her teeth to chatter. She immediately thought of the Indians she and Zac had seen. Were these Cortina's men? Had the dreaded bandit general reached this far into Texas? And where was the army? Weren't they supposed to protect Texas citizens from Indians and bandits?

The brush next to her rustled, and she nearly screamed with fright when George appeared at her side. She fell into his arms.

"It's some Mexicans stealing several hundred head of cattle," he told her.

"Do they have any of ours?" she asked fearfully.

"Our ranch is too far away."

"Are they Cortina's men?"

"I don't know, but I didn't ask. There were forty or fifty of them."

"Will they come after our herd?" she asked.

"Probably," George answered.

"What will you do?"

"Fight."

"But how can you fight so many?"

"If we don't, they'll take everything we have."

Rose had almost forgotten that the frontier wasn't as safe as Austin. She had forgotten that George and his brothers might have to fight and die for their land.

"Get everything loaded up. We're moving out."

George's order terrified her. "Why? Do they know we're here?"

"No. We're going to scatter the herd."

Panic seized Rose. "What can you do against so many?"

"Nothing much, but I can't watch them steal those cattle and not try to do something about it. There aren't enough of us to steal them back, but if we can turn the herd, start them stampeding back toward their home ground, maybe their owners will have time to catch up."

"I want to go with you."

"No. You and Silas will take the wagon and start toward the ranch. The rest of us will catch up with you before dawn."

"But you don't even have a horse."

"I'm hoping Silas will lend me his."

Silas nodded his agreement.

Rose knew there was no use arguing with George, not about fighting.

"They're coming," Salty said, racing up to the thicket where George had set up his ambush.

"How many are in front?"

"Just two. Alex and I already took out the lookouts."

George grinned. "I wish I'd had you in my command during the war. We could have given them some sleepless nights."

"You sure all you want to do is turn the herd?" Salty asked.

"It's all we can do," George said. "If we try killing as many as we can, we'll have half the outlaws in Mexico on our backs. I won't endanger Rose's life, not for somebody else's longhorns. Now take your position. When you hear my yell, come out shooting."

Salty grinned. "You think the Rebel yell will put the fear of God into these bandits?"

"It always worked on the Yankees. It ought to scare the hell out of this rabble."

George's whole body trembled with excitement. Like a wild stallion with the smell of a rival in his nostrils, he could hardly wait to signal the attack. It felt good to be back in command. He only wished he had enough support to wipe out every bandit who dared cross the Rio Grande. He'd even be willing to take the fight to Cortina's own backyard.

Now if he only had command of one of the Texas forts . . .

George didn't complete the thought. The lead steer emerged from the brush. Digging his heels into his mount's side, George let out a blood curdling Rebel yell and directed a fusillade of bullets just over the heads of the oncoming longhorns. It was followed immediately by a similar outburst from four other points in the brush. The point riders were swept out of their saddles before they had time to unholster their guns.

Staring wild-eyed at the onrushing men, the lead steer threw up his head, gave out a bellow of fear, and turned on the longhorns immediately behind him. In seconds the whole herd was racing back down the trail and toward their familiar feeding grounds.

Knowing the other bandits had to run with the herd or be trampled, George and his men followed behind, filling the night with enough yells and gunshots to keep the herd running at full speed for twenty or thirty miles.

Rose had never had anything to do with a stampede, and she didn't know how to interpret the succession of sounds: first the eerie silence, next an awe-inspiring eruption of sound followed by the thunder of thousands of feet, then the gradual return of silence.

She didn't ask Silas what was happening. She didn't want to know. She only wanted George at her side and those bandits as far away as possible. She didn't even want to think of what it would be like if they attacked the ranch.

She concentrated on the things she needed to do when they reached home. As uninspiring as that was, it was better than wondering if she would ever see George again.

The sound of hoofbeats in the distance caused the muscles in her stomach to relax.

"That'll be my husband," she said.

"How do you know it's not the bandits?" Silas asked.

"George would never let them find us," Rose replied.

Even though she didn't know anything about war and battle tactics, she knew George would make sure she was safe. He had already turned his life upside down doing just that.

She saw him the moment he broke cover. His face was wreathed in a broad grin. He looked happier and more relaxed than she could remember ever seeing him. She realized his happiness came from having commanded his men in a successful battle action, and her heart sank.

It must have been just like being in the army again.

Rose didn't realize until now how much she had come to depend on George's not returning to uniform. But if it made him this happy . . .

"That's one herd I doubt will reach Mexico," George said when he rode up. It only took a few moments for him to exchange his seat on Silas's horse for one on the wagon next to Rose. "Maybe they'll catch a few of those bandits along with the cattle."

"Did anybody get hurt?" Rose asked.

"Nobody on our side," George answered. Rose listened without comment as he gave Silas a brief rundown of the encounter.

"I wish I'd been with you," Silas said.

"I wish you could, too," George replied. "I haven't felt this good in a long time. It's a shame we can't get a company together and drive them out of Texas altogether."

"I'm sure the governor would be agreeable," Salty said. "After tonight, a command like that would be yours for the asking."

Rose felt something wither inside. She had slipped another notch in George's heart. After tonight his determination to return to the army would be stronger still.

"No. It was fun," George said, "but a married man has more important things to do than chasing bandits and outlaws for a living." He put his arm around Rose. "If not, he shouldn't have gotten married."

All over her body, Rose could feel the knots of tension, the tight balls of fear, ease and fade away. George wouldn't leave her. He didn't want to leave her.

She had been right to marry him.

George was surprised at how glad he was to be back on his own land, to recognize familiar landmarks, even to see a well-remembered, mean-tempered steer or cow. Everything was so different from Virginia he had never even thought of trying to like Texas. He was stunned to find he now thought of it as home.

Did he owe this new feeling to Rose and to his marriage?

It was impossible to tell, but nothing had remained the same since the day he entered the Bon Ton. He expected it would continue to change. That excited him, but he was worried about the effect it would have on the boys.

He didn't know how he was going to tell them about Rose. It would have been awkward enough without Jeff. With him, it was nearly impossible. They had almost reached the house. If he waited much longer, they'd see for themselves.

Salty and the four men he had hired to help with the roundup, Silas Pickett, Ted Cooper, Ben Preyer, and Alex Pendleton, had gone off to look for the twins. George and Rose continued on to the house by themselves.

"Nervous?" he asked her.

"A little. You?"

"Yeah."

"It's Jeff, isn't it?"

He nodded.

"What are you going to tell him?"

"That you're my wife."

"And?"

"The *and* will be up to him."

A shriek erupted out of the brush along the trail. It was so sudden and unexpected that both horses sidled nervously. George wasn't the least bit surprised when Zac exploded from the brush.

"You're back," he shouted at Rose, completely ignoring his brother. He climbed up on the wagon and hugged Rose until her bonnet was knocked askew and her hair was in danger of coming down.

"You brought her back!" he exclaimed, turning to George. "I didn't think you would." The shining happiness in Zac's eyes more than compensated for anything Jeff might say. Zac's world was back on its axis.

"Why did you come back?" Zac asked after he'd settled himself on the wagon between Rose and George.

"Rose and I got married," George said. "And a wife is supposed to go home with her husband."

George waited for Zac to say something. His reaction would probably be a barometer for the others.'

"Can I have your bed?" Zac asked, excitement springing up in his eyes.

George's shout of laughter snapped the bands of tension which had been gathering for the last hour at the base of his skull. He had spent all this time worrying how his brothers would react, and all Zac cared about was getting a larger bed.

"We'll have to see."

"That means no. You can't fool me."

"It means you caught me by surprise. I haven't had time to think about it. One of the other boys may need it. If so, you could have his bed."

"Little kids never get anything," Zac complained. "I'm going to run away to New Orleans."

"I hope you won't," Rose said. "Who would help me with dinner?"

"Not Tyler. He'll light out the minute he sets eyes on you."

"Did Tyler stay home with you?"

"Yeah, and he's been a son-of-a-bitch the whole time."

"I think I hear Monty's influence here," George said, giving Zac a stern look. "You're not to use such language again."

"Tyler does."

"I'll have a word with Tyler *and* Monty. No six-year-old should be cussing."

"I'll soon be seven," Zac informed his brother. "Will I be old enough to cuss then?"

Rose nearly overset George's gravity by giggling shamelessly.

"Not at seven, eight, or twelve."

"Damn," Zac said, then looked up at his brother, conscience-stricken. "I didn't mean it," he pleaded. "It just slipped out."

"That's what frightens me. I think it's time I sent Monty on a long trip."

"Send Jeff. I like Monty."

That ingenuous remark had a sobering effect on George. He grew even more unhappy when he saw the expression on Tyler's face when he emerged from the house just after they pulled up in the yard. Tyler had a bowl in his arm and was mixing something.

"What's she doing back?" he demanded.

"We got married," George said.

Tyler gaped at Rose for a full second, his hand arrested in

the act of stirring. Then he cast the bowl to the ground and ran off around the corner of the house.

"Tyler was making stuffing," Zac said, looking at the discarded bowl. "It doesn't look like stuffing to me."

"I seem to be forever apologizing for my brothers," George said.

But Rose seemed to take Tyler's disappearance in stride. "He'll be back in time for supper." She picked up the bowl, inspected its contents, then turned them out for the chickens.

"I'd better get started on dinner. The twins will be home before long. I'll let you bring in the luggage. Zac, I need eggs and firewood. I'm sure you haven't gotten either for Tyler. I require them right away."

Both brothers snapped to, Zac with a good deal more alacrity than George. Zac only had to gather the eggs, split some wood, and pour out the milk. George had to plan what he was going to say to his brothers.

In the end, he didn't have to say anything. Salty had already broken the news.

Monty rode his horse practically to the steps, leapt down, burst into the kitchen, and grabbed Rose in a bear hug. Without giving her time to drop the spoon she was using to stir a pot of beans, he picked her up, whirled her around, and gave her a big kiss on the lips.

"Thank God George came to his senses. Now I can eat again."

"Don't you ever think of anything but your stomach?" Rose asked, laughing.

"Yeah," Monty replied, flashing the grin that Rose knew would someday destroy more than one woman's peace of mind, "but I sort of got the feeling you were off-limits. Besides, you haven't had to eat what Tyler's been dishing up the last few days. I swear he's trying to poison us for liking your cooking better than his."

"Put my wife down," George said, a slight edge perceptible

in his voice. "You're allowed a kiss, but that hug is more than brotherly."

Monty still held Rose in his arms, her feet dangling off the floor, her chest smashed against his. The old wicked gleam flared in Monty's eyes, and Rose feared for a moment he would bait his brother. She was prepared to ladle beans over him if necessary, but Monty smiled good-naturedly and set her down.

"I won't cause trouble, even though it's mighty tempting with George looking as serious as a Mormon."

Hen stepped forward, shoving his brother aside. "I'm glad you're back. I never thought George would make such a sensible marriage." He gave Rose a restrained peck on the cheek.

"You can give her a real kiss," Monty said, goading his twin. "George won't mind."

Hen stepped back from Rose, flashing his twin an angry glare as he did so.

"Thank you so much for your welcome," Rose said. She felt her stomach flutter uncomfortably. "I appreciate it very much."

"Not as much as we appreciate—"

"Monty, if you mention my cooking one more time, I swear I won't fix dinner. A woman likes it when a man enjoys her food, but she likes to think she's appreciated a little because of herself."

"When I think of you, I just naturally think of food."

Disgust was written all over Hen's face. He hit his brother on the shoulder so hard Monty almost lost his balance. "What she's saying, you dumb cluck, is she'd like to think you'd want her here even if she couldn't cook a lick."

Monty hit him back. "I'm not a dumb cluck, even if I don't know pretty things to say to a woman."

"You'll know when the time comes," Rose said when the two boys started hitting each other in earnest, "but if you get into a fight in my kitchen, you'll go to bed hungry."

"I suggest you wash up and cool down," George said. "And put on something clean. I want tonight to be a little festive."

"It won't be if Tyler and Jeff come," Zac said.

Hen scooped up his little brother, held him over his head, and threatened to boil him in the wash pot before dinnertime.

Zac screamed with delight.

"Leave it to Zac to go straight to the nub of the issue," George said.

"Three of your brothers like me," Rose said. "A lot of wives start with less."

"Maybe—"

"Tyler will come around. He's just mad at me for driving him out of the kitchen. As for Jeff, well, I'm not sure he really dislikes me either. But you can't do anything about it, so stop worrying."

"I wouldn't if it were just myself."

"Well, don't because of me," Rose said, standing on her toes to give him a quick kiss. "I survived the good ladies of Austin. After that, I should hardly even notice Jeff."

But she did. They all did.

Everyone came to dinner, including Salty and the new hands. Jeff didn't speak to anyone. He didn't look at George. He seldom even looked up from his plate. He never once turned his gaze toward Rose.

At first nobody spoke much. They were all taken up with the serious business of eating. After subsisting on Tyler's cooking, and their own when they couldn't stomach Tyler's any longer, they were anxious to make up for lost time. Probably everyone except Rose and George ate too much. As they sat back to let their food settle, the conversation turned to the coming roundup.

"The other boys ought to be here in a day or two," Salty said. "How long it'll take us to be ready for the drive will depend on how big a herd you want to take."

"Silas has already showed us how to build a corral and chute for the branding," Monty told George. "That ought to cut the time in half."

"And make it easier on us," Hen said. "It's no picnic throwing a five-year-old steer bigger than your horse."

"While we have the hands to help us, I want to go through the herd and cut all the bulls we don't intend to keep," George said. "We can brand anything you missed and cull what we want to sell at the same time."

"That will probably take an extra month," Silas said.

"I want to count the herd, too," George said. "If bandits were to run off a bunch tonight, we wouldn't know how many we lost."

"We lose more to the McClendons taking one here and there than we do to bandits," Monty said. "I'd like to run every one of them out of the state."

Jeff's head snapped up.

"Don't say a word," George said to his brother. "I won't have us arguing among ourselves. Understand?"

Everyone knew this wasn't a request. Even Jeff.

The discussion about the roundup continued, but the tension had returned. It seemed to grow more intense with each passing minute.

"We'd best be heading to bed if we plan to be chasing cows before dawn," Salty said, getting to his feet. "It was mighty good, ma'am. We'll rustle our own grub in the morning."

"You'll eat with us as long as you're at the house," Rose said. "When do you want to leave?"

"Is five too early?"

"It sure as hell is," Monty exclaimed. "Damnation, my dogs don't even get up that early."

"Then we'll have to see about reforming your sleeping habits," George said. "And your language. Zac's beginning to sound just like you."

"Son-of-a-bitch!" Monty exclaimed, turning on his youngest brother.

"That's exactly the phrase I had in mind," George said.

Monty had the grace to blush.

"I'm not going to try to tell you what to say out on the range, but everything changes the minute you ride into this yard. That goes for the hands as well," George said to the men as they left the room.

Salty nodded his acceptance.

"Surely Rose has heard—" Monty started to say.

"She probably has, but there's no reason she has to go on hearing it. Would you want people cussing around your wife, or the girl you were sweet on?"

"We'll watch our tongues," Hen promised. "We didn't mean any disrespect, ma'am," he said to Rose. "Monty just never pays any attention to what he says. Come on, let's go to bed before you say something else stupid," Hen hissed to his twin. They left the kitchen amid a sequence of fiercely whispered exchanges.

"Time for you to hit the sack as well," George said to Zac. Tyler had left with Salty and the others.

"Can I have your bed?" Zac asked. "You promised, remember."

"I promised to think about it," George said. He had noticed Jeff's sudden attention, and he braced himself. "You might as well go ahead and take it. I don't think anybody else wants it."

"Yippee!" Zac yelled. He jumped up, gave his brother a hug, and raced out of the room to tell everybody the good news.

"Where are you going to sleep?" Jeff asked. The anger in his voice was palpable.

"If you two will excuse me, I'll go help Zac," Rose said. "I don't trust him not to sleep on the bare mattress rather than put on fresh sheets."

George was relieved. He didn't want Rose to have to live with the memory of whatever Jeff might say.

"I'm going to sleep with my wife," George said. "You will agree that's appropriate, even if she is a Yankee."

George didn't understand why his reply should cause Jeff to relax. He'd thought it would send him through the roof.

"I can't imagine you'll be happy in the loft."

Now he understood.

"Rose and I will sleep in the bedroom." He nodded over his shoulder to the door behind the coats.

Jeff looked thunderous.

"That's Ma's room!" he shouted, his face red with fury. "Do you mean to say you'd put that—"

George interrupted his brother. "Before you say anything, remember two things. First, Rose is my wife. You can't say anything you please about her and expect me to forgive and forget. Second, you'd better say everything you have to say now. If you repeat any of it to Rose, I'll knock you down."

"I can't believe you're doing this!" Jeff exploded. "My own brother. Are you so desperate for a woman you had to get married? You could find one in just about any town in Texas. They usually seem ready to throw themselves at your feet."

"I'm not desperate for a woman, Jeff. I have my appetites just like everybody else, but I'm not ruled by them."

"You must be ruled by something other than your brain. If it's not your stomach or your groin, what is it?"

"Something you're too full of hate and fury to understand," George said.

"Don't tell me you love her," Jeff said. "I won't believe you could love a Yankee, not even if you swear to it."

"Okay, I won't."

"God, I just realized. You'll soon have half a dozen Yankee brats running about the place."

"There won't be any children," George said.

Jeff stared at his brother. "What other reason could you have for marrying . . . her?"

"We all have Pa's blood in our veins. Do you think I'd take a chance on fathering sons like him?"

"What did Rose have to say about that?"

"It's none of your business," George said, "but she agreed."

For a moment Jeff looked nonplussed.

"But to put her in Ma's room," Jeff continued. "To let her sleep in Ma's bed."

"You know Ma would agree," George said. "Besides, she lived

here less than two years. It's not like any of us were born there."

"What will the twins say?"

"Nothing, and you know it. You're the only one who can't get over the fact Rose's father fought for the Union."

"You're damned right I can't."

"Well, you're going to have to. Rose is here to stay."

"You mean you'd choose that woman over your own flesh and blood?"

"If there's any *choosing* to be done, you'll do it, not me. I've already made my vows."

"Well, I didn't take any. It's a waste of time to ask me to accept her."

"I'm not asking you," George said. "You know what the choice is. It's up to you."

"I'm not taking her," Jeff said as he jumped up from his chair. "And I'm not taking you as long as you're married to her."

"Then you'd better pack your bedroll. I imagine you'll be more comfortable with Salty and the boys."

"You're kicking me out?" Jeff asked, his eyes wide with disbelief. "And all because of a Yankee bitch who managed to get you so hot you would marry her just to get her into bed?"

George came to his feet with a rush. Grabbing a handful of Jeff's shirt, he dragged him across the room like a rag doll.

"Be glad you only have one arm. If you had two, I'd beat you senseless. I'd make you apologize to Rose, but I don't want her to know that one of my brothers would sink low enough to call a lady names. Now get out of here and don't cross that threshold again until you're ready to treat Rose with the respect due my wife and your sister-in-law."

"I'll never do that." Jeff grabbed up one of the coats and one of the slicks and stormed out of the kitchen.

Rose couldn't sleep. She knew George couldn't either. But it wouldn't do any good to talk. They couldn't fix what was wrong by talking. At least not yet.

Their first evening home had been a disaster. So disastrous that she had resorted to a lie to make things easier for both of them.

She had heard Jeff leave. Everybody in the house had heard him. He had stormed into the boys' room, seen her saying good night to Zac, and muttered a foul expletive.

Monty had knocked him down. Only because he got to him before Hen. Fortunately, before things got completely out of hand, Jeff got to his feet and stormed out of the bedroom. George was in the breezeway. When he let him pass, Rose decided he hadn't heard what Jeff said.

For that she was profoundly grateful.

"I'm sorry," she muttered to the twins and quickly returned to the kitchen.

"Anything wrong?" George asked, following her back into the kitchen.

She couldn't tell him what Jeff had said. It would solve nothing and only add to the burden he carried already.

"I guess I was hoping Jeff wouldn't take it so badly."

"He'll cool off. He's a lot like Pa. He never stayed mad long. It was just too much trouble."

"That's Monty," Rose said. "Jeff is different."

And she knew George knew it. She let him unpack most of their clothes while she cleaned up in the kitchen. It gave him time alone. It gave her time alone, too.

"We never did get to finish papering this room before the war started," George said when she finally entered the bedroom. "I don't guess the boys had any reason to after Ma died."

"We've got plenty of time now," Rose said with as much enthusiasm as she could muster. She put the last of her clothes away, but George didn't move. He stood staring out the small window into the night. He seemed moody and preoccupied. Rose cursed Jeff in silence. She climbed into bed. Still George looked out the window.

"I don't know why you're not tired," she said. "I'm worn out. If I'm to fix breakfast at five o'clock, I've got to get to sleep."

George turned toward the bed, but he looked right through her. "I don't feel quite right," she said. "I think I'll go on to sleep. Why don't you sit up for a while if you're not sleepy?"

"Are you sick?" George asked, bringing himself out of his abstraction.

"Just tired, I think. Maybe I'm coming into my time a little early."

George's gaze focused immediately.

"I do sometimes," she said.

"Are you sure that's all?"

"I'm sure."

"Okay." George leaned over and kissed her.

Even then she felt that something stood between them.

"I'm sorry your homecoming wasn't any better."

"It'll get better."

But she didn't believe it. When the door closed behind George, she felt as if he had closed it on her.

Why had she thought that all she had to do was marry George and all of his doubts would disappear? Why had she been so foolish as to believe that all she had to do was become his wife and she would take precedence over his family? Why had she left the kitchen? She wished she knew what had passed between him and Jeff. Then she would know what she had to fight.

But she knew anyway. She had his family to fight. George probably didn't know it himself, but he loved his family more than he loved his wife.

That hurt Rose deeply.

There was no appeal from that. It wasn't a matter of reason, something she could argue against. It just was. She knew that if her being his wife broke up his family, it would always stand between them.

Still she wanted him to come to bed. She'd be content to just hold him as she had done that night in Austin. She didn't think she'd ever been so happy as when they'd lain side by side, their arms around each other, her husband wrapped in sleep.

And in her love.

Why had she sent him away? He needed her. He desired her. She could have used that to help bind him to her.

But she didn't want to hold his affections through the bed any more than she wanted to do it through her cooking. She wanted him to love *her*, not her accomplishments. It didn't matter that George seemed to think of her accomplishments as part of her. She knew there was a difference.

She had been foolish to think her only problem was to convince him he wanted children. That might prove easier than convincing him she was more important to him than his family. Or at least as important. And she now knew she wouldn't be happy until she had achieved exactly that.

# *Chapter Sixteen*

Closing the door on Rose was like a physical pain. He could almost feel the skewering of the enormous pressure of his physical need which had been building in him since his marriage. It took a few moments to restore his equilibrium.

He was almost annoyed by the enormity of his physical response to Rose. He had so many questions that needed answering, but his mind could only focus on the one question about which there was no doubt: his desire for Rose.

It was torture to be around her and not be able to touch her, to kiss her, to claim her as he had in his dreams time and time again.

But he couldn't. If he didn't mean to be a proper husband to her, he should leave her untouched. Only George didn't know if he could.

But rather than tease his mind and body with what he couldn't have, George tried to turn his mind to his family. They had trapped him between two forces. Jeff's anger he had expected. The importance of keeping the family together had surprised him.

He hadn't known how much he cared until Jeff stormed out the door. Rose was right about that. He would do anything for his brothers. He would have come home without Jeff's encouragement. He might have waited longer, he might even have enlisted at some army outpost first, but he would have come home. They were his responsibility. He wouldn't run from it any longer.

He guessed he'd gotten that much from his mother.

He wanted to get to know his brothers. He needed time to begin to understand them, to help them know each other better, to help them *want* to become a tightly knit family, to seek out and nourish the hidden parts of them their parents' legacy had left arid, infertile.

He worried about Tyler. Nobody seemed able to reach the boy. It was up to George to find a way to break through Tyler's isolation and draw him back into the comradeship of the family.

Now his marriage had given him another person to try to understand, to weave into this network of threadbare souls.

George asked himself if his changed attitude toward his family had anything to do with his marrying Rose. Maybe he hadn't been just reacting to Peaches's slander. If he hadn't been aware of how he felt about his family, why couldn't he have misunderstood his feelings for Rose?

He wasn't talking about liking her, or finding her attractive, or even wanting to make love to her. He was talking about wanting to marry her because he couldn't imagine his life without her. What would he do if it came to a choice between keeping the family together or sending her away?

That question scared him to death.

Up until this minute he'd have been sure he would sacrifice Rose. Yet now when the possibility was staring him in the face, he didn't know what he would do.

His feelings went much deeper than he had suspected.

Stupid of him. He'd been so busy trying not to think about wanting to touch Rose, kiss her, make love to her, he had lost sight of all the little steps which led up to love. Pleasure in her company, the excitement of seeing her first thing in the morning, of her comforting presence at the end of the day; to wonder if she was happy, what she was like before they met, if she had ever loved anyone else.

He didn't know if what he felt was fascination, lust, or a deep-felt longing that would never go away.

But he knew he couldn't think about her without feeling that delicious contentment. There was something about her that he needed. And it had nothing to do with the physical needs of his body. He was surprised to find he resented not being able to make love to her tonight, that he was tempted to say to hell with her cycle. Yet, that wasn't what made the difference.

Simply put, Rose embodied everything he needed to be happy. How could he even consider giving her up?

He couldn't. He hadn't.

But what about Rose? Wasn't it possible she would be better off with someone else? It wasn't fair to deprive her of the chance to have a family. There were many good men looking for wives. Surely she could find one to love, to make her forget him. Maybe it would be better if she went farther west where the feeling between the Union and the Confederate states wasn't so strong.

But no sooner did he think of sending Rose away than he knew he couldn't do it. He might not know the true nature of his feelings just yet—and that made him feel rather foolish—but whatever his feelings, they were tenacious.

He just hoped they were honest and honorable as well.

The first week of the roundup was hell. The work was brutal. The heat was murderous. And the tension was homicidal. Jeff never came near the house or mentioned Rose's name, but his anger hung in the air like a sword over their heads.

Tempers stretched to the limit were sent hurtling over the edge by his forked tongue. George counted himself lucky that neither Monty nor Hen had shot Jeff. The only thing that prevented a blowup was that with ten men working the cattle, George was able to keep Jeff away from the twins nearly all the time.

Branding, cutting, and counting calves was nothing compared to driving a fifteen-hundred-pound longhorn from the brush. They didn't want to leave their familiar haunts. Many of them had grown up without being herded or bothered. Quite a few had never been branded. The twins had done their best, but keeping the rustlers at bay, watching for Cortina's bandits, and trying to stay alive had taken up too much of their time. Every fifth or sixth animal was an unbranded bull.

The longhorns wouldn't come out of the brush without being driven. Some slept during the heat of the day and grazed at night. They turned foul-tempered when anything disturbed their sleep. George was glad he had been able to find some Mexican *vaqueros* to go in after them. The *vaqueros* had a knack for understanding the longhorns and knowing how to come out of the brush alive.

He also hoped that hiring the *vaqueros* would help build up some loyalty to his ranch. He couldn't pay them a wage, but the beef and hides he gave them would help support their families. He hoped it would make them less likely to steal from him or allow their friends to do so.

Once the *vaqueros* had flushed the longhorns from the brush, it was up to the rest of the men to herd them to the corrals. Driving the wild-eyed, mean-tempered beasts anywhere was hot, exhausting, and dangerous. The men needed fresh horses every couple of hours.

Some of the cattle couldn't be rounded up. They were wilder than deer and just as fast and agile. They swam like ducks, jumped like antelope, and fought like wounded boars. When aroused, they would attack anything that moved.

One day George heard the bleating of a calf. Almost immediately he heard the sound of steers stampeding through the brush. At first he thought they were running away. Then he realized they were running toward the calf calling for help. Within minutes a dozen steers were closing in on the thicket where the distress call came from. George heard a terrific disturbance from within the thicket. Even at a distance, he could see the chaparral shaking. Suddenly a wolf exploded from the brush chased by half a dozen longhorns. Even running for his life, the wolf couldn't match the longhorns' speed. Right there before George's eyes, they chased the wolf down and ground him beneath their hooves.

George decided not to disturb this thicket until they had time to calm down, but both the unwanted bulls and the poor-quality cows would have to be culled if he was going to upgrade the herd. He would give some to the *vaqueros*. Some more would be butchered by the rustlers. Those left would be shot for their hides and tallow.

The work of branding was hot and rough, but using the pens made it possible to brand the full-grown bulls as well as castrate them without as much danger of being killed. With five ex-Confederates, five Randolph brothers, and as many as ten Mexicans, the work progressed steadily. George intended to work his way over every inch of their land and a good bit more besides. No one else had a ranch within fifteen miles. Theoretically every cow belonged to him and his brothers.

But not everyone agreed. Hardly a day passed that he didn't come upon a bleached cow skeleton. Some of them must have been killed even before the war. There were no ranches around, but there were people who thought they had a right to Randolph beef. Jeff might believe they only took what they needed to survive, but George soon decided that "what they needed to survive" seemed to be a steady diet of beef.

Having come upon a homestead here and there, George found himself agreeing with the twins. He saw no signs of farming, of domestic livestock, of people determined to build up a homestead which could support them and their family. He saw untended, weed-filled gardens, an old cow, maybe a bony mule, and run-down cabins. Yet no one looked hungry.

It wasn't hard to guess why.

"They're all part of Frank McClendon's clan," Hen told him. "Mean as snakes and lazy as hogs. One of them got himself a job with the Reconstruction, and now they act like they can do anything they want."

"Well, they're through living off our beef," George said.

George had expected trouble—he rarely passed a day without seeing someone watching, either on horseback or on foot— but none came. The McClendons lived to the east of the ranch. That was the area George worked first. After three weeks they had cleared everything they could move out of the breaks and tangles. Nothing remained but about fifty rogue steers.

And he gave those to the *vaqueros* to shoot for their meat and hides.

"Do you have any family left?" George asked Rose.

She could feel him slipping away and there was nothing she could do about it. She might have had a chance if she had been able to see him for more than a couple of hours each day, if she had a chance to talk with him alone, if she hadn't started her cycle.

As it was, they met only at the table. Breakfast was a quick scramble to eat and get on with the work. Supper was no better. Everyone came in exhausted, covered with dust, sweat, thorns, and innumerable cuts, burns, and abrasions. By the time they had washed, tended their wounds, and eaten dinner, it was time to go to bed.

"Only my uncle's wife and children," she answered. "They don't seem like family. I've never even met them."

George shared her bed, but he was too exhausted to do more than give her a hasty kiss and a quick good night. She understood that it must be difficult for him to touch her and then go to sleep with nothing more than a chaste kiss, but she longed for the little intimate touches, the brushing of finger-tips, a small hug, an arm slipped around her waist.

Nothing.

She had tried to talk to him. He listened, but after a day of giving orders, he had no desire to talk. And neither did she, not really. She couldn't talk about the things that touched her most deeply. They had already made a deal. She was the one trying to change the rules after they had been agreed upon.

"Shouldn't you let them know you're married?"

Once in a while she would catch him looking at her in the strangest way. It was almost as if he were looking at a stranger, studying her, trying to figure out who she was, what she was. Other times he looked right through her. That was when she knew he was thinking about his brothers.

She started to wonder if she had made a mistake in thinking George could come to love her. It was pretty hard to fall in love with a woman you barely had time to think about.

"They wouldn't care, not since my uncle was killed. They think everyone who lives in Texas lives on a plantation and owned hundreds of slaves."

Rose told herself this was a bad time. Things would be better after the cows were rounded up and sold. But she knew that every passing day made it harder for George to change. He had been at his most vulnerable in Austin. He had moved away from her ever since.

She considered asking him to take her to Austin, anything to get away from the family, but she couldn't expect him to stop the roundup when she had everything she needed for the next several months.

Except his love.

"Surely there's somebody else. How about your father's family?"

Every time she saw him stare at Jeff's empty chair, she knew that his feelings for his brothers were stronger than for her. She knew it every time he looked at Tyler with that crease between his eyes. She knew it when she saw him make a point of spending a few minutes with Zac every evening.

Even when he didn't have time to spend with her.

"They wanted him to become a minister. They disowned him when he went to West Point."

And his brothers' behavior had done nothing to allay his fears about the bad blood in his family. Jeff was sharp-tongued and cruel. He seemed to look for ways to make the twins furious. Monty and Hen were in savage moods most of the time. They were merely beastly the rest of the time. Tyler hardly recognized anybody's existence. Only George and Zac seemed to have any emotional equilibrium. Maybe George was right. Maybe they were all crazy.

"Then you really are alone in the world."

They might be, but George wasn't, and it was George she loved.

She couldn't go forward and she couldn't go backward. She would go crazy if something didn't happen soon.

"Not anymore."

George's nerves were stretched to the breaking point. Rose had told him that this was the time when she could conceive, so for the third night in less than a week he lay in bed next to her, unable to kiss her, unable to touch her. The other nights he'd slept under the stars, dreaming of lying next to her, of holding her in his arms.

When he was away, it seemed that staying away from her was the hardest thing he'd ever done. But when he lay next to her, a forbidden zone of two feet between them, it seemed much harder.

For a solid week he'd tried not to think of her when he was in the saddle and an angry cow was coming at him. He tried not to remember the warmth of her eyes when he was about to place a red-hot branding iron on the side of a fifteen-hundred-pound bull already pushed to the point of madness by castration. He tried not to think of her as he made his plans or gave out the instructions for the day. He inevitably lost his train of thought and confused everyone.

The hardest task of all was trying not to think of her when he slept at the ranch because he knew he couldn't have her. It had never seemed harder than tonight. She was awake. He knew it. He could tell the difference in her breathing. He knew she was lying there, waiting.

Waiting for what?

He didn't even want to think about it. What would any woman want from the man she loved? The one thing he couldn't give her. Maybe his father had been able to tell women he loved them in order to secure his momentary pleasure, but George couldn't do that. When he told Rose he loved her, he would mean it.

But he wanted her. God, how he wanted her! His whole body was rigid with aching. He had to do something. He didn't think he could lie there for five more minutes without exploding.

Maybe if he just touched her. He wouldn't do more than kiss her or hold her in his arms. He might be burning with unsatisfied desire, but it wasn't so strong he would forget himself and impregnate her.

"It's still not safe," Rose said when George reached out to her.

"I know. I just wanted to touch you. That's all right, isn't it?"

"Yes," Rose answered.

George felt himself relax. Despite his best effort, he had been thinking about her all day. He just wanted to feel her skin under his fingertips, feel the softness of her breasts, taste the sweetness of her lips. He wouldn't do anything else.

"I'm sorry I haven't been able to spend more time with you," he said as he let his hands move across her stomach. The thin material of her gown felt soft and warm.

"I understand," Rose said. Her voice sounded wispy, uncertain.

"It's not much of a way to treat a wife."

"I haven't complained."

She didn't flinch when he moved his hand over her breast. But his own body hardened with desire. He could feel her nipple firm under his touch. That inflamed him more.

"You don't feel crowded, do you?" she asked. "I told you I never would tie you down."

"It's not that."

He didn't want to talk. He wanted to let his mind bury itself in the sensations coming through his fingertips. He wanted to think of nothing but the one thing he had forbidden himself.

"What is it then?"

"I feel guilty," George managed to say. "More guilty than I've ever felt about anything."

"Don't."

But he did. He felt guilty about asking her to marry him when he knew he couldn't give her children or the kind of home she wanted. He felt guilty about her loving him when he couldn't love her back. He felt guilty wanting to make love to her so badly every muscle in the back of his neck was stretched tight. He felt guilty because his actions were out of sequence with his emotions.

His hand slipped inside her gown. Her skin was warm and soft. His breath caught when he found her nipple. He expelled it in a long, shuddering sigh as his fingertip teased the hardened peak.

He felt her body grow tense, and the tension in his body became even worse. But he couldn't stop. He rolled up on his elbow. He let his head sink until his lips touched her warmth.

He could feel her chest rise and fall under his hand. She was breathing faster, not as deep.

So was he.

He freed the near breast from her gown, and while he continued to explore the other with his hand, his fevered lips began to circle one nipple. He let his lips brush softly against her skin as he moved in circles around her breast. She smelled of violets again. Faintly. He liked it.

With his tongue he began to trace circles around her nipple. She tasted warm and soft. His tongue found and teased her nipple. The sharp intake of breath, the sudden stiffening, the involuntary arch against him only inflamed his desire. Taking her nipple between his teeth, he gently nibbled at it.

Her tiny gasps goaded him on.

Taking her nipple into his mouth, he suckled it, gently at first, harder as his own desire grew more engulfing. His hand cupped her other breast, drawing it toward him, burying his face between them.

Rose put her hands behind his head and drew him closer to her. George went over the edge.

Deserting her breast, he took her mouth in a searing kiss, a kiss fueled by a week of longing, a week of thinking of her at least once every five minutes, a week of nights tortured by the thought of her body, a week of winding his nerves so tight he was about to explode.

It was a long kiss, a harsh kiss, a desperate kiss. His need so inflamed his senses he was barely conscious that she kissed him back with equal desperation.

Even as he covered her neck and shoulders and breasts with torrid kisses, his hand moved down her side until it caressed her thigh. He didn't know if the moan came from him or Rose. It hardly mattered. They were both under the sway of their overwhelming need for each other. Neither one wanted to halt the forces that were driving them to a union which had been the focal point of their thoughts for more than a week.

George's hand slipped under the hem of her gown, past her knee, and arrived at the middle of her inner thigh. With a barely perceptible sigh, Rose relaxed her body, waiting for his entry.

But even as his own body throbbed painfully from nights of restraint, George felt himself hesitate, felt the heat cooled by a wave of ice-cold fear.

He saw a seven-year-old boy cowering before his father, a hand raised in rage descending again and again until the child couldn't stand up. He heard his own screams of pain and fear, saw the horror in his father's eyes as he realized what he had done to his own child. He saw his mother, a weak woman lacking the courage or strength to defend her children, gather him into her arms, her tears of grief dropping on his face. He saw his father drunk and dangerous for days afterward. He saw the whole household moving about in fear.

And desire lay dead in his breast.

"I'm sorry," George rasped as he erupted from the bed. He drew on his pants and shirt, snatched up his socks and boots, and was gone as quickly as a cool breeze on a hot summer's day.

Once away from the house, George stopped to allow his pounding heart to slow to a reasonable speed. Gradually he felt some of the tautness leave his body, gradually he was able to take a deep breath. Finally, heaving a great sigh, he sat down to put on his boots.

He couldn't go back. Not tonight or any other night until her fertile time was over. He had come to terms with his need for her, but there could be no compromise on anything else. There must be no children. Not ever.

Maybe he ought to send her back to Austin. He could visit her regularly. It wasn't a long trip on horseback. Especially if he rode a fast horse. It might be better for her. It would certainly be easier for him.

But every time he thought he had decided to talk to Rose, he came up with another reason why he couldn't do without her. Before long he gave up.

Even if the womenfolk of Austin had been willing to welcome Rose with open arms, George knew he couldn't tell her to go. It would have hurt her deeply. Besides, he had gotten used to her being around. He liked it. He *needed* it. She had a hold on him he couldn't shake. As for the danger that he would give in and sleep with her before it was safe, well, he would just have to sleep at the camp. It was worth a few nights on the ground to avoid a lifetime of regret.

But as he walked the hours of the night away, as he mulled over thoughts he had never had time to contemplate in the busy hours of daylight, he realized that not having children would be as much of a loss to him as it would be to Rose.

Something else he owed to the legacy of his father.

For several minutes Rose had lain without moving, her body rigid with desire. And pain.

Then as her muscles started to let go of the tension, the tears started. There were no heartrending sobs, there was no convulsive heaving of the chest, just a silent flow of salty tears down her cheeks, across her lips, onto her pillow.

Once again life had held out something to her, allowed her to see, to touch, to hold, to cherish, then had snatched it away just as she thought it had become her own.

She didn't know how much more she could endure before she broke down altogether. She now understood that just as love can create, it can also destroy.

"Could you take Zac with you today?" Rose asked when George entered the kitchen. The rest of the boys were still washing up.

"He'd only be in the way."

"I've got a surprise for him," Rose explained. "Tomorrow is his birthday."

George felt terrible. He'd gotten so caught up with the roundup and sorting out his feelings for Rose that he'd forgotten Zac's birthday. He remembered how important birthdays had been to him as a child. It must be even more important to Zac. Just more proof he'd make a lousy father.

"He's dying to see the roundup. You can tell him it's his birthday treat. That way he won't expect to go every day."

"I'll take him," George said. "I'm just sorry I didn't think of it."

"You can't think of everything. You've had a lot to worry you these last few days."

"That's no excuse."

"It's more than enough. Stop blaming yourself."

George actually looked forward to having Zac with him. For a short while at least. Before he reached the branding corral, the boy had peppered him with so many questions he was tempted to take him back. By the end of the day he wished he had.

"You make sure to wash up extra carefully tonight," George told Zac as they dismounted that evening. "If you don't, Rose might not let you come to the table. You're covered with enough dirt to plant a garden."

"I got to pour the milk," Zac protested.

"I'll pour it. I'd rather do that than have to smell you all night long. Of course, if you get done in a hurry, you can still pour it."

Zac was little, but he wasn't stupid. He took twice as much time as he needed. Everyone had a chance to get to the kitchen before he did.

When he bounded in the door, he saw a cake with seven flaming candles and a stack of presents at his place. His eyes grew as big as saucers.

"Is it all for me?" he asked, looking from George to Rose.

"Every bit of it," Rose assured him. "I don't know of anybody else who has a birthday."

"Wow!" Zac exclaimed. "I never got presents before. Or a cake."

George knew he couldn't have done anything about the birthdays Zac had missed, but it made him feel worse than ever. Even if he'd remembered Zac's birthday, he'd never have thought of getting the child a present or of asking Rose to make a cake.

Yet she had thought of everything. But then she always did. It seemed to come naturally with her. And not just big things like birthdays. Hardly a day passed without her doing something. Even for Jeff.

She would be a perfect mother. The look of pleasure on her face as she watched Zac's happiness made George feel good that she was enjoying herself, bad that her marriage to him was preventing her from having children.

"Chaps!" Zac shrieked when he unwrapped a very long brown package. "My own chaps."

Zac threw himself on his big brother and hugged him until he nearly broke his neck.

"How did you know I wanted chaps more than anything else in the world?" he asked, his eyes shining with happiness. "I never told anybody."

George opened his mouth to deny he had had anything to do with this wonderful surprise, but Rose shook her head ever so slightly. George realized that Zac would give her credit for the cake, but only a big brother could think of anything as wonderful as chaps. Rose wanted him to take the credit because Zac would like it better that way.

George swallowed his pride.

"What else could a man want when he has to ride through the brush?"

"But you won't let me. Can I now?"

"If you don't mind having Rose pick the thorns out of your hide."

"She doesn't pick out your thorns," Zac pointed out. "She doesn't pick out Hen's and Monty's either."

"We don't want her to see us cry," George said.

"You don't cry," Zac said, laughing because he was sharing a joke with his big brother. "You don't make a sound at all. It's Monty who makes all the noise."

"Rat on me, will you?" Monty said, making a playful grab for his little brother. Zac wisely hid himself in George's arms.

"You and Tyler hold George down while I rip the little rascal apart," Monty said to Hen. Hen and Tyler pretended to try to break George's hold on Zac while Monty tickled every part of the little boy he could reach.

Zac shrieked with laughter.

After the older boys tired of their play and turned back to their dinner, Zac ventured from the safety of his brother's arms to open his other presents. A shirt and a belt were cause for happy laughter, but a new pair of boots sent him jumping into George's arms again.

"You'll have to thank Rose this time," George said, determined not to take any more credit no matter what Zac or Rose wanted. "She picked them out especially for you."

It struck George all at once that Rose had been responsible for the happiest moments he'd enjoyed since he reached home. His brothers, too. He couldn't remember when they'd laughed so much. Even Tyler.

More guilt that he didn't love her. More guilt he couldn't give her children.

George forced his mind from those thoughts. He and Rose had crossed that bridge with their eyes open.

*No, she didn't. You never told her you didn't love her. And you didn't tell her until after you were married that you didn't want any children.*

*But she knew I didn't love her.*

*That doesn't make any difference. Many people who don't love each other have families.*

George wanted to run away. The weight of shame over the way he'd treated Rose, his obligation to his family, the responsibility for the ranch were beginning to pile up on him.

He hadn't come even close to solving the problem with Rose. His family, either. He didn't know whether he was doing the right thing with the ranch. They could lose the entire herd on a drive to St. Louis. He wasn't sure that any of them except Monty were cut out to be ranchers.

This must have been how his father had felt when things started to fall apart. George had never felt any sympathy for his father, only rage. Now he understood, and it scared him.

"My fertile time is over." Rose said it casually as she put away the remains of the cake, as though her words were of no importance.

George froze in his tracks. His brothers had just left the

room, Zac anxious to try out his chaps, Hen willing to teach him how to put them on. George had paused, searching for a way to tell Rose how much he appreciated what she had done. Some way that didn't make it sound like he was thanking her for a job well done.

"I just wanted you to know, in case you felt you had to sleep out at the camp."

It was an invitation. It was also the moment for him to decide what he was going to do about his marriage. A series of circumstances had allowed him to postpone making a decision. Now nothing stood in his way. He had to make some commitment to this woman or let her leave. He couldn't keep her here forever, loving him but waiting and wondering.

He nodded his understanding.

He could see the disappointment in her eyes. He could see it in her face, too. Her expression froze. She looked like something beautiful but inanimate.

"Thanks for the birthday party," he said, feeling on firmer ground. "But you shouldn't have given me credit for the chaps."

"I knew Zac would like them better coming from you."

"I know, or I wouldn't have let him thank me."

He paused. How did you tell a woman who looked at you with love in her eyes that something she had just done was sweet? It would be almost insulting.

"I don't know how you always seem to find just the right thing to do. I never can."

"Maybe certain things come more naturally to a woman," Rose said, a thin smile curving her lips. "You're doing more than enough as it is."

"Considering the way things are going at the camp, I don't know. I certainly can't get them to enjoy an evening as much as this."

"It's the things you do that make times like this possible," Rose said, a warmer look coming into her eyes. "There's much more to the success of a family than birthdays and presents."

She was trying to tell him something, but he didn't know

what it was. But that wasn't surprising. His family had never been happy. He had no experience of any times except unhappy ones.

"Maybe, but I don't seem to know what they are. Maybe I should turn the family over to you. You'd do a much better job."

He was feeling sorry for himself. No, he was still feeling guilty about forgetting Zac's birthday. And frustrated that he was still dithering, like a foolish adolescent, about Rose.

"If you think I could get Monty to listen to anything I had to say on the subject of cows . . ." She left it hanging.

George smiled, and the tension inside him eased. "I guess I'd better stick around a little longer. And if I'm to do that, I've got to talk to the twins before they go to bed."

He also had to have some time to think. Rose had clearly told him she wanted him to make love to her. He wanted it, too. He wanted it so badly he was surprised she didn't see it in his face. But he had a couple of things to get straight in his own mind first.

He knew that tonight was crucial for both of them. He knew what he wanted to do, but he wanted to make sure he was doing it for the right reason. It was vital that he be sure.

Rose lay in the bed. Wide awake. Waiting.

Would he come?

He hadn't said anything. He had just walked out.

They had reached a crisis point. At least she had. If she wasn't important enough for George to come to her tonight, then she wasn't important enough to be his wife. It hurt to say that, even in her thoughts. She had come too close to lose now.

No matter what happened, she would never forget George. Even if she never saw him again. She could never love anyone as she loved him. For the rest of her life she would measure every man she met against him.

She had memorized his features, his changing moods, whole

conversations, entire scenes. She knew every movement, every expression. He was part of her fiber. He would always be.

She wouldn't forget his brothers, either. She felt as if they were part of her now. And that was odd, considering the fact that *they* felt she was an outsider.

She thought of the ease with which she had fitted into the Robinson family. She had felt welcome from the first. By the end of the first week, she felt like she had always been a part of them. Why couldn't that happen here?

But she was a survivor. She had endured before George appeared in Austin, and she would survive if she never saw him or his brothers again.

The sound of an opening door caused her thoughts to snap like a thread, her breath to stop in her lungs. Footsteps in the kitchen. The handle on the door lifting.

George had come!

# *Chapter Seventeen*

She waited in the dim lamplight, the wick turned down to conserve precious fuel. He continually marveled at her loveliness. He couldn't understand how any man could let her father's fighting for the Union blind him to her beauty. Inside and out.

She looked so vulnerable. So fragile. So afraid of what he was going to do.

Or not do.

"I wasn't sure you would come," she said. Even her voice sounded anxious, as though she was afraid the slightest misstep might drive him away.

"I had some thinking to do."

"So did I."

George felt a tremor of uneasiness. It had never occurred to him that Rose might also have some questions which needed resolving. Fool! Why did he always think he was the only one who had to make decisions? He realized now he'd been doing that with the boys as well.

With Rose, too. He'd been taking her for granted, assuming she'd always be there, waiting, willing, forgiving, whenever he decided to turn to her.

George approached the bed. He sat down on the edge, facing Rose.

"Do you have things straight in your mind?" she asked.

"More than before."

He wished she would turn the wick up. He couldn't see her expression. He wanted to know how she felt about what he was going to say.

"You mind if I go first?" she asked.

George felt his stomach knot. There was nothing of the happy, comfortable Rose of earlier that evening. She seemed terribly serious. Unhappily so.

"No."

She didn't start right away. She didn't look at him either. And that made him even more nervous. If she found it so difficult to find the right words, it could only be because she felt they were words he wouldn't like. She looked up, straight into his eyes.

"I don't know why you asked me to marry you. Quite frankly, I've been afraid to ask."

She lowered her eyes. She seemed reluctant to continue.

"You know I love you," she said. "I never made a secret of that."

He didn't know how to respond, didn't know what to say.

"I'm afraid that love betrayed me into making some promises I don't think I can keep," she went on.

The queasiness in his stomach grew worse.

"I said I understood your fear of responsibility, that I would never tie you down. I do understand, but I can't go on living here waiting for you to decide you want to come to me, fearing you will change your mind any minute. That used to be enough, at least I used to think it was, but it's not anymore."

Was she about to tell him she wanted to leave?

"When I came here, I had a fantasy about St. George rescuing me. I knew it was unrealistic, just a child's fairy tale, but I believed if I could stay here a while, somehow things would work out."

"But they didn't."

"I fell in love with you. Then Zac seduced me with his impish grin. Next I became awfully fond of Hen. I even like Monty when he's not shouting or trying to stampede me by the sheer force of his personality. I don't mind Tyler, and I worry about Jeff."

"You learned to care about all of us."

"You've got a wonderful family. They are so bright, energetic, and fiercely loyal. Each of you has so much love to give, but you're afraid to reach out for fear it'll be refused."

"They haven't refused you."

"No, but they're holding back. They're waiting for you. They won't let themselves love me as long as you don't."

George was stunned. It had never occurred to him that his brothers' decisions might rest on his own. It was an even greater shock that they would hold back from something they wanted just because of him. And to think he'd been holding back because of them.

If Rose was right. . . .

"No one can live here as I have and not become deeply involved with your family," Rose continued. "It hurts to still be on the outside. I don't think I can stand it any longer."

"You want to go back to Austin?"

"No!" She spoke softly, but the intensity was unmistakable. "I want to stay here for the rest of my life, but I can't. Not the way things are. I thought I could, but I can't. Can you understand how I feel?"

*Can you? You've never thought about anything from anybody's point of view but your own.*

He was trying, but he'd been so absorbed by his own fears, his concern for his family, he hadn't learned to see anything from someone else's point of view.

And much to his shock, he also hadn't had time to consult his own feelings. He had to now because Rose was on the point of leaving them. Of leaving him. And clearer than anything he'd ever known in his life, he knew he didn't want her to go.

"I'm beginning to," George said, "but you're wrong about not being accepted by the family. There are times I think Zac loves you more than he loves the rest of us."

"Zac wants to love me, but even though he doesn't understand what he's doing, he's keeping his distance, waiting for you to let him know it's all right."

"You think he can understand things like that?"

Rose looked at him as if she thought he was handsome and wonderful but something of an idiot.

"All of them understand. Look at Monty. He used to tease me. When it became clear there was something between us, he backed off. If he thought you loved me, he would start to tease me again, but like a sister this time."

George had seen what Rose was talking about but had just assumed that Monty was being difficult as usual.

"Even Jeff is waiting. He may decide to leave. He may decide to come back. But until you make up your mind, he's going to wait."

George felt worse than before. Not only had he failed Rose. He'd failed his family as well.

"I never meant for this to happen," he said.

"I know. The last thing you wanted was a woman to complicate your life."

"After watching my parents, I decided not to risk making their mistakes. Then I met you, and everything started to change. You ask why I married you. I couldn't do anything else. That may seem a stupid thing for a grown man to say, especially one who's set himself up to tell everybody else what they ought to do, but it's the truth. My feelings for you have grown stronger every day, but I can't tell whether I just like you a lot, whether you've made me so comfortable I can't bear to give you up, or whether I'm drawn to you because you're the most beautiful woman I've ever seen."

"Is that all?"

"No. I keep telling myself I'm crazy to keep doing exactly what I don't want to do, what I never meant to do. Then I realize I don't *not want it* anymore, that I actually like it very much. But when I look inside and see I'm still the same person, I start to wonder about my motives. Am I feeling this way because I want to use you for my own pleasure, or have my feelings really changed enough that I might have grown to love you without knowing it?"

"And what did you decide?" The anxiety in her voice was plain.

"I realized I don't know what love is. I've never seen it. I don't count Ma's love for Pa. It made her blind to what he was. I don't think love blinds you to truth. If it does, I don't want it. My feelings for you are very strong, but I don't know if they're strong enough. Everything else doesn't cease to matter when I look at you. I couldn't count the world well lost as long as I could hold you in my arms. No matter how much I want you, I can't forget my brothers. I just know I can't let you leave."

Rose hardly dared let herself hope again. What made her think anything was going to change now? George was married to his brothers and his obsessive fear of being like his father. What chance did she have against such powerful forces?

Yet even as her brain told her that George still hadn't made a commitment to her, that he still hadn't been able to decide she was more important than his family, she realized he had made another step forward. Small, but still a step forward. He had decided that in the face of all his difficulties, he didn't want her to leave.

Maybe he did love her and just didn't know it.

She wanted to believe that. She wanted it desperately. But

could she stand another disappointment? It didn't help to know that George had never promised her anything, that she had done this to herself. It had happened, it was nobody's fault, but she was the one who was suffering.

And George. He suffered, too.

George was trying to learn how to love. Could she desert him just when he was about to reach out to her? And not just as a lover. He was reaching out to save himself from the morass of his own doubt, from the terrible sense of worthlessness about to drown him.

She wanted to be his lover, not his savior, but she realized it might not be possible to be the one until she had been the other. He had reached out and saved her against his will. Didn't she owe him the same?

Maybe, but she didn't want to stay with him because she owed him something. She wanted him to stay with her because he loved her, because he couldn't do anything else.

*That's exactly what he said, you little fool. He said he married you because he couldn't do anything else.*

He did love her! He was approaching knowledge slowly, unable to see his way, unable to catch sight of his goal, but he was coming, steadily, inexorably.

But how long could she wait? Could she withstand disappointment once again?

She could stand anything as long as George loved her. She knew that. She might not like to admit it, she certainly didn't want to have to endure it, but like George, she would stay because she couldn't do anything else.

"I'll stay if you're sure you want me," she said.

"Even though I can make no promises?"

"Do you want me even though I can't make any either?"

His answer was instantaneous. "Yes. And I will make you one promise."

Rose felt disappointment. She knew he was going to promise to take care of her. She also knew it was no longer enough.

"I promise to try to learn to love you. I want to."

Rose was so happy she almost jumped up and threw her arms around George. She'd have done it if she hadn't been afraid it would cause him to withdraw. He did love her. He only needed some more time to realize it.

"And I promise to wait as long as it takes."

Rose felt as if they were pledging their vows for the first time, that this time their lives were truly bound together. If he made love to her tonight, their marriage would truly begin. She reached out and took his hand.

"Are you going to stay with me?"

"Are you sure you want me to? I can't leave you untouched. I tried, but I can't any longer."

"I don't want you to."

George felt his whole body tremble with hunger. Even as his fingers took hers in his grasp, he felt the heat of desire begin to spread through his loins. He knew if he didn't leave now, he'd never be able to tear himself away from her.

But he didn't want to leave. Tonight he had decided he wanted Rose with him for the rest of his life. And he would do what it took to keep her here.

George felt the tension flow from his body. Not the tension caused by Rose's invitation. Not the tension of anticipation that caused his muscles to quiver. But the tension that kept his senses from focusing entirely on the fulfillment of a longing that had been tearing him apart for weeks.

George moved up on the bed until he lay alongside Rose. For the first time he felt as if he belonged here. He didn't feel the fear of his own failure or the nagging guilt about his intentions. He felt happy. At ease.

He felt content.

Almost without conscious thought, he reached out and let his fingers move over her skin. More than an act of passion, it was an act of commitment. It established a line of communication between them. It said he wanted her; he desired her. It also said he would continue to want her for the rest of his life.

His head sank until his lips brushed the top of her breast, scattering feathered kisses across her velvety smooth skin. His lips said he wanted her, that he desired her. They also said he would cherish her, that she was precious to him. That he would care for her as long as he was able.

The subtle scent of violets assailed his nostrils. He usually liked it, but tonight he wanted to inhale Rose's scent, not something from a soap.

Yet the scent seemed to fit her. Strong, yet not heavy or clinging. Like Rose herself.

He tasted her skin. It tasted faintly of moisture. Moisture produced by the warmth of the night. Moisture produced by uncertainty. By desire.

He, too, felt damp. The fire building inside him would soon cause him to break out in a fierce sweat. Already his body had begun to swell with urgent need. George shifted to get more comfortable, to be able to roll on his elbow so his lips could range over still more of Rose's tempting perfection. But as he planted a chain of kisses across her shoulder and along her collarbone, his body grew taut with need. His right hand covered Rose's breast, caressing it through the thin cotton of her nightgown.

Responding to the primeval urge to capture and possess, he claimed her as his own. He encompassed her with his passion, surrounded her with his desire, draped her in his need, covered her with his heat.

Rose moaned softly. She rolled toward George, bringing her body into full contact with his. The feel of her against his whole length stretched George's self-control to the limit. Using every bit of restraint he could muster to keep from throwing himself on her, he raised himself until he could kiss Rose's closed eyelids. A kiss dropped on the tip of her nose, a more demanding kiss on her parted lips.

Rose moaned again and wiggled against him. Her mouth responded to his, and George deepened his kiss. Her arms wound themselves around his neck as she pushed her body hard against him. Her breasts, firm and full, pushed hard against his chest, their firming peaks burning his skin. Her scent filled his nostrils; the moisture of her skin mingled with his. The taste of her mouth invited him to ask for more.

George moaned. And not softly. It was the moan of a man deep in the toils of desire. Even as his tongue forced its way into Rose's mouth, his hands slipped the straps over her shoulders and freed her breasts from the light restraint of her gown. With a growl of desire, he attacked one nipple with his hungry mouth, the other with his fingertips.

Rose's response was instantaneous and dramatic. Her hands gripped his head and pressed him hard against her body.

Gripping the bed to keep from devouring her in a single gulp, George focused his mind on Rose's breasts rather than his own need. He had waited so long he intended to go slowly, to savor every minute, every touch, every taste. To savor the sound of her gasp of shock when he took her firm nipple between his teeth. To savor her excitement as he teased her with his hot tongue.

When George realized he was more aware of his restraint than he was of the pleasure of exploring Rose's body, he threw restraint to the winds. He would take his leisure some other time. Tonight he would explode if he had to wait another minute.

Rose helped him slip her gown down her body and under her hips. She seemed to be in more of a hurry than he was to remove all barriers between them.

She seemed unaware of her nakedness. He was aware of nothing else. He couldn't get enough of her. His eyes, his lips, his fingertips, every part of him wanted to explore her body in frantic haste. All failed to do anything more than fan the flames that were even now lapping around the edge of his senses.

Driven by a desire which had been ignited on that day long ago when he first saw her in the Bon Ton, he quickly came out of his clothes and joined her on the bed.

"This may be uncomfortable at first," he said as he parted her thighs.

Rose's body relaxed, welcoming him. She arched off the bed as his fingers sank into her moist heat. Moan after soft moan escaped her lips as he plunged inside her, preparing her for his entry. He should have waited longer, should have taken more time to be sure she could accommodate him, but when she threw herself against him, he lost all ability to wait.

"This will hurt, but only for a moment," George said as he poised himself above Rose.

Then he claimed her. The way men have claimed their women since time began. With their bodies. With their minds. And with their souls.

It took every bit of restraint he possessed to ease into her body rather than plunge in. Rose practiced none of his control. Even as he prepared himself to break through her virgin's sheath, she threw herself against him, forcing him deep into her.

George abandoned control. Riding the bucking of his desire with wild abandon, he drove straight toward fulfillment. He only slowed his rhythm so that Rose could keep pace.

But as he felt the wave of sweet agony begin to swirl higher and higher around him, he rushed ahead, bringing them both to a shattering release of the tension which had held them in bondage for so long.

They lay side by side for some time. Neither of them spoke. As his senses returned to normal, George found it hard to believe he had just made love to his wife. But he only had to turn his head or reach out to discover that Rose was really there, warm and inviting.

The feeling of contentment had returned. He could feel it spread over him like a comforting blanket. If he'd had any doubts that he'd done the right thing, he had them no longer.

It was the first feeling of true peace he could remember experiencing in his whole life.

\* \* \*

George woke with the first rays of sunlight.

His gaze fell on Rose. She lay facing him, her eyes closed in sleep. He slowly raised his head and rolled up on his elbow so he could get a better look. He didn't know how it was possible, but she looked even more lovely in sleep. Her slightly disordered appearance provided just the right feeling. As if nothing in the world could threaten her rest.

But something disturbed George's repose. Rose's nearness. She was only inches away, one arm across her body. His lips were a mere breath away from hers, her barely clad breasts, the alabaster perfection of her neck and bare shoulders.

He could feel the heat of desire start to rise within him. He could still feel the glow from last night.

He wanted Rose. He had known that from the first, but he'd never known she could make such a difference in the way he felt. He wasn't sure what that difference was. He only just this minute realized he felt different about everything. But he knew it was better.

He'd never felt so good, or so good about himself. He couldn't explain that either, but he wasn't going to try. He was just going to enjoy it for as long as it lasted.

It would end. Not even Rose could make life something it wasn't, but he knew that this feeling would never be far away. Only as far away as Rose. All he had to do was reach out.

He touched her cheek. It felt soft and cool. Dry. He brushed her lips. They felt dry, too. Apparently she felt none of the heat that even now was causing drops of moisture on his skin.

George trailed his fingers across the planes of her face, brushed past her ear, whisked them down the slim column of her throat, and feathered them across her shoulder. He didn't know why it felt so enjoyable just to be able to touch her. He'd touched women before, but it hadn't been anything like this.

It was more than a physical hunger for her body, a stirring need to find release for his own sexual drive. It was a need to know her, to discover all there was to learn about her body. To linger over her lips. To see if kisses felt better in the hollow of her shoulder or the hollow of her throat. To determine if the skin was softer on her breast or her lips. To discover where his touch excited her the most. She was a labyrinth of secrets, and he must learn the answer to every one.

Rose stirred under his touch.

He kissed her awake.

"What time is it?" she murmured.

"Daybreak."

"I've got to get up," Rose said, trying to sit up. "They'll be wanting breakfast soon."

George pulled her back down next to him. "They can wait a few minutes longer." His hand dipped into her gown and cupped her breast. Rose's gaze flew to his eyes.

"We can't. If we're not out when they come into the kitchen, they'll know what we're doing."

"I don't care if the whole world knows," George said as he slipped Rose's gown over her shoulders and drew her to him. "We're man and wife."

"But—"

"No buts," George said as he pushed her gown down her body. "I've never felt so free in my whole life. I don't know how I'll feel once I step through that door, but right now I don't care. I need you."

George was shocked to realize he had just told Rose he needed her. He did, more than he had ever imagined possible, but he hadn't felt he could admit it to anyone. But he just had, and it had been easy.

That made him feel even better. He wondered what new wonders Rose could work in his spirit.

But he would save that for later. Right now he wanted to wrap himself in the wonders of her body.

"Jeff, I've changed my plans. Stay after the others leave, and I'll explain."

George had ridden out to the camp with the twins, but he had taken almost no part in their teasing banter as they rode along. He felt like a man reborn. All because of Rose.

He must have her. No matter what he had to do. No matter what he had to give up. It had seemed so difficult before, so complicated. Now it seemed easy, natural.

"What are you going to do now?" Jeff asked. He was as sulky as ever. Obviously nothing had changed with him.

"I talked it over with the twins. It's too late in the season to make a drive to St. Louis. I don't know if we'd make it before winter. With the dry summer, I doubt we could find enough grass and water."

"Then wait till the spring. I told you that before."

"We can't wait that long," George said. "I want you to go see King now."

"In person?"

"Yes. Go to his ranch if you have to, but talk to him yourself."

"There's nothing to talk about. We don't have any money to buy cows."

"I want to make a trade. He'll make a drive to St. Louis in the spring. It'll be easier for his men than for us. They have the experience, the manpower, the knowledge of the trails. Offer to trade him steers for cows. It won't be a problem to drive the steers to his ranch. Find out if he'll trade and for how much. I'd like to get one cow for every two steers."

"Whose idea is this?" Jeff demanded.

"Mine," George said.

"That's about the only sensible idea you've come up with since we got back," Jeff said, "but I don't know if King will go for it."

"Neither do I, but if anybody can talk him into it, you can."

Jeff looked startled, then distrustful, as if expecting a trick.

"What makes you say that?"

"You're very persuasive when you want to be. You're also tight as a tick with money. We need the very best deal we can get, and you're the one to get it for us."

Jeff looked a little flustered by the compliment. He had apparently expected some sort of argument when George asked him to stay behind. His defenses had been up. His jaw set, his teeth clenched. Now he looked surprised.

"Suppose King won't trade?"

"There must be other ranchers shipping out in the spring. Or agents looking to buy a herd. You might even find someone willing to take our herd with him for a commission. I don't like the idea of going that far until you boys have had a chance to go over that trail with somebody who knows it. Ask him if the twins can go with him next spring."

"How much should I ask for?"

"As much as you can get, but don't settle for less than twelve dollars a head. If you can't get more, we'll have to take them ourselves. Otherwise we might as well sell them for hides and tallow."

"When do you want me to leave?"

"The sooner the better. I asked Rose to see that your clothes were ready to pack."

Jeff's expression went from sulky to sullen. George ignored it.

"There's also something else I want you to do while you're in Austin," George said. He went over to his horse and returned with something long and slim wrapped in a cloth.

"That's your sword," Jeff said. "Is something wrong with it? I doubt they have anybody in Austin who can work on anything as fine as that."

"Nothing's wrong with it," George said, handing it to Jeff. "I want you to sell it."

"Sell it! Why? We're not that short of money."

"I want you to sell it and buy a wedding ring for Rose."

Jeff looked thunderous.

"Take it to McGrath and Hayden. Ask for Jim Hayden. I've already spoken to him. He knows the ring I want. He'll give you a good price."

"Damn, I won't do it. I can't sell your sword to buy a ring for—"

"You'd better think before you finish that sentence," George warned. "And while you're thinking, try to remember you're speaking about my wife."

"But—"

"There are no buts, Jeff. You seem to think your getting mad will change everything, but it won't. Rose is going to keep on being my wife no matter what you do."

"I keep hoping you'll come to your senses and—"

"And do what? Send her back to Austin? Divorce her? What for? She hasn't done anything except take better care of us than our own mother."

"How can you say that?"

"Because it's true. Pa never took care of anybody. And Ma never took our side against him. Maybe you don't remember, but I do." His eyes grew just as hard as Jeff's. He remembered the beatings when his mother had stood by, helpless. He remembered the anger he'd harbored against her for her weakness. "Rose would kill me if I tried to do half the things to Zac that Pa did to me, and you know it."

"I'm not buying a ring for that woman. Even if I were, I wouldn't sell your sword to do it. It's sacred."

"It's nothing but a sword, Jeff. It only reminds me of four terrible years I'd just as soon forget. You see a cause, the beliefs we fought for. I see the boys I commanded shot to pieces, some so badly mangled I didn't even know who they were."

"I still don't think you ought to sell it."

"I can't use the family's money. That ring has to come from me. And this is the only way I can do it."

"I won't do it. I can't."

"Which? Buy the ring for Rose or sell the sword?"

"Both."

George looked at his brother's twisted, unhappy face and some of his own anger faded. He could have been the one to lose his arm. How did he know he wouldn't be just as angry and bitter?

"Jeff, you're going to have to let go of the war. Right or wrong, it's over. There's no going back, no doing it over again. If you keep looking over your shoulder, you're going to make yourself miserable and everybody around you unhappy."

"How am I going to forget?" Jeff shouted, waving his stub in George's face.

"By letting go of the hatred. You may be mad at the Yankees, but you're taking it out on us."

"If you're talking about Rose—"

"I am, but I'm talking about the twins as well. And Zac and Tyler. And me. Nobody is happy when you're around. Haven't you noticed how they all fall silent when you join us?"

"They can't stand being around a cripple."

"Believe it or not, they love you. They'd show you, but you won't let them."

"That's a damned lie. They can't wait to get out of the room. Monty practically falls over himself."

"Why should he stay? You haven't said a nice thing to him since you got back."

"He's a bigoted, narrow-minded, stubborn, irritable—"

"No more than you."

Jeff looked as if he would explode with rage. "Monty's ten times worse than I ever was."

"Ask Rose if you don't believe me."

"I wouldn't ask her anything."

"You should. You might learn some things that would surprise you. Help you, too."

"If you mean to start relaying Rose's advice, you can save your breath."

"I only mean to give you one piece of advice," George said. "You're going to have to choose between your family and your bitterness."

"You're just trying to force me to accept Rose. You know I never will."

"I'm telling you that you're in the process of alienating the only people in the world who have reason to love you no matter how much you try to act like a miserable, hate-filled bastard.

Rose is a part of that family now. In a few years Monty and Hen will marry. You can't reject their wives without rejecting them as well."

"They won't marry Yankees."

"Probably not, but that choice won't be yours. You have to be prepared to accept them no matter who they marry."

"I can't do that."

"Well, you give it some thought on your way to Corpus Christi. You think about it while you're talking to Mr. King. You think about it when you're selling my sword, and you think about it while you're buying that ring for Rose. You decide what's more important to you—this family or your anger. You can even spend a few extra days in Austin if you need to be real sure. If you decide for the family, we'll be only too happy to see you sleeping at the house once again. If not, you'd better send the ring."

"Are you telling me to leave?"

"I'm telling you to make a choice. I'm not going to let you destroy this family."

"You're doing that with your Yankee wife."

George thought Jeff's words would make him mad, but thinking about Rose made it impossible for him to get angry.

"You should have been at the house yesterday. My *Yankee* wife gave Zac a birthday party. None of his brothers remembered his birthday. None of his brothers thought to bake a cake or buy him presents. Just my *Yankee* wife. She used the money we paid her to buy our brother chaps. Do you know how that made me feel?"

"Did he like them?"

"He didn't come down to earth for hours. And you know what else my *Yankee* wife did? She made me take credit for buying them. By this time I was so disgusted with myself I could hardly hold my head up. The only thing Zac really wanted for his birthday, and I didn't know."

Jeff didn't say anything.

"I've never seen that boy so happy. Monty and Hen started teasing him. Even Tyler seemed to enjoy it. All four of them ended up wrestling in one big knot on the floor. Have you been able to give the family an evening like that? I haven't, but my Yankee wife did. People suffered on both sides during this war, Jeff. I know that won't change what happened to you. It won't bring Pa back either, but neither will remembering."

"So if I don't forget about this"—he waved his stub at George—"and Pa, and all the rest, I'd better go."

George heaved a weary sigh. It seemed his words had no effect. But he couldn't stop trying.

"None of us will forget the war, Jeff. It'll always be part of us, but it's only a part. As the years go by, that part will become smaller and easier to bear. But we've got to start now, when it's hardest."

"I can't ever forget what her father did."

"I didn't ask you to forget it. Rose won't. I just ask you not to hold it against her. You'll never be welcomed into any man's home if you can't have respect for his wife."

"Tell me you love her," Jeff said, flaring up, all his anger distilled into his challenge. "I've never heard you say it. I don't believe you can."

"Would it change your mind about Rose?"

"It might. If you meant it. But I don't believe you do."

Hissing impatiently, George started to turn Jeff's question aside. This wasn't about him and Rose. But then maybe it was. He didn't know. Jeff had asked the question. Maybe it would give him one of the answers he needed.

"I realized a few days ago I didn't know what love was."

"Ma worshiped Pa," Jeff objected, indignant. "She was obsessed with him."

"That's one of the reasons I was so afraid of marriage. I loved Ma, but I didn't want to marry anybody like her. To me love was helpless, suffocating, painful. It wasn't until Rose came that I realized that love was strong, that it meant standing up for yourself, saying things nobody wanted to hear. I also know it means giving of yourself because it makes somebody else happy. I don't know if I love Rose. For a while I was sure I didn't, but—"

"I knew it. I knew it!"

"—but now I'm not sure. I know I need her, that I can't imagine living the rest of my life without her. Is that love? I think it's part of it. I know I want her. She comforts my spirit and body as nothing ever has. That's part of love, too. I also know I'm never as happy as I am when I'm with her."

"You sound like you're obsessed."

"Maybe that's also part of love. I don't know, but I'm going to learn. It's embarrassing sometimes. I feel like a child. But I learn a little something every day. It's like a whole new way of living. It's a willingness to give up control. To make a commitment and have faith it'll work out."

"It sounds like you've gone crazy," Jeff said, scowling.

"Maybe that's part of it, too. Whatever it is, it's something I want more than I ever thought possible. And Rose is the only one who can teach me. I'm not giving her up, Jeff, no matter what it costs me."

"Hell!" Jeff barked. "You are in love with her."

# Chapter Eighteen

George's sixth sense saved them.

Rain threatened. The heavy, humid atmosphere seemed to unsettle the longhorns. Just as the men had finished for the day, a particularly wild steer broke through the fence taking most of the day's gather with him. By the time they had located the herd and put a bullet through the head of the instigator, it was too late to go back to the ranch. They had skinned the steer, cooked as much of the meat as they could eat, and wandered off to sleep, dead tired. They wanted to get as much rest as they could before they got wet.

Something woke George. It might have been the wind moaning through the trees. Or a splintering limb. It was too dark to see. Storm clouds obscured the moon. The only light came from the dying embers of the fire.

One of the dogs was awake, his head pointed downwind. He growled low in his throat. He looked toward Monty, whined uneasily, then looked back into the night. He growled again.

George didn't know how he knew they were about to be attacked. He just did. Reaching for his gun, he fired into the blackness.

"Someone's coming at us from the creek!" he shouted to his sleeping crew.

The raiders came with a rush, riding their mules and scrub ponies through the center of camp and firing indiscriminately.

The crew scrambled out of their beds, desperately trying to reach any cover they could find. By the time they found their weapons, the raiders were gone. It was impossible to tell how many there were. They wore dark clothes and must have blackened their faces.

The attackers rode straight through to the Mexican camp about fifty yards away.

The raiders found no one at the camp. The *vaqueros* were as adept at disappearing into the brush as the longhorns. George could hear the noise of a wagon being overturned, crockery breaking, metal clanging noisily against metal. The raiders were trying to ruin the Mexicans' supplies and equipment.

Then they turned and rode back through George's camp, a thundering, charging mass in the dark. George guessed there must have been thirty or forty men. His crew wouldn't have stood much chance against such overwhelming numbers if it hadn't been for one rifle, firing with nerve-racking regularity, that picked off one after another of the raiders. By the time the last of them had raced through the camp, four men were swaying in their saddles.

"Hen, is that you?" George called out to the rifleman. He received no answer.

The raiders turned and headed back again, scattered along a broad front this time, but the deadly rifle picked off three more. The attack broke before they reached the camp. The raiders melted into the dark, the hoofbeats fading quickly into the thick atmosphere.

"The McClendons, the goddamned sons-of-bitches!" Monty cursed, emerging from his cover behind the log he sat on while he ate his meals. "I thought they'd have come before this if they were coming at all."

"Are you sure it's not the Mexican bandits we stampeded coming back from Austin?" Salty asked.

"Naw, it had to be the McClendons. No self-respecting bandit would be caught dead on one of their nags."

"It doesn't matter who it is, they both want the same thing," George said. "Make sure everybody's all right. Salty, do we have any medicine?"

"Not for gunshot wounds."

"If anybody's hurt, we'll have to take them back to the house." But nobody seemed to be hurt.

"See how the *vaqueros* are doing, Monty," George said.

"I'll warrant they were a hundred feet into the brush by the time those sons-of-bitches passed through our camp."

"Check on them anyway." Monty headed off.

"Looks like we'll have to post a guard from now on," George said.

"Just like the army. Do we stand guard in pairs or alone?" Silas asked.

"One's enough. The dogs will be more help than an extra man."

"You ought to let young Alex stand the first watch. He's always the last to go to sleep."

"Where is Alex?" George asked. "Has anybody seen him?"

"No, now that you mention it," Salty said.

Without a word, Hen plunged into the surrounding darkness, heading toward the clump of bushes where Alex had bedded down. Alex always liked to have something to sleep under. He had come from the hills of Alabama and didn't trust wide open spaces. They made him nervous, he said. He liked woods better anytime.

He was a skinny lad, looking much younger than his twenty-three years. He had a happy disposition and was a favorite of everyone. He and Hen had become particularly fast friends. George had never understood it—they were so different. With a sinking heart, George followed Hen.

Hen put his hand out to part the branches over Alex's bed. He froze, his hand still in midair. From the way the boy hunched his shoulders, the muscles becoming steel-hard, George didn't have to ask any questions. He knew what he would find.

Even after four years of war, the sight made George sick to his stomach. A shotgun blast must have caught him at close range about the time he got to his feet. He was unrecognizable.

Instinctively George reached out and gripped Hen's shoulder. He felt the muscles hunch, the tension build, but Hen didn't shrug him off.

"He meant to head for Santa Fe come spring," Hen said, his voice low. "Said he knew a girl out there. With sandy hair and freckles."

"We'll write. I'm sure she'd want to know."

"He wanted a place in the hills. Never did sleep good on flat land."

"We'll bury him on the highest hill we can find," George promised. "First thing in the morning."

"Hadn't we better get ready in case they come back?" Salty asked.

"The sons-of-bitches won't come back," Monty said, contempt in his voice. "They're cowards. They expected to catch us by surprise. They'd attack women and children before they'd face us again."

"The house!" George exclaimed. Cold fear gripped him. The McClendons must have headed for the ranch when their second attack failed. Rose, Tyler, and Zac were alone.

He started for his horse at a dead run. The men came streaming behind him.

Rose didn't notice the sound at first. She was telling Zac a story. It was particularly important she tell it well because Tyler was listening. He pretended to be asleep, but she knew he wasn't. He thought he was too big to be interested in stories, but she remembered she had enjoyed them as late as the time her father left for the war.

"But when the prince came to the castle, he couldn't get in. Vines covered the doors and windows."

"He could chop them down," Zac said.

"He didn't have an ax," Rose replied, a little cross at Zac's constant interruptions.

"How could he chop wood for the stove?"

"Princes don't carry axes, you stupid boy," Tyler said, sitting up in his bed. "They dress up in shiny armor and carry swords."

"Somebody has to cut wood," Zac insisted. "How will the princess cook breakfast?"

"Don't you know anything?" Tyler said, exasperated. "Princesses don't cook."

"Rose does."

"Bless you, child," Rose said, giving Zac a kiss on the top of his head, much to the boy's disgust, "but I'm not a princess. The palace woodcutter cuts the wood," she said, hoping to end the quarrel. "A prince never carries an ax. It's not very princely."

"Oh," said Zac, apparently satisfied.

"Now let me see, where was I? Oh, I remember. He walked all the way around the castle looking for a way in, but everything was covered in vines. And the vines had lots of long, sharp thorns."

"Like cat's claw?" Zac asked.

"Ssshhh!" Rose said. "Did you hear that? It sounded like gunshots."

"Probably Monty getting a turkey. He said it was time you cooked another one."

But Monty wouldn't shoot that many turkeys. Nor would he miss that many times.

"Something's wrong," Rose said. She jumped up and ran to the door. The boys followed. Outside the shots were much louder. And there were a lot more of them.

"It's the camp," Tyler said. "Somebody's attacking the camp. I've got to go help."

"Wait!" Rose said.

"They'll need me."

"They may come here," Rose said.

Tyler froze.

"They wouldn't come here unless . . ."

"There may be two groups of them," Rose said, unwilling to allow her mind to finish Tyler's thought. "Anybody who would attack the camp would attack the house."

"I'll go find out," Tyler volunteered.

"No. The men can take care of themselves. We've got to be ready in case they come here. Get every gun you can find. And all the ammunition."

"Do you know how to shoot?"

"Well enough. Don't forget, I'm a colonel's daughter."

"Can I shoot, too?" Zac asked.

"I want you to load."

"But I want to shoot."

"This is no time to argue. Tyler and I may not be able to leave the windows. Someone will have to load our guns. Can you do that?"

Zac nodded, his eyes positively dancing with excitement.

This was nothing more than an adventure to him, like a battle from one of her fairy tales.

"Quick, try to hide the bull. But if you hear them coming, get back here as fast as you can."

Rose checked the field of fire from each of the windows while Tyler gathered the guns and ammunition.

"I'll cover them from our bedroom," Tyler said. "You cover them from the kitchen."

"I want us all in the same room," Rose said. "If we have to make a run for it, I want us all together."

The stack of rifles and boxes of ammunition in the middle of the floor amazed her. Hen and Monty must have stocked the house in case they had to withstand a prolonged attack. Tonight she was grateful they had.

Zac burst into the room.

"They're coming!" he shouted. "I heard them coming along the creek."

"How many?" Rose asked.

"Hundreds," Zac replied.

"You sit right here in the middle of the floor. Keep the lantern turned down low. No matter what we do, don't you stop loading. Our lives may depend on it."

Zac didn't look like he was having as much fun now. Sitting in the middle of a dozen boxes of rifle shells took away some of the excitement.

"I bet they'll go for the horses and the corral."

"We can't help that," Rose said.

"I could sneak out behind the house—"

"No!" Rose said, her voice almost a shriek. "I can't risk your being out there without cover."

Rose heard panic in her voice, and it shocked her. How could she expect the boys to remain calm if she didn't? She would need all her concentration. Still she felt the fear rising in her like oil up a wick.

She would not panic. Her father had been an officer. He

had endured many battles, but he had never panicked, not even under fire.

Neither would George. And he would be depending on her to keep her head, to make sure that nothing happened to his brothers. She thought of what these two boys meant to George, what they meant to her, and started to get mad. She didn't know who was about to attack the house, but only base cowards attacked women and children.

Anger slew her fear.

"When you see them coming, pick out one man and aim for him," Rose told Tyler. "Don't even glance at anybody else. It'll ruin your aim."

Her father had taught her that. Pick your target, he would say, and forget there's anybody else out there.

"Start over here with me," she told Tyler. "Change to the other window if they go around."

The raiders burst into the yard at a gallop. They seemed to pop out of the darkness without warning.

Both Rose and Tyler fired as fast as they could. The attackers, apparently expecting to take the house by surprise, were driven back in confusion.

"Keep firing," Rose ordered as she handed her empty rifle to Zac and picked up another one. "We've got to keep the pressure on them."

The concussion of the rifle shots inside the room almost deafened Rose. She was certain the noise would permanently scramble her brain, but she concentrated fiercely on the men who were even now preparing for a second run at the house.

"Do you know who they are?" she asked Tyler.

"McClendons!" the boy shouted at her without slowing his firing.

"Who's the leader?"

"The old man. The one who looks like he's been smoked and cured."

"I'll aim for him," Rose said. "You get the one closest to you."

She discarded a second rifle just as they started a second charge. She peered into the heaviness of the night, waiting for the grizzled old man to appear.

"They're circling the house from both sides," Tyler warned.

"Get to the other window," she called without taking her eyes off the heavy black mist that shielded the raiders from her view. Rain had started to fall, making it even harder to see. Maybe it would wet the raiders' guns, making them harder to fire.

They burst out of the darkness almost at her window. Startled by the suddenness of their appearance, Rose nearly failed to shoot. Gathering her wits quickly, she aimed for the old man. She missed, but she had the satisfaction of seeing shock on his face. She must have come close.

When he turned she saw the tear in his sleeve. She had hit him. She fired again and again without hitting him, but she did hit one of the others. She discarded her rifle without looking back, picked up the next one, and resumed firing.

"How are you doing on your side?" she asked Tyler.

"I winged a couple. They're drawing off, but there're so many of them."

"Do you think we can hold them off?"

"Not if they decide to rush the breezeway."

"I don't think they will," Rose said, surprised she had a definite opinion about fighting, something she knew nothing about. "The old man looked pretty surprised when I hit him. And that bullet couldn't have done more than graze him."

"What are they doing now?" Tyler asked. "I can't see anything."

"I don't know. I'm afraid they're going after the bull. Did you hide him, Zac?"

"I couldn't find him," the boy answered. "They came too quick."

Rose heard a single shot in the distance. She didn't hear a second. The raiders had obviously shot at something. The single shot meant they had hit their target. She felt sick. They had found the bull. George would be enraged. It would destroy all his plans.

"Tyler, grab a rifle and follow me."

"What are we going to do?"

"We're going to chase them off. They don't know the ranch, and they can't see us in the dark. We ought to be able to get a couple of them before they know we're out there."

"But they'll kill us once they locate where our rifle fire is coming from."

"We aren't going to stay out there. Zac, you stand by the door. Don't open it until you hear my voice. Do you understand?"

The child nodded.

Rose hadn't gone five steps outside the door when she wished she were back inside. She had never realized how comforting it was to be behind a thick wall. No bullet could penetrate those logs. Out here there was nothing to stop them.

"They're by the corrals," she whispered to Tyler.

"I bet they're pulling them down, the bastards," he hissed back.

They were. They tied several ropes to each post and one by one pulled them out of the ground. They probably would have burned them if it hadn't been raining so hard.

"Sons-of-bitches!" Tyler hissed and raised his rifle.

"Wait!" Rose hissed. "We've got to shoot together. We won't get more than one or two shots before they see us."

"Let's get the men pulling up the posts."

"No, let's go for the old man and the man next to him. If we get them, maybe the rest will leave."

"Okay."

"Three quick shots, then head for the house as fast as you can go."

"Gotcha."

Rose waited until the men in question were still. "Now!" she hissed and fired as rapidly as she could.

She saw the old man flinch before she turned her rifle on the man next to him. She fired both her shots, grabbed Tyler by the arm, and hollered, "Let's go."

She didn't try to hide or be quiet. The raiders had to know where the rifle shots came from. They knew they would be trying to get back to the house. Using the speed of their horses, they would try to get to the house before Rose and Tyler.

Rose ran as fast as she could, but she was no match for Tyler's long legs. He was in the house before she was much more than halfway there. Then she heard the sound of hoofbeats. Someone was bearing down on her at breakneck speed. No, it was two of them. Fear gave her limbs extra speed. She would make it, but it would be close.

Then she stumbled and fell. Over a dropped rifle.

Oblivious to the mud that covered her, she leapt to her feet. The men were practically on top of her. She feinted to one side causing one rider to miss her, but that brought her directly into the path of a second. He aimed his gun straight at her.

The explosion was terrifying. But Rose felt no pain. Her legs didn't buckle under her. She kept running. She made it to the porch, dashed through the door, slammed and locked it behind her.

Zac stood at the window, a rifle in his hands, his face white as a sheet.

"He was going to hurt you," Zac said.

"He fired before I could," Tyler said as he rammed his rifle through the window and peppered shots into the night. "And the little bugger hit him."

"He was going to hurt you," Zac repeated.

Rose realized the child was in shock. He had shot the man when he was about to kill her, but now reaction had set in. That scared her. He was too small to suffer such a fright.

Rose ran to Zac and grabbed him up in her arms.

"It's okay," she crooned. "You're a very brave little boy." Zac didn't move. He felt like a wooden doll in her arms. Glancing out the window, Rose saw that both raiders were gone. "You saved my life," she said to Zac, gently taking the rifle from his grip. "Your brother is going to be very proud of you."

"When is George coming?" Zac asked.

"Soon," Rose assured him. "I'm sure he's on his way right now."

"They're leaving," Tyler called out. "They're riding off." He started toward the door.

"Stay here," Rose ordered. "It could be a ruse. They may have chased their horses off to draw us outside so they can kill us."

Tyler regarded Rose thoughtfully. "You'd make a good Indian fighter," he said. "I'd never have thought of that."

Rose was so surprised she couldn't think of anything to say.

She felt Zac's body relax a little. Then his arms flew around her neck in a viselike hug. Rose thought she would strangle, but she didn't loosen his grip. When he started to shake, she held him closer, hoping her warmth and nearness would give him the comfort he needed.

She had shot her first man tonight, too, but the only feelings she had were relief that the danger was over and anger that these men had tried to kill them. She knew she would have no compunction at shooting again if they came back.

"George is coming," Tyler called.

"Don't go out. It may be a trick."

"They're coming at a gallop. Only George and the twins could ride like that in the middle of a rainstorm."

Rain was coming down hard now. It was impossible to see anything at all.

"Turn up the lamp and set it in the window," Rose said. "But stay down just in case."

Unable to peel Zac's arms from her, she picked him up and moved to the door. She opened it slowly. When nothing happened, she opened it further and stepped outside.

Gusts of moisture-laden wind reached her far back in the breezeway, but she pressed forward. She wanted to see George. She needed to know he was all right.

He came out of the gloom like a boulder in advance of an avalanche. He was off his horse and sweeping the two of them into his arms before she could even call his name.

"Are you all right?" he asked, burying his face in her shoulder, Zac crushed between them. "Where's Tyler?"

"I'm right here," Tyler said, emerging from the bedroom with the lamp turned as high as it would go. The light barely illuminated the faces of the others gathered close behind George.

"Did they attack the camp?" Rose asked, her grip on George not loosening.

"They hit us first."

"Anybody hurt?"

"They got Alex," Monty said, pushing his way past Rose and George, still locked together. "Did they do any damage here?"

Rose let her arms slide from around George. "They killed the bull. Zac tried to hide it, but they came up too fast."

Uttering a particularly foul curse, Monty rushed off into the night. Hen and a couple of the men followed him.

"Come inside," Rose said. "I'll fix some coffee and warm up the stew. You're dripping wet."

"What happened?" George asked.

While Rose made coffee, sliced bread, and heated a venison stew, she told George about the attack. "If Zac hadn't shot that man, I wouldn't be here right now."

With the return of his big brother, Zac's spirits had made a remarkable recovery. The light had returned to his eyes, energy to his limbs. He couldn't wait to tell George all about his part in the shootout.

"He was a real mean-looking fella," the boy said, delighted at the way the room full of grown men hung on his every word. "I was sure he would shoot Rose dead right there in the mud."

The condition of Rose's dress was proof enough of that.

"So I grabbed a gun and shot him."

"But you don't know how to shoot," George said.

"I'm a natural," Zac answered, proud of himself. "I just pointed the gun, and I hit him."

"Rifle," Tyler corrected, disgusted with his little brother's attempt to show off. "And you couldn't have done more than wing him. He rode off fast enough."

"He didn't shoot Rose," Zac said.

"And that's all that's important," George said.

The conversation became general until Monty returned. He was like a gust of wind himself, entering with all the compressed energy of a giant spring.

"They shot the milk cow, the filthy bastards," he said, going straight for the coffee Rose held out to him. "But they didn't get the bull. The lazy beast was snuggled up under a bit of chaparral trying to keep his precious hide out of the rain."

"They would have if Rose and I hadn't driven them off," Tyler said, determined to get his portion of praise for the night's work.

"You left this house?" George said. He sounded so shocked and furious that Tyler wilted instantly.

"It was my decision," Rose said, coming to Tyler's rescue. "I was mad they would attack children. Then when they shot your bull—"

"They didn't," George pointed out.

"I thought they had," Rose insisted, "and it made me mad. They couldn't see us in the dark, so Tyler and I took a few shots at them."

"Atta girl," Monty said, grinning.

"That was a crazy thing to do," George said, throwing his brother a fierce glare. "You could have been killed."

"I could have been killed in my bed," Rose shot back. "Besides, I didn't see why I should wait here, quivering with fright, while they tore down the corral and worked up their nerve to attack us again. I thought we could drive them off, and we did."

George still looked unhappy, but he didn't say anything more.

"They may try again," Salty said. "We ought to set a watch on this place as well as the camp."

"That'll stretch us real thin," Monty said. "Anybody got any ideas how we can do it and finish the roundup?"

For the next hour they kicked around ideas about what needed to be done. By the time they had figured out a plan and worked out a schedule for who would guard what when, the sun was coming up.

The rain had stopped. Everything looked fresh and new.

Except the men.

"Where is Hen?" George asked suddenly. "I haven't seen him in hours."

"He went to look for the bull with me," Monty said.

"Did he come back with you?"

"Sure."

"He didn't come in," Salty said. "I remember it was just you and Ben."

"You sure? He was right on my heels at the door."

"I wasn't paying much attention, but I think he went into the other side of the house," Ben volunteered.

Monty dashed out of the room and was back inside a minute.

"He's not there. Hasn't been there as far as I can tell. The rifles and ammunition are still on the floor."

Rose felt a sudden apprehension. She went to the bedroom. She didn't have to count the boxes to know that several were missing.

"He went after the McClendons," Monty said. "That's got to be it. I should have gone myself."

"No, you shouldn't," George contradicted. "You'd get yourself killed. You can't go up against thirty or forty men."

"Hen did."

"We don't know what Hen has done, but he's not going to face that crowd. He's too smart."

"I'm going to help him."

"You're going to stay here and have your breakfast. Then we're going back to camp and get on with the roundup."

Monty looked ready to fight. "He's my twin. I can't leave him out there alone."

"He's my brother," George said, "and if I know anything about him, he wants to be out there alone. He's a wolf, Monty. Those men are in more danger than he is. You're a bear. You would charge right in the middle expecting to take them by force."

"What do you take me for, some kind of fool? We didn't hold this place for four years by ourselves by getting our heads blown off."

"He doesn't think you're a fool," Rose interceded. "He's just worried about you."

"Well, I'm worried about Hen."

"We all are, but you won't help matters by charging into the middle of you don't know what. He'll come home when he's ready. Now sit down. Breakfast is almost ready."

Twenty minutes later the uneasy silence was broken by the sound of a single horseman riding up to the house. Monty jumped up and hurried to the window. "Son-of-a-bitch!" he exclaimed. "It's Hen, and the damned fool is leading a milk cow."

"Everybody sit down," George said when the whole crew seemed ready to dash for a window or the door. "Act like you hadn't missed him."

A little later, after he'd washed up, Hen entered the kitchen, sat down in the place Rose had set for him, served himself, and started eating. About the time he swallowed the second mouthful, just before the room exploded with curiosity, he lifted his head and looked at George.

"Zac, you'd better go milk the cow. If George has to drink coffee for breakfast, he won't be worth shooting."

Hen flashed George a rare smile and turned back to his breakfast.

\* \* \*

"I don't ever recall being more frightened in my life. Not even during the war," George told Rose.

They were lying peacefully, side by side, enjoying the afterglow of their lovemaking. George still had to remind himself that Rose had married him, that she would be his wife for as long as they lived. It still seemed hard to believe.

Their lovemaking had been particularly intense tonight. Maybe it stemmed from the danger of the previous evening. Maybe it stemmed from realizing he could have lost Rose. Whatever the reason, he felt closer to her than ever.

"I can't believe it took me so long to realize they would attack the house," George said, wondering for the dozenth time if his survival instincts had deserted him. "You could have been killed before I got here."

"Tyler was wonderful. I don't think he's a very good shot, but he's fearless. I think he almost had a good time."

"Not as much as Zac. That little rascal is still chattering about what happened."

Slipping out of George's embrace, Rose sat up in the bed. "I haven't had a chance to tell you until now, but I'm worried about Zac. He didn't have a good time. He was white as a sheet after he shot that man. I had to pry the rifle out of his grasp. He didn't recover until you got here."

George felt the harness of responsibility settle a little more heavily on his shoulders, the bands of guilt draw a little tighter around his chest. Would he manage to get Zac and Tyler to adulthood before something else went wrong?

Thank God he wouldn't have any children of his own.

"I'll try to spend a little more time with him."

"Don't let him know why you're doing it," Rose said. She chuckled softly. "Zac is very proud of himself. It would hurt his pride if he knew I told you of his weakness."

"But you just said he was petrified."

"He was, but didn't you just tell me you had never been more scared in your life?"

"Yes."

"Do you want me to announce that to your brothers? Monty would love to know. So would Tyler."

"Of course I don't."

"That's exactly how Zac feels. He has finally done something wonderful in his own eyes. He needs that if he's ever to grow up and think himself your equal."

George turned so he could face Rose.

"I don't know why I ever thought I could manage this family without you."

Rose turned pink with pleasure. "You'd have managed somehow."

"No. I've finally accepted the fact that I can't do all I once thought I could."

"You're not thinking of leaving, are you?" Rose asked, her eyes searching his, fear somersaulting through her stomach.

George moved closer. Putting his arm around Rose, he drew her close.

"I'm not thinking about leaving anybody, anything, or anywhere. Especially you. I'm just learning to accept the fact that I need help. I'm also finding out I'm terribly happy you're here to give it."

Rose snuggled a little closer. "Anyone could do what I've done." She believed what she said, but she fervently hoped he would deny it.

"Not without loving each of my brothers as much as I do. I realized that when I was racing here, cursing myself for being so stupid, hoping I wasn't too late. I knew that somehow you'd keep the boys safe."

Rose couldn't think of anything to say, so she squeezed her husband a little harder.

"I realized something else during that nerve-racking race through the rain and mud. You know, you can rack your brain over something until you're so confused you don't know what you think. Then along comes a crisis, and everything is perfectly clear."

"That happens to everybody."

"I've been wrestling with my feelings for you and getting nowhere at all. I no sooner thought of those bastards riding up on you while you were asleep than I had no indecision at all. I was just as afraid for you as I was for the boys. I know I'll have to let go of them someday, but I could never let go of you. Even if I didn't need you as much as I do, I wouldn't want to give you up."

"A woman likes to feel important to her husband," Rose said, snuggling down even closer.

George sat up and pulled away so he could face Rose. "You don't understand what I'm saying. I love you. I finally discovered what it is, and I love you. I have for some time now, only I didn't know it."

She wanted to believe him. She wanted it more than anything else in the world, but she had to be sure.

"Are you sure? It's easy for a person's emotions to become exaggerated during a crisis."

George gripped her by the arms and drew her to him.

"I love you, Rose Thornton Randolph. I love you so much I feel like I'll explode if I try to keep it inside me. I love you because you love us so much. I love you because you're beautiful, because I want to make love to you for the rest of my life. I even love you because you're crazy enough to attack the McClendons for shooting a bull they didn't shoot." He put his fingers over Rose's lips to still her protest.

"But there's something different about it now. It's little things. When our eyes meet at a distance and you smile—you can't know what a lift that gives me. It makes me want to do something foolish. When you catch your skirt on a splinter or prick your finger on a dried bean hull and you come out with one of the words you've learned from Monty. I even like the way you wipe the perspiration from your forehead when you're standing over the stove. Isn't that crazy?"

Rose wondered if a person could die from too much happiness. If so, she had about five minutes left. Surely George wouldn't talk so foolishly unless he really meant it. It was hard to give in, to allow herself to be vulnerable again, but it was even harder to hold back from something she had wished for so ardently for these last months.

"No crazier than me liking the way you seem to stand a little taller whenever you look out at your land. I'm particularly fond of you when you're forced to drink coffee. You look like you'd rather drink from a mudhole."

George tickled Rose until tears ran down her face. Then he put his arms around her and kissed her enthusiastically. "Anybody listening to us would think we're crazy."

"No, just in love."

"Do other grown people act like this? Do they feel like they're fourteen all over again?"

"I don't know about anybody else, but I like the way I feel. I hope I go on feeling this way for the rest of my life."

"And you still don't mind not having children?"

Rose wished George hadn't asked that question just now. It was the only thing about her life that made her sad. She would have preferred to enjoy his declaration without remembering that it came with a price. But there was no point in avoiding it.

"Yes, I mind. It was very lonely being an only child. Living with the Robinsons helped, but I always wanted brothers and sisters of my own. As I got older it changed to wanting children. Now I don't know whether I want them more for myself or for you."

"For me? Why?"

"I've tried to tell you what a wonderful man you are. It's not just me. Your brothers and all the men who work for you agree. I can't think of anything more exciting than watching your sons grow up wanting to be like you, watching your daughters hope to find a man only half as good as you."

George shuddered. "Just trying to bring up Zac and Tyler scares me to death."

"You don't have to get defensive. I won't try to talk you into changing your mind, but I *will* try to convince you you'd make a good father."

"What for?"

"Because you deserve to think well of yourself. I don't know what your father did or why you think you're going to repeat all his mistakes, but you deserve to be able to look at yourself with pride."

George was shocked to find himself swallowing hard. Worse, he had this odd watering in his eyes. For one terrifying moment he was afraid he might actually lose control of his emotions. He had learned to accept a lot since he'd met Rose, but this was too much.

He held Rose a little closer. "I don't know why it took me so long to realize I loved you. It gives me cold chills every time I realize how close I came to losing you. For such a wonderful person, I'm remarkably dense."

Rose twisted around until she could kiss him on the nose. "Well, you finally figured it out. That's all that counts."

George dropped his head until his lips caressed the top of Rose's breast.

"You sure you're happy?"

"Deliriously," Rose answered, twisting around so he could reach her more easily. "You?"

"Completely."

The two of them surrendered to the desire which was washing over them like storm-tossed waves. Soon they were conscious only of each other.

# Chapter Nineteen

In the days that followed, Hen didn't smile again. He insisted they bury Alex Pendleton next to their mother. He said Alex had never had a mother he could remember. Now he would, and Mrs. Randolph would have someone to look after.

Hen refused to say anything about what he had done that night beyond that he'd brought in a milk cow he'd found "wandering lost on our land."

Less than a week later they found out.

The brothers rode home from the range to find an army lieutenant and a detachment of six men camped in the yard. Old man McClendon and two of his clan were there as well.

"Let me do the talking," George warned his brothers.

"Why?" Monty demanded.

"Because I never know what you're going to say."

"You're not the only one with any brains around here. I can—"

"Keep your mouth shut," Hen growled. The unexpected sharpness of his twin's order stunned Monty into silence. At least for the moment.

"Are you George Randolph?" the lieutenant asked.

"Yes," George answered as he dismounted. His gaze cut to where Rose had emerged from the house, Zac at her side. The boy broke for George.

"They say you killed somebody," Zac said, clinging to George for assurance. "I told them you didn't, but they wouldn't believe me. They wouldn't believe Rose, neither."

George knelt down to give Zac a reassuring hug. "Either," he corrected, taking the boy's hand in his as he stood up and turned to the officer. "What's this about somebody being killed?"

"I'm Lieutenant Crabb," the young man said. "Mr. McClendon here says one of you killed two of his kin. The others swear to it."

"What do you mean by *one of you?*" George asked.

"You, or one of your brothers, or one of the men who works for you," the old man shouted.

"You might as well include the rest of the county," George answered quietly. "I have six brothers counting this little rascal here. At the moment, I've got fifteen men working for me."

"He's come to arrest you for murder," one of the younger McClendons shouted.

"You can't arrest me because *somebody* killed one of your kin," George said.

"Texas is under Reconstruction," the lieutenant said. "Certain laws have been suspended."

"Which ones?" George asked, his gaze pinning the lieutenant down. "The ones which protect honest citizens from murderous attacks in the middle of the night? The ones which protect women and children from being murdered in their beds? Or just the ones which are supposed to protect honest citizens from charges leveled by men in the Reconstruction office?"

"What are you talking about?" the lieutenant asked.

"I'm saying that this old man and his clan stampeded through the middle of our camp six nights ago and murdered one of my hands. And I'm not saying *someone* did it. I'm accusing him," George said, pointing straight at old man McClendon. "And every man here will swear to it, won't you, boys?"

They nodded their assent.

The lieutenant turned to McClendon, but the old man's eyes gave nothing away.

"And I'll swear he attacked this house right after that," Rose said, stepping forward. "I wounded him in the left shoulder. Make him take off his shirt if you don't believe me."

"He says he got that wound when your men attacked his

family. He says your men wounded more than half a dozen of them."

"You can see the bullets embedded in the logs," Rose said, pointing to the easily seen scars on the house. "You can tell from the color of the splinters they're fresh."

The lieutenant looked undecided.

"I can show you our camp if you like," George volunteered. "We've cleaned it up, but you can still tell what happened. I can also show you young Alex's grave. It's under that large oak." He pointed.

Even at a distance, the mound of fresh earth was visible.

"But why should they have attacked you?" the lieutenant asked.

"They've been living off our beef for years," Monty burst out, unable to contain himself any longer. "We're rounding them up to sell. Now they'll have to go to work or starve."

"That's a lie," old man McClendon shouted. "Not one of my kin has ever killed a beef of yours."

"You own no cows, so how do you explain the beef on your table?"

"We buy our beef," the old man said. "Every one of us will swear to it."

"If you do, you'll be lying." Hen's voice was low, but it vibrated with such rage he drew every eye. "I can prove you've been stealing our beef."

"That's a very serious accusation," the lieutenant warned.

"As serious as murder?" George asked.

"Can you show me your proof?"

"Not until the rest of our men arrive. Once we get in the middle of that clan, I don't trust them not to murder us all."

"This is the United States Army," the lieutenant said proudly. "No one would touch us."

"You're either a fool or you haven't been in Texas very long," Monty snapped.

The ride to the McClendon homesteads was long and

uncomfortable. George had left Salty and Silas at the house with Rose and Zac. The rest of them rode together in a tight bunch. Hen led the way, but George made sure that he and Monty rode between the McClendons and Hen.

The McClendons rode pretty easy in the saddle at first, but as they got closer to their land, George noted they seemed to be getting a little uneasy. When Hen turned east at a blasted oak, they grew visibly nervous. When Hen headed toward a grove of pecans lining a broad shallow in the creek, the McClendons disappeared into the nearest thicket. The lieutenant and his men just sat there with their mouths open as they listened to the sound of the McClendons crashing through the brush. When the sounds had faded away, Hen led them into the creek.

"Dig there," Hen said, dismounting on a sandbar in the middle of the creek.

Less than a foot below the surface their shovels bit into leather. More than a dozen hides, all of them with the brand clearly readable.

"They were so sure of themselves they didn't even bother to cut off the brands or burn the hides," Monty marveled.

"They've been doing this since before we got here," Hen said, "and nobody's stopped them. They sure didn't expect anybody to stop them now that they're hooked up with the Reconstruction."

"The Reconstruction isn't here to cheat the local ranchers," the lieutenant said, his discomfiture making him defensive.

"Now I know you haven't been in Texas long," Monty said. "You should have been here a month ago."

"Why do you say that?" the lieutenant demanded.

"Ask at the land office when you get back to Austin," George said. "What do you mean to do about the McClendons?"

"Can you swear it was the old man who killed that boy?"

"None of us can say who did it," George admitted. "They surprised us, came up on a black night. We didn't find Alex until after they'd gone."

"I don't see how I can arrest anybody on that."

"But you were going to arrest me on no more."

"I have an order for your arrest. I don't have one for him."

He showed George the order.

"My wife is the goddaughter of General Ulysses S. Grant," George told the lieutenant, still staring at the order, his temper rising faster than a Roman rocket on the Fourth of July. "We can easily prove it if you like. I don't think he'd be pleased to know you arrested her husband on a charge trumped up by proven cattle rustlers"—he pointed to the hides—"especially since you say you can't arrest those same cow thieves even though they tried to kill his goddaughter and her family. You've got a dozen witnesses who'll swear to it. Some of us may be ex-Confederates, but we're honorable men."

"He's sending George a pardon," Monty announced. "With that he'll be just as good as any carpetbagger. Wouldn't be surprised if it's not in Austin already."

"A pardon?" the lieutenant asked.

"A presidential pardon, courtesy of General Grant himself," Monty explained. "You don't expect a man like the General to enjoy having his goddaughter's husband living under a cloud, do you?"

"We can prove that, too," George added.

"General Sheridan is supposed to be dropping in on us any day now to see how she's doing. Maybe you'd like to stay around and say hello to him. I hear he's a mighty powerful man. Knowing him could make a world of difference in your career."

"I thought you hated Yankees," George said to Monty after the lieutenant and his men had headed back to Austin. "I never thought you'd hide behind one."

"I'm not hiding, but I don't see any sense in not using what's right in front of us. There's going to be more trouble with the McClendons. They won't let it lie. We don't need the army on our backs as well."

"You think they'll try again?"

"They never did a day's work I know of. They're not going to sit back and let us take the food out of their mouths."

Rose didn't feel comfortable with Silas. She didn't have a reason for it, and that made her feel a little guilty. He seemed to be watching her. He was supposed to. That's why George had left him at the house, but he wasn't watching her like Ben or Ted or either of the new men George had taken on since the McClendon raid.

He watched her furtively. No, that wasn't it. He did it openly. It was like he was waiting for her to do something. Only she had no idea what.

"Not much to do around here," he said.

"Not much for you," Rose replied. He had watched her being rushed off her feet all morning. Offering a helping hand wasn't Silas Pickett's idea of how to treat a woman. He sat at his ease close to the door so he could keep a watch for anyone coming into the yard, his chair leaned back against the door jamb, his feet on the bottom rung. She had a momentary hope the chair would slide out from under him, then felt guilty for harboring such an uncharitable thought.

"I'm surprised George makes you work at all. Most men with a lot of gold stashed away would take their wife and head for Austin, or maybe New Orleans, and take it easy. Not live in this godforsaken briar patch and break his back for a pack of crazy wild cows."

Rose was preparing the second of two wild pigs for roasting. Monty was taking out his anger at the McClendons on the local wildlife. In the last week they had dined on deer, antelope, turkey, pig, and rabbit. If there hadn't been so many men to feed each day, most of the meat would have gone to waste.

"Neither one of us likes living in town," Rose told him.

"What's the point of saving all that money for your children? Seems like his brothers don't want it either."

"I don't know what your idea of money is, but I don't consider a few gold pieces anything to get excited over. The way my supplies are disappearing, that won't last us more than a few more months."

"I don't mean a handful of gold. I mean boxes of it. Thousands upon thousands of coins."

"You must have a very active imagination to think George would have any way of getting that kind of money. They lost everything in the war."

"I guess he hasn't told you, then."

"Hasn't told me what?"

Rose didn't like the way Silas was looking at her. It wasn't very friendly. In fact, it was downright antagonistic.

"Men usually tell their wives. They won't tell another man, but they need to tell someone. It's no good if nobody knows. Of course, maybe he doesn't want his brothers to know. Wants it all for himself."

"I think you've been out in the sun too long. Your wits are addled."

"Of course, he could be waiting. It wouldn't be advisable to turn up rolling in riches all at once. A much better idea to seem to have gotten it from a cattle ranch. Rather clever man, your husband."

"I think George is remarkably clever," Rose said, "but I haven't the slightest idea what you're talking about. Now unless you mean to help me with this meat, I wish you'd go find Zac. That boy can vanish faster than an icicle in a hot stove."

"I'll get him in a minute. I don't want him just yet."

Something in his voice warned Rose that things had changed, that the situation could become dangerous.

"What do you want?" She made sure she had a firm grip on the knife she had been using. It was sharp enough to cut through sinew, gristle, or small bones.

"I want to know what your husband has done with all that gold."

"What is this fixation you have with gold? Is it because of the gold they spent in Austin? It wasn't much, and it's almost gone."

"I'm talking about a half million dollars in gold."

Now Rose was certain Silas was deranged. "It's common knowledge his family left Virginia destitute. His friends had to buy this place for them."

"Captain Randolph led a raiding party on a Union Army wagon train carrying a payroll of over half a million in gold. In the confusion, the wagon carrying the gold disappeared. They never found it."

"What makes you think George's father had anything to do with it? Presumably there were other men in his patrol."

"That wagon train was near his home when it was ambushed. Nobody in that train would know the surrounding countryside like Captain Randolph."

"Assuming there was a payroll and that George's father took it, it couldn't have anything to do with George or Jeff. Neither of them saw their father after they enlisted."

"He could have sent them a letter."

"So he could, but the letter could have gotten lost. The treasure could have gotten lost, or the wagon could have gotten lost. This whole thing could be your distorted imagination. I don't know who told you this fairy tale about George having gold, or knowing where it is, but he's wrong. Knowing George, if he did know where the gold was hidden, he'd return it."

"He's not such a fool," Silas said, laughing.

"Not everyone prizes gold above honor."

"Half a million?"

"Half a million, especially a half million we neither have nor know anything about."

"I don't believe you."

"Obviously, or you wouldn't still be going on about it. Look around. Does this look like the home of a rich man?"

"He could have it hidden."

"George and his brother walked from Virginia driving that bull before them. Now, if you know how they could have managed to transport five hundred thousand dollars worth of gold without anybody knowing, you know a lot more than I do."

"They could have left it in Virginia."

"I'm surprised you're not off somewhere prospecting," Rose said. "I never knew anyone with a worse case of gold fever."

"Probably," Silas said, getting to his feet. "I always did dream of striking it rich. It sure beats working for it one dollar at a time."

"I won't argue with you there, but about the only way to get rich quick is to take something that belongs to somebody else. I can't imagine anyone who was brought up on the same principles as my husband doing something like that. You wouldn't, would you?"

"Ma'am, a man never knows what he'll do until he's faced with the temptation. A half million dollars is a mighty powerful temptation. Now where did you say that boy was likely to be hiding? I don't want to be looking behind every bush between here and the camp."

"You're most likely to find him along the creek," Rose said.

She was relieved to see Silas go. She wasn't afraid of him, but he worried her. A man with gold fever could be dangerous. And right now they didn't need any more danger. She would mention it to George tonight. It probably wasn't anything, but it was best to be on the safe side.

"King said he'd be happy to trade. He said he'd rather give them to us than have Cortina slaughter them for hides and tallow. The army is going after his raiders, but everybody knows it won't do any good. They can't go into Mexico after him."

Jeff had gotten back from Corpus Christi the night before and had barely stopped talking since. Rose couldn't remember seeing him so animated. She would have given a lot to know what had brought about the change and whether it was likely to last very long.

George did love her, deeply and truly—she was convinced of that now—but she didn't want to put his loyalty to a test. The claims of his family were of much longer standing than her own.

"He said he'd take the steers to St. Louis next spring if we want. We'd have to take our chances on the trail, but they're offering the best price we'll ever find, maybe as much as thirty dollars. We could lose them, too. What with rustlers, stampedes, and Indians, it's a fifty-fifty gamble. Or we can wait until next spring and sell to a buyer."

"What do you think we ought to do?" George asked.

"Trail north with King. If anybody's going to get through, he's the man."

"Where do we get the money to pay the men?"

"King will take the herd now. It would save him worrying about getting up with us next spring. He agreed to give us twelve dollars a head now and the rest when we sell."

George was pleased with his brother. For the first time he'd been able to put aside his own troubles and concentrate on his job.

Jeff's expression changed without warning. All of the bottled-up anger was there again. "There's something else," he said as he reached in his pocket. "Seems the sheriff in Austin has been holding this for some time. Took him a mighty long time to realize you were the George Randolph on this letter."

George took the envelope. It had been opened. "You read it?" He wasn't upset. Just curious.

"Part of it. I couldn't finish it."

That made George even more curious. The letter was from a Colonel Jonah Marsh.

"What does he want with us?"

"Read it yourself. Read it to all of them," he said, gesturing to his brothers. "They'll be happy to know our father is a real, honest-to-God hero."

George was stupefied. There had to be some mistake. He opened the letter and started to read.

*Dear Mr. Randolph,*

*I had meant to write you earlier, but the rigors of re-
turning to civilian life have up until this time prevented
me from having the time I felt necessary for this letter. For
months I've felt a growing, urgent need to tell you and
your family about the last months of your father's life. He
was a truly remarkable man. The Confederate cause owes
much to his leadership and his bravery.*

George looked at Jeff, unable to believe what he was reading.
"It gets worse."

George didn't know why he did it, but he handed the letter
to Rose. She took it, unsure of what she was expected to do,
then began to read.

*I only knew your father briefly. He joined my regiment
after the battle of Atlanta. Because of his age and experience, I immediately gave him a command. It was the best
decision I ever made. He was like a father to those boys.
There was no trouble too small for his—*

Rose broke off as Hen jumped up with a curse and slammed
out of the room. She looked at the others, but only Zac met her
gaze.

"Go on," George said without looking up.

*—too small for his attention. He was tireless in his efforts
to weld them into a single-minded fighting unit.*

*We couldn't do more than harass Sherman as he ripped
the heart out of Georgia, but it wasn't long before he and
his men came to know your father by name. He gave them
cause.*

*He was fearless. When he thought the danger was too
great for the youngsters in his command, he went in
himself. I can't tell you of the wonders he achieved. He
was intrepid. But while he had many great successes, it*

*was his valiant courage which finally brought about his
death.*

Rose paused. All the sons were aware their father had been
killed, but she wasn't sure they would want to hear about it
in a letter. Only Zac showed any interest. Tyler's face looked
blank. George and Jeff's expressions showed tightly controlled
anger. She thought Monty would pop from the effort he was
making to control himself. Feeling more unsure than ever,
she continued.

> *Mine was a small unit. Sherman sent a large patrol
> against us hoping to finish us off so he could continue his
> march to the coast unhampered. They caught us by sur-
> prise. We needed a diversion to give us time to melt into
> the surrounding woods. Without warning, your father rode
> straight at the Union patrol, straight for their leaders. I've
> never seen anything like it. Firing with both hands, using
> every weapon he possessed, he knocked a half dozen men
> out of the saddle. Even though he rode into the teeth of
> their fire, he got so close the line broke before he got hit.*
>
> *Our troops got away with no casualties. We sent a spe-
> cial detachment into the Union camp for his body. After
> what he had done, he had to be laid to rest by the men he
> died for.*

Rose looked up, but she got no reaction. Monty got up from
his seat and walked over to the window and looked out, but
he didn't say anything. She resumed reading.

> *He didn't leave much beyond his pistols and uniform,
> but we've entrusted these to one of the men who means to
> head west when the fighting's done. He will look you up in
> Texas. His name is Benton Wheeler.*

"Salty!" Zac exclaimed happily.

*He was in your father's command, so he can tell you even
better than I what a fine man he was. Know we all share
your loss, but we realize our loss as friends and fellow soldiers can't compare to the loss felt by his family. He was a
credit to his name and his country, God rest his soul.*

*My blessings go with you and your family.*

*Sincerely,*
*Col. Jonah Marsh*

"Son-of-a-bitch!" Monty cursed.

"Watch your tongue," George said. "Rose is here."

"I wouldn't care if God himself was here, I'd still damn the
bastard," Monty said, his anger so great he could hardly remain still.

"That's not the worst of it," Jeff said. "They're going to have
a parade in his honor in Austin. They're expecting all of us to
be there."

Monty emptied out his bag of curses. Rose marveled he
could have learned so many this far from civilization.

"You're not going, are you, George?" Monty asked.

George didn't answer. He sat staring before him.

"I won't go," Jeff said. "I don't care what they do. If any of us
has to go, it'll have to be you, George. You're the oldest."

George didn't answer.

"A parade!" Monty said, furious. "You wouldn't get Hen to
go if you held a gun to his head. It'd serve them right if I went
just to tell them what a weasel they were honoring."

Rose knew that William Henry Randolph hadn't been a
good father. She couldn't imagine what he had done to cause
his sons to hate him so, but she felt that ignoring the parade
would only make things worse.

"I know this is none of my business," Rose said, afraid to
speak but feeling she must, "but they're honoring what your
father did, not your father himself. I'm not trying to change
anybody's feelings about him, but wouldn't it be better if you
could put them aside long enough for the parade?"

George got to his feet. Rose had never seen such a pain-filled look in his eyes. She had always felt he had a shell which somehow protected him from the extremes of emotion.

But this was pain, deep and searing. Not bitter or angry like the twins. Not even belligerent like Jeff. He had been hurt where he was most vulnerable. Where he was still vulnerable.

"The boys can do what they want," George said, still staring into space, his voice, dull, lifeless, "but I won't be there."

He turned and walked out of the kitchen.

"That takes care of that," Monty said with a kind of grim satisfaction. "George is the only one who could have gotten us to go."

"Did you get the ring?" George asked Jeff. He had followed Jeff into the bedroom.

"Yes," Jeff replied. He dug in one of his pockets and handed George a small packet made from a piece of paper folded over many times. "He had it waiting. He said he knew you'd be back for it soon."

George unfolded the paper until it yielded up its secret, a gold band set with a large yellow stone. He knew it was a topaz, but the names of stones were meaningless to him. Rose wanted it. That was all that mattered to him.

"Did you get enough from the sword to cover the cost?" George asked without removing his gaze from the ring.

"Yes. I could have gotten more, but I made him promise not to sell it for at least a year."

"Why?"

"You'll want it back. You may not want to remember the war, but you'll want your sword. I figure by then we'll have enough money to pay for it. And even if you don't want it, your children will."

George stared at his brother. He could hardly believe he was talking to Jeff.

"You want to know what's brought about this change in

me," Jeff said. He smiled, a self-conscious, humorless smile. He looked like a man who had come to accept, without any degree of enthusiasm, something he would never like. "I'll never forgive you for marrying Rose any more than I'll forgive life for taking my arm. It's not a matter of wanting to or not. I just can't. But you're my family. With this thing," he said, glancing down at his stump, "you're all I'm ever likely to have. Besides, you're the only people who look at me without making me feel like a freak. It does come in handy in closing a deal, however. It takes a hard man not to feel a little sorry for my having lost my arm for the cause."

George felt a tremendous sense of relief.

"You'd make a sharp deal without depending on that arm. As for the sword, I don't want it back. And there aren't going to be any children to inherit it."

"What the hell do you mean? Unless I'm badly mistaken, that woman is looking forward to a swarm of little bluecoats romping about the place."

"You remember what our father was like. Do you seriously think I'd tempt fate to repeat itself?"

"For God's sake, George, you're nothing like Pa."

"Maybe not, but that's a chance I'm not willing to take."

Rose sat for a long time over her coffee. It grew cold before, with a fatalistic sigh, she got to her feet. She knew George's self-doubts were tied up with his father, but she didn't know what to do about it. She didn't know if she *could* do anything, not unless she could get him to talk more about it. She didn't know when he would be ready, but from the look in his eyes, it wouldn't be soon.

"He's never said a word about me bringing back his father's things," Salty told her. "I was sure one of them would."

"He will. He just needs more time."

But as the days went by, she grew less hopeful. George had placed the colonel's letter on a shelf where anyone in the room could see it. It seemed to exercise malevolent power on all the brothers. Even Zac, who had no memory of his father and virtually none of his mother, was affected by it.

At last she couldn't stand it any longer. She took the letter and put it in the bottom of one of her drawers.

The boys noticed its absence. Rose saw each one of them glance at the shelf as they came in, then pause a moment when they realized the letter wasn't there. But the atmosphere improved almost immediately. It wasn't long before they were in pretty good spirits.

The roundup was nearly complete. There had been no more trouble with the McClendons, and they would soon begin the drive to King's ranch. They had secured their ranch, they would have their breeding stock, and they would have some money. They were on their way to establishing the Randolph ranch as a permanent and profitable business.

And they had done it together. None of them would say it, but Rose knew they were all proud of themselves.

"I think the ranch ought to have a distinctive brand," she said one evening.

"We have a brand," Jeff reminded her.

"And a name," she added. "You don't want people calling it the Randolph place, do you?"

George eyed her, a kind of expectant amusement in his eyes. It made her squirm, but she refused to back down.

"I agree," Monty said, suddenly enthusiastic. "The running 'S' isn't our brand. It came with the place."

"What would you like?" George asked.

"It ought to be something distinctive, something people associate with us," Jeff said.

"And something not easy to change into another brand," Hen added.

"I can't think of anything that satisfies all those requirements," George said. Then he looked straight at Rose. "Do you have any ideas, boys?" But his eyes never left Rose.

"We could use—" Monty began before Hen elbowed him

in the ribs. "What the hell!" Monty exploded, rounding on his twin.

"He doesn't have any ideas at all," Hen said to George. "None of us does."

Rose was tempted to leave the room. They were ganging up on her. Even Monty, who was usually too single-minded to understand anything less subtle than a blow to the head. She would have given anything to wipe the grin off George's face. Hen was just as bad. She plunged ahead. After all, it was her idea.

"I did have one suggestion I thought you might consider," she said, giving George back his look, stare for stare. "Since there are seven of you, I thought you ought to use the number seven."

"There's only six," Zac corrected.

"You mustn't forget Madison," Rose reminded him gently. "George hasn't."

That succeeded in wiping the smile from George's face, but Rose wished it hadn't.

"And I think you ought to put a ring around the seven. The Circle Seven sounds good. It also makes it harder to change the brand."

"A square block would make it even more difficult," George said. He was teasing her. She knew it.

"I like the sound of Circle Seven," Monty said.

"I still want to know why Rose thinks we ought to use a circle," George said.

"Does it matter?" Monty asked.

"Yes," George insisted.

He was determined to pry the reason out of her. Well, he could have it, Rose thought, but he would be sorry.

"I thought of a circle because it represents the unbroken and unending love that holds this family together. Every time you see it, you'll know why you're working so hard."

She'd never seen them look more uncomfortable. She'd

have to remember that men didn't deal well with real emotion, especially not when there were other men around.

"If we're going to include Madison, we ought to include you," Zac said. He was the only one immune to the significance of Rose's words. "It ought to be the Circle Eight."

"You play your cards right, young man, and you can have a wonderful career fleecing wealthy dowagers and beautiful heiresses," Rose said, wanting to hug Zac. "You really can't call it Circle Eight, though it's sweet of you to suggest it. It would have to become the Circle Nine when the next one of you gets married, and then the Circle Ten. If you didn't, the other wives would feel hurt."

"She's right," Jeff said. "I vote for Circle Seven."

There were no objections.

"When did you think of that?" George asked Rose as he slipped into bed next to her. She moved into his arms as if she had been waiting all day for nothing else.

"A few days ago. It occurred to me that the ranch had no name. As soon as I thought of the name, I realized it could be a brand as well."

"I mean the part about the ring."

Rose hesitated. She didn't want to ruin his amorous mood.

"Every now and then people need to be reminded of the things that are most important to them. Especially your brothers. You face the world in a circle, women and children in the middle, ready to fight all comers, yet you don't even suspect how much you depend on each other."

George held Rose a little tighter, his lips against her cheek. "We owe you a great deal."

Rose twisted in his arms until she faced him, her lips on his lips, her breasts against his chest, her thighs against his thighs. "I think every man ought to pay his debts," she said, covering his face with nibbling kisses.

"Should I start now?" George asked, biting her neck.

"I'm counting on it," Rose countered, finding her own point of sensitivity.

The brothers heard their brother's yell from across the breezeway. They weren't sure what caused it, but since it wasn't repeated, they figured the damage wasn't too severe.

"I'm not going with you," George said. He didn't know he'd made the decision until the words were out of his mouth.

"Of course you're going," Monty said, his tone sarcastic. "You know you don't trust us out of your sight. No telling what kind of mistakes we'll make."

"A month ago you'd have been right, but not anymore."

"What's so different now?"

"I don't like leaving Rose by herself. I know the McClendons have gone into hiding, but I don't trust them not to come out the minute our backs are turned."

"Leave Salty here."

"He's staying, but I'm staying, too."

"I didn't realize you were so taken with the married state," Monty said, giving his brother a dig in the ribs.

"Neither did I until I thought about being gone for several months. That put everything in a different light."

"I'll bet it did."

"Don't be vulgar," Hen told his twin. "He is really worried about the McClendons."

"They won't show their faces again," Monty said.

"I don't know. I wouldn't trust that old man not to attack the devil if he turned his back."

"I'm tired of the McClendons," Monty said. "Who's going to be in charge of this drive? I hate taking orders from George all the time, but at least he's got some sense."

"And nobody else does?" Jeff demanded.

"Certainly not you."

George interrupted what promised to turn into a heated argument. "You know, when I came home I thought it was my responsibility to hold this family together. I worried myself sick about every decision I made. I didn't realize until later that I can't hold you here. You'll only stay as long as you *want* to stay."

"So?" demanded Monty.

"The four of you can all be in charge."

"That's crazy," Monty said.

"You have all the skills you need to get the herd to King's ranch. Nobody knows more about cows than you, Monty, or Jeff about the business end. Hen can be in charge of seeing you get there safely. And Tyler can fix anything that breaks."

"Maybe so, but ain't nobody else can make these fools work together," Tyler said.

"Excruciatingly put, but true," Jeff added.

"You can't desert us now just because you've got an itch that needs scratching," Monty said, giving a knowing nod in Rose's direction.

"I'm not deserting you," George said, ignoring Monty's jibe. "I'll run this ranch as long as you want me to, but I can't do everything myself. It's not fair to you or me to try. It's especially not fair to Rose. You're going to have to learn to do your part without me standing over you. If you can't manage one drive together, you're no better than an ordinary cowhand."

"He's right," Hen said. "We spend too much time fighting. That's something Pa would do. Well, I don't mean to be like Pa. And I don't mean to let any of you."

The brothers stared at Hen. It was a long speech for Hen, and it was especially forceful. George couldn't remember when he cared what anybody else did.

"You can begin by deciding on the route. Jeff's just come back from Corpus Christi, and Ben comes from Brownsville. Between them they ought to be able to figure out the best route."

"You sure about this?" Rose asked George as she listened to the brothers become embroiled in deciding on their route.

"I'm sure," George replied, slipping his arm around her waist and dropping a kiss on her head. "It'll be hard on them at first, but they'll soon get the hang of it."

"Are you certain?" she asked after a particularly loud outburst from Monty.

"They think they're ready to knock each other down, but they're not. There's a good deal of affection in their bickering."

"No matter what you do, don't tell them that."

George laughed. It had a ring of contentment to it. "I won't. I'll let them discover it for themselves. That'll be even better."

"I could go to Austin."

"Even if I wasn't worried about you, they need to do this alone. You ought to understand. You're the one who told me to stop trying to do everything alone."

"I know. I just wanted to be sure. I didn't want you staying on my account."

"I can't think of any better reason for staying," George said. "Not even Zac. And the bull runs a distant third."

Rose decided that if George was going to talk like this, they could have a very satisfactory couple of months together.

# Chapter Twenty

George entered the boys' bedroom where Rose was getting their clothes ready for the trip to King's ranch.

"What did you do with that colonel's letter?"

The question caught Rose by surprise. She had thought they'd all decided to act as if it never existed.

"I put it away. It was making everybody moody and irritable."

She could see George was agitated. She paused in folding a pair of Monty's pants, hugging them to her chest.

"I don't see why that letter upsets you so much. I know your father was hard on you, but can't you be a little bit proud of what he did? He died a hero, George. That ought to be worth something."

"It doesn't change anything." George avoided her gaze, as he always did when the subject of his father came up.

"Why not? I didn't like it when my father decided to fight against the Confederacy, but I was still proud of him."

"You don't know anything about my father."

She resumed her folding. "Then I guess it's time you told me," she said.

He raised his eyes to meet her gaze. "No."

Rose finished folding the pants and slammed them onto the pile. "Your father has stood between us from the moment I met you. You can't keep going around with this locked up inside. It'll destroy you in the end."

George didn't respond. He just kept staring at her.

She brushed aside a lock of hair which refused to stay out of her face. "It'll destroy our marriage."

"I won't let it."

"You won't be able to stop it. It bothers you more than Jeff's arm bothers him. You just don't think so because you don't shout at people or go off and sulk for days at a time."

"Talking won't change anything."

She picked up a plaid shirt and started to fold it. "You won't know until you try. I love you, George. I want to feel that you love me just as much. But I can't, not when you shut me out. It tears me up to have to sit here, helpless, while you die a little bit inside."

"It'll make you hate him, too." He picked up a spur that Zac had left lying on the floor.

Rose could hear the pain in his voice. She hated to do anything that would cause him to hurt even more, but he had to come to terms with his father's ghost or it would haunt him for the rest of his life.

"Your father can't hurt me except through you." She lifted another basket of clothes onto the bed and started to fold them. "Are you going to tell me, or do I have to ask one of your brothers?"

George sat down on his old bed. He spun the rowel of the spur with the end of his finger.

"You won't understand anything about Pa if you don't understand that I worshiped him. He was handsome, tall, athletic, smart, charming, popular, and rich. Nobody had a pa like him. I was proud of who I was because he was my pa. And, dammit to hell, I loved him."

George threw the spur down, got up, and walked over to the window. Even with his back to her, Rose could see the convulsive movement of his throat muscles as he struggled to keep his emotions in check. She ached to go to him, to throw her arms around him, but she knew he had to do this alone.

"You know what hurt me the most about that letter from his colonel? He said Pa was like a father to his men, that no concern of theirs was too small for his attention." George spun around to face Rose. "There was a time when I would have given everything I owned for five minutes of his attention."

He still looked in her direction, but she could see his mind going back through the years, seeing himself as he used to be.

She kept folding clothes.

"There was a time when he took me everywhere. He taught me to ride and hunt. He would lay a welt across my back with his crop if I did anything wrong, but I worked myself to exhaustion to please him. It stopped one day, and from then on I ceased to exist. Somewhere I failed him."

Rose felt herself shaking with rage that any man would beat his son for missing a shot or would turn his back on a son who adored him. If she could, she would have resurrected George's father just to tell him how much she despised him.

She finished putting Monty's clothes in neat stacks and moved to Tyler's bed.

"When he wasn't chasing other men's wives, he was busy gambling away everything he'd inherited. Or he was drunk and getting into fights. It got to where people would turn their backs when they saw him coming."

George fell silent for so long that Rose finished Tyler's clothes and moved to Hen's bed, but she didn't break the silence. George was so deep in his memories that she doubted he was even aware of her presence.

"Tom Bland, one of Pa's cousins, had the place next to ours. Tom had been Pa's best friend since they were boys. He wasn't married, and after a while he sort of adopted us. He used to help Ma out when Pa was away, or broke. He even took us boys under his wing, taking us on hunts, introducing us around, giving us advice. He used to send Madison money at school. You might say he was more our father than Pa. If we turned out right, it's because of him."

George surprised Rose by going to his bureau and taking out a picture in a heavy gilt frame. He handed it to her. It was a daguerreotype of a very ordinary looking man. Even with a heavy beard and mustache, Rose could see the kindness in the man's eyes. She was surprised that George had a picture of Tom Bland. He didn't have one of his mother or father.

"Pa took it into his head that Tom and Ma were cheating on him. When he couldn't provoke Tom into a fight, he seduced his sister. Tom had stayed loyal to Pa through everything, but he couldn't stomach that. He told Pa not to set foot on his property again or he'd have him whipped. Pa struck Tom and challenged him to a duel. Everybody tried to stop them, but Pa killed Tom thirty minutes later, right there on Tom's front lawn, in front of his sister and mother."

Rose handed the picture back to George. He looked at it a long while, bitterness gradually etching his face into sharp lines.

"Now do you understand why we hate him so?"

Rose nodded. At last she finally understood the terrible legacy of this evil man George must call father. She was so horrified she didn't know what to say. Her heart went out to George. It was easier for the twins. They hated their father without feeling guilty, but George had loved him. He felt responsible for his father's change. He wasn't, of course, but how could she convince him?

She understood better why he didn't want children, but she didn't know whether he was more afraid *he* would be like his father or that his father's blood would turn up in his sons and daughters. It was a cruel curse, especially for a man like George who took his responsibilities so seriously, who valued family above everything else.

She had to help free him from this yoke of misery, but she didn't know if she had enough influence over him. In order to be free, George must come face-to-face with everything he most feared.

"You're going to hate what I'm about to say," Rose began, "but I think you ought to go to that parade in Austin."

"No!" After the quiet manner in which he had told her about his father, she wasn't prepared for the vehemence of his response.

"Not because of your father," Rose hastened to add. "For yourself. If you don't, you'll feel guilty about it for the rest of your life."

George looked at the picture again. "You're wrong. I'd never forgive myself if I went." He put the picture back in the bureau.

"You ought to do it for the grandchildren," she said, ignoring his interruption. "Your father's being a hero is something they can be proud of. You'll be giving them something that was denied you."

George looked on the verge of another outburst, but he controlled his anger. "Then let their fathers go."

Rose wasn't interested in the boys or their children. Just George. She lifted another basket to Hen's bed and resumed her folding. It would have been so easy to remain silent, to concentrate on folding the frayed and threadbare clothes she had washed so carefully, but she had promised herself to take care of George. She'd never expected it would be easy.

"Just the other day you told the boys you weren't going to shirk your responsibilities as the head of the family. Well, this is one of them. You may be angry at me for saying it, but all of you are going to have to come to terms with what your father was. You're not punishing him by hiding from it. You're punishing yourselves. It's your responsibility to take the lead, to show them it's time to put this behind them. This parade is just a part of it."

"I can't."

Rose couldn't stop. She had to reach the center of the problem, George's dislike and distrust of himself.

"It's also time you stop blaming yourself for what happened and being afraid you will turn out to be like him. Children are rarely exactly like anybody."

"How can you be around this family"—a sweep of his hand took in the whole room—"for twenty-four hours and not see Pa's stamp on all of us?" George demanded, his anger unleashed. "Hen kills without the slightest twinge of conscience. Monty bullies anybody he can and enjoys it. Tyler doesn't give a damn about anybody alive, and Jeff isn't concerned with anybody but himself. As far as I can tell, Zac would perjure his soul to be on the right side of an argument. Just the thought of fathering a houseful of children like that causes me to break into a cold sweat."

Without warning, he took off his shirt. "See that?"

Welts. More than a dozen faint scars across his back.

"Pa did that in one of his drunken fits. Do you think I could live with myself if I did that to a son of mine?"

Rose had thought she was beyond being surprised by the cruelty and brutality of this man. George was right. She could hate his father. What kind of man would beat his son like that? She couldn't imagine what it must have been like to grow up knowing the blood of such a monster ran in your veins.

"Nobody said you can't have the same traits as your father. The question is whether you let them defeat you or twist you into a different shape."

"You can't always control what life does to you."

Rose knew that. It was easy for her to be logical, to weigh evidence and make rational arguments, but George had to live with the memories, with the passion, anger, and the viciousness still vivid in his memory. It was impossible to rationalize that away.

"George, there's nobody in the state of Texas more ready and willing to assume responsibility than you. What do you think you've been doing when you try to teach your brothers to get along, when you figure out how to improve the herd, round them up for market, or drive them to Corpus Christi? When you teach Zac how to ride, or let him help you and Salty with the shed? It comes so naturally you don't even realize it."

"I've never liked being the one to make all the decisions."

"Yes, you do," Rose contradicted with an indulgent smile. "Why do you think you enjoyed the army so much, or chasing Cortina's men? You may not like responsibility, but you'd never be happy taking orders. And you'd never be happy away from your family."

George didn't look convinced.

"All those traits your father gave you can be used for good. Look at what you and the boys have done since you got back. Hen wouldn't hesitate to sacrifice his life to protect any one of us. And though Monty can be irritating at times, he's the hardest-working hand on the place. Tyler works without complaint even though he hates everything about ranches. Jeff's fiercely loyal to you. And Zac would lie to God if it meant he could spend more time with you."

George looked less glum. She didn't know whether he was listening or had decided to occupy his mind with less depressing thoughts until she had finished.

She picked up her three baskets. "Come with me to the kitchen. I've got to start dinner."

No matter what crisis they might be facing, the rituals of daily life couldn't be ignored. Dinner not being on the table at seven o'clock would be a crisis in itself.

"There's a lot more if you would only let yourself see it," Rose said as she took down a large bowl. "You're so afraid of failing you don't want to try, to trust. Why?"

"Because I failed my father."

"No, you didn't. Something went wrong inside him. Get me some potatoes."

"If I could just be sure of that."

He was listening. If she could only get him to *believe*.

She took down a pan and poured some water into it.

"Is there anything Zac could do that would make you turn your back on him?"

"Of course not," George answered from inside the pantry. "He's a scamp, and I doubt he can tell the difference between what's wrong and what he wants to do—I'm not sure he cares that there is a difference—but there's a lot of good in him."

"Did you hear what you just said?" Rose asked as he emerged with a basket of potatoes. "If Zac can't destroy your affection for him, then you couldn't have destroyed your father's affection."

"You really believe that, don't you?"

"Can't you?" she asked, taking the potatoes from him.

"I don't know."

"You interpret everything you do in the worst possible light. Let me tell you what I see. Let me be your eyes and conscience." She rinsed a large potato in a pan of water and started to peel it.

"I can't do that," George said. "My mother loved my father so much she was blind to his faults. I could never be sure you wouldn't do the same. I've got to *know* I can look at myself and be proud of what I've done. I want your approval, but I've got to have my own as well."

Rose paused, knife still in the potato, the peel dangling into the water. "Okay, look at yourself all you want, but you've got to see what's there, not a bunch of ghosts from your imagination."

"You can be a fierce little tiger when you want," George said, a smile finally lightening the solemnity of his expression.

She sliced off the peel and started a new cut. "We're talking about my happiness as well as yours. I don't mean to let a dead man take it from me."

George's smile grew even broader. Coming up behind her, he put his hands around her waist. "You'd make a good mother. You'd make your children proud of themselves whether they wanted to be or not."

"And you'd make just as good a father," Rose said, forgetting her potato for the moment. "They'd love being your children."

"I'll think about what you said, all but the last part," George said, dropping a kiss on the top of her head. "I'm very glad I married you. I wish Ma could have had some of your strength. It would have been better for all of us. She failed us all, even Pa." He turned Rose around until she faced him. Neither one of them were conscious of the potato or the knife. "That's part of why I love you. You're strong enough for both of us. You won't let me give in. You fight for what you think is right. Don't ever change. I depend on you."

"I won't if you promise to believe in yourself only half as much as everybody else does."

George kissed her upturned lips. "I promise to try. Now I'd better go check on the boys and make sure they haven't killed each other."

Rose would have liked some more positive proof of his happiness, but she was enormously relieved to have finally made some progress. She dipped her now-dry potato in the water and started peeling once more.

"Don't forget to set a fire under the wash pot before you go. I'm fixing a turkey for Monty. It's nice to know I don't have to cook another one for at least two months. I'm sure the turkeys will appreciate the break, too."

Rose felt she had hardly laid her head on the pillow before it was time to get up again. The boys wanted to leave on the drive before dawn. Tyler had talked them into letting him cook. She didn't know why since they all hated his cooking, but the boy seemed to feel he was a natural-born cook, and he was impervious to opinions to the contrary.

She packed enough food to last three days.

The day passed quietly. George and Salty were building a shed for the bull. They probably could have gotten their work done twice as fast without Zac underfoot, but there was no way he would stay in the house with Rose when he could be with his brother.

She sat under the shade of the oak next to the well, rocking and drinking some persimmon tea. She watched Zac helping George with everything he did, slowing him down, but never exhausting his patience. George answered all Zac's questions, making the boy feel like an equal part in what they were doing.

Without warning, she envisioned George performing the same tasks with his son, *their* son, and her eyes filled with tears. She had to find a way to convince him to have children. And not just because the thought of remaining childless made her infinitely sad.

Because of George. There would be a great hole in his life without them. He didn't know it yet. How could he with his brothers acting like a houseful of babies? But they'd be gone in ten or fifteen years. Then he'd realize what he'd missed.

George had been almost dancing with excitement all evening. Okay, George never danced with excitement. He probably never would. He was too down-to-earth for that, but he was obviously excited about something. She could see it in his eyes. If she had had any doubts, they were erased when he gave Zac permission to sleep out with Salty.

"I don't want Salty to get so comfortable that somebody could sneak up on him," he explained to Rose. "With Zac about, it's doubtful he'll get any sleep at all."

With everyone gone, including the dogs, Salty slept away from the house to prevent a surprise attack.

George and Rose retired to their bedroom to get ready for bed. George's excitement continued to grow even though he made no attempt to make love to her. She hoped he wasn't coming down with a fever. She only had a few days left while it would be safe to make love, and she wanted to spend every night in George's arms.

She put on one of the nightgowns she'd bought in Austin, the one with the yellow ribbon, and sat brushing her hair until it glistened, its rich mahogany hues highlighted by pure ebony. In the dim light her hair looked especially dark and rich. She was glad.

She wanted to look her best for George.

"You through with that mirror?" George asked, a trace of impatience in his voice. "If I didn't know better, I'd think we were getting ready to go to a ball."

"I've never gone to a ball."

She was sorry after she'd said it. It upset George.

"But I'm sure I'll go to hundreds when you're the richest cattleman in Texas."

"You deserve to have some fun," George said. He knelt next to her chair until she could look straight into his eyes. "You shouldn't be stuck out here working from dawn to dusk, your beauty fading away with no one to appreciate it."

Rose leaned over and kissed George's upturned lips. "I hope my looks aren't fading quite that fast. I don't want to turn into a hag before I'm twenty-one." She put her finger on George's lips when he tried to interrupt. "But I don't care as long as you're with me. I'm not sure I'd like going to a ball. I'd hate to embarrass you."

"You couldn't embarrass me."

"I would like to go to New Orleans, however. Zac has piqued my curiosity."

George looked more serious than ever.

"I don't know why you married me. I can't give you any of the things you deserve."

"I don't know either," she said, hoping to lighten his mood.

"I deserve a big house in New Orleans with servants and wrought-iron balconies, balls every night, jewels and gowns, and rank upon rank of adoring lovers." She sighed in mock distress. "You can't imagine how disappointed I am that your cows are only going to make you moderately rich."

"I'm serious," George said, a smile cracking his face.

"So am I. I don't give a damn, if I may borrow a phrase from Monty, about balls and jewels and servants as long as you love me."

"Then I don't suppose you'll want this."

She didn't know what he was talking about until she glanced down at his open hand. Nestled in the deep cup of his palm was a ring set with a golden stone.

She gasped.

"Where did you get this?"

"I found it hanging on a mesquite bush."

"Don't be absurd. It's just that it looks exactly like the . . ."

". . . like the ring you saw in McGrath and Hayden's window."

Rose nodded.

"That's because it's the same ring. I had Jeff buy it on his way back from King's ranch."

"But it was so expensive."

"That doesn't matter—"

"I know it's depressingly unromantic and ungrateful of me, but it *does* matter. You wouldn't spend the family's money. How did you pay for it?"

George looked uncomfortable. She hated to ruin his fun, but she had to know.

"Tell me. Please."

"I sold my sword."

Rose was stunned. To a man who had fought in the war, no memento was as cherished as his side arms. Her father would have died before he parted with his.

But George had sold his sword to give her a wedding ring. She felt like crying from pure happiness. The silly man, didn't he realize this meant he loved her at least as much as his family? Didn't he realize she would save and scrimp, for the rest of her life if necessary, to buy his sword back for him?

George took her hand in his and slipped the ring on her finger. It was all she could do to keep from throwing herself in his arms and dripping tears all over him. She couldn't even see the ring for her swimming eyes. She could barely make out his dear, precious features.

For once she could look at him without thinking of how handsome, or how strong, or how big and safe he looked. He was a man, *her man*, who needed her and didn't even know it. He was so strong and invincible and brave. But inside he was just as vulnerable as any child. He didn't know that. Neither did anybody else. And she wasn't about to tell them.

It was enough that she knew.

Yet her happiness was not without alloy.

She knew he gave her the ring because he loved her, because he wanted to give her something she had wanted very much. But she also knew he gave it to her out of guilt. He had denied her children. This was only a token payment.

She could see him making payments for the rest of his life, and she renewed her vow to change his mind. It was bad enough that he was afraid to let himself have something he really wanted. It was intolerable that he would feel guilty about it.

But that was for another time. Tonight she wanted to bask in his love, to let her soul spill over with happiness knowing he loved her enough to make such a sacrifice for her.

"It's beautiful," she told him, "but you know I didn't expect a ring."

"That's part of the reason I wanted to give it to you," George said. "You never expect anything, but you've given me so much more than I ever thought possible. It's about the only thing I can do for you."

Rose drew him to her, nestling his head between her breasts.

"I don't know what I have to do to convince you I'm happy just as I am."

"I've made you live in a dog trot, forced you to cook and clean for half a dozen men, do without female companionship, give up any hope of having a family. There wouldn't be a long line forming at the marriage bureau if every other woman was to get the same."

"They would if you were thrown into the bargain," Rose assured him. "You couldn't get rid of me no matter how hard you tried."

"I still don't understand that," George said, his mouth nuzzling her breast through the thin material.

"I hope you don't expect me to explain it with you scrambling my wits like you are."

"I can do a much better job than this," George said, hunger and amusement cavorting in his eyes.

"I hope so," Rose said, her voice growing a little unsteady. "I'm counting on it."

For the next half hour Rose forgot all the questions plaguing her, all the arguments she needed to marshal to change George's mind, even the significance of his sacrifice for her ring. She was only conscious of what he was doing to her body. She yielded happily to his every suggestion.

It was so hot they couldn't sleep. They got up and took chairs out to the yard. The moon flooded the landscape with light, but the night was virtually soundless. Even the crickets down by the creek had fallen silent. Everything seemed to be saving its energy for the coming day. The breeze rustled the brittle leaves in the trees along the creek and in the endless brush. Rose could imagine a wolf or panther stalking its prey somewhere in the night and was thankful for George's presence.

It was hard to believe that after spending her whole life in a town she could feel safe out here, miles from anyone, unknown dangers lurking in the vast distance. Even the threat of Indians didn't bother her.

Not as long as George was here.

She didn't know what other women might think of him. She had grown up without girlfriends and had exchanged no confidences. Still, she imagined that many a young woman, attracted by his looks and the aura of command about him, would be disappointed to find him so quiet and thoughtful, so content to stay at home.

Rose found it reassuring.

She remembered the ache whenever her father had left, his happiness whenever he was assigned to a new outpost, his restlessness during furloughs at home, her feeling of always being second-best.

She would never feel that way with George. There was no place he'd rather be than with her.

"I've been thinking," George said. He was standing, looking back at the house. "We ought to add on. One room isn't big enough for five boys."

Especially if Madison returned. George didn't say that, but she knew he thought it. He would never give up hope that his brother would come back.

"How much more room do you think you need?" Rose asked.

"You need a room of your own, one besides the bedroom or the kitchen. And we need someplace to eat that isn't right next to the hearth."

"This isn't Virginia," she said, laughing. "Texas ranch houses don't have parlors and dining rooms."

"We will, even if nobody else in Texas does."

Rose smiled indulgently. "And what else do you want?"

"I don't know. It's hard to say how long the boys might be here. If some of them decide to live here with their families, well, it's hard to say."

It would depend on how many children they had. George wouldn't say that because he knew it would hurt her, but Rose knew what he meant.

"They might prefer their own homes," Rose said.

"We could build them on the ridge along the creek," George said, pointing to a small rise that extended for several hundred yards.

"In that case, you won't have to enlarge the house."

"We'll see."

Rose's body tensed, and she looked up quickly. There was something different about George's tone of voice. Something different about his expression, too. He turned to the corrals.

"I think we ought to build a barn, too. The bull is too valuable to leave out as long as there are wolves and panthers about."

Was he talking about barns because he wanted to or because he wanted to keep her from asking what he really meant about enlarging the house? It was on the tip of her tongue to ask when Zac came running up. He was so out of breath it was several seconds before he could utter a sound.

"The McClendons are coming," he gasped at last. "They've already crossed the creek."

# *Chapter Twenty-one*

"How far are they from the house?" George asked. He instinctively looked down the lane as though he expected to see them come riding up.

"I don't know. We saw them at the oaks where Monty hunts turkeys. Salty was showing me what to do when we heard them," Zac explained.

"At two o'clock in the morning?"

"I couldn't sleep. Neither could Salty."

"Not with you peppering him with questions, I'll bet. Where is he now?"

"He's watching them."

"What are you going to do?" Rose asked.

"Try to talk them into leaving. Zac, you stay here and help Rose."

"That's not fair. I want—"

"This has nothing to do with fair," George cut him off. "Rose needs your help." You didn't question George when he used that tone of voice, and Zac knew it.

George hurried to their bedroom. He took down a jacket and filled the pockets with shells. He also took down an extra rifle.

"I'll be back as soon as I can, but don't expect me before dawn."

"You will be careful, won't you?" Rose asked.

"Very careful. There's a great deal I'm looking forward to, and I don't mean to let the McClendons cause me to miss it."

George decided to go on foot, but he soon regretted his decision. His boots weren't made for walking, much less running. But he couldn't afford the time to saddle a horse or the sound of its hooves.

He didn't have to go very far. The McClendons were hardly a half mile from the house.

"Pssst!" Salty hissed from the midst of a thicket along the creek.

George darted into the shadows.

"How many are there?"

"Six. The old man's leading. They're coming slowly. They've even wrapped their horses' hooves. They're trying to get close enough to surprise us."

"Good. I've got a surprise for them."

"Something else you ought to know. Silas is with them."

"Silas! But he left on the drive to Corpus Christi."

"He must have sneaked off and come back."

"Why?"

"I don't know. I figured you might."

"How would I know? I never talked with him more than in the ordinary way."

"He must have a reason."

"I know, and that worries me."

"What do you mean to do?"

"Ask them what they're doing here."

"Wh—" Salty started to chuckle. "I'll bet you didn't learn that tactic in the army."

"No, but this is one battle I don't want to fight. This might be only a decoy. I'm hoping the main group isn't coming up behind the house right now."

"I don't think so. They wouldn't have gone to so much trouble to muffle their approach if they were trying to divert your attention."

"That's what I'm betting. Let's hope we're both right. Now let's head back toward the house. They've got to take this path through the brush. When they reach the bottleneck, we'll stop them. You on one side, me on the other."

By the time George and Salty had retreated the two hundred yards back toward the house, George was certain there was no other attacking force. It was just old McClendon, his four sons, and Silas. For some reason, nobody else from the clan was included. George and Salty took up their positions in the brush and waited. It wasn't long before they were close enough for him to hear them talking.

"How do you plan on making him tell you where the gold's hid?" the old man was asking Silas.

"You get your hands on that kid and his woman, and he'll tell you anything."

"I wouldn't turn over no gold for no woman," McClendon said, scoffing at such reasoning.

"Neither would I, but George Randolph isn't like you or me. He thinks people are more important than gold."

"Fool," McClendon said.

"You sure there's as much as you say?" one of the boys asked. "Don't seem likely they coulda drug all that much from Virginia without nobody knowing."

"There's half a million, and they brought it with them. Where do you think they got all the gold they've been flashing about Austin?"

"I'm heading for New Orleans the minute I get my share," one of the boys said. "I mean to have me a whole room full of women. And I won't let them put on nothing but them black stockings."

"I want one of them fancy houses chock full o' servants to do anything I want."

"Including jump in the bed with you?" another giggled.

"That, too," his brother agreed.

"Can't none of you spend that gold till we get our hands on it," the patriarch declared. "You'd better be remembering what you're supposed to do when we get to the house. Tell 'um again," he directed Silas.

"We leave our horses at the corral," Silas began. "George and his wife sleep behind the kitchen, Salty and the kid across the breezeway. Two of you circle around until you get—"

"It's a little dark out for a pleasure ride, McClendon," George called when they came abreast.

"I guess that accounts for you wandering so far off your land," Salty called out from the other side of the trail.

Realizing they could be caught in a cross fire, the raiders involuntarily jerked on their reins and reached for their weapons. Their mounts responded by throwing up their heads, snorting, and dancing nervously about, turning one way and then the next. They had been riding in close formation, and the ensuing confusion made it impossible for the McClendons to do more than be a danger to each other.

"What do you want here?" George demanded. "You didn't come in the middle of the night for a friendly visit."

"We've come for the gold," Silas replied.

"What'd you go and tell him that for?" old man McClendon hissed. "Now he'll be on his guard."

"We had to tell him sooner or later," Silas replied. "You can't hold a man up without telling him what you want."

"Particularly when we don't know where he's got it hid," one of the boys added.

"I don't have much more than a hundred dollars left," George said. "Why do you think the boys have gone to sell some of the herd?"

"I'm talking about that Union payroll," Silas said.

"I don't know anything about a payroll."

"I mean the one your father stole."

"You must be drunk, Silas," George said. "Do you know what he's talking about, Salty?"

"Your father captured a Union patrol that was supposed to be escorting a half-million-dollar army payroll," Salty called back. "The money was never found. Your father said it was a decoy patrol, that the gold went some other way."

"His father stole that gold," Silas insisted. "George spent nearly a year in Virginia after the war. I figure he found it. The gold he's been spending in town is part of it."

"You figured wrong."

"How would an ex-Confederate like you get his hands on gold?"

"From the sale of a small piece of land left us by an aunt," George said. "You can check the court records if you like."

"I don't believe you. You brought that gold back and hid it. You don't have to worry. We won't take all of it."

"How much would you take, Silas?"

"Half. You won't get to keep any if we tell the Reconstruction people about it."

"And once you get the first half, you won't want to come back for the second half?"

"Half is enough for me."

"What about the McClendons? Maybe they think stealing gold would be easier than stealing cattle."

The younger McClendons, muttering curses, showed signs of wanting to charge the hidden voices.

"Don't get riled," the old man ordered his sons. "They can shoot you out of your saddle before you get ten yards."

"If I did have this gold, I'd rather turn it over to the army than you," George said. "At least I could sleep easy in my bed."

"There's no need to feel uneasy," Silas assured him. "There's six of you and there's six of us. Half seems fair. It'll give us all something to start over with."

"Silas, I don't have any gold. I never had any. If I did have it, I'd turn it over to the army."

"I told you there weren't no gold," one of the boys hissed.

"He's just trying to make you think he ain't got it," another said. "Them Randolphs is slick as muskrats."

"You boys hush," the old man ordered. "I ain't believing nobody, not until I see for myself."

"It would save a lot of trouble if you would just give us the gold," Silas called. "We won't bother your wife or your little brother. We'll just ride out of here and you'll never see us again."

"For the last time, I don't have any gold, and I don't know anything about it. Second, if I did have the gold, I don't believe you'd ride out and leave half of it here. You wouldn't be satisfied until you had it all. Not when the McClendons are too lazy to work cattle in a country where cattle practically take care of themselves. Men who'll steal cows won't walk away from gold."

"You're making a big mistake."

"No, you are. You're taking a chance on getting killed for something that doesn't exist. Now I'm tired of talking. Turn around and start back toward the creek."

"We'll be back," old man McClendon said.

"I figured you would," George said, "but when you do, know I mean to kill as many of you as I can."

"There's more than forty of us," the old man said. "There's only one of you."

"There's only one of you, too," George replied, "And I mean to get you first. Cut off the head of a snake, and the body dies. You're the head, McClendon. You're the evil which infests your family."

"I'll kill you, Randolph," McClendon shouted. "I'll kill you and every one of your kin."

"A few hundred thousand Yankees tried and failed. I figure any one of them was a better man than you."

George put a bullet into the ground in front of McClendon's horse. The animal reared in fright, throwing the old man, then galloped off into the night.

"Now get out of here."

McClendon hobbled after his retreating party.

"You think they'll come today?"

Rose had taken George his dinner out in the brush overlooking the trail. He had decided the middle of the afternoon was the safest time to eat.

"I expect they'll come tonight. They've got to capture us alive. They need me to tell them where the gold is, and they need you and Zac to force me to do it."

"I tried to tell Silas there wasn't any gold," Rose said.

"Once people get it in their heads there's a fortune to be had just for the taking, they won't believe it doesn't exist, no matter what you tell them. That would mean they would have to give up hope, and people will do just about anything to keep hope alive."

"Well, you can tell Silas and that evil old man I have hopes, too, and I don't mean to give them up."

"And just what are they?"

George motioned for Rose to sit down next to him. He didn't dare take his eyes off the trail, but he liked having her close. Rose obliged by settling herself next to him while he ate his dinner.

"I dream of living here for the rest of my life. Of years and years of seeing you ride up to the house ready for your dinner, of seeing your sons riding all around you—"

"We've been over that already."

"This is my dream," Rose reminded him. "I'll dream what I like."

"Okay," George said, going back to his food. "What else?"

"I dream of girls, too. There are too many men around this place. You need a few daughters. They would make you feel like a new man."

George grunted. Rose doubted it was in agreement.

"I dream of evenings when we sit on the porch and watch the sun go down, of winter nights spent before the fire, of summer days spent picking wild plums or having a picnic in a pecan grove. I also dream of seeing all your brothers here with their wives and children."

"The house wouldn't be big enough to hold them."

"It's summer," Rose said. "The children play half the night while the grown-ups sit outside, catching up on the news, reminiscing about the times they had when they were young."

"You really are caught up on the idea of children, aren't you?"

"I can't help it. A future without children seems so empty."

"Why?"

"I'm not sure I can explain it. I know they're a lot of work, that they'll bring heartache and sorrow, but I can't imagine anything more wonderful than facing the last years of my life surrounded by my children. But that's only part of my dream."

"What's the rest?"

"It's mostly about you."

"Don't I get to hear it?"

"If you want."

"I want," George said, giving her a quick kiss.

"It's nothing much out of the ordinary. Just things I like about you."

"Tell me."

Rose chuckled contentedly. It was hard to believe she could be so complacent in the midst of trouble. Maybe after Indians, bandits, and rustlers, she was getting used to danger. But then things always seemed less dangerous when she was with George.

"I like watching you with your brothers. You're never so happy as when they're around you, usually all talking at once, arguing for their point of view. Of course you know they'll do whatever you say—"

"I'm not that bad."

"—so you can enjoy it. I also enjoy watching you with Zac. You never seem to be too busy for him even though he can be annoying."

"Is that all you like about me? George the patriarch, George the indulgent big brother?"

Rose ducked her eyes so she wouldn't have to look at him. "I also like George the lover. I doubt I'm very good at it yet, but I do like it."

"You're more than good," George said, giving her a nuzzle. "If I weren't afraid there were McClendons lurking about even now, I'd show you just how good."

Rose sat up with a jerk. "Not here, you wouldn't, not in the dust and the briars."

"Even here."

"You're not going to treat me like one of your old cows," Rose protested. She sounded indignant, but she was secretly pleased. It thrilled her to think George could be so strongly attracted to her he would make love to her in the brush. She had started a treasure chest of memories, the times when George had been so moved he had done something completely untypical. So far she only had his knocking down Luke Kearney and asking her to marry him. Making love out-of-doors would make a nice addition. She'd have to see what she could do about arranging a picnic.

In the meantime, however, the McClendons were about, and she had a lot to do before nightfall. As much as she didn't want to let go of this moment, she would never forget the look on old man McClendon's face when he'd charged the house over a few cows. She didn't even want to think what he might be willing to do for half a million dollars.

George handed her his empty plate.

She got to her feet. "You won't stay out here too long, will you?"

"Just until Salty gets back. Once I know how many are coming, I'll know what to do."

A few minutes after Rose left, Salty returned through the brush.

"McClendon's bringing the whole tribe," he said. "They're probably half an hour away."

George looked at the sinking sun.

"We've got another two hours before it's really dark. Do you think they'll wait?"

"I wouldn't depend on it. There're so many of them they might think they can attack anytime they want."

"That's what I was thinking. Was Silas with them?"

"Yes."

"So they're still convinced I've got the gold?"

"Seems like it."

George cursed. "Then they mean to kill us in the end."

"We'll stay here as long as we can, but I doubt we'll be able to hold the house for long."

George and Salty had returned to the house. Having made his preparations for the attack, George was now going over his plans for their escape.

"I packed as much food as I could," Rose said.

"And I've hidden our horses," Salty added. "We ought to be able to get to Austin under cover of dark."

The minute Salty mentioned Austin, George knew he wasn't going to run away. It might be crazy to attempt to fight off so many, but a man had to make a stand somewhere. He couldn't just keep moving on if he ever wanted to amount to anything. And George knew he wanted to do more than just amount to something. He wanted to create something, he wanted to leave something behind.

He wanted children.

Just the thought gave him an unexpectedly comfortable feeling. It was like another gear in his life clicking into place. Another piece of a puzzle which, when complete, would tell him who George Randolph was. He knew it was the right piece because it felt good.

He wanted to tell Rose. He wanted to share this moment of discovery with her, but there wasn't time. If they were to have any future, with or without children, he had to concentrate on the McClendons.

"We have to have someplace to go, somewhere they won't find us."

"We could go into the brush," Salty said.

"That won't stop them for long. They're more at home there than we are."

"I know where we can hide," Zac said. "In the cave."

"What cave?" George asked.

"The cave in the creek. Under the pecan trees." They stared at Zac. "It's big enough for all of us. I go there all the time."

"So that's why I can never find you," Rose said.

"Can we get there without being seen?" George asked.

"Sure. I do it all the time."

"Then you and Rose take the food and ammunition there right now," George said.

"I don't want to go without you," Rose objected.

"It'll be best for Salty and me to stay. If they do attack while you're at the creek, don't fire on them. I don't want them to know where we've gone."

Rose realized that if they abandoned the house, the Mc-Clendons might destroy everything in it. She hated to think of losing the beautiful bedroom furniture, but there wasn't anything else in the house that was really important to them.

Except the picture of Tom Bland.

She hurried into the boys' bedroom. She opened the drawer and quickly retrieved the picture. She was about to turn away when she noticed the protruding corner of a second picture frame. Rose pushed aside the shirts covering it.

Surprise stilled her breath. It was a picture of George's family taken in front of their Virginia home, probably just before they came to Texas. Zac was still a baby in his mother's arms.

Her gaze was immediately drawn to the tallest boy standing behind his mother. A tender smile softened her features. George. He looked so young and so serious. Not as handsome as now, but it was easy to see in him the man he was to become.

Inexorably her gaze was drawn to the man standing at the right of the group. She was stunned. William Henry Randolph didn't look a thing like she'd expected. He was the best-looking man she'd ever seen. The only one in the picture who was smiling; his charm transcended the limits of the tintype. It was almost impossible for her to believe that the father George feared and the twins despised could live inside that gorgeous man. There was no weakness, no dissipation, no viciousness written in his face. He looked like the answer to any woman's prayer.

Her gaze shifted to Aurelia Randolph. She was a pale woman, fragile, shy, and tired. She was easily outshone by her husband—she had none of the energy, the vitality that practically jumped out of the picture—but she was still very beautiful. Rose felt a twinge of jealousy that any woman could look that lovely after bearing so many children.

It was easy to identify the rest. Tyler off to one side, a loner even then; the twins on either side of their mother. She assumed it was Hen who rested a protective hand on her shoulder. Jeff completely overshadowed between George and his father. And the smaller version of George must be Madison.

She rummaged through the drawer to see if there might be more pictures, but she found none. She wrapped both pictures very carefully. It was possible they would be the only mementos of George's life before the war. He would need them to keep the memories fresh.

The attack came five minutes after Zac and Rose left the house. It wasn't a frontal assault. They came from all sides, through the brush, from the corrals, across the yard.

"We can't hold them very long like this," Salty called from across the breezeway.

"Just keep firing as fast as you can," George replied. "If we can break this first attack, we'll have a chance."

Ordinarily two men wouldn't have been able to stand off so many, but the builders of the house had cleared the ground for at least fifty yards in all directions. George and Salty had a clear shot at each McClendon the moment he broke cover. Within fifteen minutes the attacking force had been reduced by a quarter.

The McClendons drew back.

"Now what?" Salty called from the kitchen.

"We wait," George called back from the bedroom. "And we load as many rifles as possible before they come at us again."

But they didn't come. Dusk came and then darkness. Still they didn't come.

"What are they planning?" Salty called.

"They're going to burn us out."

"How do you know?"

"It's the only way. They've already lighted the torches."

Salty could see an ominous glow through the brush.

"What can we do?"

"Get out before we become sitting ducks."

Gathering up his rifles and stuffing all the ammunition into his pockets, George dashed out the door, through the breeze-way, and straight for the creek. Salty followed.

"They're getting away," one of the McClendons called. Shots peppered the night around them.

"Forget them," another voice called. "It's the gold we're after."

"But we don't know where it is."

"Silas says he knows."

George and Salty reached the creek, crawled through the brush, and slipped over the bank. "Now where's Zac's cave?" George muttered.

"Down here," Zac's voice called to them out of the night.

The dry summer had reduced the creek to a thin ribbon. But the violence of the periodic floods was evidenced by a creek bed up to twenty feet wide and six feet deep. A thick grove of towering pecans bordered the creek on both sides where it took a sharp turn. Swollen currents had carved out a network of tunnels between the deep, thick roots. The air was thick and dank, but it was blessedly cool.

"It's quite a cave. A dozen people could hide here."

"They'll never find us," Zac said proudly.

"Maybe not, but I don't mean to give them a chance. We'll stand watch."

"I'll help," Zac offered.

"Not yet. Salty and I will take turns. You and Rose need your sleep. We don't know what they'll do tomorrow."

"Are you sure we can't help?" Rose asked. "Hiding while you take all the risks makes me feel like a coward."

"We don't have any choice," George said. "They outnumber us. The only way we can hope to win is by attrition. If they catch even one of us, it'll be over. If we have to run, we'll need all our strength."

"Do you plan to run?"

"No, but I'm not going to risk our lives foolishly. Now get some sleep. I'll call you when it's morning."

"Do you think they'll come looking for us?" Salty asked. It was about three o'clock, time for him to take over the watch. He had joined George in the brush along the far bank of the creek.

"Yes. When they don't find any gold, they're going to be sure we took it with us. At the least they'll think I know where it's buried."

"I shouldn't have hired Silas. I never liked him much."

"You can't tell what's in a person's mind. It could have been any one of the others." George was silent for a few minutes. "He was a fool to tell McClendon. He would have done better to come to me himself. That old man won't share anything with anybody, including his own sons. He means to kill Silas once he gets his hands on the gold."

"Do you believe what they said, about your father, I mean?"

"I was going to ask you the same thing."

"I don't know. He was daring enough to do anything. He would have taken the gold if he wanted, but I don't think he would have done it for his family."

George laughed harshly. "He never did anything for his family."

They sat in silence for some time.

"Why didn't you tell me you knew Pa?" George asked.

"He said I wasn't to say anything until you asked," Salty said. "He said you might be so angry you wouldn't want to know anything about him."

"I was, but I guess I keep hoping I'll learn something that will explain him to me. I doubt Pa himself knew why he did things. He probably just turned any way the wind blew him. Still, I keep hoping there was something more to him than that."

"There was," Salty said. "He knew he'd made a mess of his life, and he hated it. He just couldn't do anything about it. That's what killed him in the end. Or caused him to get himself killed."

George gave a snort of contempt. "Pa wouldn't kill himself. He liked himself too much for that."

"He hated himself," Salty contradicted. "He knew he was a failure, knew he'd disappointed you and your brothers, and he couldn't live with that."

A few choice expletives cleaved the night air. "You expect me to believe that, after the way he treated us? What about my mother?"

"I'm afraid he didn't think much of women. Maybe they came too easy. I don't know."

"How do you know all this?"

"I was under your father's command. I was in his last patrol."

"So you're one of the ones he treated like a son."

"That hurt, didn't it?" Salty said.

"More than anything else that son-of-a-bitch ever did. I would have given my right arm for him to be a father to me."

"He knew that."

"Then why the hell didn't he do something about it?"

"Because he couldn't."

"Because it was more fun to keep on drinking and chasing women than it was to take a kid riding."

"Your father never talked to any of us," Salty said. "He just listened. But he couldn't sleep that night before he rode into Sherman's lines. I think he'd already made up his mind what he was going to do. I sat up with him, just listening. He talked all night."

"I bet he had a lot to tell. I'm not surprised you weren't strong enough to ride into battle next day. Or couldn't you stand to be anywhere near him?"

"He just talked about two people. Tom Bland and you."

George had expected many things, but never that.

"And what did he say?"

"That you two were the greatest mistakes of his life. Nothing else mattered."

"Not even my mother."

"He said he told her, but she wouldn't believe him."

"Told her what?"

"Not to marry him, that he was rotten, that he would break her heart."

"That's one prophecy he certainly lived up to. What excuse did he have for Tom Bland?"

"None. He hated Tom as much as he loved him."

"That makes no sense."

"He saw in Tom all the things he should have been. He hated it even more when you boys turned to Tom. Each failure made him hate Tom even more."

"Either you're crazy or Pa was. I never heard such nonsense."

"It was as though the better Tom was, the more your father wanted to destroy him. Anyway, he seduced Tom's sister just to goad Tom into calling him out."

"And killed him because he was so good he couldn't stand to let him go on living?"

"I don't think he meant to go that far. The drink muddled him a bit."

"Nothing muddled him. He was evil to the core."

"He wasn't so evil he couldn't feel remorse. He used to mumble things about Tom. I didn't understand them. I don't suppose they made sense to anyone but him."

"I don't think he felt any remorse about killing Tom," George said angrily, "but I'm glad something bothered him. I only wish he'd suffered half as much as the rest of us."

"He did, mostly over you."

George didn't want to hear any more. He had finally come to accept the fact that his father had no redeeming qualities. He couldn't afford to hope again.

"You're not going to tell me he gave me a single thought after ignoring me all those years. I won't believe you."

"I don't know how often he thought about you, but he was proud of you."

The curses George spat out would have shocked even Monty.

"He talked about you a lot, mostly a sentence here and there, but we all knew he was proud of you. That's one of the reasons the boys were so willing to confide in him. They figured if he could have such an interest in you, he might be willing to listen to them."

George felt like getting up and walking away. He didn't believe a word of it. But what upset him the most was he *wanted* to believe it. He *needed* to believe it. No matter what Salty told him, he would continue to sit there, waiting, hoping for something that would allow him to respect his father just the tiniest bit.

"Your father knew he wasn't a good man, but he knew that you were."

"Don't make stuff up, Salty," George said. He could feel the need to believe growing greater all the time. If he could only trust Salty to tell him the truth.

"He said that while you were still a child, he could see you were going to become the man he should have been. He also saw that you adored him, that you would do your best to be like him. That's when he decided to drive you away so he wouldn't ruin you."

"Surely you don't expect me to believe that Pa became the most disliked man in Virginia just to keep me from trying to be like him."

"No. I doubt he did anything he didn't enjoy, but he did want to protect you. That's why he ignored you."

"So I could grow up without any guidance at all."

"He said he knew you were strong enough. And you proved him right."

George had almost succumbed, he had almost believed, but that was too much. Not once in his whole life could he remember his father saying anything about his strength of character. In fact, his father had berated him for being weak and too willing to talk when action was called for. He had mocked his skills, his friends, his dress, his interest in going to West Point. He may have felt some remorse over killing Tom—George would like to think he had at least that tiny bit of humanity in his soul—but he'd never believe he admired his son in any way.

"He gave me something for you. He made me promise to make sure you got it."

"How did you know where to find me?"

"He told me how to reach this place. He knew you'd be here. He said you'd come because your brothers would need you."

George teetered on the edge again. There were times he wished he could forget he'd ever had a father. He never wished that more than now.

Salty went over to his bedroll, opened it up, and withdrew a sword. He held it out to George. "He wanted you to have this."

George couldn't touch it. No matter how much he wanted to, he couldn't. It would mean he believed. It would mean he was vulnerable. If he gave in just once, there would be no way back, no barrier from all the pain he'd walled off for so many years. He couldn't take that chance.

"Why would he give me his sword?"

"He also sent you a letter." Salty went back to his roll and extracted a crumpled envelope from its depths. The wax seal was badly cracked, but it was still unbroken.

"He wrote that the night before he died."

George felt as if he had been turned to stone. He couldn't move. He stared at the envelope in Salty's hands. He desperately wanted to take it, but he was afraid. He was so near the edge now, he might never get back.

Then he remembered what Rose had told him, that he was so afraid of having things go wrong that he wouldn't let himself live, that he would deny himself the chance to have the things he wanted. If he didn't have the courage to read his father's last words to him, how could he have the courage to face the rest of his own life?

How could he deserve a wife like Rose?

Quickly, before he could change his mind, he took the envelope, ripped open the seal, and took out the single sheet. There was only one sentence written on that page.

*"Remember me the way I died, not the way I lived."*

George could feel the walls crumble and fall. He could feel the tempered steel within him bend and melt. He could feel the freeing of something inside, something small and undefinable, but something quite essential. For a moment he felt unwell; then it passed away. He felt worse and he felt better. He felt tremendous disappointment, regret as well, but he also felt relief.

Maybe he could believe after all.

# Chapter Twenty-two

"They gotta be here somewheres," one voice said.

"They probably headed for Austin. They had the whole night to get away."

"While we was digging up half their yard."

"I never did think there was no gold, but Pa won't listen. He means to make that man tell where he hid it. He said he'd peel the hide off that woman inch by inch if he had to."

George had been mad before, but what he experienced now was something completely new. He could feel rage boil through him like the surf on a rocky shore, a mighty current driving it higher and harder. This must have been how his father had felt when he lost control of his temper.

The thought frightened George so much, the rage began to recede.

"We've got to lure them away or they'll soon find us," George whispered to Rose. "Salty and I will draw them off. You and Zac stay put. Don't move no matter how much gunfire you hear."

"Why should I hear gunfire?" Rose asked.

"We can't draw them off unless we attract their attention, can we?"

Rose didn't look reassured.

"Don't expect us back before nightfall," George said.

"Be careful."

They could do little more in the cave than crawl on their hands and knees, but George managed to get his arms around Rose. "I've never had anything to come back to, but I do now. You can be sure it's going to take more than a few dozen McClendons to keep me away." He kissed Rose quite vigorously.

"You and Zac might as well take a nap. It'll make the day go faster."

"What are you going to do?"

"I don't know, but I'm going to convince old man McClendon it's not a good idea to come around here again."

"How?"

"I'll find a way."

Then he was gone. He just crawled out of the cave and disappeared.

Rose was uncomfortable. George wasn't like himself. There was a ruthlessness in him she had never seen. Determination she knew and expected. But this was different. This frightened her. She wasn't sure she liked it.

"Can't we at least see what's going on?" Zac begged.

They had spent a long, tense, boring day hiding deep in the cave waiting for George to return. She had stayed awake, but she had encouraged Zac to sleep. Now he was bursting with energy while she could hardly keep her eyes open.

"You're not to go near the opening," Rose said. "You never know when one of them might be crossing the creek. And keep your voice down."

"But they won't catch me. You never did," challenged Zac. "Neither did George."

"That may be true," Rose admitted, "but this is no game of hide-and-seek. If those men find you, you know George would give himself up, don't you?"

The boy nodded.

"They won't believe there's no gold. They'll kill us all. Now do you understand?"

Zac nodded again.

"Good. Now why don't you tell me a story. I don't think I could think of another one if you held a gun to my head."

Rose woke with a start. She had fallen asleep with Zac telling her a story about the dog he was going to have George buy for him when they sold the herd. She wondered why she felt so warm until she realized that Zac had pulled a quilt over her. He really was the dearest boy. She'd have to do something really special for him when everything got back to normal. In the meantime she'd better see about something to eat. It was dark enough in the cave to be late afternoon. She sat up expecting to find Zac right next to her.

He was gone!

She felt a desire to spank him within an inch of his life even as fear for his life caused her breath to come quick and shallow. Maybe he was just near the entrance. She scrambled through the labyrinth of roots, all the while cursing herself for falling asleep. Zac would never have left had she been awake.

The mouth of the cave was deserted. Zac was truly gone. She had to find him. She would never forgive herself if anything happened to the child.

She didn't even want to think about how George would feel. From the way he acted this morning, he wouldn't stop until every McClendon was dead. That would destroy George and all her dreams. She couldn't allow that.

Rose crawled out of the cave and listened. After a few moments she heard shots somewhere far to the west. So George and Salty had drawn the McClendons off. She felt a little better. The fewer McClendons left, the more likely nothing had happened to Zac. Rose crawled back into the cave, picked out a rifle, checked to make sure it was fully loaded, and started out again.

After half an hour of searching she had found no trace of the boy. She also found no McClendons. It was as though they had never been there. She didn't dare approach the smoldering remains of the house—McClendons were bound to be there—but she didn't think Zac would have gone to the house. She wondered if he might not have returned to the cave by now.

But she didn't make it back to the creek. She had hardly gone twenty yards when old man McClendon leapt out at her from behind a thick tree trunk. He wrenched the rifle from her hands.

"I knew you'd turn back to your den." He chuckled. "I know about those caves. I hid there once myself from some Indians. I thought you'd find them."

It was useless to struggle. He might look old, but he was amazingly strong. Besides, she wouldn't get two yards before he gunned her down.

"We're going back to wait for your husband," McClendon said. "I don't expect he'll stay out much longer."

Rose knew she couldn't allow McClendon to drag her back to the cave. If he ever got her inside, George wouldn't be able to save her.

She struggled just enough to slow him down, trying all the while to decide where to make her stand. But no place seemed to be a good spot. Rose soon realized that if she was going to do anything, she had to do it soon. She thrust her foot between McClendon's legs to trip him. At the same time, she hit him in the middle with all her strength.

The old man hardly flinched. He didn't stumble. He hit her just above the temple with the butt of his rifle. Rose collapsed in a heap at his feet.

"I'll crack your skull if you try anything like that again," he threatened.

Rose offered no resistance when he picked her up and started dragging her toward the creek. She fought to remain conscious. She had to warn George. Summoning all her strength, Rose let out a long shriek.

"George!"

The sound lingered in the heavy afternoon air like a shimmering light, but Rose didn't hear it. McClendon's long, thin fingers closed around her throat, cutting off her air. All she heard was a ringing in her ears before blackness engulfed her.

An hour earlier George and Salty had abandoned their attempt to decoy the McClendons and started back to the cave. They had almost reached the creek when the cry turned George's blood cold. It galvanized him into action. He sprinted across the open plain separating him from the creek, vaulted over the brush into the creek, and ran down the gravel-strewn bed toward the cry which still rang in his ears. He came to a shuddering halt when he saw McClendon dragging Rose's inert form toward the creek.

A murderous fury unlike anything he'd ever known exploded inside him. He felt a cold-blooded desire to kill, to destroy without mercy this man who threatened someone he loved. It was as though some beast had lain, safely chained, buried deep inside him for years. But the need to fight for his life, and the lives of those he loved, had stripped away the softness and unchained the monster.

It was as though his father had come back to life and taken over his body.

Even as he stood facing McClendon, trying to decide what to do to protect Rose, George fought off the blood lust, the animal rage. Whatever he did, he would do it because he must, not because he couldn't control himself.

"Let her go, McClendon," George called out. "I've told you already, there's no gold. There never has been."

The old man looked up, surprised. Then an evil grin spread over his face. "I sent the others away," he said. "They believe you've gone to Austin. I knew you wouldn't. You're too stubborn. But you're not stupid. All I want is the money. You just tell me where it is, and I'll let your woman go. I don't want them boys to know I got it. They'll just waste it on whores. They won't have a cent left by Christmas. Not me. I don't aim to be poor again."

Salty had come up behind George during the exchange with McClendon.

"I'm going to try for a shot," George whispered.

"Where? Even if you shoot him in the head, he might still get a shot into Rose."

"I know. I'm going to try for his elbow. Watch him a minute."

George disappeared inside the cave. He emerged moments later carrying a single dueling pistol.

"Keep an eye out for Zac," he said to Salty. "I don't see him anywhere."

George vaulted out of the creek bed onto the flat ground above. He stood facing McClendon.

"Tell me where the gold is or I'll kill her," McClendon said, his grin even wider.

"You're bluffing, old man," George answered. "Let Rose go or I'll kill you where you stand. And don't think I can't do it. My father taught me to shoot the pips out of a playing card at twenty paces. Wouldn't let me sleep one night until I did it twenty times in succession."

Uneasily, McClendon eyed the pistol hanging at George's side, but he didn't let go of Rose.

"You won't kill me," George continued. He started walking toward the old man. "If I did have any gold, I wouldn't have told anybody where I hid it. You'd never find it if I was dead. And you won't kill Rose because you know I'll kill you."

"You'd better not push me too far," the old man threatened.

George kept walking.

"You don't mean to let us go. You've got your kin out there somewhere. No more than half a dozen followed Salty and me. It wouldn't surprise me if they were all around us this very minute. As soon as I tell you where the gold is, you'll call them in and kill all of us."

George continued walking.

"Don't come any further," the old man cried. "I'll kill her."

"Then I'll kill you. You still won't have any gold."

George had come close enough to see that Rose had regained consciousness. He also saw a thin streak of blood trickling down her temple.

The beast inside him leapt up, snarling. Every feeling of compassion, every desire to spare the old man's life, went dead in his breast. He had never felt so calm in his life, never felt so sure he could kill.

He wasn't himself any longer. He had been shoved aside. Someone else was in control of his body.

"I'm going to kill him, Rose," George said, ignoring McClendon. "As soon as you feel able, fall away from him. Then make for the creek as fast as you can. They'll be coming out of the brush."

"You're a fool if you think you can get away," the old man said, backing up, dragging Rose with him. "The boys will hunt you down out there."

"That won't do you any good, will it?" George taunted, still walking toward the old man. "You'll be dead and in hell."

Even as George felt his body tense, his arm begin to rise, he made one last attempt to fight down the blood lust which filled his brain. Never in his life had he acted out of blind rage. He would kill to protect Rose, he would exterminate the entire McClendon clan if necessary, but he wouldn't kill out of rage. He must always be able to face the consequences of his actions.

Gradually George felt the grip of insane fury begin to loosen, the light of reason begin to return. At the same moment, the old man stumbled over a root, and Rose pushed away from him. As she started to run, the old man raised his gun and fired.

George saw Rose stagger and fall. He fired almost instantly. Without waiting to see if he'd hit the old man, George raced for Rose.

"It's just a scratch," she said, pointing to the place on her shoulder where blood stained her dress. "I'm not hurt."

Gunfire erupted all around them.

George pulled Rose to her feet and, in a crouching run, raced toward the creek and over the edge. Salty was firing as rapidly as the rifle would let him.

"They're coming from everywhere," he said. "I don't know how long we can hold them off."

They took up rifles just as the McClendons burst through the brush. With deadly determination, George and Rose picked them off one by one. It wasn't long before the charge slowed.

Then it stopped.

George waited, but nothing happened. He waited longer. Still no shots. Still no charge from the brush.

"Anybody out there?" he called out.

Silence.

He didn't dare leave cover. He didn't know what was going on, but he was convinced the McClendons were still there.

"Anybody there?" he called again.

After a time, a voice answered, "Yeah."

"There's no gold," George said. "There never was. I tried to tell the old man, but he wouldn't listen. You're welcome to dig up every square foot around the house."

"We already have," the voice answered.

"There's no use in anybody else getting hurt."

There was a long pause.

"You still out there?"

"Yeah."

"You going to leave us alone?"

Another long pause. George thought he could hear them talking, but he had no idea what they were saying.

"Can we come get Pa?"

"Yes."

Moments later a tall, thin man who looked exactly like McClendon must have looked years ago stepped out of the brush. He paused a moment, then walked over to where his father lay.

"I told him there weren't no gold. I told him rich people didn't work hard like you. But that Silas fella kept swearing he knew where it was. All we had to do was get you outta the house."

"What happened to Silas?"

"Pa killed him. Got so mad when he couldn't find no gold he just shot him."

The man looked down at his father.

"I told him not to bother your woman. No man puts up with nobody messing with his woman, I told him. It makes 'um madder than hell. But he wouldn't listen. Pa wouldn't listen to no-body. Thought he knowed everything. Now look what it's got him. And the rest of us," he said, looking at the wounded men who were beginning to get up off the ground.

And the men who didn't.

"You boys sure know how to shoot. Told Pa that, too. He said you was from back East. He said nobody back East except mountain folks knowed how to use a gun. I told him about that brother of yours, how he picked off Klute and Buddy without nobody even seeing him, but Pa wouldn't listen to that neither."

"What are you going to do?" George asked.

"Take him home and bury him next to Ma. She'd like that. Me, I wouldn't care if the coyotes got him."

George watched as the man picked up his pa and draped him over the saddle of a horse someone led out of the brush. The old man was dead. George had lost his battle with himself.

"I meant to shoot him in the elbow," George said, more to himself than to Rose and Salty. "I just wanted to make sure he couldn't shoot Rose after I hit him."

"You did," Salty said. "But he could use both hands. He was drawing a bead on you while you were helping Rose up. I had to put a bullet into him. Only I'm not as good as you, so I aimed for something bigger than his elbow."

George felt a tremendous flush of relief. He had won. If he could do that when Rose's life was in danger, he could always do it.

"I'll go see if they're really gone," Salty said. He climbed out of the creek and disappeared into the brush.

"Do you think they'll come back?" Rose asked.

"Not anymore," George said, feeling almost like his old self. "That man is different from his father. Where have you hidden Zac? I didn't see him when I went to get my pistol."

"I don't know," Rose answered. "I was looking for him when McClendon caught me."

"Do you mean he went off without telling you?"

"I'm afraid I fell asleep."

"When I find him, I'm going to take every inch of skin off his hide," George swore.

"He didn't mean—"

"I know, but he nearly caused you to get killed. I can't excuse that."

But George didn't have to look for Zac. At that moment a tiny form propelled itself out of the brush and straight over the creek bank into George's arms.

Before George could say any of the things boiling in his brain, Zac shouted, "Look, George. I brought the army."

George looked up to see an army officer on horseback, covered in general's braid and dozens of ribbons, emerge from a side path through the brush. A patrol of eighteen men followed.

"I'm Phil Sheridan," the man announced. "Can you tell me where I can find George Randolph? I've got a pardon for him."

# Chapter Twenty-three

George stared at the smoldering remains of their home. The logs were too thick to burn, but the roof was gone. Virtually everything inside had been destroyed. Every inch of floorboard had been ripped up. Chests and cabinets smashed. Every pot and cupboard emptied. Tins and boxes ripped open and cast on the floor. There were so many holes in the yard it looked like a prairie dog town.

They had even dug into the graves of Mrs. Randolph and young Alex.

"You can't live here," Sheridan said.

"No," George agreed. "We'll move to Austin."

Rose's gaze flew to George's face.

"I'll have my men clear away the debris," Sheridan offered.

"It'll give them something to do while they're waiting for Cortina's men to strike again. You don't have to worry about those McClendons, either. That's something else we'll clean up."

"You can't give up," Rose pleaded to George. "Not after you've worked so hard."

"I'm not. We have a parade to attend, or have you forgotten?"

Rose had never imagined a smile could be so cheerless. But it made her proud of him. Very proud.

"Besides, you can't stay here while we build another house, a real house this time. It'll take too long. It has to be big enough to hold at least a half dozen Yankee brats."

Rose felt her heart lurch violently in her chest. "Are you sure?"

"Absolutely. I'm positively looking forward to the responsibility. I welcome the challenge of guiding their teetering footsteps along life's treacherous path. I long to sit, Solomon-like, in judgment of their disputes. I'll be a repository of wisdom, a fount of knowledge, a treasure chest of counsel."

"You sure it's a bunch of kids you're after?" Salty asked. "Sounds to me like you're running for governor."

Rose and George laughed.

"You do know I can't stay in Austin after the parade," Rose told George. "And there's no use arguing. No woman in her right mind would stay away while her husband was building her house."

"But there's no place for you to live."

"I'll live where you live and sleep where you sleep. In the open or in the cave. It doesn't matter, but I'm not staying in Austin."

"Maybe I'd better give this idea of having children a little more thought," George said with an attempt to appear serious. "I don't know if I can stand a houseful of girls as stubborn as you."

Rose's face softened with emotion. "You're not doing it for me, are you?" she asked.

"Of course I am. They'll be my gift to you for all that you have been, are, and ever will mean to me. But they'll also be my gift to me. They'll be my belief in the future, in myself, my triumph over the past. I couldn't have done any of this without you."

"For an ex-army man, he's sure given to a lot of high-flown sentiment," Sheridan remarked to Salty.

"Sounds like it," Salty answered, grinning. "I guess it's a good thing he didn't reenlist."

"Reenlist?" General Sheridan directed a penetrating look at George.

"Yeah. For a while he thought about going west to fight Indians."

"You think he would? Any man who can hold off forty men practically by himself could make colonel in no time. And if Grant took an interest in him, there's no telling how high he could go."

"I don't think he's interested," Salty said, watching George and Rose as they walked arm-in-arm toward the oak sheltering the two graves. "I think he's got a whole different tribe of little Indians in mind now. And Rose is the only general he's going to put up with looking over his shoulder."

# Author's Note

The period of Reconstruction after the Civil War was a truly reprehensible postlude to our bloodiest and most tragic war. The greatest misfortune, however, was not that it happened, but that it went on so long. In Texas, outside rule lasted for nine long years.

On June 19, 1865, General Gordon Granger landed in Texas and declared the state under military rule. Most of the soldiers were stationed in coastal cities where they created problems with the local citizens. After a black army garrison terrorized Victoria, the white officers refused to let any professed Union man or black be jailed by local citizens. Black troops burned the town of Brenham to the ground, but no soldier was ever brought to trial or admonished. Other soldiers raided Brownsville with similar impunity.

In 1866, the United States Congress devised the *ironclad* oath, which barred people who "had ever voluntarily borne arms against the United States or yielded a voluntary support to any 'pretended' government hostile or inimical thereto" from holding office at state or local levels. In 1867, General Charles Griffin extended it to include all persons who had ever held a state or federal office *before* the Rebellion. This interpretation included mayors, school trustees, clerks, public weighers, even the cemetery sexton.

It wasn't until after 1869, during the administration of Governor Davis, that the tax burden became ruinous. Six million dollars of taxes were levied against an estimated eight hundred thousand dollars needed to run the government. Most were land taxes which ruined the planters and farmers but left the businessmen relatively untouched. Twenty-one percent of Texans' income went for taxes.

Texas rule did not return to the hands of Texans until Davis was forcibly ousted from office in January 1874.

I've taken two liberties with history. First, I've moved the problems with skyrocketing taxes forward about five years. Second, the army did not attempt to stop Cortina's raids or eliminate Indian and rustler raids. It wasn't until 1875 when Captain L. H. McNelly organized his company of rangers that any effective measures were taken against Cortina.

With the exception of General Sheridan, all characters and incidents in this book are products of my imagination.

There is a real Randolph family of Virginia which numbers among its members President Thomas Jefferson, Supreme Court Justice John Marshall, and Confederate General Robert E. Lee. Any similarity to members of this family, living or dead, is purely accidental.

# ☐ **YES!**

Sign me up for the Historical Romance Book Club and send my FREE BOOKS! If I choose to stay in the club, I will pay only $8.50* each month, a savings of $6.48!

NAME: _____

ADDRESS: _____

TELEPHONE: _____

EMAIL: _____

☐ I want to pay by credit card.

☐ **VISA**   ☐ **MasterCard**   ☐ **DISCOVER**

ACCOUNT #: _____

EXPIRATION DATE: _____

SIGNATURE: _____

Mail this page along with $2.00 shipping and handling to:

**Historical Romance Book Club**
**PO Box 6640**
**Wayne, PA 19087**

Or fax (must include credit card information) to:

**610-995-9274**

You can also sign up online at **www.dorchesterpub.com**.

*Plus $2.00 for shipping. Offer open to residents of the U.S. and Canada only. Canadian residents please call 1-800-481-9191 for pricing information. If under 18, a parent or guardian must sign. Terms, prices and conditions subject to change. Subscription subject to acceptance. Dorchester Publishing reserves the right to reject any order or cancel any subscription.